**The W**
**by Linds**

ॐ

*Quinn was so close—so pulverizingly male.*

It took everything Kerry had left not to turn and lay her head against his strong, broad shoulder. Somehow, she knew Quinn could handle big loads and responsibility. He was built for it not only physically, but emotionally, too.

As he stepped away, Kerry keenly felt the loss of his nearness, his care. Opening her eyes, she fell captive to the smoky blueness now banked in his gaze as he studied her in the silence strung between them. For the first time in years Kerry felt another stirring deep within her heart and lower body; it was the stirring of desire for a man. For Quinn Grayson. Even though he was a tough, no-nonsense marine, he had an incredibly surprising and wonderfully tender side, too. It was a beautiful discovery for Kerry.

Because right now she needed someone exactly like Quinn…

# The Rancher, the Baby & the Nanny
## by Sara Orwig

*'What about last night?' Wyatt couldn't resist asking. 'You didn't feel anything when we were together?'*

'Look, you're experienced and worldly enough to take care of yourself,' Grace said.

'You didn't answer my question.' Wyatt studied her intently.

'I would have to be blind not to notice that you are a very good-looking man, Mr Sawyer. But that's the end of it.'

'So, I'm the only one in that room last night who felt any sparks between us?' he asked softly, moving closer to her. Her eyes widened.

'Yes, you were.'

'Oh, I think not,' Wyatt said, reaching out to unfasten the barrette that held her hair. 'Still don't feel anything when I get close?'

'I don't think so.'

'I think you do. Where's all that blunt honesty of yours now? Tell me if you feel anything when I do this.' He wrapped his arms around her.

'Mr Sawyer!'

'The hell with that,' he whispered, and leaned down to cover her mouth with his own.

# Available in November 2003 from Silhouette Desire

# The Will To Love
## LINDSAY McKENNA

# The Rancher, the Baby,
# & the Nanny
## SARA ORWIG

SILHOUETTE®
DESIRE™

*Silhouette, Silhouette Desire and Colophon
are registered trademarks of Harlequin Books S.A.,
used under licence.*

*First published in Great Britain 2003
Silhouette Books, Eton House, 18-24 Paradise Road,
Richmond, Surrey TW9 1SR*

The publisher acknowledges the copyright holders of the
individual works as follows:

The Will To Love © Lindsay McKenna  2002
The Rancher, the Baby & the Nanny © Sara Orwig 2003

ISBN 0 373 04882 3

*51-1103*

*Printed and bound in Spain
by Litografia Rosés S.A., Barcelona*

# THE WILL TO LOVE
## by
## Lindsay McKenna

**SILHOUETTE®**
**BOOKS**

*proudly presents seven more fantastic stories*
*from*

*Lindsay McKenna's*

*exciting series*

# MORGAN'S MERCENARIES

*Meet Morgan's newest team:*
*courageous men and women destined for*
*greatness—fated to fall in love!*

## LINDSAY MCKENNA

A homoeopathic educator, Lindsay teaches at the Desert Institute of Classical Homoeopathy in Phoenix, Arizona. When she isn't teaching alternative medicine, she is writing books about love. She feels love is the single greatest healer in the world and hopes that her books touch her readers' hearts.

To the innocent and brave men, women and children
who lost their lives on 11-9-01.
You will be in our hearts and memory forever.

# Chapter One

*January 14: 0545*

It was a bad day getting worse by the moment, Corporal Quinn Grayson decided as he eased out of the dark green Humvee once it stopped against the curb. Above him towered the massive, dark gray concrete headquarters building for U.S. Marine Corps Camp Reed. It was barely dawn, the sky lightening to a pale gold color on the eastern horizon as he took the concrete steps two at a time.

The only thing good about the day was that he was going to see someone in Logistics whom he truly admired and respected: Morgan Trayhern, who was a living hero to the Marine Corps. Feeling his mood lifting slightly, Quinn wove in and around the crowds of swiftly moving personnel, all dressed similarly to himself in desert-colored utilities. The helmet on his head always felt heavy, and he was glad to take it off as he stepped through the double doors and into the building itself.

The noise level inside was low, but the faces of the office pogues were filled with stress and anxiety as they hurried like bees in a stirred-up hive. The H.Q. was organized chaos, Quinn decided. And why wouldn't it be? Two weeks ago the worst earthquake in American history had turned the Los Angeles basin upside down and inside out. Millions of helpless victims desperately needed food, water and medicine. Worse, there were no highways left into the basin; they had all been destroyed by the massive quake.

The only way in and out now was by helicopter. From the platoon he was assigned to assist in the emergency operations, Quinn saw only the tip of the iceberg as far as rescue efforts to the civilian populace went. Yesterday evening he'd been in the loading area with his platoon, piling food, water and medicine into the choppers, when his sergeant, Sean O'Hara, had ordered him to go see Morgan at 0600.

Turning now, Quinn headed up the stairs to the second floor, where Logistics, the heart and brains of Operation Sky Lift, was located, and where Morgan had an office. En route Quinn passed a number of office types descending rapidly, their hands filled with files and, more than likely, orders.

Pushing the stairwell door open and striding forward, Quinn located Morgan's office halfway down the passageway, which was also crowded with busy personnel. Tension was high; he could feel it. Shrugging his broad shoulders, as if to rid himself of the accumulated stress he felt in the building, Quinn halted in front of the open door and rapped once with his knuckles. Morgan Trayhern was behind the green metal desk, head down, writing a set of orders for a woman officer in a flight uniform. Quinn saw the black wing insignia sewn into the fabric of her suit and knew instantly that she was probably a helo pilot.

Morgan lifted his head. His scowl faded. ''Quinn! Great, you're here. Come in.'' He raised his hand and beckoned him into the office. ''I'll be just a moment.''

''Yes, sir,'' Quinn said. He took a step inside and stood at attention. The woman pilot, a Marine Corps captain, nodded toward him.

''Ma'am. Good morning.''

''Good morning, Corporal. At ease, please,'' she said.

Quinn nodded and relaxed into an at-ease stance behind her, near the wall. ''Yes, ma'am.''

''You had coffee yet, Quinn?'' Morgan rumbled

as he signed the second and third sets of orders before him.

"No, sir." Quinn kept his helmet, which was splotched with desert camouflage colors of yellow, brown and gray, beneath his left elbow and against his hip. He noticed Morgan was dressed in civilian attire—jeans and a red, long-sleeved cotton shirt with the cuffs rolled up to just below his elbows. He looked out of place in the marine-green office.

Gesturing to his right, Morgan said with a grin, "Grab a cup of java, then. I managed to scrounge up my very own coffeemaker. A rarity, you know. Help yourself, Son."

Quinn smiled slightly and moved toward the machine. "Yes, sir. Thank you, sir."

Blowing out a breath of air, Morgan put the pen aside and gave the thick set of orders to the helicopter pilot. "There you go, Captain Jackson. Congratulations. You and your copilot are now responsible for Area Six. We've transferred the other team to Area Five.

"Yes, sir. Thank you, sir. We'll do a good job."

Morgan smiled up at her. Captain Jackson was in her middle twenties, with short black hair, intense gray eyes and a sincere face that was currently filled with excitement. H.Q. had just gotten a whole new batch of helicopter pilots transferred in yesterday from other Marine Corps bases around the U.S. Having new pilots on board would give the hardworking

helo crews stationed at Camp Reed a desperate and
much-needed rest from the twelve-hour days they'd
been putting in for the last two weeks. Pilots could
fly only so long without sufficient rest and recoup
time before they began making critical mistakes.
Jackson was one of many personnel scheduled to
come to Morgan's office today for orders.

"Good luck out there, Captain." Morgan rose.
"And be careful, you hear? Things are unstable
right now. We've already had a helicopter crew
murdered by a survivalist group in Area Five."

She came to attention. "Yes, sir, we'll be careful.
Thank you, sir."

"Dismissed," Morgan murmured. He stood and
watched the woman, who was nearly six feet tall,
big boned and athletic, turn on her heel and quickly
march out the door. Swiveling his head, Morgan
gave Quinn Grayson a warm look. The corporal had
just poured a cup of coffee. Moving to the machine,
Morgan poured himself one, too.

"Come with me, Quinn. Now is about the only
time today I might get to see Laura. You remember
my wife?"

"Yes, sir, I do." He sipped the coffee tentatively.
It was fresh and hot, and he savored it. "She's here,
too?" How could that be? Quinn knew Laura lived
in Montana, near the headquarters Morgan kept for
Perseus in Philipsburg. Quinn and his fire team had
been selected to be part of two different Perseus

rescue missions in Iraq, where pilots were that had been shot down in the No Fly Zone earlier in the year. He and his team had been flown back to the secret headquarters in Philipsburg, an out-of-the-way place only a few tourists and trout fishermen found in the summer. It was a perfect hiding spot, Quinn had thought. He'd met Morgan's lovely blond-haired wife there by accident, when she'd brought over recently baked cookies for all of them. It was a thoughtful gesture that was as surprising as it was unexpectedly generous. Quinn had relished his share of the chocolate-chip cookies, and so had his grateful men. He had found Laura to be beautiful, elegant and sensitive. Quinn thought Morgan was the luckiest man in the world to have a wife like that. Cookies during a briefing. He'd never get that in the Marine Corps. No, he liked working with Morgan and Perseus. But he wondered how Morgan's wife had wound up in the midst of this disaster.

"We were at a hotel in south Los Angeles, celebrating New Year, when the quake hit," Morgan explained as they left the office and headed down the stairs. "Laura was trapped in wreckage." At the bottom of the stairs, Morgan pushed open the door. Gesturing toward the end of the passageway, he took quick strides toward it. Quinn, who was six foot tall, and shorter than Morgan, had to lengthen his stride to keep up with him.

"Your wife was trapped?" he asked with a scowl as they moved out the doors and into the brightening day. The sun was going to rise soon and already the darkness of the night had fled.

"Yeah," Morgan muttered. "Thank goodness a Marine Corps rescue officer and her dog located Laura."

"Is she all right, sir?" They hurried down the stairs toward the hospital a block away. The world around them was already in high gear. The shrieking whine of jets at the nearby airport filled the air, along with the deeper chugging sounds of diesel truck convoys loaded with supplies lumbering across the base. A whole fleet of helicopters were taking off one by one, hotfooting it out of Camp Reed with the first supplies of the day for desperate people across the disaster area.

Quinn drew abreast of Morgan as he walked swiftly toward the hospital.

"Laura suffered a broken ankle. She had surgery here. Then, shortly after the surgery, she developed a blood clot. They had to string up her leg with a pulley, and she was tied down like a roping calf." Morgan grinned wryly. "My wife is not one to lie in bed all day and do nothing. We had to wait until some blood-thinning drugs were flown in from Seattle for her." He rubbed his hands together. "Today, she gets out of her contraption and into a wheelchair. The doctor says the clot is dissolved and her ankle is stable enough for her to be a little more active.''

''Almost two weeks in a bed would drive me nuts,'' Quinn muttered. It would. He was restless by nature, and loved the outdoors and the strenuous activity demanded of marines.

''Yes, well...'' Morgan chuckled ''...if it hadn't been for a tiny baby the team rescued from beneath the rubble, Laura would never have survived bed rest. She's been taking care of Baby Jane Fielding for the nurses. And the hospital staff bring up other infants so Laura can hold them and bottle-feed them. They've been keeping her busy.''

Quinn smiled knowingly. There was no doubt about Laura's maternal side. He liked that about women in general, although in his world, he saw mostly women marines, with tough, demanding jobs. Still, he saw that nurturing side in many of them, too. It was something he enjoyed about women, in or out of the service.

They hurried into the chaotic, busy hospital and up an elevator. Quinn was glad to escape the bustle once they arrived at the private room where Laura Trayhern sat in her wheelchair, an infant wrapped in a pink blanket in her arms.

''Hello, Quinn.'' Laura greeted him warmly as he approached. ''You look well.''

''Thank you, ma'am,'' he said, nodding to her and smiling. The infant was suckling strongly on a bottle of milk. "I'm glad to hear from Mr. Trayhern that you're doing okay."

"I'm fine." Laura lifted her face toward Morgan as he bent and gave her a kiss on the brow. Then he gently stroked the baby's dark, soft hair.

Quinn saw the man's face change remarkably. For a moment, he glimpsed the love burning in Morgan's eyes for his wife of many years. And when Morgan ran his fingertips caressingly across the baby's hair, Quinn saw tenderness replace his normally stoic expression. But as Morgan's fingers lifted away, Quinn saw the same hard mask fall back into place. Despite that, there was no doubt in his mind that Morgan loved his wife and the orphaned baby.

"Come over here, Son. Let's sit down and go over this new plan that you're going to initiate for the basin."

Moving to the two metal chairs near the venetian-blind-covered window, Quinn excused himself from Laura. Morgan handed him one of two red folders and sat down. Opening his copy, Quinn saw a set of signed orders with his name at the top. The other members of his fire team were named, as well.

Scowling, Morgan studied the folder opened in his lap. "We're initiating a basin-wide plan B today, and you're a part of that effort—you and your fire team. It's a trial balloon. A work in progress, so to speak. We don't know if it will work or not, so you're an experiment of sorts. We can't afford to put a full squad of ten men into each area. Camp Reed doesn't have the personnel to pull that off. But by splitting up a squad into two fire teams of five people each, plus their leader, we have a chance to do something rather than nothing.'' He looked squarely at Quinn. ''So you're it. You're our test case. You're to play it by ear and see where the energy flows in this changing situation. You're the only fire team we're putting in there for now. If it works, we'll insert others later.''

''Five marines in each given area?'' Quinn asked.

''That's right. We've divided the basin into twelve quadrants. These are huge blocks of real estate. We're talking ten to twenty square miles, depending upon the location, the population of the area and so on.'' Scratching his head, Morgan gave Quinn a rueful look. ''Believe me, Logistics has been wrestling with this nightmare. The basin has no law enforcement. Without backup, the police in some areas can't do what they've been trained to do. There are no highways to drive on to get to a problem area. They're pretty much limited to handling problems within walking distance of their base of operation.''

Morgan pulled a sheet of fax paper from his file folder and handed it to Quinn. ''This is Deputy Sheriff Kerry Chelton. She is the only surviving member of the law enforcement agency in Area

Five. Kerry contacted us by radio a week ago, and I've had the pleasure of talking with this young woman a number of times. Damned intelligent and resourceful. She found a gasoline generator, some fuel, and managed to retrieve a radio from the sheriff's building, which collapsed and killed everyone inside it. She calls us every night with reports. Beautiful woman, isn't she?''

Taking the paper, Quinn saw the photo on it. For no explainable reason, his heart contracted instantly. The black-and-white picture showed a woman with dark hair, cut to just below her ears. With her heart-shaped face, full but compressed lips and wide eyes, she was a very attractive woman, Quinn decided. The head shot showed her in her law enforcement uniform. The resolve in her large eyes was obvious. She exuded confidence.

''Yes, sir, she's a looker, no doubt,'' he murmured.

''Kerry has been in regular contact with our radio group at H.Q. She's been helping us formulate stage two of our rescue efforts.'' Sighing, Morgan said in a low voice, ''There's a lot of people out there dying right now. We just can't get to them soon enough. The water mains are broken, so there's no fresh water supply, or at least, not enough for the millions that are trapped out there. And food, while less of a problem now because people can go to their homes and eat whatever canned goods they find, will be disappearing shortly, too. Kerry has been scouting as much of Area Five as she can every day and giving us nightly reports. She's telling us what the needs are, and we've been trying to organize community groups in each area to help stabilize the situation. We're trying to find local police, state troopers, sheriff's deputies—anyone in law enforcement—to become the hub of this wheel we're building. Without law and order, chaos continues."

"Yes, sir, I've been hearing plenty about that gang in Area Five."

"Humph. Those survivalists. They call themselves Diablo—or Devil. And you, Quinn, are going to be taking them on." Morgan gave him a hard look.

"I'd like nothing better, sir. They killed two marine pilots in cold blood. That's reason enough to go after them." At the thought, anger tightened his chest. Yet when Quinn studied Kerry's photo again, his heart sped up and thumped violently for a beat or two. Part of him was eager to meet this inventive woman. Another more prejudiced part of him didn't believe a woman could be *that* resourceful. Yet Morgan obviously admired and respected her, so she had to have the right stuff. In Quinn's experience, women were not especially handy or practical. Nurturing others was one thing, but there really wasn't much place for that in the Marine Corps. And he really didn't like the integration of females into male slots in the corps. Not at all.

"At 0800, Quinn, you are to go to LZ Echo with your fire team. The pilots of that Huey will take you and your team into Area Five. They're going to drop you at a destroyed shopping mall parking lot. Deputy Chelton will meet you there. She has a makeshift H.Q. set up nearby with that generator. What she needs now is help." Morgan eyed him with a slight, twisted smile. "Firepower, in other words."

"And who's in charge, sir?"

"Both of you will be."

Quinn frowned. "But sir, to run an operation like this...going after Diablo...why should a civilian have *any* say over what we do?" He struggled with his choice of words and tone of voice. The term *civilian* had sounded disrespectful. Instantly, he was sorry for how he'd framed his objection.

Trayhern's face darkened, and his blue eyes turned icy for a moment. "Listen to me, Quinn. That woman just lost everyone she ever cared about two weeks ago. Most people would be so stunned with such grief and loss they couldn't think straight. Kerry has single-handedly set up a base of operations for Area Five. She has tracked Diablo. She's been like Lara Croft, Princess Xena and Supergirl all wrapped into one. Without her constant input, her observations and suggestions from the field, we wouldn't be launching this second phase so soon.

She's been able to help us define what is needed out there.

"Your fire team was chosen because you have emergency medical training. We're desperate for medical intervention out there. Without Kerry's guidance, we couldn't have formulated this concept we're starting to put together to help the folks. Your team is an experiment. If it works, we'll do more of it."

Stung by Morgan's censure, Quinn lowered his gaze and looked at the file. Kerry's photo stared back at him. She wasn't smiling, but she had a softness about her face. Her nose was thin and fine. Her eyes were far apart, her gaze clear and direct. Swallowing hard, Quinn nodded. "Yes, sir, I hear you."

"Don't go in there with a chip on your shoulder about women," Morgan warned him in a growl. "The last thing I need on this mission is a man who's prejudiced about what women can or can't do." He reached out and tapped Kerry's picture. "She's the kind of woman I like to hire for Perseus. Kerry thinks on her feet. She's creative. Trustworthy. And she doesn't miss anything. Maybe it's because of her training in law enforcement, but she has an eye for details. And without her input, Quinn, we would be up a creek right now. She's just about the only one out there who has radio contact with Camp Reed. Ask yourself how she managed to jury-rig that. No, I think she's one hell of a person. And

I want you to go into this assignment with that same attitude.''

Chastened, Quinn felt his heart contract when Morgan called Kerry trustworthy. Maybe he was still feeling the pain of his breakup with Frannie Walton, a civilian secretary he'd met in Oceanside nearly two years ago. Since then, he'd had a lot of trouble trusting any woman. After the way Frannie had treated him, he'd crawled into a dark hole of hurt, his pride wounded. She'd been a social climber and on an emotional level, Frannie had been anything but reliable or trustworthy. Quinn had been raised in the backwoods country of Kentucky, where women were still women. They didn't try and take a man's job away from him. Nope, they were good wives, raised kids and stayed home to cook, clean and be mothers.

Rubbing his chest above his heart, Quinn tried to pay attention as Morgan explained what was expected of him and his fire team.

''You're to set up an H.Q. with Kerry. She's your civilian liaison or counterpart. Without her, you'd be a duck out of water. She knows the turf, the people and the area. Twenty-seven years old and a graduate of law enforcement, she was on the fast track in the sheriff's department.

''Right now, Kerry needs help in continuing to organize the people, to keep peace and to stop the slide into chaos that's happening more and more.

People are desperate. They need water, and are willing to steal from others to get it. Kerry is trying her best to locate a well in her area, but so far, no luck. Even if they do find one, there's no guarantee it will have clean water, given the lack of sewage facilities.''

"Our mission, then," Quinn murmured, "is threefold, right? We're to try and hunt down Diablo and corral them. We're to help Kerry Chelton set up an H.Q. And lastly, we're to help organize the area so it doesn't disintegrate into turf wars over water and food?"

"You got it," Morgan said, satisfaction vibrating in his voice. "Now, you may find that one of those three takes priority. We don't know which one that might be yet, so be flexible and let this thing evolve as the situation develops. Kerry has been working hard for two weeks to set up some kind of organized response. She's been instrumental in bringing civilians together and getting them to work with one another. What she needs is muscle. And that's where you and your team come in. You're military, and people will respect that more than anything. With Diablo ranging across Kerry's area, people are going ballistic. Your presence alone should help calm a lot of fears." Morgan turned to another page in his file.

"The Diablo have an MO—modus operandi—of going into a house they think might have a stash of food or water. They move in small groups, maybe

one to four men. The men talk with the house owners, pretending to be part of the rescue effort, and
ask if they have children.'' Morgan's voice deepened with fury. ''If the answer is yes, one member
will find and hold the child hostage, at gunpoint.
Then the rest of the pack come out of hiding and
ransack the house for food, water, money, jewelry.
The home owners are helpless. They can't stop
them. They don't want their children hurt. To date,
Diablo have already killed five people, not including
the two Marine Corps pilots. They don't tolerate any
rebellion by anyone.''

''They shoot first and ask questions later,'' Quinn
muttered, anger stirring in him again. It was one
thing to prey on adults, quite another to involve innocent children. His mouth flattened. Right now,
he'd like nothing better than to get his hands on the
leader of that gang.

''Exactly.''

''Do you know who's heading up Diablo?''

''No, but Kerry thinks she knows and is trying to
piece it together for us. She's been trying to shadow
their movements.''

''That's dangerous.''

''Sure it is,'' Moran agreed, ''but she's fearless,
that woman. She's been tailing them without their
knowledge whenever she gets a chance. She calls in
their last position, and that helps us keep tabs on
them, and to protect helicopter crews flying into that

area. Right now, it's a cat-and-mouse game. We keep changing our landing area to outwit Diablo and get basic goods to the civilians. And on days when she can't detect them in Area Five, the helo goes back to the original LZ, which is her H.Q. set up at the destroyed shopping center. That's where you'll be flown into today.'' Morgan's mouth quirked. ''But that'll go only so far. What we need is the gang captured and extricated. We've got a brig cell waiting for those bastards.''

''Then you've come to the right team, sir. We'll find them and be Thor's hammer to 'em.''

Grinning sourly, Morgan studied the marine, whose face was dark with anger and set with determination. ''Thor's hammer'' was an old saying in the corps. Morgan could recall many times when, as young officers during the Vietnam War, he and his friends at an officers' club would toast to Odin, Norse king of the gods. The Norse god of thunder, Thor, hurled thunderbolts at his enemies. Yes, Quinn was no doubt going to be Thor's ''hammer''—his lightning bolt—in this situation. Morgan had full confidence in him.

''We're counting heavily on you, Quinn. You've worked twice with me on important missions and I know you're a warrior at heart. You have the medical background. If anyone can track down Diablo, you can. You come from Kentucky hill people, and they're the best hunters and trackers in the business.

That's one of the reasons I chose you—you're one hell of a bird dog on a scent.''

Laughing shortly, Quinn nodded. ''Yes, sir, I am.''

Morgan straightened and placed his hands over the file. ''Just try to get along with Deputy Chelton, okay? That's the one fly in this ointment. I know you'd rather work with men. That's your background and I understand that. But Kerry is exceptional, Quinn, and I feel you two will make a hell a team. Dodge is infested with bad guys, so to speak, and she needs some muscle to help get them out of there.''

''Then you've come to the right person, sir.'' Quinn felt a lethal resolve flow through him as he met and held Morgan's deep blue gaze. ''We won't let you down. My team and I have been together nearly two years. We know each other's thoughts, and we've been battle tested. I want Diablo more than most, sir. I don't believe in using children as shields. That's unforgivable.''

''It is,'' Morgan agreed unhappily. ''Everyone's traumatized by the quake. Having these survivalists roving around and adding to the chaos, endangering and scaring children and killing adults, isn't acceptable. We all need to pull together, work together in order to survive this nightmare.''

''I'll try my best to work with Deputy Chelton,''

he promised Morgan. More than anything, Quinn wanted Morgan's respect.

"Do your best, Corporal Grayson. She's an exceptional woman, not to mention a savvy police officer. We're lucky to have her." Morgan held out his hand. "Good luck, Quinn, to you and your men. Get your gear together, take this set of orders and hotfoot it out to LZ Echo for an 0800 takeoff. Kerry's expecting you."

As Morgan shook his hand, Quinn tried to ignore the photo of Kerry Chelton resting in his lap on the opened file. A woman. What bad luck. Somehow, though, Quinn would try to make the best of it. Was she another Frannie? A social climber? Could he trust this Kerry Chelton?

His emotions smarted at those unanswered questions. Where he'd grown up, women didn't become police officers. They were wives and mothers and that was it.

And he was going to jump from the frying pan into the fire today. Figuring out how much or little he could trust Chelton would be his first order of business. Until he knew that, they were technically all at risk, and Quinn wasn't about to get his head shot off because some woman was involved in the plan.

No, he'd go in distrusting her completely.

# *Chapter Two*

*January 14: 0830*

For the first time since the earthquake, Kerry Chelton felt hope. It wasn't much more than a thin, fragile thread, but it began to take root in her traumatized heart and lifted her flagging spirits. Dressed in the dark green slacks and tan, long-sleeved blouse that was her sheriff's deputy uniform, a silver badge over her left pocket, she stood at the ready on the massive asphalt parking lot of the destroyed shopping center as she watched two U.S. Marine Corps helicopters landing.

A sudden, unexpected sense of joy enveloped her. She was getting help. Help! Oh, how badly she needed some.

Putting her hands up to protect her eyes from flying debris kicked up by the rotors, she surveyed the group of twenty people standing around her. Patient and respectful, as they were waiting eagerly for the first Huey, which was carrying a crucial supply of bottled water, to land. The water would be distributed at the other end of the shopping complex, where Kerry had had her people build a makeshift depot out of bricks and other material taken from destroyed buildings. On other days, when Diablo was ''active'' in her area, Kerry would redirect the helo to a safer LZ. The supplies would be distributed from that location instead. This morning there had been no activity with Diablo, so the original LZ was put into use.

Her gaze moved to the second Huey, which she knew was bearing the five marines Morgan Trayhern had sent. Morgan had been her lifeline since she'd cobbled the generator and radio together. His deep, soothing voice over the radio day after day had given her hope and kept her sanity intact. Now he had sent her reinforcements to help keep Area Five stable. Morgan had spoken enthusiastically of the leader of this fire team, Corporal Quinn Grayson, who was a marine as well as an EMT. God knew, Area Five needed medical intervention! She could hardly wait to meet him.

Deep within her, Kerry knew she was still pulverized by shock because of the recent traumatic events. She had felt nothing, emotionally, for two weeks. Now a trickle of hope wound through her pounding heart as the Huey with the marines landed within two hundred feet of her. Kerry spread her feet apart in order to remain standing against the buffeting wind. As the Huey powered down, she saw the door slide open.

The first marine to jump down had to be Quinn Grayson, Kerry decided. She could tell by the authority in his stance that he was the leader. Tall and broad-shouldered, he clutched an M-16 in his hands as he warily looked around. When he turned and snapped an order, four more marines disembarked, on guard and alert.

Instantly, as she watched him walk away from the helicopter and eye the knot of people around her, Kerry liked Grayson. He was looking for her, she knew. She was his contact. Stepping forward, she saw him halt and stare at her assessingly. Was she friend or enemy? Pain in the butt or help? Her heart fluttered wildly in her chest for a moment. That was an odd reaction, Kerry thought, as she walked quickly toward him.

She hadn't smiled in two weeks, but she did now—a smile of welcome, but also of relief. Although she could carry a heavy load on her broad-shouldered five-foot-eleven frame, this disaster had stressed her out completely. And Grayson looked strong, capable and powerful as he stood there looking at her through narrowed, dark blue eyes. Kerry felt his gaze move over her as she closed the distance between them. Behind her, she heard the footsteps of her volunteers as they moved toward the other Huey. As usual, they would carry the boxes of precious water to the ''store'' at the other end of the shopping center for distribution.

As Kerry drew within ten feet of Quinn, her heart soared unexpectedly, with such a rush of happiness that it shook her completely. The marine had an oval face with a firm-looking chin. Though his lips were thinned, she could see he had a wide mouth, with laugh lines deeply indented at each corner. His nose was long and straight, the nostrils flaring as she approached, as if to pick up her scent. He seemed as much wild animal as human to her, and yet the quality of danger surrounding Grayson made Kerry feel secure for the first time since the quake. This marine knew how to protect; she could feel it in her bones. His black brows made dark slashes above his glittering blue gaze. The color of his eyes reminded Kerry of the glacial ice up in Alaska, where she'd taken a cruise with her now deceased husband, Lee Chelton. The color was most unusual—almost unearthly—and Kerry thought it looked like the color of heaven, such was its ethereal beauty. Quinn's pupils were large and black, and she saw intelligence gleaming there, as well as surprise. Why the surprise? she wondered, as she lifted her hand to wave, her mouth pulling into a relieved smile.

"Corporal Grayson? I'm Kerry Chelton. Welcome to our little corner of the world."

During the helo flight in Area Five, Quinn had decided to keep things on a business level and not be very friendly. Now, as the tall, willowy woman in the sheriff's deputy uniform held out her cut, dirty hand, he felt his resolve falter. The black-and-white photo he'd seen of Kerry Chelton had done nothing to prepare him for the woman before him now, her short, tousled brown hair rife with gold highlights as it framed her heart-shaped face. Maybe it was the look of relief in her huge gray eyes that touched his hardened heart. Or, maybe it was the way the corners of her mouth softened and her lower lip trembled as she welcomed him.

Quinn didn't know what magic was at work, but suddenly he transferred his weapon to his left hand and thrust out his right hand to enclose hers. Kerry Chelton looked utterly worn-out. He saw the dark smudges beneath her incredibly beautiful eyes, which now sparkled with unshed tears. Something inside him made him want to open his arms, pull her into them and hold her. The relief in her gaze, the sudden emotion revealed in her dirt-smudged face, got to him. She was melting his armor with her unsure smile and sparkling tears, Quinn thought as he saw her swallow convulsively, struggling to hold back her emotions. Because he'd been so hurt by a woman, Quinn struggled to remain wary. Somehow this woman was opening him up and he had no control over it. The last thing Quinn wanted was to allow himself to get emotionally close to her.

Her hand was warm and firm in his, though he was careful of how much pressure he exerted on her long, slender fingers. Shocked by how dirty she was, he reminded himself that none of these people had water to wash or bathe. Her hair was mussed, in dire need of a comb, shampoo and water.

''I'm Corporal Grayson,'' he told her, speaking loudly in order to be heard over the shriek of the helicopters.

''Pleased to meet you. Come on, let's go to my 'office.''' She grinned and pointed toward the shopping center. Wild, fleeting tingles ran up her fingers and arm and cascaded into her heart, which was thumping without pause. Grayson's stony persona, combined with the fact that he was a marine, gave her such hope. If the truth was known, Kerry wanted to simply fall into his arms to be held. She knew that wasn't possible—that it was only her knee-jerk reaction in the midst of the shock and trauma—but there was something wonderfully secure about this marine. She'd seen his icy blue eyes turn warm as their hands met in welcome. And the way he'd wrapped his long, strong fingers around hers had made Kerry feel protected and…something else. She couldn't identify the emotion right now, with all the activity going on around her.

Quinn raised his hand in a silent order for his team to follow him as Kerry took the lead. On his left shoulder, a radio was attached to the epaulet of the camouflage jacket he wore over his flak vest. Pressing the button and turning his head to speak into it, he told the helicopter pilots of both birds to lift off, that contact had been made.

The Huey helicopters, flown by Lieutenants Galway and McGregor, had off-loaded the water. The helo's engine changed pitch and, within a minute, lifted off to head back to Camp Reed. Quinn walked with his men spread out behind him like a V of geese following their leader. They each remained on guard, their rifles locked and loaded. Quinn wasn't taking any chances. They were in enemy territory as far as he was concerned. Ahead of them, Kerry walked quickly toward a makeshift structure with a roof that was nothing more than a piece of corrugated tin laid awkwardly on top. The "house" had been painstakingly put together with wire, broken blocks and other material obviously retrieved from the destroyed shopping center. The entire three-story mall, which was at least a quarter mile long, had collapsed. Quinn had not seen this level of destruction yet, and he felt stunned by what the powerful quake had done. It was unimaginable to him. Unthinkable. Horrifying.

Kerry halted in front of the small shack in the midst of the rubble. "This is it, Corporal Grayson." She gestured toward the hovel. "My home." It hurt to say those words. Her real home, a block away from the sheriff's facility, was now nothing but broken brick, shattered glass and a twisted roof.

Quinn halted near Kerry and looked at the structure. There were several yellow wool blankets strung across the front, one serving as a door. Looking around, he saw the team of volunteers trundling the boxes of bottled water toward the other end of the shopping center.

Kerry followed his gaze. "They're taking the water to our distribution center," she told him.

"There's no fighting about who gets what?"

Shaking her head, Kerry said, "Not yet…but people are real desperate, Corporal. Real desperate."

At that moment, a little black-haired girl around seven years old stumbled sleepily from behind the blanketed door. She was dressed in a grungy pink flannel nightgown that showed off her toothpick legs and the red socks on her feet. As the little girl rubbed her sleepy eyes, Kerry instantly moved forward and scooped her up in her arms.

Turning, she said to Grayson, "This is Petula. Her parents are…well, in heaven…." She sent Quinn a pleading look, obviously asking him to play along with her. "I found her trapped in her home and we dug her out ten days ago. Petula stays with me now...."

Mouth turning downward, Quinn watched as Petula, who had shining brown eyes and long black hair, wrapped her thin arms around Kerry's neck and rested her head on her shoulder.

"I'm hungry, Kerry," she whimpered.

"I know, Pet, I know," Kerry soothed, moving her hand gently across the child's tiny shoulders. "I'll see what I can find, okay?"

Quinn's scowl deepened. Like each of his men, he had on an eighty-pound pack filled with food. "I've got an MRE—meal ready to eat—with eggs, bacon and hash browns. How about if I get that warmed up for her?"

Heart expanding, Kerry bit back her tears. "Oh... that would be wonderful!" Relief washed over her as she stood there holding Petula in her arms. Since Kerry had found her, the little girl had cried often, wanting her parents, and Kerry had told her they'd gone to heaven and would watch over her from there. There was no way she would tell Petula that her parents were trapped inside their house, dead. Each day Kerry tried to keep the child busy with small activities, and she slept with her each night after she finished her patrol of the area, keeping her arms wrapped around the little girl to give her a sense of safety in a world gone mad.

Turning, Grayson gave his men orders to spread

out, reconnoiter the entire shopping center area. His
fire team consisted of three privates and a lance corporal. He assigned Private Orvil Perkins, a Virginia
hill boy, to guard the center against fighting or stealing, and make sure the distribution of water went
quickly and quietly. Then he gave LCPL Beau Parish orders to check out the rest of the shopping center with Privates Cliff Ludlow and Lewis Worth.
Parish was a North Carolina Eastern Cherokee In-
dian, and a damn fine tracker and hunter. Right now,
Quinn was grateful that his men had been with him
nearly two years and could be trusted. They each
carried a radio on their left shoulder, so could stay
in touch no matter where they were. At the first sign
of trouble, Quinn would be notified.

He turned to Kerry. "Do members of the Diablo
gang wear any kind of special clothing or symbols
so my men might see them coming?"

She nodded. "Yes, they wear white headbands."
Grimacing, she whispered, "But they aren't always
so obvious. When one or two infiltrate a neighborhood, they look like us." She glanced down at herself and gave a wry grimace. "Unclean and smelly.
They only put the headband on after they've taken
a hostage."

"I hear you," Quinn muttered with a scowl.
"Okay, men, spread out. Be eyes and ears at this
stage. Anything odd, call me immediately. I'll be
here with Deputy Chelton trying to come up to

speed on what we're up against. When you're done with your reconnoiter, come back here. Understand?''

The four marines nodded.

''All except you, Perkins,'' Grayson ordered. ''You stay at the distribution center. Look like you mean business.''

Once his men headed off to follow his orders, Quinn glanced over at Kerry, who was gently kissing Petula's smudged forehead. A sudden, unexpected ache built in him as he watched her full, soft lips caress the child's wrinkled brow. What would it be like to be caressed like that? To capture her mouth beneath his?

His thoughts were so startling, coming as they did during the present situation, that they rocked Quinn completely. On the way here, he'd been mentally trying to shut out Sheriff Deputy Chelton. Well, that was going to be impossible. She was more attractive in real life, even if she was dirty and unkempt. And her natural, womanly warmth reached out and touched him on this cold, windy January morning.

His scowl deepened as he watched her gently rock Petula. The child had her arms around Kerry's neck, her eyes closed as she snuggled tightly beneath her chin. Kerry seemed so very maternal to Quinn in that moment. And when she lifted her dark, thick lashes to look at him, he growled, ''Come on. Let's get this girl and you something decent to eat in there.''

He pointed toward the hovel Kerry called home. The idea that this pile of bricks, broken boards and drywall could be called a shelter left a bad taste in Quinn's mouth. But such were the living conditions for many Americans on this fourteenth day after the killer quake. Thinning his lips, Quinn pulled back the blanket to allow Kerry and the child to enter.

Inside, Grayson locked his rifle and set it down. Under no circumstances did he want Petula fingering the trigger mechanism and firing it off by accident. That would be unthinkable, so he made certain the safety mechanism was secure.

"Have a seat," Kerry invited softly, kneeling down on the floor, which she'd covered with some Oriental rugs she'd found at the shopping center. At least they didn't have to sleep on dirt like a lot of other people had to do.

Quinn grunted and went to a corner where he saw a hole dug in the ground, charred bits of wood and ash around it. Shrugging out of his pack, he set it on the floor, careful not to lean it against the rickety wall, which probably wouldn't take its full weight.

"Helluva place you live in," he muttered, opening the pack with quick, sure movements.

Kerry raised one eyebrow. "Corporal? Could you watch your language? This little girl here doesn't need to hear cursing.''

Biting back a reply, he nodded. "Yeah, you're right. Sorry," he replied, glancing uneasily at Kerry, who was sitting cross-legged on the rug, the child in her arms, the girl's head resting against her breast as she sucked her thumb. Kerry was smiling down at Petula and gently threading her fingers through the child's tangled black hair.

"Is this your first time in the basin?" she asked Quinn.

"First time," he answered. He pulled out some food packets. In all, he had twenty. Lining them up in order of breakfast, lunch and dinner, he opened the first one and put a heating tab beneath it to warm it up.

Kerry's mouth watered as the odor of bacon and eggs filled the space. Her stomach clenched in hunger as she watched the marine handle the MRE with deft, sure movements. There was nothing soft or vulnerable about Corporal Grayson. No, he was all-business. The dark look on his face told Kerry a lot. Shock was written in his eyes, even though he tried to hide it from her as he worked quietly.

Taking utensils from his pack, he readied the plate of eggs and bacon. The look on Kerry's face as he handed it to her made him flinch inwardly.

"How long since you ate last?"

Shrugging, Kerry said, "I don't know. I'm so busy, so tired most of the time, that I forget about things like that."

Quinn watched with fascination as she sat Petula in front of her, gave her the warmed tray and placed the fork in her hand. Immediately, the child began stuffing the eggs into her mouth, hot or not.

"Take it easy...." Kerry whispered to Petula. "If you eat too fast, you'll throw it up, honey. And you want to keep down what you're eating. Okay?"

Petula didn't understand how sensitive her hungry, fatigued body could be, so Kerry monitored the amount of food the child took in. Halfway through the unexpected feast, Petula yawned, rubbed her eyes and murmured, "I feel sleepy...."

Setting the plate aside, Kerry smiled gently and eased the girl onto a blanket, beside a stuffed purple dinosaur near her pillow. Getting up on her hands and knees, Kerry drew a second blanket around her and tucked it in.

"Go to sleep, honey. Your stomach is full for the first time in a long time, and all your energy is going there to digest it." She ran her hand soothingly across Petula's thin back, and very soon the child fell asleep, her arms around Barney.

Quinn motioned to the MRE. "Why don't you eat the rest?"

Kerry frowned. "There are so many people out there starving. If I ate it, I'd feel guilty."

"Eat," he ordered, studying the way her blouse hung on her frame. She'd probably dropped a good ten pounds or more in the last two weeks. Seeing the hungry glint in her eyes, Quinn added, ''Look, I need you strong, awake and healthy. So dig in, will you?''

Casting him a glance, she picked up the plate and sat down opposite him. ''You're a pragmatic person, Corporal Grayson.''

''When you're in a war, reality is the name of the game. You're a cop. You must understand that,'' he said gruffly, then regretted his harsh tone. He watched as she carefully spooned up a mouthful of eggs and started chewing. The look on her face was one of pure pleasure. She closed her eyes.

''Mmm…I never thought eggs could taste so good….''

If someone felt guilty right now, it was Quinn. The hollowness in Kerry's cheeks told him more than he wanted to know.

''How long, really, since you ate last?''

Sighing, Kerry opened her eyes. ''Probably twenty-four hours or more.''

Quinn reached down and pulled out a canteen filled with water.

''Here. You're probably thirsty, too.''

As she took the dark green canteen, her fingers met his briefly. Kerry absorbed his touch. The look in his eyes was predatory and assessing. ''You don't miss much, do you?'' There was a wry note in her voice as she set the MRE aside, unscrewed the lid of the canteen and drank deeply of the proffered gift of water.

After a moment, Kerry forced herself to stop drinking. She had to think of others, too. Reluctantly, she put down the canteen, wiped her mouth with the back of her hand and then started to replace the cap.

"You're not finished."

"Yes, I am."

"No, you're not. Drink up." Quinn hooked a thumb toward his pack. "I've got a gallon of water in there. More than enough for the three of us."

Kerry hesitated. She remembered once more those who were thirsty outside her hovel. She had heard too many squalls of infants dying of thirst. Seen too many desperate parents looking for water for their children. Her fingers tightened around the canteen, which rested on her knee.

When Kerry hung her head, her knuckles white as she gripped the canteen, understanding hit Quinn like a steamroller. Frowning, he lowered his voice.

"Listen to me, Kerry. I was in the Gulf War. I was over there in the worst of it. I saw a lot of people die of thirst—men, women and children. It wasn't fair. And it wasn't right. But the first thing you have to do is take care of yourself. You're the only one here who has the information we need. You can't short yourself just because people out there need water, too. Without you, this whole operation in Area Five would fall apart. I need you strong. Thinking. Not weak and unable to put two thoughts together.''

His voice was gentle with understanding. Kerry lifted her head and drowned in his lambent blue gaze, which was fraught with emotion. Slowly, she picked up the canteen again. Taking off the top, she lifted it to her lips and drank deeply. For the first time in two weeks, she was able to drink all the water she really wanted. What a luxury!

Wiping her mouth, she gave him a sad look. ''I still feel guilty.''

''That's okay,'' Quinn rumbled. ''Life isn't fair. It isn't ever gonna be. You've earned the right to the water, and—'' he gestured toward the half-eaten MRE ''—the rest of this food.''

Grimacing, Kerry handed the canteen back to him. ''Thanks,'' she whispered.

''Eat.''

''I can't....''

''Why not?''

Rubbing her stomach, she gave him a helpless look. ''I've been so long without good food that if I ate that, I'd throw up, Corporal. I'd be better off eating a crust of bread, or some crackers....''

Wincing internally, Quinn said nothing. He pulled one of the lunch MREs toward him, tore it open and took out a handful of crackers. ''Here, start with these. We'll slowly build you up in the next day or two so you *can* eat regular food."

Kerry took the crackers and peeled off the plastic with shaky fingers. Her stomach growled, embarrassingly loud.

"I guess my belly knows it's going to get fed."

Moodily, Quinn watched as she daintily ate each cracker as if it were a priceless gift. A look of pleasure suffused her face once again as she tasted the morsels. It hurt to watch her. This was America, the richest nation on earth, and people were starving to death. The terrible reality of that slammed into him. Kerry Chelton was gaunt looking. So was Petula. And so were the men who had taken the bottled water off the Huey earlier. Everyone had obviously dropped weight. Alarmingly so. As Quinn sat there listening to Petula breathing softly in her sleep, cuddling her purple dinosaur, and watching Kerry eat each cracker as if it were a feast, rage rose in him.

It was a rage of frustration. Flying in, he'd seen how every road in the basin, large and small, had been ripped up and torn apart by the massive earthquake. No vehicle, no convoy could possibly get through to give the people a consistent supply line of food. Now, as he sat here with Kerry and the little girl, the human side of the disaster was brought home to him in a way he'd never thought he'd see in the United States.

"You know," he said, his voice rough with sudden feeling, "things like this happen overseas. You see it on television. You see the destruction. Yeah, you feel bad, but it doesn't reach you or grab your heart and gut." Looking around the hut she'd fashioned as a strong wind blew in through the many cracks in the walls, he said, "But now it's happening here. In America. Our home." With a shake of his head, he held her darkened eyes. "God, it's just sinking in…this disaster…."

Without thinking, Kerry reached out, her hand covering his momentarily. "It's a nightmare. And it's unraveling by the minute, Corporal Grayson." Her gesture had been an attempt to try and soothe his obvious shock over the conditions around him. But once she realized what she was doing, Kerry jerked her hand away. Heat stung her neck and flowed up into her face. What on earth was she thinking, touching him like that? Glancing up, she saw his blue eyes suddenly become stormy. What *was* that emotion she saw for a split second on his hardened features?

Unsure, Kerry said, "Don't mind me. I'm a toucher. I found out a long time ago that people respond better if you reach out and just touch them. Stabilize them. It sends a message, a good one."

Nodding, he rasped, "I'm reeling, all right. I won't tell my men that. I'm sure they're just as shell-shocked by what they're seeing right now as I am." His hand tingled pleasantly where her fingertips had grazed his hairy flesh. Her touch was un-expected. Wonderful. He wanted more. Much more.

"When we're alone, call me Quinn. Out there—" he nodded toward the blanketed door "—call me Corporal Grayson. And I'll call you Deputy Chelton."

"Agreed." She saw his face thaw a bit. Maybe Grayson wasn't the unfeeling military machine that he'd projected earlier. He certainly looked like it, but Kerry knew that in law enforcement as well as the military, one had to hide behind an armored facade, show no emotion, and get the job done no matter what.

"Call me Kerry. Formality is necessary some-times, but not always. We're a team. I'd like to think of you and your men as friends come to help us."

Friends. Well, Quinn wanted to say *Friends, hell. I'd like to be your lover.* Having no idea where all these crazy, intrusive thoughts and feelings were coming from, he quirked his mouth.

"Yeah, we're one big family in a hurt locker."

Laughing softly, Kerry said, "Spoken like a ma-rine." "Hurt locker" was a navy slang term for someone being in a world of trouble. Since the Ma-rine Corps was part of the navy, and because she had worked with military personnel in the past on a number of investigations, Kerry was familiar with the terminology. She saw Quinn's eyes shine with laughter for just a moment.

"And I have a feeling you're just one big softy underneath that tough marine-green facade of yours," she teased gently.

"Humph. We'll see."

Kerry motioned to the sleeping child. "She touched you. You knew she was hungry. The first thing you did, Quinn, was try to help her. And me." Her throat closed up for a moment. Bowing her head, Kerry felt tears jamming into her eyes. Unable to look at him, because she didn't want him to see the tears, she got to her feet and turned away. If she didn't, she was going to burst into tears—tears she'd fought off since the night of the quake. And right now wasn't the time or place to let them flow.

Clearing her throat, she whispered in a rough tone, "Come on. I'll get one of the women to stay with Petula. I need to show you how things are working around here."

# Chapter Three

*January 14: 0950*

Sylvia Espinoza, a teenager of nineteen, came to stay with Petula so that Kerry could begin to show Quinn the layout of the area. The sun was shining strong and bright in the eastern sky when Quinn and she left her makeshift home. The day was chilly, and Kerry shrugged into her dark green jacket. As always, she wore her pistol around her waist and kept her flak jacket on beneath her blouse. With Diablo roving around, Kerry didn't want to take any chances.

As she fell into step beside Quinn, she felt more relief sheeting through her.

"I feel like we're going to make it now," she

confided to him. Around them, the world was waking up. People slept out in the open on cardboard, with whatever blankets they could find. To sleep in one of the remaining buildings would be foolhardy, given the continuing aftershocks. A roof or wall caving in could kill them.

Quinn glanced at Kerry's profile, which was set and serious. Her brows were drawn downward, her lips pursed. She had wrapped her arms across her chest, her hands beneath her armpits to keep them warm. January mornings in California were typically cold. Quinn made another mental note to call in for warm clothing for him and his men—and her.

"What do you mean?" Looking ahead, he saw that they were skirting the shopping area and heading toward the distribution center. In the distance, he saw one of his marines standing at ease, M-16 in place, as a long line of people waited patiently to receive bottled water.

Giving a short laugh, Kerry said, "Oh, I know this is going to sound stupid. Naive, really. I'm a police officer. I know better." She held his sharp blue gaze and her smile faded. "But just having you and your team here makes me feel better."

"In what way?" Quinn hoped she wasn't expecting miracles they couldn't deliver. There was just too much devastation and not enough people power to rescue even those most affected.

"Oh," Kerry murmured, "for two weeks I've shouldered all the responsibility of trying to set up a logistical network to help people. I did receive training in disaster relief for our county, and it sure has come in handy. Without it, I wouldn't have had a *clue* what to do first."

"You've handled this area single-handedly?"

"Yes." With a sigh, Kerry whispered, "When the quake hit I had just gone out to my cruiser in the parking lot at the back of the sheriff's building, Quinn. I remember hearing this god-awful roar—like a freight train bearing down on me. I looked around, but it was dark and I couldn't see a thing. I didn't figure out what was happening until the first shock hit."

Quinn slowed his pace and stopped, turning to face her. The emotions and pain in her expression ate at him as she stopped before him, looked down and began gnawing on her lower lip, obviously struggling not to cry. Without thinking, he reached out and slid his hand down her arm.

"It's okay," he murmured. As a trained EMT, he knew the effect touch and a gentle voice could have on someone who was in trauma. It was obvious to him that Kerry was still in shock. Deep shock. She refused to look up at him. He wanted to touch her again, so he rested his hand lightly on her slumped shoulder and stepped toward her until their bodies were nearly touching. What she needed, he realized, was to talk it out, to get some of those nightmarish memories out of her in the same way a sick person needed to discharge an infection in order to feel better.

"Tell me about it?"

The deep, concerned tone of Quinn's voice tore away the last of Kerry's defenses against the horror she could still see, even with her eyes tightly shut. His hand resting on her shoulder sent warm, wonderful sensations lapping through her. His attention, his obvious care, dismantled her monumental efforts to put a lid on the boiling cauldron of trauma she carried daily within her.

"I don't know if you're ready to hear it," she said unsteadily.

Quinn patted her shoulder awkwardly. Hell, if he was honest with himself, he really wanted to open his arms and draw Kerry against him. That's what she needed most. With all the people around them, however, Quinn knew that wasn't wise. She was a leader and needed to be seen that way by the people of the area. And he didn't want his stature as head of the fire team to be compromised, either. So he remained where he was, even though his heart was crying to him to embrace Kerry. Hold her, rock her and ease the awful pain he saw revealed in her pale features.

Biting down hard on her lower lip, Kerry tried to control her escaping emotions. "Oh, this isn't going to be good, Quinn. I don't think you want a crybaby on your hands right now...."

Chuckling softly, he said, "Listen, Kerry, I've

seen horror. I know trauma. I think I've got an idea of what you're going through. One thing I found out a long time ago was that it helps to talk it out with someone you trust. Someone you feel safe with.''

Lifting her chin, Kerry tried to smile, but failed. ''You make me feel safe, Quinn. I can't explain it. The moment I saw you come off that Huey, I knew everything was going to be okay. Maybe that's foolish and idealistic, but that's how you impressed me.'' Easing her hands from beneath her armpits she waved them helplessly, her voice wobbling as she said, ''The sheriff's building collapsed in on itself, Quinn. All three stories.'' Kerry shut her eyes. Hot tears scalded her eyelids. She felt his hand grip her shoulder more tightly, as if to buttress her against the pain she was sharing with him.

''Go on...'' Damn, it was tough just to stand here and not hold her. Quinn watched as two tears wound down her pale cheeks, leaving a silvery path in the light film of dust on her skin. How badly he wanted to give Kerry a warm, luxurious bath, so she could relax. She needed to clean herself up to feel halfway human again. He was glad she'd said he made her feel safe. His heart had soared at that whispered admission, and emotion still vibrated in his chest, like a flower that had discovered the glory of the sun. She made him feel good about himself as a man.

Sniffing, Kerry wiped her eyes self-consciously. Raising her head, she looked around, worried that others might see her crying. In the two weeks since the disaster, she hadn't shed any tears. People were looking to her for strength, for answers and for organization. They looked to her for help. It was a horrible burden to carry alone.

"This is tougher to talk about than I thought," she admitted, taking a short rasping breath.

"I'm here for you, Kerry. Just talk it out. That's best." And it was. To get a victim of trauma to talk was part of the healing process.

"Well…" She looked up at him and was stunned to see the tender flame burning in his blue eyes. That hard, armored marine mask had dissolved. The man who stood in front of her now took her breath away. His well-shaped mouth had softened, his lips slightly parted. The gentle strength she saw in his face made him even more handsome.

"I'm listening…."

"The building collapsed, Quinn. I was thrown off my feet and rolled around in the parking lot. The cruiser I was going to climb into flipped. I was lucky I wasn't crushed. I remember seeing the back end of the car suddenly shooting upward. The streetlights went off. Everything went black. So black… The roar around me was incredible. I've never heard anything like it before. I remember getting thrown against the cyclone wire fence—smashing into it. I heard the building going down. Dust…dust was everywhere. I was choking on it. I couldn't see. I was covered with it. I don't know how long the shock lasted…."

"The initial quake lasted two minutes."

"It felt like *hours*," Kerry whispered unsteadily. She blinked back the tears, mesmerized by his tender expression. How badly she wanted to take one more step toward him and sink into his arms. Somehow, Kerry knew that Quinn Grayson would hold her. Hold her, help her and heal her. Right now, her heart was wide-open and she was feeling so many emotions for the first time since the quake. It was him, she realized belatedly—his care, his attention, the touch of his hand resting gently on her shoulder, that had allowed her this moment of healing.

"Hours…" she repeated, and slowly shook her head.

"Then what happened?" Quinn asked, trying to keep his voice steady. He saw the ravages of horror in Kerry's wide, tear-filled eyes. Her mouth was a slash against the awful feelings she held within her, and it hurt him to see her suffering. How much he wanted to take his thumbs and erase the tracks of those tears. But Quinn knew the value of letting a person cry. When he'd worked as an EMT, they'd had an old expression: better out than in. In other words, it was better to cry, scream or talk about the incident rather than hold it inside. If a victim tried to suppress the hurt, it became like an ugly infection that would debilitate the person sooner or later.

"The building collapsed," Kerry said, all the energy draining out of her as she stood with that cold

January sunshine against her back. "Do you know how many people died in there, Quinn?"

He shook his head, seeing the grief now shadowing her face. "No...no, I don't, Kerry."

"I—I had so many friends in there, men and women I'd worked with for years.... Since Lee got killed, they'd rallied around me, helped me so much through that hellish year after I lost him...." She stopped and sniffed. Embarrassed, she raised her hand and tried to wipe away the tears. It was impossible. They were leaking out of her eyes steadily now. She felt as if a huge volcano of grief was imploding in her chest. A lump was forming in her throat, keeping her from saying anymore at the moment.

"Lee?" Quinn asked, stymied.

"My husband. He was a sheriff's deputy, too...." Kerry took a ragged breath. "I was married to Lee for three years. H-he was killed in the line of duty. He didn't like to wear his flak jacket under his shirt, so he rarely did. He got a call one night on duty, and when he went to the scene, a gang member shot him point-blank in the chest. If he'd had his vest on, it would have saved his life. But he didn't...."

"Damn," Quinn whispered, his fingers digging momentarily into her shoulder. "I'm sorry, Kerry. Really sorry." And he was. It was obvious she loved her husband. Quinn could see the warmth burning in her tearful gray eyes when she spoke of him.

Wouldn't it be wonderful if some woman loved him that way? Yes, but it was never going to happen.

Pushing aside his own problems, Quinn focused on Kerry. She lifted her hands and wiped her face. All the gesture did was spread the dust, leaving muddy smears. Withdrawing his own hand, he groped for the canteen and a cloth he carried in one of the pockets of his uniform.

"Did you lose all your friends in there?" he asked, as he uncapped the canteen and poured some of the precious water onto the dark green cloth in his hand.

"Y-yes. Every one of them. We had a shift change going on at the time. After the first shock ended, I got to my feet. I was stunned. It was so dark. There were no lights. The quake had torn up the lighting system and it was awful. I managed to find my flashlight and started back toward what I thought was a building." Opening her hands, she looked down at them. Her nails were jagged, and her hands were dirty and covered with cuts.

"I tripped and fell so many times in that chewed-up asphalt parking lot, Quinn. It was pulverized rubble, just like you see here at the shopping center." She swept her arm around them. The once smooth surface was now a vast stretch of jagged chunks of asphalt and dirt that looked more like a plowed field than a parking lot.

"But you got to the building?" Quinn capped the canteen and hung it back on his web belt.

Kerry nodded and sighed heavily. "Yes, I managed to get over to it. But I could smell natural gas. The lines had been broken. I knew I was in trouble. As I got closer to the building, I couldn't believe it. All three stories had pancaked down upon one another. Three stories had become a half story of concrete, steel and glass rubble." Shaking her head, she whispered, "All I could do was stand there. I just couldn't believe it. I didn't hear anyone crying out for help. Nothing. I felt so helpless. So very helpless. I stumbled and staggered all around that building, but there was nothing left of it. Over a hundred people were in that structure…so many of them my friends…." She covered her face with her hands.

How alone she was, Quinn realized, her grief reaching out and grabbing him hard. *To hell with it,* he thought, stepping closer and putting his arm around her shoulders. "Come here, Kerry. Let me clean you up a bit." And he raised the dampened towel.

When she lifted her head in surprise, he smiled at her. It was a smile, he hoped, that said *Relax, I'm going to help you.*

With the first stroke of the soft terry cloth against her cheek, Kerry released a tremulous sigh. She stood very still against him while he cleaned her face as if she were a lost child in need of care and love. Every stroke was gentle. The coolness of the cloth against her skin felt good. Cleansing. Quinn was so close, and so pulverizingly male to Kerry. It took everything she had left, emotionally, not to turn and lay her head against his strong, broad shoulder. Somehow, Kerry knew Quinn could handle big loads and heavy responsibility. He was built for it not only physically, but emotionally, too.

His gentleness was surprising and unexpected, however. All too soon, he was done cleaning her face. Stepping away, he dropped his arm from her shoulders. Inwardly, Kerry cried over the loss of his nearness, his care. Opening her eyes, she fell captive to the smoky blueness now banked in his eyes as he studied her in silence. For the first time in years, Kerry felt another stirring deep within her heart and lower body—the start of desire for a man. For Quinn Grayson. Even though he was a tough, no-nonsense marine warrior, he had an incredibly surprising and wonderfully tender side to him, too. It was a beautiful discovery for Kerry. Right now, after the last two hellish weeks, she needed someone exactly like Quinn.

"Has anyone ever told you that you're really a mother hen in disguise?" Kerry tried to keep her voice light and teasing, for if she didn't, she was going to break down in unrelenting, body-shaking sobs. She hadn't yet cried for the loss of all her friends, and the emotions threatened to hit her hard now.

Grinning crookedly, Quinn handed her the damp towel. "Yeah, I've been accused of that by my fire team from time to time. It's my job to care for my people.''

"You're good at it," Kerry whispered shakily. She took the towel and rubbed her hands free of dirt. "And this is a wonderful gift…. Thanks for listening to me, Quinn. And thanks for the spit bath. I know I'm dirty as all get-out. There's no water to waste. But I long so badly for a hot bath…." She sighed. "Now, *that's* a dream. A faraway one…"

Quinn said nothing, watching as she scrubbed her slender wrists and artistic fingers free of dirt. Once they were clean, he saw many fine pink scars across them, as well as healing cuts. "What are these from?" he asked, pointing to her hand.

"Those? Oh, I spent hours at the building trying to pull away rubble and debris to find someone…anyone…." Kerry handed the cloth back to him. When his fingers met hers, she absorbed the warmth like a greedy beggar. Right now, she felt like an emotional thief on the prowl, stealing energy from Quinn, who was giving so unselfishly to her. That wasn't right, but Kerry couldn't help herself. Quinn seemed to bring out every emotion she hadn't allowed herself to feel for the last two weeks. That caught Kerry off guard, and she labored beneath the violent ebb and flow of her grief, rage, frustration and sadness.

"Any luck?" he asked, tucking the cloth back into the large pocket in the thigh of his cammos.

Shaking her head, Kerry felt sadness overwhelm

her once more. "No…none. Not one survived. I stayed there all the next day, Quinn, but I couldn't find anyone alive, or hear any cries for help. It was just so…devastating."

Looking around the shopping center, Quinn could see people moving about. Here and there, he saw small campfires, with people huddled around them for warmth. They were cooking a meager breakfast. Probably preparing whatever food they could find.

"The natural gas odor got so bad, I had to leave. I was afraid of an explosion," Kerry related.

"We heard at the base that there were a lot of explosions and fires after the quake."

Nodding, Kerry said, "Yes, there were. There aren't now. The pipelines have all been shut off."

"So how did you get involved in all of this?" He swept his arm around the area.

"By accident, I guess." Kerry shrugged. "I retrieved what I could out of my cruiser—the shotgun, the emergency medical kit, my shoulder radio—and went looking for a place where I might find some electricity, a generator. Uppermost in my mind was to get help. There was a hardware store two blocks down from the sheriff's building and across the street from the apartment where I used to live. I went there and dug out a small gasoline generator. About five blocks down, there was a small electronics store. I broke into what was left of it and found a radio that hadn't been destroyed. The gas station was still standing for some reason, and I managed to siphon off gas from a car that was nearby. I carried the container of gas to the generator, and got it fired up and working. Once it was on-line, I hooked up the radio and started calling for help. By chance, I got lucky and zeroed in on Logistics at Camp Reed. From there, I talked to Morgan Trayhern, who, thankfully, was able to get you here. You and the supplies.'' Kerry grimaced. ''I needed a place for a helicopter to land, so I set off to try and find a big enough clearing. The shopping center was a mile away, so I came here. The asphalt parking lot was chewed up, but the area was clear of downed power lines and there was no natural gas or propane around. I told Morgan about it, and that's when he started ordering the Huey to fly in as often as it could during the daylight hours to deliver food, water and medicine.''

''And so you set up your H.Q. here as a result?''

''Yes.'' Kerry smiled softly. ''I asked for volunteers to help me move the generator and radio to this place. The people who lived in this area pitched in with their hearts and souls. They're wonderful, Quinn. Most of them have lost family members. But they rallied and helped me. Over the last two weeks, this neighborhood has really pulled together in order to survive. These people are great. The area has a mix of nationalities—lots of Koreans, Hispanics. Elderly folks on a fixed income... It's a poor area of Los Angeles. But everyone—'' she glanced over at him ''—and I mean *everyone,* has helped. They understand that the only way they're going to survive this is to work together as a team.''

''So there's been no fighting among them for food or water?''

''None. They're a tribute to the human race, Quinn.'' Kerry wrinkled her nose. ''But then, a week ago, Diablo started infiltrating, and it has been hell ever since. We aren't prepared for such a group—men who take and don't share. There aren't any guns available to fight them off, either—the houses are crushed. You can't dig inside to find anything, not with aftershocks happening dozens of times a day.'' Touching her holster at her side, she added, ''I'm the only one with a weapon. But I can't be everywhere. If I go somewhere, I have to walk. I can't just hop in my cruiser, lights flashing, and go to the scene where I'm needed.''

''I understand,'' Quinn said. His admiration for Kerry skyrocketed. She was an incredibly resourceful woman. Single-handedly, this stalwart person was helping hundreds of people survive. And as Quinn looked around, watching quake survivors get up from their shabby, crude sleep areas, he began to understand that Kerry was a very special person. Her bravery, her strength under the circumstances, was worthy of a medal. Her cool-headed efforts, her ability to organize and be a leader when the world was in chaos around her, spoke volumes.

''Let's get to your distribution center,'' he told her with a slight, tender smile. ''Let's see what we

can do to help you and these folks out a little more.''
He knew his first priority was to close down the bad
guys if possible, but even now, he could see his
mission changing, just as Morgan had warned that
it might.

Hope spiraled strongly in her breast. As Quinn
gazed at her, Kerry felt her heart expanding with
such joy that it overshadowed all the sadness she
was feeling. There was a burning look in his eyes
meant for her alone, and she knew it. Somehow, her
sharing the awful trauma with Quinn had forged a
new and wonderful connection between them. Kerry
was as scared as she was euphoric. Never had she
felt like this. As she walked at Quinn's side once
more, she told herself it was because she was traumatized, her emotions stripped and vulnerable.
Quinn represented help and survival, she tried to tell
herself sternly. And that was all. But no matter what
she did, she couldn't quite make herself believe that
completely. No, there was another emotion, a special
one, growing between them. She had seen it banked
in his narrowed eyes…and she was afraid of it.
Afraid, and yet eager at the very same time.

# Chapter Four

*January 14: 1015*

Private Orvil Perkins gave Quinn a look that spoke volumes. The thin, wiry marine was surrounded by civilians who had desperate looks on their faces and in their eyes as they asked him question after question. As Kerry and Quinn approached, the crowd of about twenty people, mostly adults, turned to face them, hope burning in their eyes.

In shock, Quinn saw that the people were all dirty and unkempt. It looked as if he'd stepped into a third world country. He'd been in some, but he'd never seen people in such a state. Even in those countries, people were able to bathe, wash their threadbare clothes and keep their hair neat and combed. Not here. These people were gaunt, with red-rimmed eyes, their hands caked with dirt. The desperation in their faces rocked him deeply.

"Is help coming?" One balding man spoke up, his voice booming across the others.

"My baby," a woman cried. "She's got a fever and I can't get it down. I can't even get to the aspirin in our house. It's too dangerous to crawl in and try to find it. Can you help me?"

"We need water," another man said. "We aren't getting enough. My animals have already died. I've got a teenage son with a broken leg. I can't move him. I need more water for him. Can you help us?"

Swallowing hard, Quinn placed his rifle across his right shoulder. Holding up his hand, he silenced the restless, anxious group.

"My name is Corporal Grayson. The Marine Corps is beginning to initiate help. You are in Area Five, as most of you probably already know. We're here to provide safety as well as continuing organization."

"When are we going to get medical help?" a red-haired woman called out angrily. "I got a little girl, six years old, and she's diabetic! I gotta have insulin or—" she choked up "—she's gonna die! You gotta help me!"

Kerry lifted her hands to silence them. "Folks, I know your stories and your needs. Today, Corporal Grayson is going to assign one of his men to write down each of your specific requests. We'll pass them along to the Huey crew that flies in our supplies. That's the best we can do. There're millions of people in the basin just as bad off, or worse, than us. Corporal Grayson is the beginning of a vanguard, but he can't do everything. He and his fire team are here primarily to protect us from Diablo.''

A sigh of relief went up from the crowd, which edged closer and closer. Kerry saw Quinn cut her a quick glance. He said nothing to her about her suggestion. They hadn't talked about it, but Kerry knew it would help defuse the anxiety if written requests were collected.

"Thank God!" a man cried. "Those bastards killed my wife!" He began to sob, and pressed his hands against his face. "All for a lousy box of crackers."

Quinn stared at the man, who appeared in his thirties. He was weeping uncontrollably.

Kerry gripped Quinn's left arm. "Folks, please get back into line for your water ration. I need to take Corporal Grayson around our immediate area, fill him in on our needs, so he can radio back to Logistics at Camp Reed. It's there that plans for the future are worked out. The more information I can give the corporal, the more potential help we can get."

"We need medicine! I need insulin!" the woman cried, desperation in her tone. "My baby's gonna die without it! Somebody has to do *something* soon!''

"I hear you," Kerry said soothingly. "And help is coming. Just get into line, Martha. Please."

The crowd began to hesitantly break up. People trudged wearily back into a ragged line to await the one-quart bottle of water that would have to suffice for them and their families for the next twenty-four hours.

Quinn felt Kerry release his arm and he glanced at her. The look in her soft gray eyes compounded the emotions he felt in his chest. As they moved out of earshot, he growled, "I never realized how bad off these people really were. Not until now…"

Mouth compressed, Kerry nodded. "You've seen only the tip of the iceberg, Quinn." Her voice broke with emotion as she added, "Believe me."

He halted and turned to face her. "You've been holding this paper bag on wheels around here together since the beginning, haven't you?"

"Yes." Shrugging, she sent the people waiting in line a compassionate look. "I'm a law enforcement officer. It's my duty to help keep the peace. To help direct people in a disaster."

"You're doing a helluva lot more than that." Giving the crowd a dark look, he returned his gaze to Kerry. "I like your idea of having them write down their needs. That woman has to have insulin for her daughter. We need them to write this stuff down, and then we can go through it like a triage, separating common requests from real emergencies. Thanks for suggesting it.''

Smiling slightly, Kerry said, ''I didn't mean to usurp your authority. It was one of the things I thought of doing once you guys arrived.''

''It's a good suggestion. Speak up on anything else you have in mind. Frankly, I wasn't trained for this kind of duty.''

''Who was?'' Kerry asked wryly, giving him a tentative half smile. She liked the way his blue eyes warmed when he looked at her. Despite Quinn's warrior toughness, he was a man with a heart. A big, generous heart.

''I read you loud and clear on that one. Let's make a circuit around the shopping center. From the looks of it, a lot of people are sleeping out in the parking lot, with makeshift tents, and cardboard for beds. I want to see the whole thing. Then we'll go back to your H.Q. and make plans. I also want to radio Logistics and try to get an extra flight out here today with certain supplies that you think are needed right away.''

''The insulin, for sure,'' Kerry said.

''Absolutely...''

As Quinn turned and began to walk again, with Kerry at his side, he wrestled with the exploding shock of seeing Americans in such a state of helplessness. He felt overwhelmed by it all. They were only a five-man marine fire team. His main mission was to hunt down Diablo, but how was he going to do that and try to help these people, too? Torn, Quinn knew that Kerry's help, as well the knowledge she'd gained from the past two weeks of dealing with this horrific situation, was absolutely essential to him in order to make good decisions for everyone here. And he knew Morgan would support his helping the people first, before trying to locate Diablo. One fire team could do only so much.

*January 14: 1515*

By 1500, Quinn had radioed in for some extra supplies—emergency items needed to keep people alive. Luckily, according to Morgan Trayhern, Camp Reed had just gotten ten more helicopters delivered, U.S. Navy choppers that would hold a lot more cargo. They were setting up a dirt landing zone at Camp Reed, a second, makeshift airport desperately needed in this escalating situation. Marines at Camp Reed were now moving supplies to this new airport so that the larger, heavier helicopters could carry more supplies in one flight to each affected area.

Kerry had looked tired as Quinn had stood outside her hovel and made the radio call. Sylvia was babysitting Petula nearby.

Quinn had shared more of his MREs with them, but Sylvia had gobbled her food down and promptly thrown up. The food was too rich for her in her starving condition. She'd cried afterward because she hadn't listened to Kerry's instructions to eat just a little, slowly, and then eat more an hour later. The teenage girl was so hungry she'd eaten like a starving dog. Quinn had felt badly for her. He'd seen the unshed tears in Kerry's eyes as she'd held the girl while she vomited. This was an unfolding and shocking nightmare to him. And it was going to get worse.

In his eyes, the only good thing about the situation was Kerry. She was a bulwark of quiet, gentle strength. Throughout the day, her home was like headquarters for the area. Anyone who needed something came to Kerry. By late afternoon, she had given away the two extra blankets she slept on to two needy families who had nothing and were sleeping out on the yellowed lawns outside their destroyed homes, huddled together to keep warm. The only blanket she didn't give away was Petula's and the ones that hung in the door of their hovel.

Once Sylvia was feeling better she took Petula for a walk, and Quinn took the opportunity to sit with Kerry outside her home. She looked drawn.

The sun was low in the sky, on the opposite side of the shopping center now, leaving the house in the shade. Kerry was sitting on the chewed-up ground sifting through at least fifty handwritten notes before her. Her brows were drawn downward, but as the breeze lifted some of the strands of her hair, she looked beautiful to him.

Opening the pack he left inside the hovel, Quinn knelt down opposite her and prepared a heating tab.

Kerry looked over. "What are you doing?" Quinn had two tin cups in hand and several packets near his boot.

"Making us some well-deserved instant coffee." He grinned at her. "Interested?" He tore open the pack and sprinkled it into the bottom of a cup, then added water.

Sighing, Kerry whispered, "Coffee?"

The longing in her voice touched him. "Yeah. Not the real stuff, and certainly not a mocha latte, but it'll do in a pinch, as my ma would say. Want some?" The moment he lifted his head, he drowned in her widening eyes. When they were alone, Quinn noticed, Kerry's official demeanor melted away. He was privileged to see the real woman behind the badge. And he liked what he saw—more than he should. All day he'd found reasons to touch her arm or hand or shoulder briefly. Quinn *liked* touching Kerry. Every time he did, he saw her expression change perceptibly. Saw her dove-gray eyes go soft for just a moment. And it made his heart sing. He felt his chest expanding and widening like a river flowing at flood stage. Kerry Chelton was affecting him like no other woman he'd ever met. And Quinn found himself dying to know all about her on a personal level.

Yet all day they'd dealt with people, with problems, trying to come up with solutions to help them. It was a pathetically useless effort, as far as Quinn was concerned. They didn't have medicine, blankets, food or water for the people, except what was being flown in hourly, and that merely helped stave off the long-term problems.

"Coffee…" Kerry sighed. "Wow! Do you know, in my dream last night, I was at a Starbucks over on Central?" She hooked her thumb over her shoulder. "Just two blocks from where I worked there was a Starbucks. Now it's gone. I used to love to get my coffee there before I went on shift."

Chuckling, Quinn created a tiny stove with some pieces of asphalt and placed the cup between them. The magnesium tab flared to life, bright and burning. Soon, the water was bubbling. "Yeah, I don't move without my coffee, so I know what you mean."

Smiling, Kerry placed her hands over the papers so they wouldn't blow away in the breeze. The sky was a light blue, the sun bright. She looked forward to the afternoons because the temperature warmed up and she could take off her coat. By this time of day, the chill and dampness of the night before was only a memory.

"You have the most wonderful soft, Southern ac-

cent, Quinn. Were you born in the South?'' she
asked as he lifted one cup off and set it aside, then
placed the second one over the burning tab. She saw
his cheeks grow a dull red as she complimented him.
Even though he'd shaved that morning, a five-
o'clock shadow darkened his face, giving him a dangerous, predatory look. It excited her.

''I was born in Kentucky. Up in the mountains.
My folks are hill people.'' Quinn held up sugar and
cream. ''Any of these?''

''Oh, yes, please. One of each?''

The sudden excitement in her voice made him
sad. Kerry's eyes were bright with eagerness for
such a small, seemingly insignificant gift. After he
tore each packet open and poured the contents into
the steaming coffee, he stirred it with a spoon.
''There,'' he murmured, and held the cup toward
her. ''Coffee for a purty lady.''

Blushing, Kerry laughed. It was the first time in
weeks that she had. Her hand closed around the handle of the cup. ''Thanks, Quinn. You are truly an
angel in Marine Corps disguise.''

''Drink up,'' he told her brusquely, unable to
meet the gentle look of thanks in her eyes. ''You've
more than earned this cup of coffee.'' And she had.
Quinn was finding that Kerry was giving away everything she had to those who were worse off than
she.

As the second cup came to a boil, Quinn removed

it and took a sip. He liked his coffee black and strong. Over the rim, he saw the look of absolute pleasure on Kerry's face as she drank.

"Ohh… I never knew coffee could taste so good, Quinn. This is delicious…." She closed her eyes and savored the taste of it.

His conscience ate at him. Back at Camp Reed, they had real coffee in huge urns, available twenty-four hours a day at the many chow tents that had been hastily erected in different parts of the hundred-thousand-acre military base. Dipping his head, he sipped his coffee with a scowl. The soft sighs of pleasure emanating from Kerry as she relished each sip ripped at his heart. She deserved so much more. She was a good person in a very ugly situation—so brave and helpful to those in need. In his eyes, Kerry deserved a medal, but she'd never get one. After what he'd seen this afternoon, Quinn knew that just surviving in this area was heroic.

Opening her eyes, Kerry smiled at Quinn, who sat with a dark scowl on his face. He seemed bothered by something, but wasn't saying much.

"You said you were born in the mountains of Kentucky. Like the Hatfields and McCoys?" she teased, trying to lighten his mood.

"Yeah, you could say that." Fighting the sadness and frustration he felt for the people around them, Quinn looked at Kerry. Just studying her attractive features and gray eyes lifted his spirits and made his heart pound a little harder for a moment.

"I was barefoot most of the time until I went to a local high school nearby. Up until then, I was home-schooled by my ma. My pa was a man of the woods. He hunted and killed what we needed for food. My ma tended a huge garden, and me and my sisters used to help her can stuff in the fall. When I wasn't book learnin', my pa would take me out and teach me how to hunt and track."

"What a wonderful childhood," Kerry said. "I was born and raised here in Ontario, California, a huge suburb of Los Angeles. I'm afraid I'm a city girl in comparison to you."

"Opposites."

"What made you join the Marine Corps?" she asked, sipping the cooling coffee with relish.

"My pa was in the corps. So were my uncles, and my granddaddy before them. It's a tradition in our family."

"Are you making it a career?"

"Probably." Quinn shrugged. "I don't know anything else. I'm not a math wizard. I don't pretend to be smart like a college graduate."

"The fact that you didn't go to college doesn't mean you aren't intelligent," Kerry pointed out. "Look how many good ideas you've come up with so far. You're good at assessing a situation and coming up with solutions."

Feeling heat steal into his face, Quinn shrugged. "I'm fire team leader. It's my job to do that."

"I feel your common sense and practical knowledge are a huge plus here. You dovetail beautifully with me and my ideas."

"Yeah, we make a good team," he admitted quietly. Glancing around, he could see people getting ready for nightfall, which would happen around 1730 this time of year.

"I was so looking forward to your coming," Kerry admitted. "Today I realized just how tired I've become—mostly because I wasn't eating much." She gave a short laugh. "You can't get far on a growling stomach. It's been tough pushing myself through my physical tiredness to keep going."

"I don't know how you've done it." And he didn't. His admiration for Kerry came through loud and clear in his voice. "You're so patient with people."

"You have to be, Quinn. That was part of my training as a deputy."

"Yeah, but a lot of it is you. You're a good person, Kerry. Mighty good, as my ma would say."

She laughed softly. "Thanks, that means a lot to me, Quinn." She gestured toward him. "So tell me about yourself. Are you married to some woman who loves the outdoors as much as you? Is she in base housing on Camp Reed with you? And do you have kids? You'd be a great father, I think."

Startled by her personal questions, he was caught off guard. "I'm not married," he told her gruffly, "so there're no rug rats around."

Kerry grinned. "Rug rats? That's a military term for kids, right?"

"Yeah. A nice term."

She tilted her head. Kerry couldn't believe Quinn didn't have a woman in his life. She'd seen a shadow flicker in his blue eyes when she'd asked.

"Sorry," she whispered. "I guess I got nosy and overstepped my bounds with you. You just seemed like you were married and settled down. I could imagine you with a couple of kids—taking them fishing and hiking in the woods. Doing the kind of things that give children a wonderful sense of the natural world that surrounds them."

Quinn finished his coffee. "I was engaged once," he admitted abruptly. "But Frannie wasn't happy that I was a marine. She was a social climber, to be blunt about it. I was an enlisted man and I found out too late that she wanted someone with more rank and status. Like an officer."

Grimacing, Kerry sipped the last of her coffee. She handed the empty cup to Quinn. Their fingertips met briefly, and again she enjoyed the contact. His demeanor made her feel solid and secure. Protection emanated from Quinn like warmth and light from the sun. And she was starved for both.

"Sorry to hear that," Kerry murmured. "At least you found out before you tied the knot."

"Yeah," he muttered, putting the cups aside, "I did. She wasn't honest in our relationship, I discovered. And if I marry someday, which won't be soon, I want truth between us. My ma and pa have been married for over thirty years and I saw, growin' up, what it took to hold a marriage together. It's a lot of hard work, but I think it's worth the effort."

Resting her elbows on her crossed legs, Kerry smiled softly. "It sounds like what I had with Lee, my husband. And you're right, in the throwaway society we're in today, people waltz into marriage like it's a one-night gig at a local club, and waltz out of it the next day."

"It's far from that." Quinn glanced down at the watch on his right wrist. According to Morgan Trayhern, one of the big navy helos was going to try and come in just before dark to deliver an extra load of supplies, including the insulin that was so desperately needed. Quinn hadn't said anything to Kerry about it, because Trayhern couldn't promise it would arrive that quickly. But Morgan had told Quinn he'd go through hell and high water to try and get it off to him by the end of the day. This one shipment would make such a difference, and Quinn wanted nothing more than to give these people, including Kerry and little Petula, some respite from the horrible circumstances they dealt with daily.

"How did you meet your husband?" he asked now.

"We were at the police academy when we met." Kerry sighed. "Lee was a lot like you."

"Oh?"

"Yes, he was born and raised in the Sisque Mountains, in a tiny logging community in Northern California known as Happy Camp. His dad was a logger, his mother a teacher at the local school. Lee could hunt black bear and cougar when he was ten years old. His father taught him well."

"I see."

"I'm twenty-seven now. We got married after we graduated, when I was twenty-one." She lost her smile. "At least we had six wonderful years together. We worked for the same sheriff's department, though we had different areas to patrol. Our watch officer gave us the same hours so that we could at least have a life together outside work. We both had the graveyard shift."

"Any kids?" He didn't mean to ask that, but he suddenly had to know. So when he saw Kerry's face go pale and her gaze drop as she pretended to pick at a thread on her dusty, dark green slacks, he suddenly felt as if he'd tramped like a bull into the proverbial china shop. Obviously he'd touched on a very poignant subject, a raw wound in her life. "You don't have to answer that. Don't mind me. I shouldn't have asked," he told her abruptly.

"No..." Kerry said in a low tone, "I don't mind you asking, Quinn. I like talking with you, if you want to know the truth...." And she did. Forcing herself to look at him, Kerry saw the angst in his eyes. Opening her hands, she whispered, "I was pregnant with our first child when Lee got killed in the line of duty. When I heard from my watch chief that he was in the hospital, I went there. I remember fainting after the doctor came out and told me he was dead. Two other deputies were there and caught me. When I came to, a few minutes later, I had horrible cramping in my abdomen. I was numb with shock. They took me home and I remember just lying there on the couch, curled up, staring off into space. I couldn't believe it, Quinn...that Lee was dead."

"I'm sorry."

"There's more...." Kerry hitched up one shoulder in an awkward shrug. "I remember finally sleeping, probably near dawn. When I woke up, hours later, the cramping was worse. It was then that I miscarried. I was three months along and the shock of his death caused it." Biting her lower lip, she whispered, "So I lost our baby, too."

Quinn could hardly bear to look at her. He heard the sadness, the helplessness, in her voice, but there was nothing he could do to soothe her loss. Not a thing. And the good Lord knew, he wanted to. He wanted to do *something* to ease her agonizing burden.

# Chapter Five

January 15: 0600

Quinn didn't have the heart to awaken Kerry at dawn the next morning. He'd just finished his three hours of duty at the distribution center, and had come back to her hovel. Quietly easing away the blanket over the door, he saw a scene that tugged at his heart.

It has gotten very cold last night, with the wind whipping and sawing inconstantly. Petula had left her bed and made her way into Kerry's arms for more warmth. Kerry lay on her side on the unforgiving cardboard beneath her, her legs drawn up toward her body. Curled in her arms, little Petula snuggled, both of them sound asleep. Kerry had her face pressed against Petula's hair.

Quinn stood there frozen, absorbing the heart-wrenching scene. It hurt him that all they had was cardboard to sleep on, now that Kerry had given the two Oriental rugs on the dirt floor to families who desperately needed something to cover up with during the cold nights. No one should live like this.

On top of everything else, he'd gotten a call that the navy helicopter wouldn't arrive until late today with the badly needed extra supplies. It had been held up because the medical items had to be flown in from San Francisco. Obliquely, he wondered if the little girl who needed insulin would survive until that afternoon. Frustration, he was discovering, was becoming his worst enemy.

Allowing the blanket over the door to fall into place because it kept out some of the biting wind, Quinn tried to be quiet as he moved about. Kerry had been up until 0100 this morning dealing with people who had problems, demands, urgent requests made worse by their rising hysteria. Word had gotten out that a marine team was here, and the news had run like wildfire across Area Five. When people heard that help had arrived, they came from miles around to the shopping center, pleading for relief.

After easing his rifle off his shoulder, Quinn slipped out of his Kevlar flak vest. He'd worn his heavy cammo jacket while standing on guard this morning because of the cold out there. When the night sky had begun to turn gray with the coming dawn, Private Cliff Ludlow had relieved him of guard duty. They had to keep an around-the-clock guard at the distribution center. Some people, beyond desperation, were sneaking in during the night to steal what little food or water might be left. Kerry couldn't stay up twenty-four hours a day to stand guard, so she couldn't stop the thievery until Quinn and his men had arrived to help.

When Private Ludlow had taken over, his eyes puffy from sleep, Quinn had purposely gone around the back of the shopping center, quietly moving among the massive piles of rubble, eyes open and ears keyed to any sounds. It had been silent, but Quinn didn't put it past Diablo to start trouble once they heard that a marine team had come in. Or the presence of the team might scare the gang away, possibly driving them into Area Six adjacent.

Now, as he quietly eased his hand into his massive pack and searched for three breakfast MREs, his mouth quirked in pain. Kerry had lost her baby due to the trauma of losing her husband. Trying to grasp how that must have felt, he shook his head. It was impossible to imagine. Taking the MREs from the pack, he quietly began to open them. More than anything, he'd like to waken them to a hot, decent breakfast. Little Petula had eaten off and on from the MRE he'd opened yesterday morning. According to Sylvia, the girl hadn't vomited once. By last night, Quinn could see the difference a little good food made for the girl. She was more animated, her wan cheeks touched with some color.

More than anything, he wanted Kerry to eat. He needed her strong and alert. She had the bad habit of giving away most of her food and supplies—even the rugs off her dirt floor—to those she saw as more needy than herself. What a big heart she had in that strong, beautiful body of hers.

Quinn quickly and efficiently fixed the three MREs, and when the enticing smells of eggs and bacon began filling the cold space within the hut, he glanced up.

Kerry was beginning to stir. Her eyes opened slightly, her lashes thick and dark against her pale flesh. The sight of the soft hair grazing her cheek made Quinn want to go over and gently tame the strands back into place, but he resisted. She slowly eased her left arm upward and rolled onto her back. Blinking, she raised her head.

He gave her a slight grin in greeting. "Breakfast is on, sweet pea."

Sweet pea. An endearment, Kerry realized vaguely as she struggled out of the deep folds of sleep that still tugged at her. Quinn sat near the door, his legs spread wide, the meals cooking on heating tabs before him. Light leaked in around the blanket at the door, leaving his hard face in shadow. The beard made him look truly like a warrior from the past. Maybe it was her sleep-fogged mind, Kerry thought as she gently extricated her arm from around Petula. Turning, she covered the child with both blankets, tucking them around Petula's bare feet.

Quinn said nothing as he savored the sight of Kerry wakening. Noticing the slight puffiness beneath her glorious, dark gray eyes, the softness of her full lips, he felt his heart mushroom violently with feelings for her. She sat up and rubbed her hands against her face.

"What time is it?" she asked, her voice husky with sleep.

"It's 0600—6:00 a.m. to you civilian types," he teased.

His voice was like rough sandpaper across her awakening senses, as delicious as a lover's caress. Lifting her head, she met his blue eyes, which were filled with warmth. Seeing the slight smile on his full mouth, she smiled shyly in return. He'd taken off his helmet, and his hair, dark and short, emphasized the shape of his large skull.

"That smells wonderful...." she whispered, moving slowly across the few feet of space to where he sat.

"Yes, and you're gonna eat *all* of your MRE today," he told her darkly, handing a plate along with some plastic utensils.

Thanking him softly, Kerry sat down nearby. She tucked her legs beneath her and balanced the warm plate on her right thigh. "Mmm...this is the best wake-up breakfast I've ever had! Thank you, Quinn. You're a knight in shining armor to me, to all of us...."

Watching her covertly, Quinn proceeded to wolf

down his own meal. So Kerry saw him as a knight…
His chest swelled with pride, and his heart hammered briefly. Tongue-tied, he didn't know how to
reply to her husky words of thanks.

Kerry slowly ate the fluffy eggs, which were
sprinkled with bits of diced red and green pepper
and fragrant slices of onion. Her mouth watered as
she spooned up the bacon. She knew she had to eat
slowly and not gulp down the wonderful meal as
she wanted to. No, she didn't want to follow Sylvia's example. Food was too precious to waste like
that.

"We had five intruders last night," Quinn told
her between bites. He stirred the hash browns with
his plastic fork, his brow wrinkling for a moment.
"Civilians, not Diablo."

"Desperate people."

Nodding, he rasped, "Yeah. It was pitiful. And
every one of them had a sad story to tell, one that
ripped my heart out. Some cried and begged me to
give them just a bottle of water. Others had family
members who are dying, who desperately need
meds. I didn't realize how bad it really was out here,
Kerry…."

Sadness flowed through her as she took another
mouthful of eggs. "I know, Quinn. It's so tragic. It
takes every bit of strength I can muster not to cry
with these people every day." She sighed, lifting her
head and looking around the hovel. Her gaze rested
lovingly on Petula, who was snuggled like a bug in

a rug, just the top of her unruly black hair visible. Kerry knew with the two thick wool blankets wrapped around her like a cocoon she was warm. For that Kerry was grateful.

"You kinda like that rug rat, don't you?"

She lifted her head and gazed at his shadowed face. "Yes, I do. Her parents are dead. I intend to keep her with me until we can find the rest of her family after this terrible crisis is over."

"And if you hadn't found her? What would have happened to her?"

Frowning, Kerry felt her appetite fade abruptly, even though her stomach was cramped and crying for food. Setting down the MRE, she whispered, "She'd probably be dead by now, because Pet couldn't scrounge enough food for herself. So many people over the last two weeks have been killed reentering their destroyed homes or a grocery store, searching for food. The quake aftershocks are powerful. Real killers. No, she'd be like a lot of others— trapped in the rubble and killed outright, or injured, with no hope of rescue."

Hanging his head, Quinn forced himself to finish his breakfast, though he was no longer hungry. "This is such a mess," he began hoarsely. "I just didn't realize the extent of it, the desperation.... Last night was bad, Kerry. As I said, I had five people— three men and two women, come to the center to steal. They were shocked to see military personnel there. It stopped them cold in their tracks."

"So, did you give them what they needed?"

Snorting softly, Quinn muttered, "First I went to the manifest inside the office to see if their names were on it, to make sure they hadn't already been given their daily ration of water and food. Once I saw they weren't listed there, I gave them supplies. Otherwise, I would have simply had to tell them that a navy helo was coming this afternoon with more supplies, and to come back after 1500 today."

Reaching out, Kerry laid her hand over his, which rested on his thick thigh. "I'm so glad you're here. I'm relieved they sent you, of all the marines available. You have a heart and soul that's in touch with the people here. Someone else might have fired at them, or denied them, but you didn't."

Her hand was warm on his, and Quinn laced his fingers through hers, giving her hand a gentle squeeze. "I have a good teacher—you." He held her gray eyes, which swam with sudden, unshed tears. How easily touched Kerry was, he was discovering. She was such a breath of life in his tight regimental world. Somehow, she was opening the door to his heart. The boldness of her touch, the coolness of her fingers made him want her even more. As his gaze moved from her eyes to her softly parted lips, the urge to lean over and kiss her nearly overwhelmed him. Kiss her? Would she allow it? Quinn thought so, judging from the warmth and admiration shining in her eyes.

Petula stirred and whimpered.

The magical moment dissolved. Instantly releasing her hand, Quinn muttered, "You'd better take care of our little rug rat."

*January 15: 1600*

"I can't believe this!" Kerry's voice was filled with wonder as she stood with Quinn behind the makeshift table, where several men and women were doling out food, water and medicine to needy quake victims who stood in ragged lines to receive the goods. The U.S. navy helicopter had left an hour ago, and the many supplies it brought had been carried to the center. Now, as she looked at Quinn, who stood with his usual scowl on his stony face, his M-16 resting on his right shoulder, she could barely contain her excitement.

"We've been given *three times* the amount of supplies we usually get!" she whispered. Not only that, but plenty of insulin, heart medication and antibiotics had also come with the shipment. It was like Christmas in January.

"What I like is that they're promising one flight a day by that navy helo," Quinn said. "That's even better news." He motioned with his left hand toward the waiting people, saw the hope burning in their dirty, drawn faces. Hope. Yes, the sight of those supplies made him feel good, too. His men stood at ease on either side of the table as each person approached, was looked up on the manifest, and then given supplies for the family he or she represented. Each bag given out contained bottled water, food and whatever medicine was needed.

"Yes," Kerry sighed. "But even more exciting is that the National Guard is up north of us, teamed up with Navy Seabees in huge Caterpillar bulldozers. They're beginning to open up roads into the basin!" Sighing, she added in a wobbly voice, "If they can make dirt roads into this area, that means trucks carrying supplies can get in and out. It also means ambulances and other vehicles can start taking out those most in need of medical help."

"Roads are the key," Quinn agreed. From talking to the copilot, a lieutenant by the name of Cynthia Mace, Quinn had learned that the efforts of the National Guard were going to be three-pronged. There were now enough bulldozers and navy construction personnel in place—north, south, and east—to start some major road building. Today was the kick-off date for plowing new routes through the rubble to the first four areas. Area Five wasn't targeted yet, unfortunately, for it lay at the heart of the quake zone. It was the hardest hit, and therefore would be most difficult to get to. But even though Area Five would be one of the last to get roads, the fact that the surrounding areas would soon be accessible by land vehicles meant that most of the helos could then concentrate on supplying aid to the hard-hit areas like theirs.

As well, there would be more aircraft available to fly out serious medical cases. The hospital at Camp Reed was chock-full. Even if a person was badly injured, he or she would have to be flown to the marine base first, and then to a hospital somewhere along the West Coast. That meant an extra flight, and right now, the airport at the base was still the only one available, and only so much traffic could come in and out of it. At the moment, many emergencies had to be wait-listed. But that would all change soon, and Quinn was glad, because there were so many people who were suffering terribly.

"Come with me," he told Kerry in a conspiratorial tone. When she tilted her head, a question in her gray eyes, he added, "Trust me?"

Laughing, she said, "With my life. Okay, I'll follow you."

Quinn knew she would normally stay at the center as the distribution began, but his marines were here to ensure the process went smoothly, quickly and quietly. Moving out the back of the center, through a door that hung askew on its hinges, he slipped his hand around hers briefly, when no one could see them.

"I have a surprise for you." Though he didn't want to let go of her hand, he knew he had to, despite the softness he'd seen in her features when he'd spontaneously reached out to her.

Kerry's heart skipped a beat as she hurried along the side of the shopping center toward her home. "I love surprises! What did you do, Quinn?'' She grinned suddenly, feeling like an elated child. Quinn made her feel so light and wonderful.

''Oh,'' he said teasingly, with a wolfish smile, ''I had that helo bring in a couple of things for you and our rug rat. By now, Beau should have everything up and in place. Come on....''

Her shack was on the other side of the center, near a department store that had pancaked in on itself. The day had turned warm, the wind had dropped and the sun felt great on her head and shoulders. Kerry had come to appreciate the afternoon warmth as never before. As she walked, her arm sometimes brushing Quinn's, she smiled gaily. ''Why do I feel like a child who is getting a surprise birthday party thrown for her?''

Chuckling, Quinn said, ''Because you are. This is from me to you.'' As they rounded the end of the department store, he pointed toward the area where she had made her home since the earthquake had hit.

Gasping, Kerry halted. Her eyes bulged. ''Oh, Quinn!'' Her hands flew up to her parted lips. No more than a hundred feet away stood a large, dark green tent, erected in front of her old shelter. Lance Corporal Beau Parish came toward them, a wide smile on his face.

''Got it all done, Corporal Grayson. Just in time, I see.''

''Great, Parish. Thanks. Go help one of the men

pack those grocery bags so those lines move faster now,'' he ordered.

''You bet.'' He nodded deferentially toward Kerry. ''Ma'am? I hope you like what we've done.'' And he took off at a jog toward the center.

''What have you done?'' Kerry whispered as she hurried toward the newly erected tent.

''Go look,'' Quinn urged, pride in his voice. He watched Kerry hurry to the tent flaps, which were open. Hearing her cry out with joy, he smiled widely.

Just seeing the blush of color sweep across Kerry's cheeks made his day. Quinn halted in front of the tent and watched her enter as if in a daze. Inside were four cots, with plenty of blankets to keep off the cold at night. The floor was a raised wooden platform, so rain would run under it and not through it, as it had in her hovel. Toward the rear was a small two-plate stove. Outside, a small gasoline-fed generator had been set up, to supply electricity for the stove as well as a small refrigerator, and best of all, a heater. The tent was snug and fully capable of withstanding the elements.

Quinn stood at the opening and watched with quiet joy as Kerry moved around inside, her hands spread open, her eyes huge as she touched everything as if to make sure it was real and not a figment of her imagination.

''I figured, since you're the leader of Area Five, you deserve to have nice digs,'' he said. ''I talked to Morgan Trayhern a couple of days ago, and he agreed. I told him what conditions you were living in with that little girl, and he promised he'd do something worthy of your position in the community."

"Oh, Quinn!" she gasped, turning toward him. "This…this is beyond my wildest dreams! A stove! A refrigerator! That means no more fear of food poisoning!"

"Look in the fridge," he urged her quietly, stepping forward and laying his rifle on one of the cots. He sat down on the opposite cot and watched her as she knelt and slowly opened the door.

"Oh… I don't believe this!" She sat back on her haunches and looked over her shoulder at Quinn, who was smiling like the proverbial Cheshire cat. "Milk! For Petula! Oh, this is wonderful!"

"There's more…. Remember you mentioned how much you like chocolate cake? Well, you see that box in there? There's a chocolate cake in it. Morgan called up the chow hall, talked to the gunny, and they made it special—for you."

Tears flooded Kerry's eyes. She sat down and gazed in awe at the small refrigerator crammed with goodies. There was milk, yogurt, fresh eggs, at least five pounds of bacon, fresh fruit and vegetables. It was an unimaginable feast. And all because of Quinn. He missed nothing. He had heard every word she'd spoken.

Sitting there in stunned silence, her hand on the

door as she stared at the treasure trove, Kerry had no words. Her heart lifted, vibrating with such joy at his thoughtfulness that she couldn't even say thank you.

Gently closing the fridge door, she turned to him. The floor of the tent was made of thick plywood, and it was dry and solid. Placing her hand on it, she twisted around and met his half-closed eyes. He sat on the cot, his elbows resting on his thighs, his hands clasped between them. The gentle smile playing across his lips infused her with the kind of happiness she'd once felt years ago, with Lee. There was a special chemistry between her and Quinn, filling her with light and joy.

"You are..." she choked out "...incredibly wonderful. I was right, Quinn—you truly are a knight from King Arthur's round table. This is too much. Too much..."

"No, it isn't. Morgan said it for me. He said you need to start eating and sleeping regularly. You can't lead if you're weak and tired all the time, sweet pea. So now you have no excuse. You have a fridge, a stove and real food. You and our little rug rat can eat well. And when we're away from the tent, I'll post a guard to ensure no one steals anything. This belongs to you and Petula."

Whispering his name, Kerry got up off the floor. Following the promptings of her heart, she approached him and leaned down. Sliding her hands across his prickly, bearded cheeks, she framed his face and pressed her lips against the smiling line of his mouth. Her actions were completely spontaneous. Kerry hadn't kissed another man since Lee. Something old and hurting dissolved in her heart as she brushed Quinn's mouth with her own. As, after a moment of surprise, his hands came to rest on her shoulders.

"Thank you…" she whispered against his strong mouth as he returned her tentative caress. "Thank you a million times over…" And her lashes closed as she drank deeply of his own proffered kiss. His hands tightened on her shoulders, and Kerry relaxed. She trusted Quinn with her life. He was giving her life, she realized belatedly as his mouth wreaked fire across her lips. He was just as shocked by her bold kiss as she was, but swiftly responded with surprising tenderness.

Her world spun and dissolved beneath his mouth, his searching exploration. Kerry knew in the back of her mind that she shouldn't be kissing Quinn at all, but the man deserved it. He was showing her daily how wonderful, how sensitive and thoughtful he was toward her and everyone else. Maybe marines were a special breed if they were all like him!

Gradually, Kerry eased away and opened her eyes. She drowned in his smoldering blue gaze, which spoke eloquently of his desire for her. Feeling suddenly shaky and unsure of herself, Kerry released him and stood up.

"I…gosh, I didn't mean to do that, Quinn…."

His brows rose. "I liked it. And I'm not sorry."

Laughing unsurely, Kerry took a step away, her hand on the tent flap. "I don't know what got into me...." She shook her head, breathless. The branding heat of his strong mouth lingered on her lips, making them tingle warmly. Deliciously.

"Are *you* sorry?" he demanded hoarsely. How beautiful she looked standing there, her hair unruly, her cheeks stained with a blush. It was her eyes, though, that told Quinn she'd enjoyed the spontaneous kiss just as much as he had.

Laughing a little, Kerry touched her brow. "No... I'm not sorry. Just shocked that I did it. This isn't like me, Quinn."

Shrugging, he felt a grin crawl across his mouth. He could still taste the sweetness of Kerry on his lips. "Maybe it's the times. The pressure. Who knows? One thing I do know, though, sweet pea— I'm not sorry it happened."

# *Chapter Six*

*January 16: 0630*

"I don't want you to go with me," Quinn said in a low voice outside the tent the next morning. Dawn was just crawling across the eastern horizon. Above him the last of the inky darkness was fleeing before the coming sun.

"Too bad. I'm going with you, Quinn, so stop being so protective, okay?" Kerry, too, kept her voice low. The morning was crisp and chilly. Today she was wearing her new marine cammo jacket and she felt much warmer—thanks to Quinn, who had radioed in for extra warm clothing for so many in Area Five. He had made sure she got a jacket, as well.

Pulling her away from the tent, where Petula and Sylvia were still sleeping, Quinn scowled. Yesterday, he'd tried to persuade Kerry not to come with him as he began to hunt for Diablo. She'd balked then, as she was doing now. After that soft, unexpected kiss, he found himself not wanting to put her in the line of fire for any reason. He had slept restlessly last night on his new cot, beneath several blankets. Kerry had asked him to stay with them. He knew Diablo was around and the new tents might draw their interest. The heater had warmed them all, and he'd noticed that Kerry, Petula and Sylvia all slept deeply and soundly. Usually, they were cold beneath their threadbare blankets and moved sporadically to keep warm.

"No one knows Diablo better than me," Kerry told him with grim determination. She pulled the pistol she carried from the black holster at her right hip. Checking it to make sure a bullet was in the chamber, she replaced the safety and strapped it back in place. "And in your uniform, you'll be a prime target for those guys. They hate authority."

"Like they won't spot you, too?"

She grinned as they stepped farther away from the tent. "Well, since I'm wearing this marine jacket, they'll probably think I'm one of you. Either way, it doesn't matter, Quinn. We're both targets, because we represent authority. I've tangled three times with members of this group since the quake hit, and believe me, they take no prisoners. You've seen that from the reports I've made. I've attempted in every case to talk to witnesses who were there. We've gotten some names. After this disaster is over, I intend to hang these guys in a court of law. They're not going to get away with these atrocities.''

"They're already up on murder charges for two marine helo pilots." Halting, Quinn slung his small knapsack, filled with water and food for a day's worth of hunting, across his shoulders. Picking up the M-16, he switched the safety off, then kept the barrel pointed downward, the gun ready to fire in his hand.

"I know," Kerry whispered sadly. "Can I help you carry anything?"

Giving her a dark look, he growled, "You aren't going to stay behind, are you?"

"No."

"Sometimes I wish you could be like other women," he groused, his umber brows dipping.

"Ouch. That sounds so old-fashioned to me. Didn't your hill women do anything but stay home and raise the kids?" she teased lightly as they began to walk toward a flattened neighborhood ahead.

"My sister, Katie, is a crack shot. She always went with Pa and me, and usually ended up bringing home more squirrels for the stew than either of us."

"And is Katie married now?"

"Nope. She went on to Glen, Kentucky, the closest town out of the mountains where our clan lives, and got an education like I did. She's a teacher now," he said proudly. "The first in our family to get a college diploma. They built a small school for the hill children about five years ago, and she teaches there."

"I see. So not all hill women are expected to just stay at home and do domestic things?"

Giving her a disgruntled look, Quinn said, "No. But it's still…odd when they don't."

"Hmm, odd as in bad? Or odd as in unique and apart from what most other women do?" She flashed him a smile, warmly recalling his heated, hungry mouth upon hers. Kerry had slept deeply last night, partly because she'd been warm for the first time since the quake hit, with that wonderful heater in the tent. Last night, she'd dreamed of Quinn. He was making love to her in a glade deep in the mountains, near a pool. It was wonderful, so primal and natural. Kerry wasn't about to tell him that, however. The look in his normally glacial blue eyes had changed. That kiss she'd given him had changed everything, she was discovering. Was that what she wanted? Had she kissed Quinn because of her own shock and trauma over the quake? To alleviate some of the stress from the horrendous responsibility she carried daily? Or was it out of relief at having a partner who would help shoulder it all? Kerry was uncertain.

She was still letting go of Lee, of their wonderful marriage. Grief didn't just suddenly end a year after your spouse died, Kerry had discovered. Her emotions were like a roller coaster, going up and down. When grief surfaced, she felt it for days or weeks, and then it would submerge again, and she'd be okay about going on alone once more.

Quinn noticed the faraway look in Kerry's face as they left the shopping center and walked carefully along a chewed-up asphalt avenue toward a long line of stucco homes that lay in shambles. In front of each home, families still slept in whatever makeshift shelter they had pulled together.

"You seem far away," he noted.

"Sorry… I was thinking, Quinn. Did you answer my question?"

"Not yet. I just felt you leave me."

A little stunned by his admission, she gave him a look of surprise. "Are you psychic or something? I did go away. I was thinking of the past."

Shrugging, he trudged down the middle of what had once been a street. "I've been accused of having a strong sixth sense. Pa said all good hunters have that gift," he said, studying the trees that had once lined the area, now ripped out of the ground and lying around like scattered toothpicks. Downed power lines and poles looked like giant spiderwebs where they crisscrossed. There was no electricity in the lines—good news, because the dark cables snaked across collapsed roofs and dusty yellow lawns.

Impressed, Kerry asked, "You have this skill with everyone? Your fire team?"

Feeling a little self-conscious, Quinn held her interested gray gaze. "Not with everyone. Just… special people, I guess."

"Well," she teased softly, "it's nice to be one of those special people in your life."

Caught off guard by her tender admission, Quinn studied her candid expression, before his gaze roamed over her face, her hair. This morning, Kerry's locks were washed and brushed. He'd made sure that toiletry items were on board that U.S. Navy helicopter, too. Now he saw that her sable hair actually had reddish highlights in it. Yesterday, for the first time, Kerry had washed her hair in a basin of precious water. Petula had gotten her hair scrubbed as well. It had done Quinn's heart good to see them smiling and laughing as Kerry had gently towel-dried Petula's long, black hair, the child seated in her lap. It was then that he knew Kerry would be a good mother.

By the time they'd passed the first two blocks of the neighborhood, it was 0600 and the sky was brightening in the east. There was no wind this morning, and Kerry was grateful. She pulled a map of the region out of the large pocket of her oversize cammo jacket.

Quinn kept looking around, on guard, the rifle clasped in his hands. Members of the Diablo gang weren't going to be easily distinguished from the people of Area Five. They were dressed just like them. The only thing that made them stand out was that, upon occasion, they wore a white headband. If the leader, a man named Snake Williams, was smart, he'd have his survivalists fade into the local population so none could be singled out. Quinn wasn't so sure Snake was that smart, but he wouldn't bet the farm that he wasn't.

According to Kerry's reports, Snake was the man's nickname. Helluva nickname, Quinn thought. No one knew his real name. But in the second incident report, one of the victims remembered hearing another gang member use his last name: Williams. The victim, a woman whose teenage son had been taken hostage, a gun held to his head by Snake as he demanded all the food she'd managed to retrieve from her destroyed home, had given the leader everything. Her son had lived.

Kerry folded the map into a small square as they continued down the next block. The street was in fist-size pieces of asphalt, and she had to be careful where she stepped, or she'd fall and hurt herself.

"So where did you go before, when you had that faraway look in your eyes?" Quinn asked now.

"Where did I go?" She looked at him and smiled slightly. "I was thinking of how I boldly kissed you the other day. It wasn't like me, and I was wondering where that spontaneity came from." Coming to a stop at the end of the block, she looked around, getting her bearings with the map in her hands. Quinn halted at her shoulder, less than a foot from her. She liked the feeling of protection he always gave her.

"Are you sorry it happened?" he asked as he watched her run her index finger along the route they were taking. Holding his breath momentarily, he hoped that she wasn't feeling regret. Why did he want that kiss to mean something beyond what it probably was? Kerry had been thrilled over the gift of the tent. It was possible she had just kissed him out of gratitude. Quinn was bothered by the fact he wanted it to mean more than that.

Looking up at Quinn's recently shaved face, Kerry savored his embracing blue gaze. "I don't know any other way to be than honest, Quinn. So here goes...." She took a deep breath. "I surprised myself by going over and kissing you. No, I don't regret it. But I'm scared, too. That wasn't like me. I keep trying to figure out why I did it. Was it because of the stress of the quake? Shock?" Lifting her fingers, she tunneled them through her hair in a nervous motion. "I haven't been attracted to any man since Lee died."

Though he nodded, Quinn felt his heart sinking.

Quirking her lips, Kerry refolded the map and slid

it back into the pocket of her jacket. "It's you, Quinn. Whatever that means, it's you. I wanted to kiss you. I like being with you. I like the way you think. Most of all, I like how you treat others. You're a true leader. You listen to your men and their ideas. You don't rule by control, you rule by soliciting their opinions, respecting their insights and experiences before you make a decision."

"And that's important to you, Kerry?"

She smiled hesitantly. "Yes...yes, it is." Opening her hands, which now had warm gloves on them, thanks to Quinn, she said, "You've surprised me, Quinn. When Morgan Trayhern said there was a Marine Corps fire team coming in here, I had this idea that you were all John Wayne, gung-ho warriors who would look at us civilians like a plague that had to be cured." Her smiled widened. "But you didn't."

"We're trained for suburban warfare," he told her seriously. "Morgan said you had the goods. You were our contact. No one knows this area better than you because you've been clawing out a life here for two weeks before we arrived. What else could I do but listen to you? Learn from you?" She was achingly beautiful as the first rays of sun shot over the horizon and touched her slightly curled, short brown hair. Once again he could see the reddish highlights, and he had a maddening urge to run his hands through the silky strands. How badly he wanted to reach out and touch Kerry.

Laughing shortly, she said, "I found that out." Her lips pulled in at the corners as she studied his frowning countenance. "I'm finding myself really attracted to you, Quinn." There, the truth was out on the table. She saw his brows raise in surprise, and then his blue eyes narrowed speculatively on her. A delightful river of warmth coursed through her heart and down into her lower body. Kerry recognized that look: it was desire. For her and her alone. Ordinarily, if a man gazed at her that way, she ignored him. But not now. Not with Quinn. Instead, Kerry absorbed his look like a starving animal.

"I guess I'm just realizing how lonely I really was," she admitted in a low tone. "After Lee died, well, I threw myself into my work at the sheriff's office. I ran a teenage drug program for the county, too, so it kept me extra busy. I didn't want to go home at night to our house. I didn't want the silence warring with my memories. It was...just too much for me to bear...so I kept super busy to take the edge off my grief and loss."

"I can understand that," Quinn said. He saw the grief in her eyes and grasped as never before what the loss of a loved one could do to a person.

"Have you ever lost someone you loved, Quinn?" She earnestly searched his scowling face.

There was such tenderness in this marine who stood inches from her. Kerry ached to throw her arms around him, kiss him and lose herself in his embrace.

"No…not really. My parents are still alive. All us kids are alive. I had my grandpa die, and that was hard on me. They lived in the holler down from our cabin, and he was an important part of my life." Looking up, Quinn saw a flight of birds wing overhead on their way toward the Pacific Ocean in the distance. They were seagulls, their white plumage shining in the rising sun. Gazing back at Kerry, he said, "But losing someone I loved and lived with? No."

"I don't wish it on anyone," Kerry whispered forcefully. "Even this quake, Quinn, is peanuts compared to the emotional mountains and valleys I've been moving through since I lost Lee."

Reaching out, he brushed her cheek. Kerry's skin was smooth, like a warm, fuzzy peach beneath his fingertips. "Thanks for telling me where you went. It helps me to understand you." *And appreciate you.* But Quinn didn't say that.

"I haven't met many women who are as honest as you are, sweet pea." The endearment rolled off his tongue. He saw Kerry's eyes widen momentarily at his grazing touch, and then her cheek became stained with pink. He positively itched to touch her again, touch her longer, and in a way that showed her what lay in his rapidly beating heart.

What was happening? Was it her? This disaster? Quinn wasn't at all sure. What he was sure of was that Kerry touched his heart big time, and his desire for her was escalating. It was so unexpected that Quinn didn't know what to do about it. In a way, he felt helpless around her. Not that Kerry flirted with him or egged him on. He'd see that warm look in her eyes from time to time when he caught her watching him in a quiet moment, but that was all. She hadn't tried to kiss him again, rub up against him or find an excuse to touch him.

Managing a crooked smile, Kerry whispered, "I like being called sweet pea. That must be a hill expression?"

Chuckling and a little embarrassed, he said, "Yeah, it is. My grandpa called my grandmother by that name for as long as I could recall. I guess..." he paused, searching for the right words "...you remind me of her. She's a gutsy old lady in her seventies now, and I've always admired her spunk and rebellious nature."

"I'm rebellious?" There was a teasing note in Kerry's tone. How she ached to have Quinn touch her unexpectedly like that again.

He shrugged. "Maybe. I don't know of any hill women who are in law enforcement. You broke the mold, as we'd say, Kerry. But I don't see that as bad. Just different.'' And wonderful. She was special to him, though he was afraid to ask himself why.

"Just don't call me by that name in front of anyone, okay? I've got a job to do and a reputation to uphold. Somehow, a sheriff's deputy being called sweet pea could be counterproductive.''

Joining her laughter, Quinn looked around. "Yeah, don't worry. I won't undermine your reputation or rank. Come on, let's head east, toward the borderland region where Area Six butts up against us.''

Nodding, Kerry fell into step at his side. By now, the whole neighborhood was awakening. Small campfires to cook on were in evidence on the lawns in front of the houses, the inhabitants huddled around them for warmth. Her heart, however, was pulsing with a need for more conversation with Quinn. Kerry sighed inwardly. Was it possible to fall in love with someone so quickly?

# Chapter Seven

*January 16: 1500*

It was near 1500 when they unexpectedly ran into the Diablo gang. Near the boundary with Area Six was a row of suburban homes only partially destroyed by the quake. Some were still intact. Quinn knew by now that a standing house meant many things to a quake victim: a way to get clothes, stored food or water, plus a roof overhead, providing there weren't large cracks running through the structure. The lucky person who had a standing or even partially standing house was a drawing card for others. Quinn had found out from Kerry as they'd walked through the devastated neighborhoods that frequently many families would gather and use that home as a central focus point for their small community. And at night, providing the house was stable, as many as forty or fifty people would crowd into the rooms and hallways to sleep, to escape the raw January elements.

The afternoon sun was strong and warm. Quinn had stuffed his and Kerry's jackets in the pack he carried on his shoulders, but was still sweating freely. The flak vest beneath his cammo shirt chafed him so badly with each movement that he wanted to tear the thing off, but didn't.

They had just come to the last square block of a neighborhood that butted up against the Area Six boundary. Three homes were standing. Kerry held out her hand to stop him. Her brows moved downward.

"Wait…" she cautioned.

"What?" Quinn saw she was studying a crowd that stood in a semicircle in front of one of the homes. At least thirty people were riveted in place, looking at something he couldn't see.

"Trouble," Kerry whispered in warning, unstrapping her pistol from her holster. "I think it's Diablo…."

Though he didn't know how she knew that, Quinn didn't question her. Immediately he locked and loaded his M-16, after taking off the safety. But before he could intercede, gunfire erupted near them. Six geysers of dirt sprayed up at their feet, the bullets narrowly missing them.

There was no time to think, only to react. Quinn saw Kerry dive for the ground, aiming her pistol to the left of the crowd.

As he lunged for the ground in turn, because there was nowhere to hide, he saw a tall, swarthy-looking man coming at them, a submachine gun in his hand. The winking red-and-yellow flashes from his gun barrel told Quinn that he was firing directly at them. Quinn grunted and rolled to the left. The man was in back of the crowd. Quinn couldn't return fire for fear of wounding a civilian. *Damn!*

Kerry? Where was she? Jerking his head to the right, Quinn spotted a car that had been upended. Leaping to his feet, he caught sight of her in his peripheral vision. She was running out in the open, pistol held in her right hand, her entire focus on the Diablo member coming at them, rifle blazing.

Bullets whined and whistled around Quinn. He had to find protection or he was going to be hit! Digging in the toes of his black leather boots, he sprinted toward the car, which was a hundred feet away.

"Get down! Get down!"

Kerry's voice carried loudly across the area.

Somewhere in Quinn's mind, he knew she was screaming at the civilians to duck so that she or Quinn could take a clean shot at their attacker. He had no time to look. Bullets whined past his head. Dirt leaped up near his right foot as he dived the last ten feet to the car.

With one final leap, Quinn landed heavily in the dirt and rolled. He was safe! Once behind the car, he scrambled upward. Where was the shooter? Where? His heart was pounding. Sweat was stinging in his eyes. Searching frantically, he heard the screams and shouts of the people. He saw them falling to the earth, hugging it and screaming out in fear.

It was then that his blood turned cold. He saw three more of the Diablo members, all wearing white headbands, at the center of the group of people. They were heavily armed.

Looking to his right once more, he spotted Kerry. His heart shrieked out in protest. She was out in the open, with no place to hide! His mouth dropped open as she sank down on one knee, steadied her pistol in both hands and fired directly at the three members.

Cursing, Quinn focused on the first Diablo and squeezed off three shots. The man went down, his submachine gun flying out of his hands. It landed harmlessly five feet away on the chewed-up street.

Kerry! Heart pounding with fear because she was a fully exposed target, Quinn steadied the rifle against the top of the car. To his horror, two of the thugs were firing at her. He saw one jerk and fly backward. Kerry had gotten him. One more to go!

Breathing hard, Quinn sighted on the big guy with red hair who was focused so intently on Kerry. There wasn't more than three hundred feet between the two of them. Squeezing off a shot, Quinn aimed for the man's bare head. He couldn't be careless. If he was, he might kill one of the civilians flattened on the lawn near where the man stood.

Kerry! In that split second before he brushed the trigger of his rifle, Quinn knew she was in trouble. She was an easy target.

Kerry kept her wits about her, despite the shrieks and screams of people surrounding her. This was the only angle to shoot the thug. The gunfire was deafening. She knew she was a target. She didn't want to die, but they were firing at her with a hailstorm of bullets.

There was no time to worry about Quinn. She'd seen him dive for safety behind the overturned auto. Good! As she steadied herself on one knee and held her pistol firm, she fired off shot after shot. They had to be head shots, because if she aimed lower one of her bullets might strike a civilian. And that would be unforgivable.

A bullet slammed into her right thigh. At first, Kerry felt only a vague, stinging heat there. She was too focused, her adrenaline pumping too strongly, to feel anything more. She saw two Diablo members go down. Satisfaction thrummed through her. *Good!* More people shrieked as the man fell on top of them, unconscious. One more to go.

It was then, as Kerry squeezed off the ninth shot from her pistol, that a bullet struck her in the head.

She didn't even see that her last bullet missed her attacker as she fell back.

*No! Oh, God, no!* Quinn saw Kerry crumple. He saw the pistol fall nervelessly from her fingers. She sagged backward, like a rag doll, limp and lifeless. With his last shot, he took out the last member of Diablo. The man crumpled to the ground, his weapon falling from his hands.

Leaping from behind the auto, Quinn sprinted toward where Kerry lay. She was on her back, her body twisted, her arms thrown outward. Sobbing for breath, his chest hurting, Quinn cried out her name as he dropped to his knees beside her.

Around him, people were starting to get up and move. Children were crying. Women were sobbing. All his focus, his heart—his life—centered on Kerry. Dropping his weapon, Quinn went into EMT mode. The A, B, Cs—airway, breathing and circulation—roared through his fragmented mind. He saw blood staining her dark green slacks on her right thigh. Worse, he saw blood on the right temple of her head. She was pale, seemingly lifeless.

Thrusting his hand out, he put his shaking fingers on her pulse. Yes! She was alive! *Thank God. Thank God.* He leaned down, trying to still his chaotic breathing in order to hear, and placed his ear near her nostrils. Was that a faint puff of air? She was still breathing! She was alive! But would she live?

Gripping the computerized radio he carried,

Quinn punched in the code to connect him with the medevac helicopter base. It was a special frequency that would tie in directly to Camp Reed, to a Blackhawk helicopter on loan from the U.S. Army, that sat waiting for just such a call from military personnel in the field. Glancing down at Kerry's soft, pale face, her slack lips, the thick dark lashes against her cheeks, Quinn felt his whole world tilt out of control.

People were running over to him, crowding around him, asking if they could help. Quinn shook his head. He waited what seemed hours for the medevac team to answer. When they did, he gave them coordinates.

"Hurry! She's critical. It's a head wound!" His voice cracked. Everything blurred as Quinn signed off. It would be fifteen minutes before the chopper arrived—the worst, most nightmarish fifteen minutes of his life as he leaned down and continued to assess her condition.

He felt the touch of a man's hand on his shoulder. Someone was thrusting a blanket forward, to keep Kerry warm. Trying not to sob, Quinn looked up— into the terrorized faces of the civilians who surrounded them.

"Y-you saved us," a woman choked out. She gripped her small boy in her arms. "Those men were from Diablo. They were going to kill my baby here, for food. Oh, thank you…thank you!" She began to weep harder.

Quinn put his hands up. "Please," he called, "give us some room. There's nothing you can do here—unless there's a medical doctor present?" He prayed there would be.

The people stood mute, staring down at him and at one another, their faces mirroring shock from this latest tragedy.

No one answered, so Quinn quickly went back to work. Inside his pack, he carried a small EMT kit for just such emergencies. Because Kerry had a head wound, it was important not to raise her feet. Ordinarily, when a person was unconscious and in shock, that's exactly what was done, to force the blood back toward the head and into the major organs of the body. But not this time.

Reaching out, he touched her curly brown hair, which glinted with red highlights from the slanting sun. Shaking his head, Quinn tried to think. But he couldn't. As he knelt at her side and applied a pressure bandage to the bullet wound in her right thigh, he wanted to scream—scream in pure frustration. Kerry couldn't die. She just couldn't!

*January 16: 1700*

"How is she?"

Quinn turned toward the deep male voice. He was standing alone in the surgery floor waiting room. Looking up, he recognized Morgan Trayhern coming toward him, his black brows knitted, his blue eyes narrowed with concern.

Opening his hands, Quinn whispered, "I don't know, sir. She's been in surgery for an hour now. The paramedic on board the Blackhawk said the wound on her thigh was clean and superficial. It's her head. She took a shot to the head." Numbly, Quinn sat down. He didn't know what else to do. He felt so damned helpless. Kerry's blood was on his shirt. On his hands. Her head wound had bled profusely, as that type always did—even when he'd helped the paramedic take care of her in the chopper on the way back to the base.

Morgan gripped his slumped shoulder. "Damn, I'm sorry, Quinn." He sat down with him on one of the red plastic chairs. "Tell me what happened?"

Quinn knew it took an act of Congress to get Morgan out of Logistics; the man was busier than anyone at Camp Reed. The fact that he was here made a powerful statement about him. Morgan cared deeply for the people in the field.

Swallowing hard, Quinn rubbed his face. Hot, unexpected tears jammed into his eyes. He looked down so Trayhern couldn't see them. Opening his mouth, he tried to gather his shocked, fragmented thoughts. He knew Morgan was expecting a report. Emotionally, Quinn wasn't with it. His heart was with Kerry in the surgery room.

"Take your time," Morgan said heavily, studying

his profile. He saw the glitter of tears in Quinn's eyes even though he tried to hide them.

Finally, Quinn managed to get ahold of himself. He sat there and talked in a rough whisper, his legs spread, his hands gripped between them. When he finished, he heard Morgan curse softly beneath his breath.

"This gang is a helluva lot stronger and more violent than we realized," he told Quinn. "We're getting reports from other areas of their activity. It's a much larger group than we realized. And there's no way a fire team is going to handle this volatile situation. There's just too many of them." He scratched his head and muttered, "I'm going to have to put together a special Recon team with a doctor in case of medical casualties, and have them find the bastards."

"Sir, what with all the needs and demands of the people in Kerry's area, we're stretched too thin." Quinn opened his hands. "This was the first day since our arrival that she and I were out reconnoitering the area. I hadn't expected to run into them. We were undermanned. We didn't have enough firepower. And they had civilians they were using as a shield so we couldn't fire back. They knew what they were doing."

"I hear you, Quinn. Damn, I hear you." Morgan sighed and stood up. "Listen, you go get cleaned up. I've arranged for you to have a room at the

B.O.Q. Take a hot shower. There will be a fresh set of clothes for you, Son.''

Looking up in surprise, Quinn muttered, ''The B.O.Q., sir?'' That was the Bachelor Officers Quarters, and only officers were allowed to stay there. Not an enlisted person like him.

He saw Morgan smile grimly. ''You're getting a field commission, Corporal. As of right now, I'm making you a second lieutenant. Orders just came down today that we're to pinpoint marines with leadership qualities out there in the field and promote them battlefield rank. Okay?''

In shock, Quinn sat there, his mouth open. He didn't know what to say. He saw dark satisfaction glimmer in Morgan's eyes.

''There will be a set of silver bars with your clean clothes, Lieutenant. I suggest you get over there, clean up and hotfoot it back here.'' Morgan glanced at his watch. ''I'm late for a meeting. I'll try to swing back by here in two hours. Just know there's a lot of people praying for Kerry right now, Son. I know how much she means to you. I see it in your face, hear it in your voice. Let's hope for the best....''

Stunned with the good news that warred against his worry and anguish, Quinn sat there for a long time trying to digest it all. During a war, it wasn't uncommon for an enlisted person to be handed officer's rank. This quake, the horrific magnitude of destruction, was a war, he realized belatedly. And

Morgan Trayhern had just made him a second lieutenant. My God.

Shaking his head, Quinn shuffled stiffly out of the
visitors' center and to the nurses' station, a beehive
of activity. He caught one nurse's attention and
asked her about Kerry.

"Hey, look, Corporal, I don't know. She's in operating theater three, that's all I can tell you." Harried, she grabbed a clipboard. "You'll just have to
wait."

Nodding and swallowing hard, Quinn turned
woodenly toward the elevators at the end of the
highly polished white passageway. Right now, all
he wanted to do was hold Kerry's hand. To whisper
to her that she would be all right. In a daze, he
walked unsteadily toward the row of elevators. The
hallway was crowded with male and female nurses
in light blue uniforms hurrying in and out of surgical
rooms where patients lay. The antiseptic odors were
cloying and sharp. As an EMT, Quinn knew what
went on in an operating room. Kerry would be on a
table surrounded by hospital staff, a doctor heading
up the team trying to save her life.

Quinn's mind gyrated with grief. With fear. Kerry
couldn't die! She just couldn't! As he pressed the
down button, the door to one elevator slid open and
he stepped in. There were five other people, all in
cammos, standing there, their faces grim. A gurney
bearing an older woman covered with blankets stood

beside them. A hospital corpsman held up a bag for
the IV flowing into her right arm.

The intense anguish he felt for Kerry nearly suf-
focated Quinn. As the elevator dropped to the first-
floor lobby of the huge naval hospital, he couldn't
wait to get out of there, and escaped hurriedly into
the cool evening air. The sun was just setting. Standing on the cracked sidewalk, Quinn barely noticed
the people milling around him like ceaseless droves
of busy ants. Instead, his gaze sought out the B.O.Q.

It felt so strange to be heading toward officers'
quarters. He'd been given a battlefield commission!
Quinn had never expected that, not in a million
years. It just wasn't done. The last time that had
occurred was during the Vietnam War, when so
many young officers were killed because they were
unprepared for jungle warfare. And without an officer to lead, the entire unit ground to a halt. Now
Quinn was an officer.

None of it really mattered, he thought as he
headed to the B.O.Q., his heart heavy with worry
over Kerry. To his surprise, his name was already
on the register at the front desk. The clerk handed
him a key to a room on the second floor, no questions asked. Quinn knew he looked filthy, what with
Kerry's blood staining the front of his cammos. He
climbed the stairs slowly, in shock, then went
through the motions of finding the small room.
Opening the door, he found a queen-size bed with
a floral bedspread, and a set of maple dressers. The

curtains at the window matched the bedspread. Different rooms were available. Some were suites and others were not. He was grateful to have any room.

Standing there, he felt torn apart. The world he'd just left was so devastated, this one so neat, clean and sparkling, with all the amenities. There was a pitcher of ice water on the coffee table in front of the leather davenport. Water! It was so desperately needed out there in the heart of the quake zone, and here it was readily available. There were so many thirsty and dehydrated people out there, many dying slowly from a lack of water. He felt as if he were in a surreal nightmare as he stared down at the pitcher. Walking past it, Quinn headed directly to the bathroom. How wonderful a hot, steamy shower would feel.

As he climbed out of his dirty uniform and let it fall on the tile floor, he thought of Kerry. She hadn't had a shower in weeks. Guilt ate at him as he stepped into the glass cubicle and felt the first hot droplets fall. As he applied soap to a washcloth, he wished desperately with all his heart and soul, that Kerry could be here with him. He wanted to wash her gently, kiss her, caress her and tell her how much she meant to him.

Standing in the pummeling stream of hot water, Quinn began to cry. He'd never done that before—cry on the spur of the moment. The experience was foreign to him. The salty tears flooding down his heavily bearded face mingled with the heated water from the showerhead above. He had no idea how the tears had started—or why. All he knew as he stood there, feet apart, the water running over him, was that he'd fallen helplessly in love with Kerry. She was an extraordinary person, so very courageous, and yet incredibly kind and compassionate. As Quinn savagely rubbed his face with the soapy cloth to erase the unbidden tears leaking out of his eyes, he felt a wave of sheer terror tunneling through his chest. Kerry didn't know how he felt about her. Quinn hadn't wanted to admit the feelings growing powerfully toward her. Not even to himself.

He'd shrugged off his feelings as something that had grown out of the trauma of the quake. But now he knew differently, and it hurt that he'd never told her. It felt as if someone was slicing up his heart with a razor blade, one deep, violent cut after another.

What if Kerry died on the surgery table? What if she became paralyzed or worse, a vegetable, because of the bullet? A beautiful life destroyed by a roving band of thugs… It wasn't fair, Quinn thought as he stood there, gasping for breath. He tried again to stop his tears, but it was impossible.

If someone had been in the bedroom, they would have heard a man sobbing hard and long. But no one was there to hear him. The sounds of his grief, of his hopes and dreams for a life with Kerry were all muffled by the walls.

Would Kerry live or die? The question tore at Quinn, and not even his tears brought him any relief.

# *Chapter Eight*

"How long are they going to keep Kerry in an induced coma?" Laura Trayhern asked. She sat in the wheelchair, Baby Jane wrapped in her arms.

Quinn sat on a red vinyl lounge chair, tension filling him. "I just talked to Dr. Edmonds. She was the surgeon for Kerry." Rubbing his bloodshot eyes, he felt fear clawing at his throat. He tried to keep his voice even and detached. Just the look on Laura's kind face broke something loose within him. Even though she was confined to a wheelchair because of the broken ankle she'd sustained during the earthquake, she had made an effort to come up and visit him. Her kindness overwhelmed him.

"And Dr. Edmonds said they were going to purposely keep Kerry unconscious with drugs?"

Nodding, Quinn muttered, "She said something about Kerry's skull being cracked. The bullet glanced off her cranium and cracked it. The doc is worried that her brain will swell because of the injury."

"I see…." Laura sighed. "But Kerry's brain is okay? The bullet didn't penetrate?"

Releasing his own trembling sigh, Quinn said, "No, thank God, it didn't, Mrs. Trayhern."

"Call me Laura." She smiled softly. "Then there's a lot of good to come out of this? The doctor is inducing her coma so her brain doesn't swell?"

"Something like that," Quinn murmured. He was exhausted. Even now, he wasn't thinking clearly. The surgery had taken five hours. He'd come straight back to the hospital after cleaning up and donning his fresh cammos, with the single black bar which was seen on each shoulder to denote his new second lieutenant status. Then he'd had to wait for Dr. Edmonds to finally appear and tell him how Kerry was doing.

Reaching out, Laura squeezed his arm. "I can tell you're tired, Quinn. Have you seen Kerry yet?"

"No, I haven't. She's in recovery right now, and no one's allowed in. They'll transfer her to ICU, the critical care unit, in about thirty minutes." He looked down at the watch on his hairy wrist. Feeling as if he were moving through a nightmare, Quinn sighed again. All he wanted was to see Kerry. To touch her. To convince himself that she was still alive. She *had* to live! She just had to! Clenching his teeth against the avalanche of wild, frightening thoughts, he glanced over at Laura. She was holding the baby in her arms, looking content and at peace.

The thought that Kerry would look like that with their baby struck him full force. He sat back in amazement. Quinn had no idea where *that* errant idea had come from. He knew he was sleep deprived. Knew that the emotional burden of Kerry's wounds weighed heavier on him than anything he'd ever encountered. Wrestling with all of it, Quinn felt like he was being torn apart, piece by piece, and he didn't know where to go or what to do with all those emotions.

"Listen," Laura whispered gently, "I know you want to wait until she's transferred to ICU, so you can see her...touch her and know that she's alive. But after that, Quinn, go back to your room at the B.O.Q. and sleep. You look like you're in shock yourself."

With a low, startled laugh, Quinn said, "Yeah... I am. I'm a trained EMT and I recognize my own symptoms, Laura." It was easy to be on a first-name basis with Laura Trayhern. She was so warm and caring. No wonder Morgan loved her. In many respects Kerry was very much like Laura, Quinn thought as he sat there holding her warm gaze. They both had that gentle nurturing quality.

"I promise to get some rest soon," he told her gravely.

"Morgan said that he's in contact with Sergeant Slater, the leader of the platoon your fire team came from. They're sending out a replacement for you now. That should make you feel better."

"It does, thanks. But all those people in Area Five will wonder about Kerry. They love her. They've come to rely on her—a *lot*. I need to get back out there...."

"In time," Laura counseled wisely. "First things first, Quinn. Make sure Kerry is okay, and then get some badly needed sleep. Morgan said for you to come to his office over in Logistics at 0900 tomorrow morning. Until then, you have nothing but downtime on your hands."

Nodding, Quinn whispered, "Thanks...."

Just then, a nurse in a light blue smock came into the visiting room.

"Corporal Grayson?" She frowned and looked at him again, studying his clean uniform and the bars on his shoulders. "Er... I'm sorry, Lieutenant Grayson? Deputy Kerry Chelton has been transferred to ICU. Mr. Trayhern said the two of you are engaged, so that makes you family. Only family members are allowed to see her at this point." The nurse looked at her watch. "You have five minutes every hour with her, sir. That's the rule."

Quinn rose to his feet, feeling uneasy with his

new rank. One moment enlisted, the next an officer. He had seen the brunette corpsman's eyes widen as she saw the lieutenant's bars on the cammo shirt he wore. "I understand. Thank you," he told her.

"No problem, sir." She turned and hurried away.

Quinn turned to Laura. "Thanks to you...and your husband. I don't know what I'd do right now if you hadn't been here."

Grinning slightly, Laura rocked the baby in the pink blanket gently. The little tyke was sound asleep. "I told Morgan he'd better concoct a story so you could get in to see Kerry. Patients in ICU aren't allowed visits from 'friends.' I wasn't sure you knew that, so I told Morgan to tell the nursing staff you two were engaged." She looked up at him, her eyes sparkling. "I hope that doesn't bother you, Quinn?"

Reaching out, he touched her shoulder. "No, ma'am, it doesn't. I'm not thinking fast on my feet at this point, and I'm grateful you are. Right now, all I want—need—is to see Kerry...."

"Then," Laura whispered, "go see her. And remember, even though a person is in a coma, they can still *hear* you. That's a medical fact. So go in there and *talk* to her. She'll be listening, Quinn. I know she will."

Swallowing hard, he lifted his fingers from Laura's slim shoulder. "Do you need help first, though? I know you came up here on your own."

Laughing, Laura said, "If you could ask the orderly who is waiting at the nurse's desk to take me back to my room, I'd appreciate it, Quinn. Thanks for asking."

Nodding, Quinn felt his heart begin to thud with dread. "I'll get him right now and then I'll go see Kerry. And I'll see Morgan tomorrow at 0900. Thanks—for everything..."

He left, walking almost woodenly. The passageway was clogged with orderlies and nurses hurrying in and out of rooms where so many injured and sick people lay. Keeping near the wall, Quinn moved like a robot toward the nurses' station where he asked the awaiting orderly to take Laura back to her room. Then he turned and headed to ICU, which was at the other end of the surgical floor. Kerry. He was going to see Kerry, finally....

The nursing station at ICU was filled with quiet tension. A red-haired corpswave behind the desk pulled Kerry's board off a hook.

"It says here that you're her fiancé, Lieutenant Grayson?" she asked, checking the second page of the document.

"Yes...yes, I am." It was a lie, but he wished it was true.

"Okay, no problem. She's in ICU 4. Just walk down there." She pointed behind her. "You have five minutes. I'll have to come and get you should you go over that time limit." Giving him a harried look, she added, "How about I leave it up to you to know when your time is up? We're busy, as you can see, so if you could…?"

"Sure, no problem," he promised her.

"Great. Go ahead, sir."

Turning, Quinn hurried toward the passageway. There were four ICU rooms, each walled with glass so that the nursing staff could see at a glance how a patient was doing. Kerry's room was on the right, the number 4 mounted in gold on the glass panel. Anxiously, he looked at her. She was propped up on a bed, with so many tubes running into her mouth, nose and arms that it scared him.

Opening the door quietly, Quinn was hit with the powerful smell of antiseptic, so strong it made him nauseous. Standing there, he eyed all the equipment on either side of the bed where Kerry lay without moving. She was on complete life support, a machine pumping for her, to mimic her breathing. Every few seconds the light blue covering across Kerry's breasts rose and fell.

Swallowing hard, Quinn moved to her side. They had placed her arms over the covers, her hands at her sides. Reaching out, he slid his fingers beneath her right hand. How cool it felt! Anxiety filled him again.

Kerry's head was wrapped in white gauze. Her right temple, where the bullet had struck, was hidden beneath a dressing. How pale she looked! Moving closer, he stared down at her, grasping her hand more firmly and lifting it against his heart.

"Kerry? It's me, Quinn. I'm here, sweet pea. You're okay. You're going to make it. You hear me?" Gently, he grazed her wan cheek with his fingers. How dark her thick lashes looked against her flesh. She was warm and dry, but unmoving. Only the monitors beeping and clicking told him she was alive. A tube protruded from her open mouth, pumping oxygen systematically into her lungs. Quinn could barely stand it, seeing her like this.

Keeping her limp fingers clasped protectively in his, he ran his other hand caressingly up and down her forearm. "Listen to me," he said gruffly, "you're going to get well. The doctor put you into a coma on purpose. The bullet hit you in the side of the head, Kerry. It broke the bone, but that was all. Your brain is okay, just a little swollen is all." He could see where they had placed a dry-ice pack against that area to reduce any swelling. He knew that she was receiving steroids by IV to reduce the inflammation, as well.

The beeps and sighs continued, steady and unabated.

Closing his eyes, Quinn felt dizzy and scared. Even though they'd said that Kerry's chances of surviving were good, anything could happen. A sudden blood clot could form. She could have a massive cerebral hemorrhage and die. Sometimes Quinn wished he didn't know as much about emergency medical procedures as he did. In this case, his knowledge scared him. He knew the possibilities, and all of them were bad.

Opening his eyes, he leaned down and brushed his lips against her cheek, which felt like soft peach fuzz. Kissing her gently, he lifted his head a little and whispered, "Kerry, I love you. Don't ask me when or how it happened. But you being hurt like this, out of the blue, showed me the truth." His fingers tightened again around her cool, limp hand. "Sweet pea, just know I'll be here for you. Tomorrow, I don't know what will happen. I'm going to go now… I gotta go sleep. When I wake, I'll be back over here and we'll talk some more, okay? Just know I love you. And I always will…."

*January 25: 1400*

The world was swirling in shades of dark and light before Kerry's closed eyes. She felt herself whirling downward, growing heavier by the minute. Taking a deep, ragged breath, she struggled against the sensations. There were noises around her, and low voices, both male and female, nearby. Most of all, she could feel someone's warm, strong hand around hers, and it was wonderfully stabilizing to her in this netherworld she floated in.

"She's becoming conscious," Dr. Edmonds said,

with a smile at Quinn, who stood on the other side of the bed, holding Kerry's hand. "Excellent. We've stopped giving her drugs to keep her in a coma and she's coming out right on schedule. This is a good sign." Dr. Edmonds removed her stethoscope and placed it against Kerry's blue-gowned chest.

Quinn stood there, breath suspended momentarily. For seven days Kerry had been unconscious and on life support. He'd been out on duty in Area Five today when Morgan had sent for him, with news that Dr. Edmonds was going to awaken Kerry. The swelling in her brain was down. Everything looked good.

Dr. Edmonds, a U.S. Navy first lieutenant, straightened up and smiled slightly. "She's becoming conscious, Lieutenant Grayson. We'll leave now, but if you need anything, Nurse Williams here will assist you," she said, gesturing to the red-haired woman who stood beside her.

"Thanks," Quinn said sincerely. "For everything..."

Dr. Edmonds grinned and pushed her short black hair off her broad forehead. "My pleasure, Lieutenant. Just stay with your lady. Keep talking to her. It will bring her out more quickly."

When they'd left, Quinn turned and faced Kerry. The tube in her mouth had been removed. She was breathing well on her own. There were still two IVs, one in each arm, going into her veins and supplying her with life-giving nutrients.

"Sweet pea?"

The words echoed through Kerry's awakening senses. She knew that voice. And she knew that wonderful endearment. Quinn! Quinn was nearby. She heard the low, off-key tone close beside her. As she honed in on the sound, she could feel the soft tickle of his warm, moist breath against her ear.

When the corners of Kerry's mouth lifted slightly, Quinn's heart soared with unchecked joy. He leaned down and pressed a tender, welcoming kiss against her lips. Her mouth was chapped, and cool to his touch.

How much he'd missed Kerry! The last three days he'd been back in Area Five, preparing for the hunter-killer team that would be flown in shortly— a team whose sole focus would be to hunt down the Diablo and capture them once and for all.

"Hey, sweet pea. I'm here. It's Quinn. I've really missed you the last three days. I've been out in your neighborhood—Area Five. I brought back a whole bunch of handwritten notes from the folks who love you, Kerry. I've got them here with me. When you're fully awake, I want you to read them. Those people really care about you. Every day I get radio reports from Morgan about you—how you're doing and what's happening. And everyone wants to know the latest. There's a lotta people pullin' for you,

Kerry.'' His voice wobbled. ''Especially me…'' He squeezed her hand tenderly.

The brush of Quinn's lips against hers was the most wonderful sensation Kerry had ever experienced. Moments later, his voice, deep and steady, filled with love for her, brought her completely out of her coma state. Despite Kerry's fragmented senses, there was no question that Quinn loved her. She could feel it in the touch of his strong, warm hand around hers, in the butterfly kiss he'd brushed across her lips. She could hear it in his low voice.

Holding his breath, Quinn saw Kerry's lashes flutter once, twice, three times. As they slowly lifted, he saw the murky gray of her eyes as her gaze settled on him. The doctor had warned him that because of the drugs, she might be disoriented for a while, but talking to her, giving her information, would help her focus and respond.

Leaning down, he kissed her brow as it wrinkled slightly. ''Welcome back, sweet pea. You're here with me. And you're safe. You're going to live, Kerry. Everything's gonna be fine. Believe me….'' And he looked deeply into her eyes, no more than six inches away from his.

Drowning in the blazing blue of his narrowed eyes, Kerry felt her heart speed up with joy. Seeing the suffering, the anxiety in Quinn's face made her want to reach out and reassure him, but she was too weak to do that. Instead, she gave him a lopsided smile.

"Hi, stranger…"

"Hi…"

"I'm okay…." Kerry whispered, and closed her eyes. It took all her energy just to try and pull two thoughts together, then speak them.

"Yes, you are." Quinn struggled with the crazy jumble of emotions tunneling through him. "I want to yell and scream and shout to the world that you're okay," he told her. "There's so many people who have been praying for you, Kerry. Who want you to pull through. And you have." Lifting her hand, Quinn gently turned it over in his and kissed the back of it. "You're going to be fine."

His words were like healing balm to her spinning and slowly awakening senses. Kerry tried to close her fingers around his, but felt incredibly weak. Fragments of his words, of what he'd told her as she'd awakened, were floating loosely, like flotsam and jetsam in the ocean of her awareness.

Just her effort to try and squeeze his hand brought tears to Quinn's eyes. Gently touching her cheek, he stroked it with his fingertips. He could see her struggling to break the bonds of grogginess, to be here with him. "Easy, Kerry. Don't try so hard. Just take your time. I'm not going anywhere. I'll be here while you become conscious. Okay? Don't fight. Everything will slowly make sense to you over the next couple of hours, according to Dr. Edmonds."

Forcing her eyes open, she met his tender, burning look. Trying to speak, she found her voice was raspy from disuse. Her throat was sore and it hurt to talk.

"You? You're okay, Quinn? The shots? Diablo…"

Seeing the fear in her eyes, Quinn realized she was recalling the firefight. "Shh, sweet pea, I'm okay. I wasn't harmed. You were. You were shot twice. Once in the right thigh. The doc said it was just a flesh wound, and it's healing well. The second bullet hit you in the right side of your head. It cracked your skull, but you're going to be okay there, too. The doc said you'll probably have one helluva headache. Do you?"

She saw the care and concern in Quinn's eyes— and the exhaustion. "Yes… My head…it's killing me."

His response melted together. He was speaking too fast for her to grasp all the words. More than anything, she was relieved that he wasn't wounded. As a matter of fact, Quinn looked wonderful to her. He was in a clean uniform, and had recently shaved. His dark hair was short and combed. Still, he looked worried. About her.

"I'll get the nurse in here to give you more pain meds through the IV," he told her. Quinn started to leave, but her fingers tightened unexpectedly around his.

"No…" Kerry whispered.

Her cry tore at him. Halting instantly, he turned back to her, his hand strong and firm around hers. "I'm not going far," he reassured her. "I'm just going to get the nurse, Kerry. I'll be right back. I promise."

When Quinn saw tears welling up in her eyes, it ripped him apart. Teardrops fell from the corners of her eyes, leaking down toward her ears. Reaching out, he wiped the moisture away with his thumbs.

"Everything's okay, sweet pea. Really, it is. It's you I was worried about. The doc says you're gonna be fine."

Unable to stop the tears, Kerry clung to his darkening features. Quinn was visibly upset over her crying, she saw, but she couldn't help herself.

"I—I just…" She choked and swallowed despite her painful throat. When Quinn's warm hand settled against her cheek to give her solace, more tears fell.

"What?" Quinn whispered, his mouth near her ear. "What's wrong, Kerry?" He was alarmed, unsure of why she was crying. Was she in that much pain from her head wound? Or was it something else? Fear clawed at him. Was her health deteriorating?

Opening her eyes, his face blurring before her, Kerry choked out in a raspy voice, "I lost Lee. I— I can't…lose you…."

# Chapter Nine

*January 17: 0900*

Quinn couldn't still his sense of urgency as he swung silently into the private room where they had placed Kerry late last night. She had rebounded remarkably, according to Dr. Edmonds, and they had desperately needed the ICU room for someone else in far worse shape than she was.

The sun was shining brightly through the partially opened venetian blinds, leaving stripes of sunlight across Kerry's bed.

"Hi!" He smiled at her warmly as he eased the door closed. "I see you're up, bright-eyed and bushy tailed."

Kerry managed a wan smile in return. She was

sitting up, with several pillows supporting her back. The orderly had just left her a tray with breakfast. "Bushy tailed?" she teased, her voice still raspy. Kerry had found out that the tube they'd put down her windpipe to help her breathe was the reason for the irritation in her throat. She was glad the tube was gone. Heart lifting, she smiled more widely. The entire room seemed to change, became lighter, and she felt happiness threading through her as he ambled toward her.

"Yeah, an old hill sayin'," he murmured. "It means you're looking real fine. Healthy."

"Mmm," Kerry said, "I'm better because you came to visit me."

Halting at her bedside, he eyed the tray resting on the moveable table across her lap. "I'm a sight for sore eyes, eh? Umm, breakfast. That's good. You need to eat and put a little meat on those bones." His mouth hitched upward.

The blue cotton gown was shapeless and hung on Kerry. Her hair was still hidden by the gauze wrapped around her head. But to him, she looked beautiful. Gazing deeply into her eyes, he saw some of the old life, those silver flecks, coming back into them.

Wrinkling her nose, Kerry offered him a slice of whole wheat bread that had already been buttered. "Want to share it with me?" As their fingers touched, she saw his blue eyes grow stormy with desire—for her.

"Thanks," he said, pulling up a chair and sitting down facing her, his right leg resting against the tubular frame of her bed. It was 0800—the earliest Quinn was allowed, by hospital rules, to visit. He'd gotten up early, shaved, showered and put on a pair of fresh cammos. No more would he take such mundane acts for granted. Being out in Area Five without water to shave or shower with had taught him that.

Kerry stirred the fork around in the fluffy scrambled eggs. She wasn't really hungry, but knew she had to eat.

"A sight for sore eyes," she said, giving him a glance. "That must be another hill saying?"

"Sure is. We have a whole other language in Kentucky."

Just being with Quinn was energizing for Kerry. She ate the eggs slowly and with relish. They actually tasted good. "I like all your expressions," she told him.

Munching on the toast, Quinn eyed Kerry closely. He didn't miss anything about her recovery. They'd already taken out one IV. She was on solid food. All those were good signs. "Stick around me," he teased, "and I'll teach you more." He wondered if she recalled what she'd said three days ago as she became conscious—about not wanting to lose him as she'd lost her husband. What did that mean? Quinn was afraid to read too much into it. Sometimes people with head injuries said a lot of things they either didn't recall later or didn't mean. Her words had meant the world to him, but the two of them barely knew each other. Their time together had been short and intense, but his heart didn't care. It wasn't at all reasonable when it came to Kerry.

"Is that a promise?" she whispered, setting the fork aside. How handsome Quinn looked. She could clearly see the desire, the care for her, in his eyes. Just the tenderness of his rough voice, the intimate tone he used with her, spoke volumes. Her heart skittered as he looked at her.

"Do you want it to be, Kerry?"

Unable to tear her gaze from his, she replied softly, "Yes…" And then she opened her hands in a helpless gesture. "I know we haven't known one another long, Quinn…."

Nodding, he set the piece of toast back on her tray. "Not long, but it's been pretty intense," he answered.

Touching her head carefully, Kerry said, "I've got a roaring headache, so I'm not going to be the best of company."

"Want me to get the nurse? Do you need a stronger pain med?" He was already halfway out of his chair.

"No…it comes and goes." Managing a slight

smile, Kerry admitted, "When my heart starts beating hard and I get scared, my blood pressure rises and that's when the pain comes on. Dr. Edmonds told me that would happen at first. With time, as the bone mends, it will go away."

"So, you need to do things to keep your blood pressure down?" Her eyes were hauntingly beautiful to Quinn, so full of life. Right now, he was scared and tentative. Did Kerry want the same thing he did? He wasn't sure, and he was too much of a coward to ask. As a marine, he might be able to storm a rampart, but when it came to this, he felt frozen by the fear of possible rejection. He watched Kerry's mobile face, so open and readable.

"Life raises my blood pressure," she told him wryly, pushing the tray aside.

"You look worried. What's bothering you, Kerry?"

Quirking her mouth, she stared down at her hands clasped in her lap. "I worry about Petula. Have you heard from her? From Sylvia? Are you in touch with them?"

"Yeah, they're both okay. I was in radio contact with Beau late last night, checking in with them to make sure everything was okay. They both miss you. Petula is getting regular MREs now, and so is Sylvia. They love the tent. The heat." He smiled. Just seeing the anxiety leave Kerry's eyes made him feel better.

"Good," she whispered fervently. "And what about Diablo? Are they still around? Or did they move into another area?"

Shrugging, Quinn said, "I don't know for sure. Morgan Trayhern is working on a plan to locate them. He realizes that my fire team can't respond as we first planned. And disease is starting to spread. He's trying to coordinate medical teams getting into our area to help stop the epidemics."

Kerry saw worry lurking in Quinn's darkening eyes. Frowning, she reached out, her fingers grazing his hand as it rested on the edge of her bed. "Are you going to be involved in getting the medical teams in there?"

Just the touch of her hand sent an ache straight to his heart. Quinn realized Kerry was a helluva lot braver than he was on the emotional front. She wouldn't touch him if he didn't mean something to her. The question was, how serious about him was she? The question almost tore out of him, but he couldn't find the guts to ask her yet.

"I don't know. I spent part of yesterday down at the brig facility going through mug shots, trying to ID the Diablo dudes we ran into. We wounded one of 'em and took out the others. The one that's still alive is here at the hospital right now, under armed guard. He didn't have any identification on him, and he's not talking to the military detectives put on the case."

Shivering, Kerry closed her eyes. "He's here?"

"Yeah." Quinn's fingers curled around her hand. "Don't worry, okay? That dude is going nowhere. The marines guarding him are brig chasers—and they're big and mean. They all hope he makes a break for it. They'd like nothing better than to take him down permanently after what he did to you." So would he, but Quinn knew it wasn't right. Let the legal system get this guy. He felt satisfaction in knowing the twenty-year-old-man was staring at a very long federal prison sentence for injuring and nearly killing Kerry. She was a law enforcement officer, and judges took a hard line and handed out long sentences to those who would do such a thing.

"I guess...well, I was wondering about him, too...." Sighing, she squeezed Quinn's hand. "I'm glad you're here with me. I'm feeling really vulnerable right now, shaky.... I was crying earlier. I don't know why, I just was...."

"Dr. Edmonds said with a head injury your emotions can go up and down like a roller coaster at first," he murmured soothingly, seeing the angst and turmoil in her eyes.

"I just didn't expect it."

"I'm here. I'll help you as much as I can, sweet pea." Quinn gave her a tender look and gripped her fingers tighter for a moment.

"I'm so glad..." Kerry's voice broke. Tears flooded her eyes and Quinn's face blurred again.

"You know, before you stepped into my life, I felt like the rug was jerked out from under me. I felt unstable and unsure, Quinn. But when you're with me, I feel okay. I feel like I'm going to get through all this hell on earth." Sniffing, she reached over and took a tissue from the box on the bedstand, dabbed her eyes and blew her nose.

"You've been through a lot, Kerry," he said, his voice a rasp. Watching her wipe the tears away made his heart ache. How badly he wanted to hold her. Just hold her. "And it's gonna take time for you to work through all the trauma. The shock. Getting shot at and injured just compounds it. Give yourself some breathing room, okay?"

Nodding, she gripped the tissue in her left hand. "It hasn't been all bad, Quinn. After all, I met you." Risking a glance, she saw his eyes narrow upon her. His mouth was thinned and set, as if he were bracing himself for whatever she might say.

"You just walked into my life and blew me away," Kerry told him brokenly. "I never realized how much of a load I was carrying by myself until you came and helped me out by sharing it. I liked your sensitivity, your care for others. I guess I had this stereotype in my head about rough, tough marines. When Morgan Trayhern told me you were coming, I wasn't thrilled pink about it, to be honest."

He grinned. "No?"

"No. I thought you'd be antiwoman or anti–law enforcement and just want to storm the beach and take over." She managed a shy smile as his grin widened.

"I respected what you'd done, Kerry. I saw how the people responded to you. I had no business coming in and trying to take over. We needed to learn from you, listen to you. And we did."

"I know." Shaking her head, she added, "Most of all, you were a wonderful leader, the best kind. I really liked working with you."

"You weren't what I expected, either," Quinn admitted. "I had a few stereotypes of my own to bury regarding you." He saw her answering smile.

Kerry was looking tired. Quinn knew she needed to sleep, so he got up and reluctantly released her hand. "Listen, you need to rest. Okay?"

Sighing, Kerry laid her head back on the pillows and closed her eyes. "I'm tired all of a sudden, Quinn." And she already missed his strong, warm hand on hers.

Walking around the bed, Quinn moved the wheeled table with the tray to one side. "Sleep, sweet pea," he whispered, leaning over and brushing a kiss on her wrinkled brow.

Opening her eyes, Kerry stared up into that blue gaze focused on her. "I feel so warm, safe and happy with you close to me like this...."

Reaching out, Quinn stroked her pale cheek.

"Then I'll make a habit of being a pest around here. I've got to meet Morgan in a few minutes. I'll come back late this afternoon and check on you."

Closing her eyes, she absorbed Quinn's touch like life-giving water to thirsty ground. "I'd like that...a lot...."

"I'll be back."

"Promise?"

"Promise."

*January 28: 2100*

Kerry looked at the clock on the wall; it was 2100. Darkness had fallen outside her private room. Most of her meal, which had been delivered at 1800, was still sitting there, untouched. Where was Quinn? There was a phone at her bedside, but she had no number to contact him. Worried, she kept glancing toward the door and then out the window.

There was a soft knock on the door and it opened. "Quinn..."

He smiled tiredly and took off his cap. "Hi. Sorry I'm late. Things snowballed today." He shut the door behind him. Turning, he saw the anxiousness in Kerry's eyes even though she tried to hide her reaction.

"I'm just beginning to realize how busy it is around this base," she murmured. How good Quinn looked! But he was tired. She could see it in his eyes and the set of his mouth. He stuffed the cap he'd been wearing into his back pocket and unbuttoned his bulky jacket. Taking it off, he threw it on the chair next to her bed.

"Twenty-five hours a day," he assured her. Moving to her tray, he said, "What's this? You haven't touched your food. How come?" And he gave her a concerned look. There was a bit of color in her cheeks as he met and held her gaze. "Aren't you feeling any better?"

"I'm okay," Kerry lied. "I was just...well, worried when you didn't show up this afternoon...."

Moving the tray back across her bed, over her lap, Quinn opened the container of Jell-O and pulled off the transparent wrapper. "I got asked to fly out to Area Five unexpectedly, Kerry. At 1500 today. I'm sorry I couldn't let you know."

"I figured something came up." She watched as he picked up the spoon and handed her the container.

"You need to eat. Get your strength back, sweet pea."

Rallying at his undivided care, Kerry took the Jell-O and spooned some into her mouth. It was sweet and tasted good.

Unwrapping a sandwich, Quinn sat down on the edge of her bed and faced her.

"Help yourself," she said between bites. "I'm not that hungry."

"I'm a starvin' cow brute," he said with a chuckle. Just being with Kerry lifted his spirits. "That's hill slang for a steer." He saw her mouth draw into a smile. Did Kerry know how beautiful she was to him? Quinn didn't think so. He was ravenous and bit into the sandwich as she continued to daintily eat the strawberry Jell-O.

"Let me fill you in on the day's events," he told her between bites. There was some orange juice in a bottle, so he opened it and poured half of it into the plastic cup for her and kept half for himself.

"Morgan asked me to fly out on a Huey shipment bound for Area Five at 1500. Even though my fire team is there, and they have a new corporal, he wanted me to reconnoiter the area for the incoming medical team that will be here tomorrow evening. I spent all afternoon, until dark, going over a street map of the area, noting information that this team will need. There's all kinds of sickness starting to crop up. Dysentery, typhoid, strep, and others. Morgan is trying to get medical teams in there to stop it, but our medical supplies can't even begin to handle the epidemics that are starting to explode in the area."

"I've been worried sick about that, Quinn. I knew it would only be a matter of time. People are drinking dirty, unsafe water. They're eating food that's rotten and germy. I'm glad Morgan has made the medical teams a priority." She brightened a bit. "Did you see Petula? Sylvia?"

Smiling, he nodded. "The first thing I did when we landed was drop in for a visit with them. They're fine. They asked about you and I told them you're doing fine. Petula cried. But it was tears of happiness."

Sighing, Kerry whispered, "That's great."

"You're missed by everyone," he told her seriously. "Walking around the area, I must have had close to thirty people come up and ask me about you. They knew you'd been wounded and they were worried."

"I lie here thinking about so many of them. I miss everyone. We bonded because of the tragedy and they feel like extended family to me now," Kerry said. She took a drink of orange juice.

"To them, you are family," he agreed. Quinn handed her half the turkey sandwich.

"Eat this."

She bit into it without a word. Her spirits were flying. The darkness, the depression she was feeling, dissolved.

"I didn't run into Diablo, either," Quinn told her, frowning. "I think the gunfight with us changed things. I'm not sure where they are right now."

"Hiding, more than likely," Kerry answered. The turkey was amazingly tasty. She realized for the first time that she was truly famished. It had to be

Quinn's presence that triggered her appetite. With her leg resting against his hip where he sat on her bed, she sponged in his presence like the earth soaked up the rays of the warming sun. The happiness in his eyes made her heart beat harder. Hope threaded through Kerry, strong and good.

"Yeah, that's what Logistics thinks. Morgan is asking me to be point man on this project to try and find them."

Frowning, Kerry whispered, "Does that mean you'll go out with another team to find Diablo?"

"Take it easy," he said, wiping his mouth with a paper napkin after finishing his half of the sandwich. "No, I'm being assigned back to Area Five as Logistics officer." He smiled at her. "I'll be working with you—again." Kerry had made it clear she wanted to go back to her area. Dr. Edmunds agreed that she could as soon as her head wound was better. The flesh wound on her thigh was almost healed.

Shocked, Kerry stared at him. "Officer?" A thrill shot through Kerry. Quinn was going to be working with her once more. She felt euphoric.

Chuckling, Quinn said, "Did you notice the black embroidered bar on each of the shoulders of my shirt here?" He pointed to his left epaulet. The silver bars Morgan had given him would go on his official marine uniform, but not on his cammies. "I got a field commission, Kerry. It sure shocked me. That kind of thing hasn't been done since Vietnam. But Morgan said they were giving it to me because of the earthquake. They need more seasoned enlisted men and women out there in the basin. They're shorthanded and they need leaders to get the help to where it's critical. They don't have enough marine officers to do that with, so they're making new ones so we can help sooner, faster, better.''

"Oh, Quinn, congratulations!'' She reached out and touched his hand.

He grasped her fingers and squeezed them gently. "It was sure a surprise to me.''

"Well deserved, I'd say. What a gift.''

"You're my gift,'' he told her seriously. "In more ways than one, Kerry.'' He lifted her hand and pressed a kiss to the back of it. "All I want is for you to eat, sleep, rest and get better. The world might have fallen apart around us, but we have each other. That's the gift to me.'' He hoped it was for her, too, but he wasn't about to put words into her mouth on that topic. Just the way her eyes turned smoky with desire made his heart beat faster. The way her soft, full lips parted made him groan inwardly.

Kerry didn't want Quinn to release her hand, but he did. He was intent on getting her to eat. Uncovering a piece of chocolate cake with a thin layer of white frosting, he divided it between them, then handed her the fork.

"At some point when the time's right," Kerry told him softly, "we need to sit down and do some serious talking, Quinn."

His heart thudded in his chest. Looking down, he muttered, "Yeah, I know. Things have been crazy of late, and our worlds have been like sheets twisted in a windstorm."

"I love your hill sayings," Kerry said. More than anything, she loved him. And how she felt had to be put on the table. Whether Quinn loved her, she didn't know, and that scared her as little else had in her life. Still, Kerry knew she had to tell Quinn how she felt.

"Two days from now," he told her, "if things go right, let's talk. Okay? I'll be back on base on the thirtieth."

Nodding, she picked disinterestedly at the cake. "Yes, two days, Quinn." Her appetite had fled once more with the fear of losing Quinn. His larger-than-life presence was exactly that—something so good, clean and wonderful that Kerry had a tough time believing that life had placed a second good man before her.

# *Chapter Ten*

*January 30:1600*

Quinn hurried into the greenhouse that was attached to the hospital. Laura Trayhern had told him that in the last two days, Kerry had become mobile in a wheelchair. Her recovery was so swift that she was spending a lot of time in the greenhouse instead of staying in her room.

He hadn't realized there was a greenhouse and solarium affixed to the hospital. It was a nice way to get the patients out of their rooms. His heart hammered. Would Kerry be glad to see him? That he'd promised her he'd see her two days ago made his gut clench. Would she understand? Pushing through the double doors, their windows steamed up because of the humidity, he entered a world of warmth and moisture.

The greenhouse was a glass-and-steel structure housing a good five thousand square feet of tropical greenery—brightly flowering orchids and tall palms that reached for the light. Where was Kerry? Quinn halted and looked around. The redbrick sidewalk was wide enough to support a wheelchair. Very few people were in the exquisite greenhouse, maybe because it was 1600. Mouth dry, he wiped it with the back of his hand and turned. Something told him to take the left fork in the path, around the huge stand of palms in the red planter that welcomed visitors into this jungle world.

He found Kerry at the end of the curving red path, a watering pot in her hands. She was watering some of the low plants along the sidewalk, one at a time. From where he stood, he could see that she wore only a dressing on her temple, and the swathes of gauze around her head had been removed. Her hair, dark and slightly curled, had been recently washed and framed her face. Most surprising, she was in civilian clothes and not a hospital gown. Kerry wore a long-sleeved, pale pink turtleneck that provocatively outlined her upper body. She had small, beautiful breasts, Quinn realized for the first time. When she'd been in her uniform or wearing a flak vest, that feminine secret had been hidden from him. Further, the jeans she wore outlined her long, curved thighs. She was leaning down, a peaceful look on her face as she dribbled water on a bright red anthurium with dark green foliage.

"I'm kinda thirsty," Quinn said, coming forward. "Can I get a drink of water from you, too?"

Kerry's head snapped to the left. Quinn's voice was low, intimate and teasing. As she sat up, she nearly dropped the watering device.

"Quinn!" Her voice was muffled by the many plants and high humidity around them. She twisted toward him. Her heart bounded and joy shot through her. He was grinning crookedly, a welcome burning in his eyes.

With a soft cry, Kerry set the watering bucket down and turned the wheelchair toward him. The look of happiness on his darkly bearded face, in his bloodshot eyes, made her smile.

Quinn crouched before her, his hands settling on her shoulders. "Hi, stranger."

"Hi, yourself." Kerry touched his bearded face. There was dirt on the side of his jaw, and his cammies were dirty, also. "And you're no stranger."

"No?" He searched her silver-flecked eyes. There was no doubt Kerry was happy to see him. He ran his hands across the silky pink turtleneck covering her shoulder and upper arms. More than anything, he liked touching Kerry. Her body was firm and athletic.

"No. How are you?" To heck with it. Kerry

threw her arms around him and drew him against her in a tight, quick embrace. Quinn came forward without protest, chuckling as he wrapped his strong arms carefully around her shoulders and held her. He smelled of sweat. Kerry knew he'd been out in the field for two days in Area Five.

"I'm fine—now." Giving her a quick kiss on her ruddy cheek, Quinn eased away. Taking off his cap, he rose and tucked it in a back pocket. "You look great." *Delicious.* He wanted her. So very badly. He wanted to claim her in every way to show her how much she meant to him.

"Thanks." Kerry laughed delightedly. Gesturing to the brick walk, she said, "Can you sit down? Do you have a minute or are you off putting out another brushfire crisis somewhere else?"

Sitting on the sidewalk, which was only slightly damp, Quinn crossed his legs and looked up at her. "I'm sorry I couldn't be here this morning when I said I would, Kerry. I know I promised." He opened his hands in a helpless gesture.

"Don't worry about it," she murmured. "Morgan came by and told me that Diablo attacked again in Area Five and that he ordered you to stay out in the field with another squad to help protect the people."

Grimacing, Quinn ran his fingers through his short, dark hair. "Yeah. We got there before they did any real damage."

"Everyone safe?" Hungrily, Kerry absorbed his

exhausted features. All she wanted to do right now was lie with him, hold him and let him know that she loved him. But it was still too soon for that, she knew.

"Yeah. They took off just as we landed in the Huey. The people were shaken up, but okay."

"Morgan said the medical teams were delayed?"

"I'm afraid so. Flight schedules are being juggled all the time because of high-priority needs. Right now, medicine is not the top dawg, but Morgan's trying to make it so."

"Why not?" Anger moved through her. "I heard cholera is breaking out all over the place," she said, trying to curb her frustration. Cholera was a deadly disease found in squalid third world countries, not the U.S.A. It shocked Kerry to realize that it was here now, only miles away from the base. That living conditions out there were worsening daily.

"Water and food still have top billing but Logistics are trying to get the medical teams in there, thanks to Morgan pushin' his weight around to get them prioritized," Quinn said with a slight smile. He saw the worry etched on Kerry's face. "Good news, though. Petula is fine, as is Sylvia and everyone you know back in Area Five. They said to send their hellos to you."

Brightening, Kerry sighed. "Oh, good! You know, deep down in my heart, Quinn, I'm a big worrywart."

Chuckling, he said, "I know." Reaching out, he captured her hand with his larger one. "Listen," he said, his voice dropping to a rough growl, "we need to talk. I need to level with you. I'm scared to do it, afraid of the outcome, but I owe you that, Kerry. And I owe it to myself."

She curled her fingers around his, light upon dark. The back of Quinn's hand was hairy; hers was white and smooth. Heart pumping violently for a moment, she licked her lips and gravely met his narrowing blue gaze.

"I know… I've got to come clean, too. And I'm scared, if that makes you feel any better?" One corner of her mouth curved upward. She saw some of the tension in his face ease. Just her touching him was helping Quinn's distress. That realization was wonderful to Kerry. Touch, for her, was so important and so healing.

"Okay, sweet pea…should I go first?"

"Yeah," Kerry said wryly, "I'm too scared. Brave ones go first."

Snorting softly, Quinn leaned over and pressed a small kiss to the back of her hand, which was warm now, not chilled as it had been days ago. "I'm a coward over matters of the heart," he confided. "But here goes…." And he took in a ragged breath and let it out.

"When you got hit out there in the field, Kerry,

something I'd been avoiding since I met you broke
loose and hit me right between the runnin' lights, in
the middle of my forehead. When I ran to your side
after the firefight, I thought you were dead. I was so
scared. Scared to death. I remember the thought
howling inside my head and heart—that this wasn't
fair. I'd just met you…thought so much of you…
was attracted to you. This couldn't be happening!''

Gazing deeply into his troubled eyes, Kerry whispered, ''So you liked me a little?''

Lifting his other hand, he grazed her flaming
cheek. ''That's an understatement….''

''I see….''

Unsure, Quinn searched her warm gray eyes,
which grew lustrous at his halting admittance. Fear
ate at him. He had to go on, had to be honest with
her. ''I didn't go into Area Five expecting to meet
a woman I'd be drawn to. I didn't know what to
expect, Kerry, but I didn't expect how I'd feel about
you.'' He ran his fingers lightly down her arm and
allowed them to come to rest on top of her small,
slender hand.

''I got burned real bad in a relationship a couple
of years ago. The gal turned on me after I asked her
to marry me. I found out then that she wanted an
officer. She was a social climber. She didn't want
some lowly lance corporal in the Marine Corps. As
soon as some green lieutenant right out of the Naval

Academy made eyes at her, she started chasing him and let me go.''

"I'm so sorry," Kerry said. She saw the anger and hurt in his expression. "That must have been awful. You were sincere. She wasn't.''

"Exactly." Quinn stared down at Kerry's hand for a moment. "So, when I met you, I wasn't expecting to…well, fall for you like that…."

His mouth was working, his brows were knitted and he wasn't meeting her gaze. Kerry could feel him wrestling within himself. Gently, she whispered, "Quinn, I wasn't expecting to fall in love with you, either, but I have.''

The words landed like bombs and exploded within him. Jerking his chin up, he saw Kerry smiling softly, tears glistening in her wide, doelike eyes.

"You—love me?''

"Yes. Don't ask me how or when it happened." She gave a half laugh and shook her head. "I sure wasn't looking for a man, Quinn. After losing Lee, I knew the universe wasn't going to put a second good man in front of me." Her smile fading, Kerry choked out the words. "But they did. They gave me you, Quinn.''

Sitting very still, he digested her tearful words. Kerry loved him. It took long, precious seconds for that realization to really sink into his wildly beating heart. Unable to catch his breath, he sat there, her hand enclosed in his, their gazes clinging together in the warmth and humidity and peace of the silent greenhouse.

Kerry had more courage than he did, Quinn realized. She'd admitted her love for him first. Getting up on one knee and cupping her shoulders, he said in a rasp, "And I've fallen in love with you…and I don't know how or when or why, either. I just know I have, Kerry."

There, the truth. The unvarnished reality of how he felt was out. He saw his awkward words touch Kerry, saw the joy leap in her sparkling gray eyes. His hands tightened for a moment on her shoulders as she raised her own hands to frame his face.

"I'm scared, Quinn. Scared to death to feel like I do toward you."

"Me, too. It's the wrong place, Kerry. The wrong time. Bad timing."

"Either of us could get killed out there in the line of duty. I almost died already. In another week, I'm going home, back to Area Five, to carry on my work there."

His hands squeezed her shoulders, firm and loving. "I know you're goin' back there. Morgan already told me."

"You'll be with me, right?" She simmered with joy and with fear as she drowned in his aqua gaze, which was filled with love toward her.

"Every moment, sweet pea. I'm not lettin' you out of my sight. We'll work that area together.

That's what Morgan has in mind—a melding of military and civilian law enforcement to hold the fabric of the place together. With both of us back there, I know we can stabilize it."

"Together," Kerry said, "like the good team we've become."

"I want to kiss you...."

She smiled tenderly. "I'd like nothing better, Quinn. I need you...." And she did. Leaning forward, she met his descending mouth. His breath was warm and moist, flowing against her cheek as he moved his lips adoringly across hers. There was such restraint in him, as if she were a priceless vase that would shatter if he put too much stress on it.

"I won't break," she whispered against his mouth, and smiled as she opened her eyes and met his gaze.

Feeling her lips curve in a smile, Quinn eased away momentarily. "You're strong, sweet pea. Strong and beautiful and every inch the kind of woman I've always dreamed of, but never thought I would meet."

Laughing softly with happiness, Kerry slid her fingertips across his hard jawline to his thickly corded neck. "Then kiss me silly...! I really need you, Quinn. You make me feel safe and warm and good all at the same time...."

Not wanting to disappoint her, Quinn eased his hands across her jaw and tilted her head just slightly to take full advantage of her smiling mouth. This time, he moved his lips against hers with a deep, searching abandon. Her breathing became chaotic. Her hands ranged restlessly against his neck and shoulders as he tasted her, cajoled her and made her a part of him as never before.

His lower body burned hotly, with almost a painful cramping sensation, he wanted her so badly. Yet Quinn knew the time wasn't right, at least not yet. They'd barely met. They needed the coming weeks and months to get to know one another better. As he glided his mouth against hers, tasted her and inhaled her special feminine fragrance, Quinn sensed they'd both know when that time came.

Lost in the explosive heat and exploration of his strong male mouth against her softer lips, Kerry sighed. Quinn was powerful without being hurtful. As he caressed her head, her neck and shoulders, as if committing it all to memory, Kerry felt as if she were the most adored person on the face of the earth. How badly she wanted Quinn in all ways. Because of the past, she needed time to say a final farewell to Lee before she embarked on a new path with this incredible man who now held her so carefully and lovingly.

Easing back, Kerry gazed up at Quinn. His shoulders were so broad and capable, and he was so near to her, so solid and warm. "I never expected this, Quinn...not now, not ever...."

Sliding his hands across her shoulders and down her arms, to capture her hands in her lap, Quinn sat back on his boot heels. His heart was thudding with longing, his chest expanding with joy. The happiness burning in Kerry's eyes was real, and it made him feel good about himself as a man.

"I didn't either, Kerry. Maybe that's why it'll work for us in the long run."

Nodding, she ran her tongue over her lower lip. Kerry liked the taste of Quinn. Her mouth tingled in the wake of his branding, capturing kiss. Trying to catch her breath, she managed a small, wry smile. "I need the time. I think you already know that."

"Yeah, I do. I'm willing to wait, Kerry. Good things are always worth waiting for, my ma says."

"Your ma is right," she laughed breathlessly. Holding his hands, she absorbed his gentleness toward her.

"We have a lot of work in front of us. And danger." Quinn's brow became furrowed for a moment. "It's gonna take months before the L.A. basin gets back on a stable footing. And it's gonna get worse before it gets better. Morgan was saying that they're now entering the critical phase, where disease is going to begin to kill off thousands of people."

Sadness settled in Kerry's heart. She looked around the quiet, empty greenhouse, breathed the fragrant perfume of orchids in bloom. "I know. I feel guilty even being here. Every time I eat a meal,

I think of the thousands of people out there who are near starvation. It's a horrible thing, and I feel so frustrated that I can't change it or fix it.''

"Nothing is gonna be a quick fix out there, Kerry.'' He reached forward and grazed the right side of her rib cage below her breast. "You need to put more weight on you before you go back out in the field, too. If you aren't strong and physically in shape, you can't help in ways you need to. You know that.''

Hanging her head, she whispered, "I do know. It's just—hard, is all.''

"That's one of the many things I love about you, sweet pea,'' he told her in a low, tender tone. "Your care of others. Your concern. You were feeding Petula what little food you could find, instead of yourself, I know.''

"Can't fool you, can I?'' Kerry's laugh was tinged with sadness.

Shaking his head, Quinn said, "No, you can't. You wear your heart, a heart as big as the mountains I was born in, on your sleeve, Kerry.'' He squeezed her fingers gently. "I love you.''

Reaching out, she touched Quinn's sandpapery jaw and held his stormy blue gaze. "And I love you, too, Quinn. I'm glad we have the time. We'll learn more and more about each other as we work together out there. I like that. I'm looking forward to being with you again. I miss you not being around.''

Kerry allowed her fingers to drop from his hard jaw, and gazed around her. "I'm lonely without you. I like hearing what you think, learning from your hill experience, about your life...."

"Every day I'm out there," Quinn told her in a quiet voice, "I'm lonely without you near me, Kerry. I feel like I'm half a person. You complete me in a way I've never been completed before. It scares me, but it also makes me feel good."

"Let's be scared together," Kerry suggested. "Life is in chaos right now. But we have one another. We have more than most. Even out of this terrible, escalating disaster, some good has come— I found you. I fell in love with you. And it's the best thing that's ever happened to me."

# *Epilogue*

### *February 1: 0600*

Quinn sat next to Kerry in Morgan Trayhern's cramped office. Logistics was in high gear since the cholera epidemic had started. They each had cups of steaming coffee in their hands as Morgan sat down across from them, his brow deeply furrowed. Quinn could see the man wasn't sleeping much; his eyes were bloodshot and shadowed with exhaustion.

Feeling for their leader, Quinn said, "Sir? Could you use a cup of coffee to jump-start your morning?" It was 0600, and the sky outside the open venetian blinds behind Morgan's desk was still dark.

"What?" Morgan lifted his head from riffling through several files on his desk.

"Coffee, sir? Can I pour you a cup?"

A vague smile twisting his mouth, Morgan said, "No, thanks… I've been up since 0400, Quinn, and if I have any more coffee, my nerves are going to start shrieking."

Kerry glanced over at Quinn. Today was her first day back on the job. Her leg was healed up sufficiently, but not fully. She'd battled hard to get back out to Area Five instead of languishing here at Camp Reed. Part of her felt guilty for taking up bed space, and eating so well when starvation was rampant in the L.A. basin now. Another part of her ached to be back with the people she worried about constantly. With Quinn and his fire team going back with her, she felt elated and hopeful.

"Well," Morgan muttered, locating the file he wanted, "finally…" He pulled it open and flattened it on his desk with his large hands. Outside his partially opened door, the office was thrumming. People were walking quickly up and down the gleaming passageway. Everyone was in a hurry. Time had run out on them. People were dying not by tens or twenties now, but by hundreds. Those numbers would reach the thousands soon if Morgan didn't get things in place pronto.

Thumping the file with his index finger, he told Quinn, "I've finally managed to get medical teams on the priority list. With word coming back daily from the helicopter flights out there, the feds are finally realizing we have an epidemic about to blow up in our face.''

''That's great news, sir. At least about the medics.''

''Yes, yes, it is.'' Scowling, Morgan rummaged around on his messy desk again. ''Kerry?''

''Yes, sir?''

''We're going to get the first medical team, Alpha, into your area.''

Clapping her hands, Kerry whispered, ''Thank you!''

''Don't be so overjoyed,'' Morgan growled. ''Your area has more epidemics than any other. Cholera, typhoid, salmonella… People are drinking whatever water they can find, and it's dirty and tainted. We're losing a lot of infants and children.''

Glumly, Kerry nodded. ''I understand, sir. Still, having a medical team sent in brings hope, and that's what the people need. They need to see the government working for them.''

''It does…'' he groused, frowning ''…eventually. When enough pressure hangs over their heads. I'd like to put a few of those overweight senators and congressmen into the basin. They'd squall like scalded cats if they were deprived of their bread and butter for more than a day.''

Quinn snorted. ''There's no bread or butter left in the basin, sir.''

''Exactly my point.''

Kerry saw the frustration in Morgan's face. Having talked with Laura, she understood his barely veiled anger. Morgan had single-handedly fought red tape right up to the president to get medical teams put on a higher priority status. More than most people in the higher echelons of federal government, Morgan knew about disease. He knew it from his time spent in Vietnam, and then in the French Foreign Legion. He'd seen deprivation, starvation and disease in Southeast Asia and in Africa. And because of his experience, he knew what would happen in the quake zone.

"I'm sending in a reconnaissance team, Quinn, to work with the first medical team. I've managed to snag Dr. Samantha Andrews, a U.S. Navy doc, to help create crisis intervention teams. She's going out with two nurses and two enlisted orderlies to see if they can start combating the epidemic."

Sitting up a little straighter, Quinn smiled. "You're puttin' a Recon team with a medical unit?"

"I have to," Morgan muttered. "If I don't, and that medical team mixes up with Diablo, they could be murdered. No, I pulled strings to get this Recon unit pulled out of Kosovo and brought here to guard them."

"That's a good idea, sir."

"You know Lieutenant Roc Gunnison? He's the officer heading up this Recon team."

"A little," Quinn said. "He was here at Camp

Reed, and my team worked together with his from time to time before he was ordered overseas.''

"What kind of man is he, Son? And don't be PC—politically correct—okay? I need the goods on this man because he's going to have to interface with Dr. Andrews. I know her. She's a strong, capable woman with a lot of guts and common sense. That's why I chose her to help create these med teams. She'll see what's wrong and know how to fix it to make the unit smoother and more reactive to the demands placed upon it.''

Nodding, Quinn said, "I'm sure you have Captain Gunnison's file there?''

"Yes, I do. I happen to know his father, a very rich man who owns a computer company. Roc is a ring knocker.''

"Ring knocker" was a term used for those who had graduated from Annapolis, a rarefied place where only the best navy and Marine Corps officers were chosen to go for an education. Quinn said, "He's the paramedic on his team, sir. And he's very good at what he does.''

"His men like him?''

"They respect him, sir.''

Grimacing, Morgan muttered, "Great." There was a fine line between like and respect. Morgan was hoping that this officer was the type of leader a team would go to hell and back for. Quinn carefully using the word respect spoke volumes, and not in Roc's favor. Scowling, Morgan rasped, "Okay, you've met Dr. Andrews?"

"Yes, sir, I have. She's a human dynamo."

Morgan saw Quinn brighten and sit up even straighter. He also saw the gleam of respect in the man's eyes for the woman doctor. Sam Andrews was a one-woman tornado in the hospital. She'd brought the facility up to speed to meet the overwhelming crisis they'd had to deal with when the quake victims started being flown in. She had been responsible for a lot of triage ideas and changes that affected the way patients were brought in and handled at the understaffed facility. She had saved lives by looking at the larger picture, and then making the necessary tweaks and adjustments that made the medical unit more responsive to the needs of the avalanche of incoming patients. Morgan liked her a lot.

"Okay, what's Gunnison's problem, Quinn? And be damned straight with me. I don't have time to pussyfoot on this one."

"Yes, sir. You know the saying, 'pride goeth before a fall'?"

Rolling his eyes, Morgan muttered, "Yes, unfortunately."

"That about sums it up, sir."

"He's pigheaded. He can't admit he's wrong?"

"Yes to both of those, sir."

"Great...!"

"He's very competitive, sir. But that's not a bad thing, usually...."

Nostrils flaring, Morgan glared across the desk at Quinn, who had an apologetic look on his face. "Except, if I'm reading between the lines on this one, your evaluation is that Dr. Andrews and Captain Gunnison are going to get along like oil and water."

"Uh...maybe like cats and dogs?"

"You've made my day, Lieutenant."

"I'm sorry, sir."

"Don't apologize." He shut the file dejectedly.

"I've seen a lot of Dr. Andrews," Kerry said, hope in her tone. "She's tough, sir. Firm and tough. I don't think she'll let this Recon officer run over her."

"Oh," Morgan chuckled, "I know she won't. Sam—er, Dr. Andrews, doesn't suffer fools lightly." He gave them a brief smile. "Thanks for your input. Both of you. Are you ready for your 0700 flight back home, Kerry?"

She smiled. "More than ready, sir. Thanks for all you've done to help them—and me. You're an angel in my eyes. A guardian angel of the best kind."

Morgan tapped his head. "Yeah? Well, I got a lot of people cursing at me and thinking I'm the devil incarnate back East in the Capital. I've been raising more hell. They're so tired of me that they're actually starting to give me what I want for these poor folks in the quake zone.''

Kerry wanted to stand up and hug Morgan. He looked like he could use a hug about now. She'd realized from further talks with Quinn that Morgan was like a one-man army on behalf of all the people out there in the L.A. basin. He was truly a knight in shining armor in her eyes.

Rising, Quinn smiled down at Kerry. ''You ready?''

She moved gingerly. Although healing, her head injury was still on the mend. Even now, Kerry moved carefully and not with her usual confidence. ''More than ready.''

Morgan lifted his hand. ''Stay in close touch. And expect that medical unit in tomorrow, possibly the day after. My people will be in radio contact with you about it.''

''Yes, sir,'' Quinn said, and he opened the door for Kerry.

Out in the passageway, they hugged the wall to avoid the stream of human traffic. Like a well-oiled machine, the Logistics department hummed in high gear twenty-four hours a day, with three shifts of people working at top speed.

Quinn opened an exit door for Kerry. There were no elevators in the building, and she would have to take the concrete steps slowly and carefully so as not to jar her head. He moved to her side. They were alone now, and he slipped his hand beneath her left elbow to steady her.

"Thanks," she whispered, looking up with a soft smile. Her heart swelled with such love for Quinn. Over the past week, now that their love was out in the open, their feelings had grown stronger, more beautiful and deeper. She cherished his touch, though it didn't come often enough. Out in the real world, they had to act with decorum and restraint. Touching or kissing wasn't allowed, unfortunately.

As she slowly took each step, Quinn at her side, Kerry said, "Do you think Dr. Andrews is going to get along with Captain Gunnison?"

Snorting, Quinn said, "No. That's like putting a fox and a chicken in the henhouse together."

"Who's the hen? Who's the fox?"

Laughing, Quinn said, "I don't know, sweet pea." He gave her a warm look. "But we'll be there to see it happen."

"My money's on Dr. Andrews. She's an amazon. A real Princess Xena."

"Roc Gunnison is nothin' to mess with, though," he pointed out. "When he thinks he's right, he'll move heaven and hell to prove it."

"Well," Kerry said dryly, "let's keep score. They're supposed to set up a medical tent city near our place at the shopping center, so we'll get fifty-yard seats to watch the battle of the titans."

His fingers closed around her elbow and he leaned

over and gave her a swift kiss on the cheek. "What kind of a bet do you want to place on them?"

Her skin tingled pleasantly where he'd kissed her, and she smiled at him. "My money's on the doctor."

"Okay, I'll back Roc."

"You marines *always* stick together."

Chuckling, Quinn said, "Yeah, I know...."

"I love you anyway."

"Whew, that's good to know!" And they laughed together as they started down the second flight of stairs on the way to their new life together.

\* \* \* \* \*

*Next month look for*
Protecting His Own

*when*
MORGAN'S MERCENARIES:
ULTIMATE RESCUE

*continues in the*
*Silhouette Sensation line!*
*Only from bestselling author*

LINDSAY McKENNA

*Turn the page for a sneak preview…*

# Protecting His Own
### by
### Lindsay McKenna

Heart pounding, Sam watched the desert-colored Humvee approach at high speed. As it drew close, Sam could see Captain Roc Gunnison in the passenger seat. Lips tightening, she tried to gird herself as he stared at her flatly through the window of the vehicle. There was no welcome in those eyes. Only hardness.

Trying to appear nonchalant, she watched as the door of the Humvee opened and her nemesis stepped out. Her heart thumped again as she studied his hard, unyielding profile.

At thirty-two years of age, Gunnison was a seasoned marine who had seen action not only in Somalia, but in Kosovo, and he was highly decorated. Medium-boned, he appeared strong, capable and athletic in his desert cammos. His black hair was close-cropped and barely visible beneath the helmet he wore. Those eaglelike blue eyes, the color of the Montana sky she'd been born under, got to her.

As he swung his head in her direction, Sam's heart thundered briefly. Their eyes met and locked. Sam felt naked and vulnerable beneath his glacial assessment. Under any other circumstances, she'd find him a handsome man, with that square face and those craggy looks stamped with experience and lined from hours spent out in the elements. Now she found herself staring almost hungrily back at him. She knew it had to be the pressure she was under. Because experience had shown her that Roc was *not* the kind of man she wanted. Not on this mission. And not as a woman.

Roc couldn't tear his gaze from Dr. Andrews as she stood outside the helicopter in her U.S. Navy regulation clothing. Despite the desert-colored flak jacket that covered her upper body, he knew she was large boned and curvy beneath that mannish clothing she had to wear. He tried to glare at her, to let her know silently that he wasn't going to take any crap from her on his mission. Yet as the early morning breeze lifted her red hair away from her long, oval face and he saw her green eyes glittering with intelligence, Roc remembered this wasn't just any woman he was dealing with.

As he stared at her across the distance, he saw her lips part slightly. That was his undoing, dammit.

He groaned inwardly. Why did Andrews have to have such a soft, full mouth?

Scowling, Roc shut the door on the Humvee. Girding himself, he hefted his pack in one hand, his M-16 in the other, and stepped around the vehicle.

"Nice to see you again, Lieutenant," he drawled.

"Liar."

Stunned, Roc took a second look at her as he threw his pack into the cargo bay of the helo. "Excuse me?"

Sam met and held his surprised gaze. "You're a liar, Captain Gunnison. And don't try and sweet-talk me because it won't work. I call a spade a spade."

So much for her soft mouth. Lips tightening, Roc stared at her. "Okay, Lieutenant, have it your way. I was just trying to be social."

"Yeah, right. I saw the look you gave me. I know where I stand with you on this mission."

He glared down at her. "We need to talk. But not here. And not now. Once we get to Area Five, you and I are going to chat. Alone."

Giving him a cutting smile, Sam said, "Fine with me, Captain. Because frankly, you're the *last* man on earth I'd ever want to have with me on a mission."

After lobbing that grenade, Sam brushed by him and leaped up into the cargo bay of the helicopter. She found her nylon seat against the bulkhead and sat down, watching as Gunnison moved lithely into the hold and sat down on the opposite side. The load master slid the door shut and it locked.

Sam couldn't steady her fluttering heart. She felt like she'd been in combat, the way her adrenaline was pumping through her veins. If Gunnison thought he could run over her or intimidate her with just a look, he was badly mistaken. Judging from the frustration she saw on his face as he strapped in, she was sure he had gotten her message. She smiled to herself. This was her mission. People needed her and her team's help.

There was no way she'd let her tension with Gunnison get in the way of that.

**\* \* \* \***

*Don't forget* Protecting His Own—*the next* MORGAN'S MERCENARIES *story— will be on the shelves in December 2003 from Silhouette Sensation.*

# THE RANCHER, THE BABY & THE NANNY

## by
## Sara Orwig

## SARA ORWIG

lives with her husband and children in Oklahoma. She has a patient husband who will take her on research trips anywhere, from big cities to old forts. She is an avid collector of Western history books. With a master's degree in English, Sara writes historical romance, mainstream fiction and contemporary romance. Books are beloved treasures that take Sara to magical worlds, and she loves both reading and writing them.

To Joan Marlow Golan and to Stephanie Maurer
with many thanks.

# FOREWORD

Stallion Pass, Texas—so named according to the ancient legend in which an Apache warrior fell in love with a US Cavalry captain's daughter. When the captain learned about their love, he intended to force her to wed a cavalry officer. The warrior and the maiden planned to run away and marry. The night the warrior came to get her, the cavalry killed him. His ghost became a white stallion, forever searching for the woman he loved. Heartbroken, the maiden ran away to a convent, where on moonlit nights she could see the white stallion running wild, but she didn't know it was the ghost of her warrior. The white stallion still roams the area and, according to legend, will bring love to the person who tames him. Not far from Stallion Pass, in Piedras and Lago counties, there is a wild white stallion, running across the land owned by three Texas bachelors, Gabriel Brant, Josh Kellogg and Wyatt Sawyer. Is the white stallion of legend about to bring love into their lives?

# One

_Stallion Pass_

"**O**h, no!" Holding a baby in his arms, Wyatt Sawyer stood at the window of his Texas ranch home and watched a woman get out of her car. As she approached the house, his practiced gaze ran over her and he immediately scratched her off his list of possibilities for nanny. She looked like a child herself. Curly red hair was clipped behind her head with a few tendrils flying loose. Her lack of makeup and nondescript gray jumper and white blouse made her seem about sixteen.

"How many nannies will I have to interview for you?" he asked the sleeping baby and shifted her in his arms. He gazed at his five-month-old niece and warmth filled him.

"Megan, darlin', we'll find the right nanny. I'm going to take the best care of you I can." He held her up and kissed her forehead lightly, then returned his attention to the woman approaching the door.

Bright May sunshine splashed over her, revealing a fresh-scrubbed look that only added to her youthful appearance. Wyatt wished he could inquire about her age, because it was difficult to imagine she was a day over eighteen, tops. Wyatt's gaze ran over her again and dimly, he registered that she had long legs. He thought about two of the women he'd interviewed who were beauties. Both times, when they'd walked into the room, his heart had skipped a beat. Three minutes into the interview, he knew he could never leave Megan with either one of them.

He sighed. Why was it a monumental task to find good help? The pay he was offering was fabulous. But he knew the drawback—they'd have to live out on his ranch. Most women wouldn't accept a king's ransom to suffer such isolation. Those from ranching and farm backgrounds weren't any more interested than city women. Either that, or applicants were looking for a prospective husband, and Wyatt had no interest in matrimony.

The doorbell chimed, cutting into his thoughts, and he went to answer it. He swung open the door and stared down into wide, thickly lashed green eyes that stabbed through him with startling sharpness. For seconds they were locked in a silent stare, a strange experience for Wyatt. He blinked and studied her more closely. Faint freckles dotted her nose.

"Mr. Sawyer, I'm Grace Talmadge."

"Come in. Call me Wyatt," he said, feeling much older than his thirty-three years. How long would it take him to get rid of her? He had gotten the interviews down to twenty minutes per nanny, but this time he planned to give her ten. She couldn't possibly be over twenty-one.

"This is your little girl?" she asked.

"My niece, Megan. I'm her guardian."

Grace Talmadge looked at the sleeping baby in his arms. "She's a beautiful baby."

"Thanks, I think so. Come in," he repeated.

When Grace passed him, he caught the scent of lemons. Her soap? He closed the door and led the way down a wide hallway, his boot heels scraping the hardwood floor. He paused and motioned her ahead into the family room, following her.

She stood looking around as if she had never been in a room like it.

Wyatt glanced around the room, which he rarely gave much attention to. It was the one room in the house that had not been changed since his childhood, with its familiar paneling, mounted bobcat, heads of deer and antelope, all animals his father had killed. Also, shelves lined with books, bear rugs on the floor, the antique rifle over the mantel.

"You must be a hunter," she said, turning to frown at him.

"No, my father was the hunter. He liked to bring down wild, strong things," Wyatt said, knowing that after all these years he still couldn't keep the bitterness out of his voice. "Have a seat, please," he said, crossing the room to sit in a rocker. He adjusted the baby in his arms and rocked slightly.

Grace Talmadge sat across from him in the dark-blue wing chair, her legs crossed primly at the ankles and her hands folded in her lap.

"So Miss Talmadge, have you any experience as a nanny?"

"No, I haven't," she replied. "I'm a bookkeeper for a San Antonio sign company. I've had my job for five years. The owner has decided to retire and he's closing his business, so I need to find another job.''

Five years surprised him. Wyatt decided she must have gone to work straight out of high school. "Then why do you want to be a nanny? You realize it means living out here on my ranch?"

"Yes, I understood that from the ad."

"If you've never been a nanny, what are your qualifications for this job? Have you been around children a lot?" Wyatt leaned forward, about ready to escort her out of his house. She had no experience, which made him cross her off his list of possibles immediately.

"Actually, no, I haven't, but I think I can learn." Her voice was soft, soothing to listen to, but Wyatt's patience was frayed from too many interviews over the past few days.

He stood. "Thank you for driving out here. I know it's a long way, but I need someone with experience for this position."

She stood, too, and faced him. "Have you had a lot of experience as a father?" she asked, a faint smile revealing a dimple in her right cheek.

Startled, Wyatt focused more sharply on her. "No, I didn't have any choice in the matter, but I'm a blood—" He bit off his words, realizing what he had been about to say. Being a blood relative was no guarantee of love or care.

"At least give me a little chance here, please," she said.

"Why do you want this job if you have no experience? You might hate being a nanny."

She glanced at the baby in his arms. "Oh, no. I could never hate taking care of a little child."

"Are you familiar with children?"

"I have some young cousins I've been around a little, but they live in Oregon, so I don't see them often."

He was beginning to lose patience, but he was worn out with interviews. "You're not here looking for a husband, are you? Because I'm not a marrying man."

She laughed, revealing white even teeth, and her green eyes sparkled. "No! Hardly. I didn't even know you when I applied for this. I have a friend in Stallion Pass, so I've heard a little about you. I suspect you and I do not have anything even remotely in common."

He agreed with her on that one. "Sorry, but some women I've interviewed do have marriage in mind, and they've been more than plainspoken about it. So if you don't know anything about babies and you aren't interested in the possibilities of matrimony, why are you willing to live in isolation with only me and my niece? Why do you want this job?"

"I've been putting myself through college. I want to pay off my college loans. I have my degree now, but I want a master's in accounting. If I have this job, I can save money, and when your little girl is in preschool, I can take classes while she's away."

"You're talking years from now. She's a baby."

"Time flies, and by then I'll have money saved. Right now, I'm paying back those loans."

"So when you get an accounting degree, I lose my nanny?"

She smiled at him as she shook her head. "No, not at all. It'll be something I'll have if I need it. Perhaps I can do a little accounting work while Megan is in school full-time. And if I don't do anything else with it, I already handle my own finances now and my family's, so I'll be better equipped to do that."

"Tell me about your family. Do they live in San Antonio?'' he asked, noticing that she had a rosy mouth with full, sensual lips. Making an effort, he tried to pay attention to what she was telling him.

"No. They're missionaries in Bolivia. I have two sisters—Pru, in Austin, who's a speech therapist and a volunteer reading teacher, and my oldest sister, Faith, who's a nurse and does volunteer work with elderly shut-ins.''

The warmth that came into her voice as she talked about her family gave Wyatt pause. He remembered his childhood friends, Josh Kellogg and Gabe Brant, who had loved their parents and siblings and been loved in return. He still remembered the shock of going to Gabe's home when he was a child and discovering that a family could be warm and loving.

"Here's their picture,'' she said, opening her purse and pulling out a photograph. She held it out to him.

"You carry a family photo around with you?'' he asked in surprise.

"Yes, I like looking at it.''

As he took the photograph, his fingers brushed her hand lightly, and he was aware of the contact. The picture showed a smiling couple, hands linked, and two brown-haired younger women, also smiling. Behind them were lush green mountains.

"These are your parents?'' he asked, studying the tall, dark-haired man and the slender, red-haired woman who looked too young to have three grown daughters.

"Yes. Tom and Rose Talmadge. They married young.''

"Fifteen?''

She smiled. "Hardly! They were eighteen. You're off just three years. They were childhood sweethearts. My grandfather on my dad's side, Jeremy, is a minister in Fort Worth.''

"Nice family," he said.

She pointed at the two younger women in the photo. "Those are my sisters. They went to see our parents last year, but I was still in my last semester at school and I couldn't go."

"So you come from a family of do-gooders, but you're going for an education in accounting and a good-paying job?"

"That's right. My family says I'm the practical one. Actually, I have a mind for figures and I like to make money. Money means very little to the rest of my family."

"Well, we have something in common there," he remarked dryly. "I like to make money, too. But I don't think your mind for figures will be a lot of help with a baby." He held out the picture. "Your parents look nice," he said.

"They're very nice," she said, taking the picture and replacing it in her purse. "I know you don't think much of me, but I come from a stable, hardworking family and I have good references. I think I can learn to take care of your baby."

Wyatt was intrigued by her. This soft-spoken, freckle-faced girl was getting to him. He knew why, though. Short of the tenuous bond he'd had with his older brother, Hank, he'd never known any kind of closeness in his family, and she was reminding him of his past in a way few people ever had. Clamping his lips together, he studied her, and she gazed back at him unwaveringly.

"Sit down and we'll talk," he said.

She sat down, crossing her ankles and looking as prim as before. She also looked as if she would run if he said boo, yet she had stood up to him with her question about his experience as a daddy. She'd nailed him on that one, all right. The first day it had taken him hours to learn to get a diaper on Megan the right way.

"The job means living out here on the ranch. It means living in this house with Megan and me," he reminded her.

She nodded. "Is there any reason that should worry me?"

"For one thing, there's the isolation."

"I don't mind that at all."

"For someone young, that's unusual. These are your prime years for finding a husband. Most women don't like isolation."

She smiled at him, her dimple showing and that twinkle returning to her eyes. "Getting a husband is not on my list of goals. I'll have your niece and I won't mind the isolation at all."

"You don't want to marry?" he asked.

"If it works out someday, but if it doesn't, that's fine, too. I have a busy life."

He didn't believe her for a minute, but he moved on to another subject. "I have a woman who is both cook and a housekeeper, and she lives on the ranch, so she'll be close at hand, but if you're nanny, you'll live here in the house."

She nodded as if it meant nothing to her.

"Since this will be your home during the week, I need to know if there's a boyfriend."

"No, there's no boyfriend. I've been working to put myself through school and I'm busy and I don't date."

"Being busy doesn't have a whole lot to do with dating."

She shrugged and he saw the dimple again. "All right. I've never found anyone who really interested me. I don't date."

"When did you graduate from high school?" he asked in a polite and legal way to discover her age.

She smiled. "I'm twenty-five. I graduated seven years ago."

Megan stirred in his arms, waking and beginning to cry.

"How's my girl?" Wyatt asked, patting her back as he stood. "Would you excuse me for a minute while I change her and get her bottle?"

"Certainly."

He left and Grace watched him go, a mixture of feelings seething inside her. Her best friend from college, Virginia Udall, had warned her at length about Wyatt, telling her of his dark past. How in high school he'd had to quit school and leave town in disgrace. She heard tales of his wildness, crazy pranks he'd done when he was growing up, the girls he'd seduced, drunken brawls in local bars. Virginia had an older sister who'd gone to high school with Wyatt. Grace had seen her high-school yearbook and Wyatt's freshman picture. She remembered staring at a picture of a boy who, in spite of wild hair that fell over his shoulders, was still the best-looking boy in the entire high school.

Of all the things she'd heard about Wyatt, the one that she could agree with completely was that he was the handsomest man she'd ever seen. When he'd opened the door, she'd been frozen for a minute, looking at thickly lashed, coffee-colored bedroom eyes, prominent cheekbones that gave him a slightly rugged look, a straight nose, a sensual mouth and firm jawline. The long locks were gone, but his black hair was still wavy and unruly, curling onto his forehead. The man was gorgeous. Small wonder he had a reputation with the ladies.

If was difficult to relate the stories she'd heard with

the caring uncle he seemed to be. She looked at the animal heads looming over her, the rifle above the mantel, the heavy leather furniture and the bear rugs. The room was masculine, lacking any feminine touch, yet she'd been told that part of the time, his brother and his wife had lived here. It was difficult to imagine a baby crawling over the bear rugs, and she wondered if the room had been that way since Wyatt's infancy. It was even more difficult to imagine Wyatt as an infant.

Was she walking into a wolf's den, as her friend had warned her? If she took this job, she would have to live here, alone with Wyatt Sawyer and a baby. Good looks couldn't mask the rogue he had been. For a moment, as she had approached the house, she'd been tempted to turn around and drive back to town. Then she'd considered the rumor in Stallion Pass that Wyatt couldn't find a nanny and was offering a huge salary. She had squared her shoulders and tried to ignore her qualms.

Wyatt strode back into the room, the baby tucked into the crook of his arm as he held a bottle for her. He sat in the rocker again, adjusting the baby and her bottle. Her tiny fingers moved over the bottle as she sucked. As he watched his niece, the loving expression on his face made Grace question the stories she had heard. The love he felt for the baby was obvious.

"Why don't you tell me a little about the job?" she suggested.

He raised his head and looked at her as if he'd forgotten her presence. Grace wondered if he still planned to send her packing. She knew he'd intended to earlier.

"You'd live here in this house and take care of Megan. I'd be around at night, but gone most of the day. The person I hire will be caring for my niece daily, so it's important that I have someone I can trust, someone who can give her tender, loving care and is competent with a baby.''

"I think I can do that.''

"It'll be an isolated life in a time when you might rather be with friends or out on a date,'' he said warningly.

She smiled at him. "Surely some time off comes with the job.''

"Yes, weekends. I'll take care of Megan then. Frankly, Miss Talmadge, you're young. I had someone who is more mature in mind, perhaps a grandmother with lots of experience handling babies. Someone who has no interest in dating. And that's another thing—if you do date someone, I don't want him out here at the ranch. No boyfriends allowed. I feel I need—''

Suddenly Megan shoved the bottle away and began crying lustily. Wyatt tried to feed her again and then he put her on his shoulder, patting her back and talking to her. When she screamed all the louder, he stood, jiggling her, talking to her and patting her as he walked back and forth.

"I don't know if she senses something has happened or if she's always been this way, but sometimes she's fussy. The pediatrician said she's in good health, though, maybe a bit colicky, or maybe she's just unhappy with the world.''

Grace set down her purse and stood, crossing to him. "Let me hold her awhile and see if a change in people helps.'' Grace reached up to take the baby from him. "You might get her more formula,'' she suggested.

"I don't think she'll take more,'' he said, looking at the almost empty bottle. "She doesn't usually finish her bottles.''

Grace smiled at him and took Megan from him, settling the baby against her shoulder, walking around and patting her back as Wyatt had done. She walked to a window and turned so Megan could see outside if she cared to look, and then she moved around the room. Megan continued to scream, and Grace held her closer and began singing softly to her. In minutes Megan grew quiet and Grace continued to walk and pat her.

Wyatt returned with a half-filled bottle, watching Grace as she moved around the room with his niece. Megan snuggled against Grace, who walked to the rocker and gently eased herself down. "Give me the bottle and I'll see if she wants more."

Grace shifted Megan in her arms and held the bottle for her. To Wyatt's surprise, Megan took it and began to suck while Grace rocked and sang to her.

With his hands on his hips, Wyatt studied the two of them. "For a woman who knows nothing about babies, you're doing a pretty good job," he said, still standing while he watched her with the baby. "Sometimes I can't get her quiet for an hour. Nothing suits her. I've taken her outside, walked her, sung to her, rocked her."

"Maybe she wants me for her nanny," Grace said sweetly, smiling at him, and he had to laugh. Grace's pulse jumped because his smile was seductive, irresistible, putting slight creases in his cheeks.

"I need to see some references before we go any further."

"I have them in my purse," she replied.

"Don't stop with Megan!" Wyatt said hastily, grateful for the baby's silence and apparent contentment.

"Tell me more about the job," Grace suggested.

"I'll be in and out. I have an office here and will have people out here sometimes when I'm working. Other times I'll be in Stallion Pass or in San Antonio. I'll have some trips to make. I don't know whether you know anything about my background or not…'' He paused and looked at her questioningly.

''Very little,'' she replied.

''A brief family history so you'll know why I have Megan. My mother died when I was a child. My father raised me and my two brothers. I'm the youngest. Jake, my oldest brother, was killed when he was in high school. Last year my father died.''

''I'm sorry,'' Grace said.

Wyatt stiffened. ''We weren't close,'' he said. ''Megan is my other brother's child. Hank and his wife, Olivia, were killed recently when their small plane crashed. They left wills appointing me as Megan's guardian.''

''I'm glad she has you,'' Grace said, and he shot her a curious glance.

''Did you grow up in this part of the country?'' he asked. No one who'd known him in the past would be pleased that Megan had become Wyatt's charge. Wyatt knew only too well the reputation he'd left behind.

''Yes. I've lived in San Antonio all my life.''

''And you have a friend in Stallion Pass who's told you about me?''

''Yes, I do. Virginia Udall.''

''I don't remember her.'' Wyatt wondered to what lengths Grace Talmadge would go to get the job. ''You must really want this job, Miss Talmadge,'' he said, unable to keep the sharp cynicism out of his voice. ''Most people in Stallion Pass aren't happy that I'm Megan's guardian. My deceased sister-in-law's family is threatening legal proceedings to take Megan from me.''

Grace raised her head, and her green gaze met his with that unwavering look that held his attention totally. ''I can easily see you love your niece and have her best interests at heart.''

"Well, you're in a minority. You also have no idea how I deal with her. Maybe I take her to bars with me. You don't know what I do.''

Grace smiled. "You would never take this baby into a bar, and I bet you put her first in your life. Am I right?''

The woman was challenging him in her own quiet way. He realized his first judgment about her immaturity was inaccurate—something that rarely happened where women were concerned.

"You're right, I wouldn't take her into a bar and I already love her as if she were my own. For a novice, you're doing all right,'' he observed.

Grace glanced at Megan who had snuggled down on her shoulder, her brown eyes wide open. "She's a beautiful baby.''

"Yes, she is,'' he said, a soft note entering his voice. "Want me to take her?''

"I'm fine and she's happy. Go ahead and sit down.''

Wyatt was amused. Grace Talmadge sounded as if this was her house and he was the one being interviewed. As he sat, he arched a brow and tilted his head. "If you were to take this job and move in, since we're both young, rumors will start. Are you prepared for that?''

She smiled at him as if he were a child with a ridiculous problem. "I have no worries about rumors. My grandparents and my parents are in Bolivia, a little far away to hear rumors. My sisters and my friends know me, and I know myself. I don't care about anyone else or any silly rumors.''

"So you hadn't heard wild rumors about me before you came out here?''

"I have heard some things. If you had lived up to

them, I would have been gone by now, but you have been nothing but a gentleman.''

Wyatt had to bite his lip to keep from laughing. ''You tempt me to throw the gentlemanly facade to the winds, but I have Megan to think about, so the order of the day is to keep this impersonal and professional. One more reason I was in hopes of finding someone older. She would be more settled. There wouldn't be this temptation to flirt with you.''

''Oh, I don't think you'll have to worry about that at all. Men like you aren't tempted to flirt with women like me,'' she assured him.

''If I'd kept this interview professional, I'd skim right past that, but somehow we slid out of professional a little while ago. Men like me?''

''You're experienced and sophisticated. I imagine you like women who share your interests. I'm bookish, strait-laced and a lot of things that don't attract sophisticated men. Flirting will be no problem, not for me and not for you. Now, how soon did you want your nanny to start?''

''As soon as possible,'' he said, once again amused. In her own mild way, Grace was still taking charge, and she had neatly answered his question and taken them back into an impersonal interview.

''I want someone for the long term, not a continual turnover of nannies that will cause more upheaval in Megan's life,'' he said.

''You have no guarantees of a long-term employee with anyone you hire. An older woman could have something happen where she would have to quit just as easily as a younger one. I'm dependable. I told you, I brought references. My college grades are a 4.0 and my attendance in college and at work was and is excellent,''

Grace replied, patting Megan's back as she rocked steadily.

"Do you mind if I contact your current employer?"

"He doesn't know I'm applying for this, but it would be fine for you to call him. Along with my references, I'll give you his telephone number."

"Maybe we better get down to details," he said, leaning back and stretching out his long legs. "You would be on duty Monday through Friday, all the time, although when I'm here, I'll spend my evenings with Megan. I want a live-in nanny who will be a stand-in for the mother Megan lost. You'll live out here. Weekends are your own. No boyfriends on the ranch, no wild parties."

Her eyes sparkled with the last. "Am I to understand, then, that there will be no wild parties here?"

Again, she amused him. "I meant you, Miss Talmadge, but no, there won't be any, not by me or by my nanny."

"I find that satisfactory."

"You're trusting."

"Sometimes when you expect the best of people, they rise to the occasion. And if you don't, I'll be gone," she reminded him, still rocking Megan, who had stopped fussing and fallen quiet.

"Very well. I have some other interviews. Let me have your references." He crossed to her and Grace gazed up at him, her pulse skittering. "I'll take Megan now," he said.

Grace handed him the baby, and as she did, her hands brushed his and tingles raced through her. "She's sweet."

"You have her vote," he said lightly. As he took Megan, her face screwed up and she began to cry again. "Hey, baby. Megan, what's the matter?" He gave Grace a frustrated glance. "I don't know what makes her fussy."

"Maybe she's cutting teeth."

"She wasn't doing this with you." He walked around, patting Megan and talking to her. Grace, meanwhile, crossed the room and removed some papers from her purse.

"Here are my references," she said, placing them on the table. "Thank you for the interview. I can let myself out."

"Miss Talmadge."

As she turned to see what he wanted, Megan's wails became louder. "Just a minute. Shh, Megan," he crooned. Her screams increased, her small face becoming red.

Grace set down her purse and crossed the room to take the baby from him. He shot her a look, but then let her have Megan, who continued to scream for a moment, then quieted and snuggled against Grace.

"Maybe she does want you for her nanny," he remarked dryly. He had his hands on his hips, and more locks of his black hair had fallen onto his forehead. "You never asked about the salary."

"If you want me for a nanny and I want the job, I suppose we can work something agreeable out."

He told her what he planned to pay, and Grace stared at him in shock, because the sum was astronomical. "With a salary like that you should be able to get any nanny you want!"

"No. Women don't want the isolation unless it includes marriage, which it does not." He didn't add, but he knew that his unsavory reputation had turned many away. "The job means devoting your life to a baby."

"No, it doesn't. The weekends are free."

As she sat down to rock Megan, his phone rang.

"Excuse me, please," he said, striding out of the room. In minutes he was back, watching her rock his sleeping niece. "I'll take her now."

"And I must be going," Grace said, standing to hand the baby to him, too aware of their hands brushing. She picked up her purse. He followed her to the door and she paused, turning to face him. She held out her hand to shake his, conscious of his brief, warm clasp.

"Thank you for the interview. I'm very interested in the job," she said, looking at Wyatt holding Megan. He stood in the doorway, watching her as she climbed into her car and drove away.

A cloud of dust stirred up behind her car as she headed off. Grassland spread in all directions around her, and she could see cattle grazing in the distance. She would be isolated, but the job sounded good. With the pay that Wyatt offered, she could pay off her student loans, save for her advanced degree, get a newer car and still put some money away. She was astounded he hadn't hired someone already.

She wasn't afraid to live out on his ranch with the man, in spite of all she had heard about him. She said a little prayer that she got the job.

When a week had passed without her hearing anything from Wyatt Sawyer, Grace's hopes for the job dwindled. Three days later she picked up the phone at work to hear a deep, masculine voice.

"Miss Talmadge, this is Wyatt Sawyer. Have you got a moment to talk?"

"Yes, of course," she said calmly, while her heart jumped with hope.

"Your references gave you good recommendations. I was impressed. I did a background check."

"And?" she asked when he paused. She held her breath.

"You passed, as I'm sure you knew you would. So would you be interested in the job as our nanny?"

# Two

"He'll seduce you. You'll get pregnant and then you'll have to take care of your baby and his while he does what he wants and forgets all about you except as his nanny!"

Grace smiled at Virginia, who sat watching Grace as she packed.

"No, he won't. I'm not his type."

"You're female. That's his type."

Grace laughed. "You don't know what type of woman he likes. I think he's all grown up now and taking on responsibility."

"Wolves don't change their spots," Virginia grumbled, tossing her head and causing her long black hair to swirl across her shoulders.

"Wolves don't have spots," Grace replied.

"You know what I mean. Aren't you scared he'll creep into your bedroom some night and—"

"No, I'm not!"

"You know he had to leave town, and you've heard the rumors that when he was seventeen, he got a girl in his high-school class pregnant. She drowned soon after. A lot of people think he might have killed her."

"I thought you said that the drowning was officially ruled an accident."

"That doesn't mean it really was an accident. I've heard that he slept with every girl in his class."

Grace turned around, her hands loaded with folded clothing. "Some of those rumors are absurd, Virginia, if not impossible."

"No, they're not. I've heard that at least three kids in middle school and high school here are his children. He had to run away. He never finished high school."

"Just stop, Virginia, and listen to me. He is paying a fabulous sum, more than triple what I'm making. I'm losing my job because the business is closing. Do you realize I can pay off my loans and start achieving my goals? And think about how much I can save."

"It won't be worth your life. Money isn't everything," Virginia replied.

"Oh, don't be ridiculous! There is nowhere else I can earn a living like this with my background. The baby is sweet, and I'm not afraid of him. He and I will hardly see each other. I'm sure he's a busy man."

Virginia rolled her eyes. "You'll be a pushover for his charm. You've only ever dated two guys, Grace. You're Miss Innocent and he's Mr. Seduction, besides being the best-looking man in Texas."

"You finally got something right there. He is very good-looking."

"He's a gorgeous stud! I've seen him in town, and he's awesome!"

"I'll have to invite you out to meet him."

"You will? Promise!" Virginia wriggled with enthusiasm.

Grace laughed. "So it's all right for you to come out and meet him, but it's not all right for me to work for him?"

Virginia pursed her lips. "That's right. You'll be living under the same roof with him. I'll be visiting. You'll be his servant. I will have an independent status." She became solemn. "All joking aside, I'm not sure the money will be worth the heartbreak. I think he'll break your heart and grind up the little pieces."

"If he does, I'll have no one to blame but myself."

"Mark my words, if you aren't careful you're going to fall for him. No red-blooded woman could live under the same roof with that gorgeous hunk and resist him. According to rumors, no woman has ever been able to resist him."

"I'm not his type, I told you."

"That won't stop him from seducing you or breaking your heart."

"I'll be careful."

"Your parents don't know anything about your taking this job, do they?"

"Not yet, but I've written them and they'll think it's wonderful. They let their daughters lead their own lives."

"And your sisters are in San Antonio and don't know anything about Wyatt Sawyer. Are you going to tell them about your new boss?"

"Of course, but my view of him may be a tad different from your view of him. Now stop worrying."

Virginia stretched and slid off the bed. "Let me carry that suitcase to your car. I *will* worry about you, by the way. He's wild, Grace. All the Sawyer boys were and two of them are dead because of that wild streak. The first died in a car wreck—he was driving a hundred miles an hour, I've been told—and this other brother thought he could fly through a snowstorm when he was warned not to. And people've always said Wyatt Sawyer is wilder than his brothers.''

''I'm taking care of his baby, not him. So stop worrying about me.''

''I'm know I'm being a worrier, but there's just cause.''

''We'll see,'' Grace said, snapping shut the large suitcase.

Early Monday morning, Grace slowed at the front gate to the ranch, drove over a cattle guard and beneath a wrought-iron arch with the S Bar brand. White pipe fencing stretched for miles on either side, and the rolling land was dotted with oaks and cedars. On a far hill she saw Herefords grazing. Far in the distance she spotted a solitary white horse galloping across a field. The ranch was a beautiful place, and she looked forward to her new job. She tried to avoid thinking about Wyatt's reputation or Virginia's warnings. Following a hard-packed dirt road, she crossed a wide, wooden bridge, boards rattling beneath her tires.

She looked down at Cotton Creek, a thin, silvery stream of water. As she neared his house, she topped a hill and saw his sprawling two-story ranch house, more houses beyond the main one, a barn and corral and an assortment of buildings beyond the house and a four-car garage. As she recalled from her first visit, the whole place had a prosperous, well-kept appearance. When she finally reached the house, she saw a shiny black pickup parked on the drive at the side of the house, a large black motorcycle parked beyond it and a sleek, dark-green sports car parked on its other side. She frowned, hoping he didn't take the baby on the bike.

When she walked up to the door and pressed for the bell, her pulse raced. All morning she'd had butterflies in her stomach, but now her nervousness increased and the butterflies had turned into stampeding elephants. The door swung open, and she looked up into Wyatt Sawyer's dark eyes and tried not to stand there tongue-tied and starry-eyed. The man was sinfully handsome!

"I thought you might change your mind about the job."

"I'm looking forward to it," she said, too conscious of him, noticing the scent of his aftershave. He stood facing her with his hands on his narrow hips, and he wore faded jeans and a T-shirt. He gazed beyond her. "Why don't you drive around back? I can bring your things in for you."

As she turned and walked away, her back tingled. She glanced over her shoulder to see that he was still standing in the open doorway, watching her. Taking a deep breath, too aware now of herself, she hurried to her car. She was wearing her simple navy cotton skirt and a white cotton blouse, and she suspected he wasn't noticing her as a woman. She wondered if he was debating with himself the wisdom of having offered her the job. He had made it clear he'd intended to hire someone older and more experienced.

When she drove to the back, he came striding out of the house, radiating energy and strength. At the same time, she couldn't stop thinking about the ugly rumors about him when he was in high school. "Just keep your distance," she said quietly to herself.

Wondering what she had gotten herself into, she popped the trunk and got out of the car.

Wyatt put a bag under each arm and a bag in each hand. "Leave 'em and I'll get everything for you."

"I can take something," she said, picking up a bag. All of her suitcases had wheels, but he could doubtless see that and evidently didn't want to bother. She had to hurry to keep up with his long-legged stride.

"As soon as we put these in your room, I'll give you a tour of the house. This is a good time because Megan just fell asleep."

They entered a spacious kitchen that had a terrazzo floor, fine oak woodwork and pale-yellow tile countertops with a copper vent over the built-in stove. Grace's spirits lifted a notch as she surveyed her surroundings. An oval oak table stood in the adjoining breakfast room, which had a large bay window with a window seat that looked out on the rolling grounds. The kitchen was light and cheerful, far different from the gloomy family room where he'd interviewed her.

Grace followed Wyatt down a wide hallway, passing beautifully decorated rooms. She noticed her surroundings, but she was more keenly aware of the man striding in front of her, holding four of her heavy suitcases as if the things were empty.

She had brushed off her friend's warnings about Wyatt, but now that she was here with him, qualms and questions assailed her. Was she entering a wolf's den, walking into trouble that might cause upheaval in her placid life? Could she possibly keep from falling for him even if he barely noticed her and treated her as professionally as possible? Were the terrible rumors about him true?

He disappeared into a room and she followed, stepping

into a large bedroom with an appeal that took her breath. It was elegantly furnished in white and blue, and another grand view could be seen through wide windows.

"This is beautiful!" she exclaimed, looking around and comparing it to her tiny bedroom at home.

"Thanks," he replied casually. "There's an adjoining bath, too. Let me give you a tour, and then we'll get the rest of your things. I'll have to warn you right now, Megan has had a little cold. She's been fussy for several days."

"That's fine. I can deal with fussiness."

"I hope so," he said, studying her as if he could read her thoughts.

"You still sound doubtful, Mr. Sawyer—"

"Wyatt. Mind if I call you Grace?"

"Of course not. Why did you hire me if you have such doubts?"

He clamped his lips together, and she realized that either he hadn't found anyone else he thought would fit the job or no one else had wanted the job.

"You didn't have a choice, did you?"

"I just want you to let me know if you want out of this. A screaming baby can shred the patience of some people," Wyatt replied.

"She won't shred mine," Grace said, smiling. "She's a little baby. But I promise you I'll let you know if I want to quit. It's not Megan who worries me."

She wanted to bite her tongue and wished with all her heart she could take back those last words. His brows arched, and he focused on her with a look that made her want to be anywhere else but in his presence.

"Ah, all those stories you've heard about me, no doubt. The wild man of Stallion Pass. Lago County's bad boy. Is that what worries you?"

She decided this is what people referred to when they talked about being between a rock and a hard place. If she told him what was really worrying her, that she was attracted to her handsome employer, that would be dreadful. But it was equally appalling to tell him that his reputation worried her. Why had she blurted out what she had?

"In caring for Megan, I may have a difficult time pleasing you," she said.

One brow arched higher, and he gave her an intense look. "I don't think that's what you were referring to at all."

"Maybe not," she said, feeling her face grow warm, "but I think we should leave it at that."

He shrugged and turned away. "Come on, I'll show you the house." He crossed the room to open a door. "Your room adjoins the nursery. I hope that's all right."

"Of course." She glanced into a pink room with a circus motif and almost as large as her bedroom. She could see the baby sleeping in her crib, a mobile of Disney characters hanging above one end. Wyatt closed the door and Grace realized how close to him she stood. She stepped back quickly and he moved past her. "We could go through the nursery, but we'll go around it, instead. My room connects to it on the other side."

This was less-than-thrilling news. Grace frowned and tried to push aside her worries.

As she walked down the hall with him, he motioned her into a room that ran the length of one end of the house. His king-size bed was covered in a deep-green comforter. Surprisingly, shelves with books lined one wall. "That's a lot of books. Do you do much reading?"

"Nope. This house is much like Hank and Olivia left

it, and the books were theirs. I'm slowly going through things and changing what I want to change."

A broad stone fireplace was at another end of the room with Navajo rugs on the highly polished hardwood floor. A bowl of chocolates sat on the corner of a desk. Wyatt picked the bowl up and offered her one. When she declined with a shake of her head, he took a dark chocolate and set the bowl back on the desk.

"You have a beautiful home."

"Thanks, but I can't take credit. My sister-in-law did all the decorating, and they stayed out here some, but not often. She preferred to live in San Antonio. The only room she didn't do over was the family room, and I'm having it done soon. I'm not living with *that* reminder of my childhood."

He sounded so bitter that Grace glanced at him sharply. "Your childhood wasn't happy?"

"Hardly."

"I'm sorry. I was fortunate there."

"It was a long time ago, and you're lucky."

"I can settle in while Megan is sleeping," she said, reminding herself to keep things impersonal. "You show me what you want me to do."

He nodded and gave her a tour of the house, part of which had been built by his great-great-grandfather; the rest had been added through the years. In the paneled room that was his office, he motioned to a stack of letters on the edge of an otherwise clean desk. "Those are applications for the nanny position. I could have kept on interviewing for the rest of the month."

Amazed, she turned to him. "If you have so many possibilities, why did you hire me? Were you in a rush for some reason?"

"Nope." He rested his hands on his hips again. "I've

interviewed too many women to count and still had all those applications. I glanced through them. I'm the new guy in the neighborhood, and a lot of single women want a date. It's not that I'm so adorable or charming. I'm just new here.''

"You're not new at all. You grew up here," she protested.

"I've been away a long time, and some people don't know me or anything about me."

"And how did you know that I didn't apply because I wanted to date you?"

Amusement twinkled in his eyes. "You didn't send me a cute, flirty résumé. You sounded quite earnest about the job. And when I asked if you had marriage in mind, you said no." His brows arched. "Did I assume wrong?"

"Oh, my, no!" she replied, and saw the corners of his mouth lift in a faint smile. "I'm sorry," she added quickly. "It's just that this is a job—dating has no part in it."

"I'm teasing. Forget it. You told me you weren't interested." He picked up the letters and walked around the desk to toss them in the trash.

"How do you know that there wasn't that one perfect, older, mature, grandmotherly type in those letters?"

"I read through them. I've had so many interviews, I don't think I can stand one more."

"So I was sort of chosen by default."

"No, not really. That day you were out here, you had a connection with Megan. That was important."

The dining room was another large room with a fireplace. As they walked into the room, she heard a baby's wail through the intercom.

"Megan is awake. You can come with me to get her."

Grace hurried with him, and at the nursery door, he

stepped aside to let her enter first, but then he moved past her to pick up the crying baby. As he bent over the crib, his T-shirt clung tightly, revealing the ripple of muscles. Grace watched the flex of muscles in his back and arms. His broad shoulders tapered to a slim waist and narrow hips. How was she going to work with this man daily and keep everything impersonal? Just watching him, she felt flushed and warm.

"Have you ever changed a diaper before?" he asked.

"Oh, yes. After my interview with you, I baby-sat a friend's three-month-old baby several times so I could practice."

"Good," he said, holding Megan on his shoulder and patting her. She quieted and he moved to a changing table, changing her diaper swiftly and then picking her up again. "I think I better get a bottle first and then I'll show you where all her things are and go over her schedule."

"Let me give her the bottle so she'll begin to get accustomed to me," Grace said. Wyatt nodded and handed Megan to her.

"Hi, Megan," Grace said softly, holding the baby up on her shoulder and patting her. From that moment, for the rest of the day, Grace was busy with the baby and learning about the house and schedules and what Wyatt expected.

"I'll take care of her at night," Wyatt said that evening when he gave Megan a bottle. "The only time you have to take over duties after bedtime is when I'm away. Whenever I'm around in the evening, I'll take care of her."

"I can help. After all, I'll be here, anyway," Grace said.

Megan was fussing and Grace and Wyatt took turns

walking her, the only thing that seemed to quiet her. At one point Wyatt told Grace to eat supper. Then she looked after Megan so he could eat.

While Wyatt got Megan to sleep, Grace went to her room to unpack. She could hear him in the nursery, talking and singing softly to Megan, and later, the creak of the rocking chair.

Grace put her clothes in a large chest of drawers, looking again at the beautiful room where she would live. Too clearly, though, she could remember Wyatt standing in it, watching her curiously with his brows arched. There were moments when he seemed to focus his full attention on her, and those moments made her pulse race.

It was difficult to reconcile the man who was rocking and singing to a tiny baby in the next room with the person who ran out on a young woman he got pregnant when they were in high school. If anyone seemed the perfect, totally caring father to a baby, it was Wyatt Sawyer. Perhaps the years had changed him.

It was after midnight and the house was quiet when she showered and dressed in her short blue nightgown. She brushed out her hair, climbed into bed and fell asleep.

She had no idea what time it was when she stirred at the sound of Megan crying. She remembered Wyatt saying he would get up in the night with Megan, so she tried to go back to sleep, but the baby continued crying until finally Grace threw back the sheet and got up. She pulled on her blue cotton robe and hurried to the nursery to check on the baby. She noticed the open door to Wyatt's room. How could he sleep through Megan's crying?

Avoiding glancing in the direction of Wyatt's bed, Grace rushed to close his door. While Megan cried, Grace switched on a small table lamp.

"Are you hungry, sweetie?" she asked softly, picking the baby up and walking her, trying to quiet her. She remembered where Wyatt kept formula and bottles and turned to carry Grace to the kitchen.

Just then the door to Wyatt's room flew open. He started into the room, saw Grace with Megan and froze.

# Three

Wyatt had heard Megan crying and then rolled out of bed, yanking on his briefs. For more than two weeks he'd been up most nights and he was groggy. He swung open the nursery door, started into the room and stopped abruptly. A light was on, and Grace was holding Megan in her arms.

Neither of them moved. He stared into her startled green eyes. Whatever surprise she felt, he was certain his was greater.

Coming out of a deep sleep, he had temporarily forgotten her presence. Now he faced a woman who looked entirely different from the person he'd interviewed and hired. Her riot of red hair was down, framing her face and tumbling over her shoulders. She held Megan gently in her arms. She looked disheveled, earthy, appealing. He felt something twist deep inside. She wore a cotton robe that had been pushed open by the baby resting against her. Beneath the robe she wore a skimpy, blue nightie that revealed lush breasts and long, shapely legs. His gaze snapped up to catch her looking at him, and her cheeks were pink. He realized he was only in his briefs.

"Sorry. I forgot," he said in a husky voice.

She turned swiftly, trying to close her robe. "I'll get her bottle. I heard her crying and didn't think you would wake. I can take care of her."

With Megan in her arms, Grace made her escape from the room. Wyatt still stood there in shock. He'd hired a beautiful woman. Standing there in the soft light, she'd looked gorgeous. He rubbed his eyes, wishing he could erase the image and go back to seeing her as plain and his nanny and nothing more. But there was no erasing the image that taunted him now.

"Hell," he muttered, and returned to his room to yank on his jeans. He raked his fingers through his hair and headed for the kitchen. "I knew I should have hired someone a thousand years old. A grandmother with wrinkles and experience."

Grace was trying to mix formula with one hand, jiggling Megan who continued to cry with the other arm. Grace's back was to the doorway, but she turned to look at him when he came in. She had her robe pulled together, but he still could imagine the delectable body underneath the cotton.

"I haven't changed her yet," Grace said. "If you'll do that, I'll have her bottle ready when you're done and I can give it to her."

"Sure," he said, without thinking about what he was answering. Crossing the room, he took the baby from her. The moment he was close enough to reach for Megan, Grace looked up at him. Her eyes seemed to envelop him and pull him into depths that were filled with mystery.

He could smell a fresh, soapy scent and that riotous red hair was an invitation for a man to bury his fingers in its softness. Her skin was rosy, perfect even with the smattering of freckles on her nose.

He dropped his gaze to her mouth, which was full and tempting. What would happen if he leaned down and kissed her? Even worse, as he stared at her unable to move, he could feel the tension snap in the air between them. Sparks sizzled and danced. He didn't want any complications in his life right now, and he sure as hell didn't want to find his nanny so physically appealing.

Tearing his eyes from her, he took the baby, too aware of his hands touching Grace as he did so. Megan had her small fist wound around the collar of Grace's robe, pulling it open and for a brief instant, Wyatt looked at soft curves and flawless, rosy skin. His mouth went dry and he moved automatically, taking the baby and turning away.

"Come on, Megan. I'll get you changed and fed," he said, hurrying out of the room. His voice was husky and raw.

When in his life had he run from a good-looking woman? He was in a sweat, too aware of Grace. She hadn't been with him twenty-four hours. He swore under his breath and looked at Megan, who was still bawling. "Sorry about my language, darlin'," he said even though he knew she neither heard nor understood him.

He changed her diaper swiftly and scooped her up, intending to carry her back to the kitchen, but when he turned, Grace stood in the nursery doorway. She had her robe belted and buttoned, but the last button stopped above her knees. She carried the bottle and came toward him. He took a deep breath, noticing that with each step, her robe flipped open, revealing brief, tantalizing flashes of her legs. He couldn't remember what she'd worn during the day or for her interview, but both times her legs had been covered almost to her ankles.

"Let me hold her. I'll give her her bottle," Grace said. "I'm not sleepy now."

Neither was he, although for the past few nights he'd thought he would have given away the ranch just to have someone watch Megan so he could sleep.

Wordlessly, he handed over his niece, once again acutely aware of touching Grace, of standing close to her, knowing he was going through some firsts in his life. When had he ever been around a good-looking woman and not flirted with her? Never until now.

"I can feed her if you want to go back to bed," he offered, unable to keep the gruff note out of his voice, fighting the image of Grace in bed.

"I don't mind," she said. "I've been getting plenty of sleep lately, and I'll bet you haven't."

"No, I haven't. Thanks," he said abruptly, then turned and went back to his room. He closed the door, crossed the room and punched his pillow hard. "Hellfire!" he whispered.

Grace's soft voice singing a lullaby came through the door, and he glared at the door with his fists on his hips. Megan was quiet, and he could hear Grace singing, hear the creak of the rocker and all too well, could picture Grace holding his niece in her arms.

What was he going to do? He raked his fingers through his hair.

Eating a piece of chocolate, he paced the room and stopped to stare out the darkened window. Yard lights lit up the fenced area around his house. Beyond that, the trees created inky shadows beneath a quarter moon. It still surprised him that all this belonged to him now. Everything had happened so fast after Hank and Olivia's fatal accident. He needed to get back to California to see about his commercial real-estate business there. He was signed up for a bull-riding event in an upcoming rodeo in Sacramento next month. He had one in San Antonio, too, the last week of July. He could either withdraw from the California rodeo, or—what he'd planned—take Megan and her nanny with him.

Scratch that plan. He raked his fingers through his hair. He glanced over his shoulder at the closed door and could still hear Grace singing softly.

He could fire her tomorrow. Just tell her it wasn't going to work out, pay her a huge lump sum and send her packing. He could find a day care for Megan—if Stallion Pass had such a thing. He shook his head. Megan had lost her parents, and he didn't want to cause more upheaval in her life. He wanted her cared for at home with someone he could rely on.

Someone mature, kind and loving who had already raised children and loved them. Not a little redheaded sorceress who had a body that was sinfully tempting and a sharp mind.

He had never been in a dilemma like this. Attractive, sexy women had always been part of his life, but not as employees. He groaned and raked his fingers through his hair, pacing the room.

Through the years, he and Hank had kept in touch, and as he'd promised, Hank had always kept Wyatt's whereabouts a secret, because Wyatt had wanted to cut all ties to Stallion Pass and his father. No one here had known anything about him except Hank. Hank hadn't even told Olivia. Wyatt remembered when Hank had called him about his will. Hank and Olivia were making wills, and he asked Wyatt if he would be Megan's guardian if something happened to both of them. Olivia didn't want her parents to be Megan's guardians, because they had little interest in their granddaughter, and Olivia considered them too old to be bringing up a baby.

Wyatt had agreed, thinking the chances of Hank and Olivia dying at the same time were very slight. But the impossible had happened.

Now here he was with little Megan and in dire need of another nanny. He didn't like the thought of going through more interviews. He paced the room and debated what to do, until he noticed the time. Grace had stopped singing and Megan had stopped crying, but he could still hear the creak of the rocking chair.

He might as well relieve Grace and let her sleep because he wasn't going to, anyway.

"Dammit," he whispered, still fighting to keep images of Grace out of his head, trying to ignore the instant desire that had ignited when he'd been with her.

He was tempted to get on his motorcycle and ride through the night. He sighed. This was one time he couldn't escape. He had a baby to care for now.

He opened the door to the nursery quietly. A small lamp was still lit. It had a pink-striped shade and circus animals around its wooden base and shed a soft halo of light, leaving corners of the room in shadows.

Grace rocked, her robe open over her knees, her head tilted against the chair. Megan was sprawled against her, her little arm around Grace's neck. With her curls framing her face, her head back to reveal the graceful curve of her pale, slender throat, Grace looked beautiful. She was both tempting and maternal with the baby in her arms. Her eyes were closed, but she rocked steadily, so he knew she had to be awake.

Megan's eyes were also closed, but Wyatt knew how easily those brown eyes could open.

He moved closer. His pulse jumped, his mouth had gone dry and he was once again on fire. He paused before he got too close.

"Grace," he whispered. "Why don't you let me take her now and you go to bed?"

Her eyes came open slowly and met his, and the effect was like a blow to his middle. He wanted to lean down and kiss her. Sparks ignited and sizzled, and he couldn't imagine that she didn't feel something.

"I'm fine. I really don't mind. I thought you'd be asleep," she said, sounding sleepy.

"I can't sleep," he snapped. "If I'm going to be up, anyway, I might as well take her."

Grace looked at the baby in her arms. Megan's eyes had come open and she stared solemnly at Grace. "She's not asleep."

"I wish I had her energy. I've always thought I needed little sleep, but she can outlast me," he said, wishing Grace would hand over Megan and get the hell out of the room. He was going to have to fire Grace. He couldn't go through this day after day and night after night.

"I hate to disturb her," Grace said. "She's awake but barely, and she's content. I'll rock her. You go to bed. If you can't sleep, go drink some hot chocolate."

He wanted to gnash his teeth. "I don't need hot chocolate," he said abruptly, and turned to leave the room. At the door he paused. "I'm going for a ride on my bike. You can reset the alarm if you want, but Napoleon is in the yard and he's a good watchdog. We've got lights everywhere around the house, too."

"We'll be fine. I'll reset the alarm if I put her down and go to bed."

He did not want to think about Grace going to bed. Under his roof, in his house, only a small room away from his. Why the hell had he hired her?

He closed the door quietly, yanked on a T-shirt and boots and pocketed his keys. He walked through the house, turned off the alarm, stepped outside and locked the door behind him.

A shaggy dog came bounding up, and Wyatt scratched his ears. "Napoleon, you watch the house, y'hear? I'll be back."

The dog trotted at his heels until Wyatt stepped through the back gate. He closed and latched the gate and looked at the big dog, a cross between a collie and a German shepherd. "You're on guard now."

The dog wagged his tail and sat. Wyatt strode across the drive into the open garage to get his bike. In minutes he roared away, racing through the night and heading up the road.

Within two hours he was back, sleepy, grumpy and as on fire as he'd been when he left. Never in his life had a woman tied him in knots like this. And she wasn't doing anything except just being there.

"Get a grip," he told himself, striding toward the house and praying Megan and Grace were asleep. He would take a cold shower, have a slug of whiskey and hope he could get a few hours' sleep. He was too aware that the sun would be coming over the horizon all too soon, and he hadn't had a good night's sleep since he had inherited Megan.

He would fire Grace. For his peace of mind, she had to go. Every time he made that decision, he thought about being in the lurch again for a nanny and all the interviews he would have to do.

Seduce her, a treacherous part of his mind told him. That way he could get some peace of mind, have a woman in his life, in his house, and still have a nanny.

No. That wouldn't work. He didn't want some starry-eyed virgin who wouldn't give Megan her full attention. Also, Wyatt knew that he had left town with a terrible cloud over his head. At seventeen he hadn't given a damn, but now he had Megan to think about, and for her sake, he needed to be a respectable, settled, upstanding citizen. The thought made him shake his head.

Since when had anyone in Stallion Pass or the next three counties thought of him as respectable? But they were going to. He never wanted to hurt Megan in any manner and he'd toss aside his wild ways for her sake.

So it came back to getting rid of Grace. He sighed. He could fish those applications for nanny out of the trash before Mrs. Perkins, the housekeeper, got them.

He peeked in on Megan and was relieved to see she was asleep and Grace was nowhere in sight. He tiptoed farther into the nursery to look at the baby, who was curled on her tummy. He leaned down to kiss her head lightly, feeling a rush of love. She had turned his life upside down, but how he adored her!

He showered, went to the family room to have a drink and finally returned to his bedroom, where he peeled out of his clothes and stretched out on the bed. Dreading the morning, he fell asleep.

Disoriented, he stirred, rolled over, looked at the alarm and sat up. It was half-past eight. That was the same as waking at two in the afternoon. Megan! He bounded out of bed, yanked on briefs and ran to the nursery. When he flung open the door and looked at her empty bed, he remembered Grace. Grace had Megan. He let out his breath, then sucked it in again as memories and problems tumbled in on him. Today he had to fire Grace.

He sighed and went to his room to bathe, shave and dress, pulling on a white shirt, jeans and boots.

In the kitchen Mrs. Perkins had made coffee and his breakfast. Wearing a denim dress with an apron tied around her waist, she bustled around, getting his plate filled and popping a piece of bread into the toaster for him.

"Good morning, Mr. Sawyer," she said cheerfully, peering at him through her bifocals, and he thought once again how unfortunate that she didn't want the job as nanny. She liked to cook, but said she had taken care of all the babies she wanted to. "I met Miss Talmadge, and she's a nice one. A good nanny for little Megan."

"Yes," he answered, thinking about the task ahead of him. "Thanks for the breakfast. It looks great."

"You missed your sleep last night?" she asked, eyeing him. "I thought your nanny was up with the baby."

"She was, but I was awake, too."

"You'll get back to your regular routine now that you have someone hired. Especially someone young and energetic like she is."

"I hope so."

He ate and then carried a second cup of coffee to his office. With reluctance, he retrieved the nanny applications from the trash and placed them on the middle of his desk. He paged Jett Colby, his foreman, talked to his assistant in California and talked to his office in San Antonio.

Then he sat at his desk and wrote a check to Grace, putting it away in a top drawer. He would break the news to her when Megan went down for her afternoon nap.

Idly he ate a piece of chocolate and stared into space, seeing Grace as she'd looked last night.

Later in the morning when he went to look for Megan, Mrs. Perkins told him that Grace and Megan were outside. It was a balmy day and he stepped out into sunshine. He slipped on his sunglasses and stood watching a moment. Megan had on a sunbonnet, pink ribbons fluttering in the breeze. She was propped and buckled into the baby swing and laughed while Grace pushed her. Grace wore another of her long, nondescript blue skirts and a white cotton shirt, an outfit that looked like a school uniform. Only too well he remembered in exact detail what she looked like under those generic clothes. Her hair was once again fastened behind her head, and the prim schoolmarm was back. But she was only a layer of clothing deep.

That was just as well. He did not want to find her attractive. And he wasn't going through another night like last night. By nightfall, Grace would be packed and out of his life.

He thought about Zoe Elder, the California blonde he'd been dating when his life had turned topsy-turvy with Hank's plane crash. Wyatt realized he could fly Zoe to Texas and cool his libido. The instant he thought of that, he knew he wouldn't. He didn't want a breath of scandal to add to his old reputation. He would wait until he flew to California to see Zoe. He and Megan had three homes now, two in Texas—one in San Antonio and one here— plus his home in California. When he was in California, he could do as he pleased without anyone caring.

"Good morning," he said, walking toward the swing.

"Hi," Grace replied, barely glancing at him.

"Hi, Megan," he said, and she squealed with eagerness.

"Want to take a break?" he asked Grace. "I've got my business taken care of this morning. I'll watch her."

"Thanks. I have some calls I need to make. I won't be long." She hurried to the house and went inside.

"We've got to get you a new nanny," Wyatt told Megan. "One who is much, much older, much less sexy, much less pretty, but just as nice. I know she's out there somewhere. Too bad Grace's mama doesn't want the job. She and her husband could move out here and she could be your nanny."

The idea of a couple held possibilities. Maybe he should advertise for a couple—a man to work on the ranch while his wife was nanny. Too bad none of the men who worked for him now had a wife who wanted to be a nanny—he'd checked that out earlier.

Grace returned shortly and Wyatt left Megan with her while he went back to his office to call Hank's lawyer, Prentice Bolton, and make an appointment. At noon, as Wyatt passed the kitchen, he stopped and went back inside. Grace was feeding Megan. The baby was in her carrier on the kitchen table, with Grace seated in front of her. Grace's mouth was pursed as she watched Megan attempt to take a bite, and Wyatt studied Grace's full, rosy lips, wondering again what it would be like to kiss her. Realizing where his thoughts were going, he moved closer to the table and tried to think about having to fire her.

"Grace, this afternoon when Megan goes down for her nap, will you come see me? I need to talk to you."

"Yes, I will," Grace said, glancing at him.

"I'll be in my office."

She nodded and continued feeding Megan, who had oatmeal in a bowl, on her chin and on her bib. Even so,

Grace was doing a better job of feeding Megan than he usually did. That thought added to his gloom.

Wyatt strode from the room. He raked his fingers through his hair and didn't want to think about having to read through all those nanny applications.

It was half-past two when Wyatt heard a knock on his open office door. He looked up to see Grace.

"Come in," he said, tossing down his pen and leaning back in his chair. "Why don't you close the door?" he suggested, wanting to avoid an interruption by Mrs. Perkins.

"Have a seat," he said, facing Grace across his desk. She sat down, still looking prim. He was amazed at the transformation in her he'd seen last night just by her letting down her hair and changing her clothes. And now he noticed things about her. Her big green eyes he'd remembered, but now in addition to her eyes, he was aware of her rosy skin, her full mouth and the clothing that couldn't hide a tiny waist and full breasts.

"You've been good with Megan."

"She's adorable."

"Thanks. I think so, too. I love her very much. So much that her interests come first in my life." He paused and Grace stared at him with an unwavering gaze. "Grace, I'm sorry, but this is not working out. I'm willing to pay you for your inconvenience and the time you've given me, but I'm going to have to let you go."

He took the check he had written in the morning out of the top drawer of his desk and got up to walk around and hand it to her. "This should cover the trouble I've caused you."

"Why isn't it working out?" she asked without glancing at the check. "I've taken care of Megan, and we get along. I can learn what I need to do for her."

"I know you can, but I was right when I first decided I needed someone older."

"What difference does my age make if I'm doing a good job and she likes me?"

Why had he thought this would be simple? Grace hadn't been simple to deal with since the moment she'd entered his life.

He looked at her. "I think if you stay, things might get much more complicated between us. I'm not looking for a relationship—"

She started laughing and he paused, staring at her. With her green eyes twinkling, she stood and waved away his check. "Keep your check, Mr. Sawyer. And I can go back to calling you mister if it keeps things more formal between us. I have no interest in dating you! Not now, not tomorrow, never!"

"You know, at the risk of sounding egotistical, I can't remember being told that before by any woman. Why not?" Wyatt demanded, feeling oddly disappointed.

"We're not the same type, to say the least! I have plans for my life and goals I want. Someday I would like to marry, but not in the next few years while I'm getting my degree and definitely not you."

"Because of what you've heard about me?"

"Well, yes, that colors it, but…" She smiled at him as if he were a confused child. "I don't want to hurt your feelings, although I sense you've had enough success with women that that can't happen."

"So why don't you want to date me?"

"Your lifestyle is too wild. Frankly, you take a lot of risks. If your reason to let me go is that you don't like the way I care for Megan, then I'll go. But if it's because you think I want to date you, please let's forget that. I'm sure there are a million women you'd rather date than me.''

"And what about last night?'' he couldn't resist asking, knowing he was rushing headlong into dangerous waters. "You didn't feel anything when we were together?''

She blinked and as her lips pursed, he could see she was biting back laughter. Wyatt wanted to gnash his teeth in frustration. She was laughing at him again!

"Look, you're experienced and worldly enough to take care of yourself,'' she said. "I'm definitely not interested in you in any manner other than as my employer, so can we just go back to nanny and employer so I can keep this job?''

"You didn't answer my question,'' he said, studying her intently. She was saying one thing, but her body language was saying another. Her face was flushed, her words were breathless and he didn't believe her. Yet he hated to think that he couldn't accept a woman telling him she wasn't interested. At the same time, the little minx wanted this job badly—he knew that. And now he was more intrigued than ever. He had expected her to flutter and blush and get coy with him or break into tears and plead for the job, but he hadn't expected her to laugh at him.

"Look, I'm in the habit of being honest,'' she said. "I would have to be blind and dead not to notice that you are a very good-looking man, Mr. Sawyer. But that's the end of it. Your kitchen is marvelous, but I really don't want it in my apartment. I can work with someone who is attractive without wanting to sleep with him. And I'm sure the same is true for you.''

Nanny job or no nanny job, she was interesting him more by the minute.

"I don't believe you."

"As difficult as it may be for your ego to accept this, I'm not interested in you."

"You'll be living here under the same roof with me," he said, "seeing me at night like last night. You don't need to date me to get me aroused and wanting you."

"I'm sorry if that happened last night. Why don't you let me take care of Megan on weeknights? You take the weekends and then we won't cross paths late at night."

This whole interview was going south quickly, and he wasn't sure how she had managed it.

"So I was the only one in that room last night who felt any sparks between us?" he asked softly, moving closer to her. Her eyes widened, and she inhaled swiftly.

"Yes, you were."

"Oh, I think not," he said, moving closer and reaching out to unfasten the barrette that held her hair clipped behind her head. "Let your hair down like it was last night. You don't look like the same woman that way," he continued. "Unfasten that top button so you'll look more like you did last night. Still don't feel anything when I get close?" he asked.

Grace wondered when it had gotten so hot in the room. Her breasts tingled, her mouth had gone dry. Her heart pounded, and she didn't know whether she could get a word out. She felt every brush of his fingers, felt too many reactions, but she wanted to hang on to this job.

"Do you feel anything, Grace?"

"I don't think so," she whispered.

"I think you do. Where's all that blunt honesty of yours now? Tell me when you do feel something. Let's see, if you feel anything when I do this," he said in a husky voice and wrapped his arms around her.

"Mr. Sawyer!"

"The hell with that," he whispered, and leaned down to cover her mouth with his own.

Grace closed her eyes as his arms tightened around her. His tongue played with hers, setting her aflame. She had been less than truthful with him about last night. She had felt sparks all right! Enough to light a bonfire. And the image of him standing naked except for his briefs was indelibly etched in her memory. He was sexy and handsome and irresistible, but she wanted the nanny job desperately. She loved little Megan; the S Bar Ranch was a wonderful place to work, and the pay was fabulous. She definitely didn't want to lose this job.

She tried to stand still, to keep from responding to him, but he tightened his arms and continued to kiss her deeply and thoroughly. He took her breath and curled her toes. Her insides had turned to liquid fire. And all her arguments and thoughts vanished like smoke in wind.

"You don't feel anything yet?" he whispered against her mouth and then went back for yet another deep kiss.

Desire roared as he continued to kiss her, one hand holding her tightly, his other stroking her nape. And then she couldn't resist responding, winding her arm around his neck, returning his kiss, tangling her fingers in his thick hair, letting go completely, forgetting everything else. The world or a job ceased to exist. She was lost, trying to take him with her.

Finally she pushed against him and he straightened, looking at her with a curious intensity that was as disturbing as his kisses.

"All right, so I felt something," she said, trying to find her voice and get some steel into it. "But *you* kissed me. We don't need to kiss. I don't want to, and you don't want to."

She moved away from him, her heart still thudding

while she wondered if she was committing the biggest folly of her life in arguing to keep her job.

"I can wear clothes that will keep you from noticing me. You'll find women to date. Neither of us wants a relationship with each other. Let me keep this job unless I'm not taking care of Megan the way you want me to. I promise you'll never see me again like you did last night."

His silence bothered her as he stood studying her. At last he said, "I don't think—"

"Look, you can get whatever woman you want. I'm sure you have all your life. You don't want me. I react to you, yes, but it means nothing. It's that simple. Let me do my job and ignore me. I know you can. I'm not irresistible. Men like you have no interest in women like me. If we work out a few things about schedules, there shouldn't be anything difficult in this for you at all. And I find Megan precious and this job perfect. I want it."

"Whatever happens, be warned now. I am not a marrying man."

Annoyed, she gave him a long look. "Be warned yourself, Mr. Sawyer. No matter how I react to your kisses, or to you, I don't want to marry you and I'm never going to."

They glared at each other, and her heart pounded. She wanted the job and he was the person who could give it to her or keep her from having it.

"Do I get to be Megan's nanny or not?" she asked as the silence stretched out.

# Four

He was sinking in the quicksand of disaster right up to his eyeballs. He hated the thought of having to interview for another nanny. This one was perfect—or would be if she were fifty years old, married and a granny.

"You said I've done a good job as nanny," she reminded him.

"All right. Stay and we'll see how it goes. During the week you get up at night with Megan. I'll take the weekends—how's that?"

"Fine. I know you're isolated out here. If you'd like to meet some interesting, pretty women, I have some friends who would love to meet you."

"No, I don't think so, Grace," he answered with amusement, thinking there was no time in his entire life he had suffered a shortage of women.

"If you dated, you might be…"

"Might be what?"

Her cheeks turned a bright pink. "You might notice me less. Although I can dress so you won't notice me at all. I just thought dating might fill a void in your life."

"No, there's no void. I do date, and Zoe's in California where I was living until I inherited Megan and this ranch."

"Good! Maybe you can invite Zoe to visit us soon."

"Maybe so," he answered darkly, watching Grace catch her hair and refasten it in the barrette. Wayward tendrils wouldn't stay pinned and sprang loose, curling around her face and reminding him of the softness of her hair, of the softness of her body. Her arms were behind her head, causing her blouse to stretch tightly across her chest and outlining her tempting, full breasts.

Too clearly, the image of Grace as she had looked last night danced into his mind. He drew a deep breath and tried to stop watching her pin her hair, but he couldn't tear his gaze away. If he had a lick of sense, he would fire her now, just yell the words and run out of the room.

Instead, he stood rooted quietly, watching her and remembering.

She caught him studying her, smiled at him sweetly, giving up catching the feisty locks. "My hair is a little unruly. I'll go check on Megan. Thank you for letting me keep the job."

She gave him a big smile and he noticed the dimple in her cheek and the sparkle in her green eyes. She turned and left the room and he watched the sway of her hips until she was out of sight.

"I think I just made the biggest mistake of my life," he muttered. How the hell could he not notice her? he asked himself, shaking his head and wiping his forehead.

That evening as he played with Megan, he was acutely aware of Grace sitting quietly on the far side of the family room. She wore her nondescript gray jumper and white cotton blouse. She was pale, devoid of makeup, sitting sedately reading a book while he played with Megan, yet he was as aware of her presence as if she was in a skimpy red swimsuit. When he was close to her, he noticed the sweet, flowery scent that he suspected was purely soap. He wondered if the woman even owned a bottle of perfume. But doing nothing, almost invisible, she was tying him in knots.

Taking a deep breath, he looked at Grace. "I'll put Megan to bed, so go do whatever you'd like for a few hours."

"Thanks, I'm quite happy reading unless I'm disturbing you." She smiled at him and her dimple showed and her green eyes were wide and innocent. Her lips were more inviting than ever.

"No, you're not disturbing me," he lied. "I think I'll take Megan for a walk."

"Tonight?"

"It's a bright moon and she likes the outdoors. I might take her for a ride with me on my horse."

"You'll be careful with her, won't you?"

"Of course, I will," he answered evenly. "I learned to ride almost before I learned to walk, and she will, too."

"That's terribly young to be on a big animal, but you're her daddy now."

It was the first time anyone had told him he was Megan's daddy, and it sounded good. It made him feel warm all over. "I am her daddy now. I'm sorry about Hank and Olivia. Whenever I think about their crash, I'm sorry, but I will be a daddy to Megan, won't I?"

"You already are. She loves you. Look how she smiles when you pick her up."

"You think so?" He looked at the baby on his lap. She lay on his legs with her feet on his stomach while he gently swayed his legs. Megan cooed and watched him and he wondered about her. "You know, I love her more than I've ever loved anyone or anything," he said, forgetting Grace and expressing what he felt. "I've never been around little children and I haven't ever wanted to marry or have children."

"Why on earth not?" Grace asked, her eyes growing round and a frown creasing her smooth brow.

"I don't want to change my lifestyle. I cherish my freedom. And, until Megan, I worried that I'd be like my father. At least, I can lay that worry to rest now." He looked at Grace. "My father was as mean as the devil."

"I'm sorry, Wyatt—Mr. Sawyer," she corrected herself quickly.

"Call me Wyatt. If you stay, we'll be thrown together all day every day a lot of the time. It's Wyatt."

"Well, now you know—you're a good daddy. Look how you are with Megan."

"She's a baby. What will I be like when she's a teenager and driving me crazy?"

"You'll be like you are now—good and kind and loving to her. Look at last night when she was crying constantly. You were as patient as Job with her. You already are a wonderful daddy for your little girl."

Her words wrapped around his heart, causing a lump to form in his throat, and he hated that he was getting emotional. Grace's words, so sweet and wonderful, had gotten to him in a way that years of harshness never had.

He looked at her and met that steady gaze. Most of the time she had him tied in knots and burning with desire. Now she'd melted his heart. He should have fired her. He stood abruptly, holding Megan in his arms. "We'll take that walk."

"Oh, good. So you're not taking her on your horse tonight."

"I might. Grace, I'll take good care of Megan."

She blushed. "I know you will. Sorry, sir," she said, and he suspected a bit of insolence in that "sir," but she looked at him with wide-eyed innocence.

He left, striding outside in the cool evening and holding Megan close on his shoulder.

"Baby, you have got some nanny. I wish I'd fired her today, but you like her and she likes you and she's good as a nanny, so here she is, driving me crazy. Megan, are you two females going to end my peaceful life?" He shifted the baby into the crook of his arm and looked down into her big brown eyes.

"I know I shouldn't take you on my horse yet—and I don't intend to, but someday I will. Someday you'll have your own horse, and we'll ride together whether Nanny Grace approves or not. C'mon, I'll show you my horse."

Wyatt walked to the pasture that held the horses, knowing Megan was too little to care or even notice. He walked back in the moonlight and sat on the porch swing, swinging her gently until long after her eyes closed.

The next two weeks Wyatt tried to avoid Grace as much as possible and still see Megan when he got home from work. Weekends were peaceful, yet by the second weekend, he missed Grace, who left the ranch on Friday evening and returned on Sunday evening. He had no idea where she went.

The first Sunday night in June as she passed the family room, he called to her. She paused in the doorway. She wore her gray jumper again and had her hair in a bun, and he wondered if she'd dressed that way all weekend or just changed to come back to the ranch.

"I have to fly to Dallas tomorrow to close a deal on a hotel I'm selling. Want to bring Megan and come along? We'll be back in the afternoon."

"You want to take both of us with you to Dallas?"

"I have my own plane. I guess you haven't seen the runway, but it's here on the ranch. I'll fly to Dallas and back tomorrow. I thought it would be a good outing for you."

"Wasn't your brother killed flying his own plane?"

"Yes, he was."

"I think Megan and I will stay here. Little babies don't need to be shuffled around, anyway."

"Grace, life is meant to be lived. It's a lot more interesting."

"Maybe, but there's no need to take unnecessary risks. It's none of my business, but I hope that you have a will with a guardian appointed for Megan."

"I'm working on that," he said, studying her, mildly annoyed. "When Megan gets older, I'll take her with me when I fly. And when she gets old enough, I'll teach her to fly."

He could see the disapproval in Grace's expression. "Fine," she said, and turned and left.

"Hells bells," he swore under his breath. And he did have a will. He knew she was right there. It had been a tough decision whether to ask Gabe or Josh about guardianship for Megan, but he had finally asked Josh and Laurie, who had eagerly agreed and seemed flattered that he had asked them.

Two days later Wyatt came home from town. He was hot and tired, wanting to have a cool shower, to stretch out and relax and have a thick steak for dinner. As he went upstairs, he heard laughter.

He paused at the door of Megan's room. The baby was propped against pillows on a blanket on the floor. Grace was on her knees in front of Megan and had her back to the door. She had a pillow in front of her face and was playing peekaboo with Megan.

"Peekaboo!" Grace said, laughing, and Megan laughed out loud, hearty laughter that was irresistible. Wyatt had never heard the baby laugh like that before and he grinned, amused by both of them. Grace leaned over Megan, talking baby talk and blowing her wispy hair, making Megan laugh again, and then Grace snapped the baby's picture.

"That's a girl! We'll surprise your daddy with your pictures. What a cutie you are! Let's have another laugh." The camera vanished and Grace held up the pillow, hiding and then popping out. "Peekaboo!"

Megan laughed again, shaking with it, her brown eyes sparkling while Grace snapped another picture. Wyatt's gaze ran over Grace's bottom and he mentally stripped off the denim skirt. His temperature jumped and he took a deep breath. Then Megan laughed again, another infectious belly laugh.

He went into the room, dropping his coat and tie on a chair.

"I don't know how you do it," he remarked. "I've never made her laugh like that." He dropped down on the floor on his hands and knees beside Grace. "Hi, Megan."

She smiled and cooed at him. He rolled on his back and swung Megan up in his arms, holding her over him, and she squealed with joy, laughing again.

Grace sat back, her legs folded beneath her, while she

raised her camera and focused on them. "Let me get your picture with her." She snapped the shutter. "Now sit up and let me take another one."

Wyatt sat up and held Megan in his arms.

Grace held up the pillow again to hide. "Peekaboo, Megan!" she exclaimed, and when Megan laughed, Grace snapped the picture.

"Okay, now I'll take one of Megan with her nanny," Wyatt said, taking the camera from Grace. She held Megan close, turning the baby to face Wyatt and smiling while Wyatt snapped a picture.

"There." He set aside the camera and took Megan, then lay back on the floor, setting the baby on his chest and playing patty-cake with her. "So what happened today?" he asked, glancing at Grace.

"That's the first I've ever heard her laugh so much," Grace answered. "I took her for a walk outside and then out to play this morning. She loves the outdoors. She had her first chicken-and-noodles today, the baby kind, and she liked that."

Wyatt played with the baby. "It's good to get home."

"How was your day?" Grace asked, and he glanced at her and then back to Megan.

"Rotten. The last years I guess my father let things slip. Then I don't think Hank paid a lot of attention to some of the businesses he had. They were Dad's and I guess Hank was just going through the motions, I don't know. Hank's wife was from a family with more money than ours. Hank really didn't have to work and he might not have wanted to. When he was a kid, he didn't want to work."

"What kind of business do you have?"

"We've got a commercial real-estate business in San Antonio and we've got some bad investments. The books are a mess. I'm getting rid of the accounting firm and getting another one.''

"Too bad I don't already have that degree and training,'' she said lightly. "Where did you live before you came back here to take care of Megan?''

"Sacramento, California. I still have my home there and my business—and that's commercial real estate, too. I'm still signed up to compete in a rodeo in Sacramento soon. And in July, I'll compete in one in San Antonio.''

"In bull riding, right? I've heard you've won national championships.''

"Yep. I love it.'' He rolled over, gently placing Megan on her back and propping his head on his elbow as he stretched out beside her.

"So you'll run businesses here and in California?'' Grace asked.

"I'm going to have to get rid of something,'' he said while he dangled a rattle for the baby. "There's too much, and I'd be spread too thin. I'll keep the ones I want, make certain I get good managers.''

"So are you keeping the commercial real estate in San Antonio?''

"Unfortunately, yes. It has some valuable properties, but there are some that my father or Hank should have gotten rid of a long time ago.''

"Who runs this ranch?'' she asked, watching Wyatt with the baby, amazed he wasn't dating constantly. He was the most appealing man she had ever met and he looked adorable, his long length stretched out on the floor, locks of dark hair falling over his forehead as he played with Megan.

"Jett Colby. You probably haven't met him yet, but he's been here for years. He's good, so there's no worry about the ranch. By the way, has Megan been fed?''

"Yes, and she should be ready for bed before long."

"Eat dinner with me," he said quietly.

Surprised, Grace's brows arched. "Thank you," she replied with a smile, "but I think I should say no. Remember, I want to keep my job. I think we should stay professional and keep our distance. Getting to know each other better would be a mistake."

He studied her, wondering about her. He was enjoying her company and he didn't want to eat alone, yet he knew she was right. "Scared we'll start flirting with each other?"

"No," she answered patiently. "I won't flirt."

"Do you ever flirt with guys? Don't you think it's fun to flirt?"

"So far I've never met anyone I wanted to flirt with, because if you do that, you might get to know each other better and get more involved with each other. There hasn't been anyone who interested me that much. Besides, I'm not the flirtatious type."

Since he was thirteen years old, Wyatt had been acutely aware that females were drawn to him. He had never met one who was young, healthy and attractive who hadn't been ready and willing to flirt with him a little.

Grace sat only a few feet from him with the baby between them. Her legs were folded under her, hidden from view, too, by her long skirt.

"Humor me. Come eat with me tonight."

She smiled at him and shifted. "You're a nice employer, and I want to keep it that way—with you as my employer. To do that, we must keep our relationship professional and impersonal. So thank you, but no." She rose gracefully to her feet. "I'll leave Megan with you."

Wyatt watched the sway of her hips as she left the

room and felt disappointed and surprised. Few women, none he could recall, ever turned down invitations from him.

With a sigh he stood and scooped up Megan. ''Come with me, sweetie. You'll eat dinner with me, won't you?''

Megan pursed her lips and blew bubbles and Wyatt smiled, kissing her lightly. ''You'll eat with me and drool on me and the conversation will be a little lopsided, but at least I can forget the day and play with you.''

Two hours later, he hunted for Grace and found her on the porch, a room that was almost all glass and had been built by his grandfather. It was filled with plants, and Grace was curled on a sofa reading a book.

''Hi,'' he said from the doorway, and she looked up, lowering her book. He held Megan, who was dressed in her pink pajamas, and he himself had changed into a T-shirt and jeans.

''Hi,'' Grace replied politely.

''Megan slept for about thirty minutes and then woke up. Would you mind watching her for the next hour? Jett called me, and they've got one of the wild bulls and some horses up at the corral. The guys are going to ride them tonight and I want to join them. You can come watch, if you'd like.''

''I'll be happy to watch Megan, and maybe we'll come watch you ride. It's certainly nice outside. Why do you have to ride?''

He grinned. ''I don't have to. It'll be the most fun I've had this past week.''

She shook her head. ''I don't know how it could possibly be fun.'' She took the baby from him, gazing up at him. ''But I'm curious enough to come find out, I suppose.''

"I just turned the thermostat down again on the air conditioner. I don't think it's working right, but we'll see if it cools down now."

"It's been a little warm today, but we've been outside a lot."

He turned and left. Thirty minutes later Grace headed with Megan toward the corral, where a bunch of cowboys sat on the fence or stood watching. At her approach, a sandy-haired man jumped down and strolled to her, holding out his hand.

"Jett Colby, Miss Talmadge. I'm Wyatt's foreman."

"Glad to meet you. I thought I'd come watch. The baby likes to be outside."

"She's a cutie. It'll be safer if you don't sit on the fence like the guys are. They don't have a baby in their arms and they can jump for safety when they need to. Just stand over there in the shade of that cottonwood and you can see plenty."

"Thanks," she said, smiling at him.

In minutes she saw why she shouldn't sit on the fence as they opened a gate and Wyatt came out on a bucking bull that looked enormous to Grace. The dun-colored animal had long horns, jumped into the air and came down stiff-legged, only to twist and buck again. Cowboys yelled and cheered while Wyatt clung to the bull with one hand. She couldn't look, turning away. After a few seconds she turned back and saw him still riding the beast.

When at last he bounded off the bull, Wyatt landed with both feet to wild cheers from the cowboys watching. The bull turned to charge him and Wyatt ran, leaping on the fence and springing over it to drop down on the other side. Cowboys sprang down, scrambling to get out of the way of the angry bull, which pawed the ground and snorted.

Wyatt came striding over to her. "Hi."

Grace gazed up at him. He looked exhilarated, far more relaxed and happy than he had when he'd come home from work today, and she realized he thrived on the bull ride and probably on the other wild things he did.

"How can you do that?"

"It's great. Makes you feel alive."

"I'd think it would make you want to stay alive and avoid moments like that again."

He laughed as he peeled off leather gloves. "I'm thirsty. Let's go up to the house and get something cold to drink. I'll take Megan now. Believe me, on the back of that bull, I forget all about lousy bookkeeping and money-losing properties."

"I'll carry her. You look dusty."

"Aw, she'll wash. Give me my sweet baby," he said, grinning and taking Megan from Grace. "When Megan gets older, I'll want you to bring her to watch me ride in rodeos. Will you do it?"

"We'll see when the time comes," Grace replied. "You're her sole parent now. Do you think you ought to take such risks?"

"Bull riding? It isn't that risky. The odds are better than when you get in your car and drive down the highway."

"I don't think you'll convince me of that one."

"What do you do to relax, Grace?"

She glanced up at him. Locks of black hair fell on his forehead and sweat beaded his face. She had to hurry to keep up with his long, easy stride. "I read a good book."

"That's mighty quiet."

"I told you—we're worlds apart. You wouldn't enjoy spending most of your spare moments reading, and I wouldn't enjoy your motorcycle or your bull riding."

"You don't like life on the wild side?"

"It's never been the way I or any of my family have lived. Besides, you have responsibility now."

"Megan? I'll be careful."

"Why do you like all these wild activities?"

He shrugged and reached to open the back gate for her, stepping aside to let her go ahead. "They're exciting. They make me feel more alive. They're a challenge and I like challenges," he said, looking at her intently, and suddenly Grace suspected he was talking about her, yet common sense said he couldn't possibly be referring to her.

"Were your brothers like you?"

"They liked the wild stuff, if that's what you mean. I think maybe we all started in defiance of our dad—or to get his attention. Then I found I liked doing the things that I did, so I've continued." He leaned closer to her. "And I've never told anyone that before. But then, no one has ever asked me why I do what I do. A lot of women are impressed by daredevil antics like bull riding and skydiving. But you're not, are you?"

"Mostly I'm a little horrified. I'll have to think about taking Grace to a rodeo, but by then you'll be older and maybe wiser."

He laughed and looked down at the sleeping baby in his arms. "I'll go put her down and then fix us cold drinks."

"Give her to me and I'll put her down while you fix the cold drinks," Grace said, reaching up and taking Megan from him.

Her hands brushed his and his chest, and she was

aware of each contact, but hoped he never knew. She held Megan close and left, knowing if she had any sense, she wouldn't go back, but she was enjoying his company and she wanted that cold drink.

When she came down the stairs, she could hear Wyatt swearing. He stood in the hall beside the thermostat.

"What's wrong?" she asked.

# Five

"**H**aven't you noticed? It's hotter in this house than it is outside. The air conditioner isn't working or the thermostat isn't working. The air conditioner is probably old as Methuselah and I'll have to replace it, but that won't do any good tonight."

He had a screwdriver in hand, and part of the thermostat was in pieces on a table beside him while he worked on the remainder.

"Want me to fix something to drink?"

"Yeah. I want a cold beer. Can you hand me that little silver screw?"

She found what he wanted and handed it to him. He tried to insert it into a tiny hole, but wires were in his way. She reached up to hold the wires so he could work. He glanced at her.

"Thanks. I'm on fire," he said, turning the screwdriver until he had the screw in place. "You can let go now."

He yanked off his T-shirt, wiped the sweat off his forehead and tossed the shirt aside, turning his back to her as he did so.

She drew a deep breath, looking at the scars on his back.

"You've got scars," she said quietly. At first sight, she thought he'd been hurt from some of the wild things he'd done, but then she realized that wasn't what caused them.

"Yeah, thanks to my old man," he said, and bitterness laced his voice. He looked at her. "It doesn't matter now. I got over letting him hurt me badly a long, long time ago, but I live with those scars."

"I'm sorry," she said, appalled that he'd had a monster for a parent and no mother.

He shrugged. "It's over, and he's dead." Wyatt bent over the thermostat. "I don't think this thermostat is the problem," he said, putting it back together. "I may have to replace the air conditioner, but we'll have to suffer through tonight." He put the cover on the thermostat and looked upstairs. "It'll be hot as Hades up there. We can go into town to the house there, but we'll have to pack, drive in and cool it down. Or we can go to a hotel. Or let's sleep in the yard. I can get cots."

The thought of sleeping in the yard with Wyatt only a few feet away sent a shock through her system, but a hotel sounded worse. "We can't go out there and leave Megan inside."

"No. I'll move her crib outside."

"You can't do that."

"Sure, I can. Sleeping outside will be the easiest thing to do. I'll get it moved now, and we can take turns with her while I get the cots up. Come help me and I'll move the crib. We'll get the cold drinks in a minute."

As they entered the baby's room, Wyatt motioned to Grace. "You carry Megan. I'll take the mattress down and then come back for the crib."

Grace picked up the baby. Megan was indeed warm, her black hair in wet ringlets against her head. She snuggled into Grace's arms, but never opened her eyes. Grace went downstairs, waiting to hold the door for Wyatt.

He came right behind her with the mattress tucked under his arm and they went outside where the air was cooler now and a slight breeze had sprung up.

"I'll get the crib," he said. "I can't believe she's sleeping through this."

"She was outside a lot today. I think that wears her out." Grace sat on the porch swing and gently moved it back and forth.

In minutes Wyatt stepped through the back door with the pieces of the crib. Grace marveled that he had taken it apart so quickly. She watched him reassemble it beneath the long branches of one of the oaks. Moonlight spilled over him, highlighting the play of muscles in his arms and back as he worked. Grace drew a deep breath. Wyatt was unbelievably handsome, with broad shoulders, a narrow waist and well-toned muscles. How was she going to sleep only a few feet from him tonight? She couldn't imagine getting ten minutes' sleep.

When he put the mattress in place and waved his hand, she picked up Megan and strolled over to the crib.

"All ready for my little princess," he said.

"Very nice, Wyatt. You're handy."

"That's a new one. I've been told I'm a lot of things, but handy…well, I don't think so. 'Course, I haven't had many air conditioners break on me, either. Now I'll finally get those cold drinks. What'll you have?"

"Just soda pop. Any kind."

He returned in minutes with a cold beer and a glass of pop over ice for her. He had a box of chocolates in hand. "Want a piece of candy?" he asked, and she shook her head.

"No, thanks. And how you eat those with beer, I'll never know."

"I'm a man of complexities," he said, and she smiled.

"When Megan gets to toddling, you'll have to put your chocolates up high."

"I will. I know they're not good for her. We weren't ever allowed to have candy at the ranch. From the time I've been on my own, I've had chocolates on hand. But it isn't out of spite. I love chocolate—it's the next best thing to kissing a pretty woman."

"Well, Mr. Sawyer, I don't care for chocolate and I wouldn't know about the other," she replied, and he grinned.

"Are you trying to remind me that I'm your employer and to drop the talk about kissing?"

"I knew you'd get it."

He grinned. "I'll sit with Megan now and you go do what you have to do inside. Then you can sit with her. I can tell you, I'm taking a cold shower before I turn in."

As Grace walked away, he raised the bottle and drank, lowering it and sitting in a lawn chair, in a moment reaching for a chocolate.

Even with the tree giving them leafy shadows, moonlight made the yard almost as bright as early evening. Down at the corral lights were on and cowboys were still riding, still cheering and clapping, the sounds muted by distance.

Wyatt sat in the cool breeze and peeled off his boots and socks. He raked his fingers through his hair and thought about the evening. Grace disapproved of his bull riding. She probably disapproved of most everything he did. And she was right—they were entirely different, yet what was it about her that had him opening himself up to her? He had told her things tonight he had never told anyone else. She was a listener deluxe, fixing those big green eyes on him and hanging on every word. Earlier, it had been a relief after an insufferable day to come home to laughter and Grace's quiet questions and interest.

And she wouldn't eat dinner with him. How many women had turned down the offer of dinner? He couldn't think of any, yet again, he wondered if his ego had gotten blown up through the years of easy conquests. He'd told her he liked challenges; what he didn't tell her was that she was a challenge. One he knew he should ignore, but how tempting to want to storm the walls she'd put up between them. He remembered when he'd kissed her and how finally she'd kissed him back.

He inhaled deeply, knowing he should try to keep a lid on that memory. Her kisses were hotter than fire. Was she a virgin? Something he hadn't dealt with since he was a kid. "And you're not going to have to deal with it now," he said to himself.

"Are you talking to me?" she asked.

He turned and stared at her. Her hair was fastened in a bun behind her head and she wore sweats. He stood up and looked fully at her.

"Have you lost your mind or are you sick? You're in sweats when it's probably ninety degrees right now."

"We're sleeping out here together, more or less. I told you I would wear clothes that would prevent—"

"Great grief, woman! Go put on something cool! I'm not going to jump you."

Even in the darkness, he could see her chin lift and

see her draw herself up. "I know you're not," she replied evenly, "but I promised you that day that I would dress so you wouldn't notice me."

"I won't notice you if you come back in a swimsuit, I promise. Just go get cool before you pass out, and I have to take those heavy clothes off you myself."

That sent her running. He could imagine the sparks shooting from those green eyes. He sat down and took another long swallow of beer. He thought about the short nightie she'd worn the first night. He had lied six ways of Sunday when he'd told her he wouldn't notice what she was wearing, but he'd try. And he'd bet the ranch she didn't come back in the nightie. Cutoffs and a T-shirt, maybe, although, except for the nightie, he had never seen her in anything that revealing.

In minutes she returned, coming across the yard in the moonlight in a knee-length cotton skirt and a T-shirt. And he was glad he was sitting in the shadows, because he couldn't keep from staring. The T-shirt molded full breasts that bounced slightly with each step she took. And the shirt was tucked into a tiny waist. He already knew about her tiny waist. And the skirt halfway revealed her fabulous legs. In those clothes she wouldn't go into melt-down, although peeling her out of the sweats had been tempting. He knew he better stop staring, but it was difficult to pull his gaze away.

Miss Goody Talmadge didn't approve of him. And his bull riding tonight had been another mark against him, so he should pay no attention to her except as his nanny. Straitlaced and virginal, she wasn't his type. Although her kiss hadn't been virginal. He glanced over his shoulder again and stood.

"That's better," he said, still thankful for the darkness because she couldn't see that he was staring. This time her hair was piled on her head in a mass of curls with loose strands falling around her face. She was really quite good-looking, and ninety percent of the time she hid it well.

"If you'll stay with Megan, I'll go get the cots now. And have my cold shower."

"Take your time," she said, moving a lawn chair slightly farther from the one he had been sitting in. She sat down, crossed her legs and took a sip of her cold pop. Then she looked up at him, and he realized he had been watching her every move. He could sense disapproval and he turned and left.

"Leave the woman alone," he whispered to himself as he crossed the porch. But he needed that cold shower because he had been thinking about her kiss, looking at her, fantasizing about her, and he was hotter than ever.

He took his time under the shower and tried to get his mind on business, on going back to California. He thought about Zoe and felt little interest. He hadn't called her for days, hadn't even returned her calls. Had their relationship been so shallow that he no longer missed it or cared? Now that he stopped to think about it, he realized he didn't care. And he needed to let Zoe know. He hadn't called her since he'd hired Grace. Sheer coincidence. He had no romantic interest in Grace, and it wouldn't matter if he did, because she wouldn't let him get within two feet of her again.

He dressed in fresh jeans and switched off the lights, going to the kitchen to get Grace another cold pop and himself a second cold beer.

He strolled across the lawn. Grace had her long legs propped on a yard chair and her shoes off. Her back was to him, and he couldn't see her face.

"I brought you another cold drink," he said when he

reached her. He held it out, and her fingers brushed his when she took it.

"Thanks," she said, sitting up and slipping her feet into her shoes.

"You can go barefoot around me," he remarked with amusement.

He pulled his chair closer to hers and turned it slightly to face her. He knew he disturbed her and she kept up a constant guard around him, but the more standoffish she was, the more he was tempted to try to break through her defenses.

"Am I bothering you?"

"No, you're not," she said. "When is the woman you date going to come to Texas to see you?"

"I'm going to break things off with her. Now that we have time and distance between us, I realize I'm not really interested. I'll call her tomorrow."

"That's good because she's been calling you about twice a day lately."

"You don't approve of anything about me, do you."

"Oh, yes, I do! You're a wonderful daddy for Megan. I don't think you could be a better dad."

"Thank you," he answered quietly. "That means a lot to me," he added, feeling pleased beyond measure. "I didn't have a role model.... Well, in a way I did. My friends' fathers were both role models. Gabe's dad was good to me and Josh's dad let me live with them for long periods of time. Josh's dad is the one who stopped the beatings. After a particularly bad one, he came over and warned my father not to lay a hand on me again. Josh's dad was full of life, but he had his moments when he could be earnest. He wasn't as large as my father, but he must have thrown a scare into the old man, because that was the last beating I received from him."

Grace reached out to touch Wyatt's wrist. "I'm sorry. My family is so loving I can't even begin to imagine what your life was like." Her hand was light and warm on his wrist, the slightest touch, yet he felt it in every nerve in his body.

"It's just as difficult for me to imagine what your life was like," he said, wanting to cover her hand, but restraining himself. She moved her hand away.

"My family was always close," she continued. "We never had a lot of money—maybe that's why money is important to me, although it isn't to the rest of my family. My dad was a minister, and then when we got older, he and my mom both wanted to devote their lives to missionary work. They've been out of the country on missions most of the time since I was thirteen. They took us with them until I got older. I've lived in Mexico, Bolivia and Peru."

"Ever been in love?"

"Not really," she said.

"You don't feel like you're missing out on life?"

"By not being in love? Hardly."

"Your parents have a good marriage from what you've told me. Don't you want what they've had?"

"Sure, someday, but not right now. I'm young and I have plans. That second night I was here, you said you valued your freedom. Well, I value mine."

"All right, what about just being in love for the thrill of it? Life's a lot more of an adventure when you're in love."

"I think you thrive on excitement. I thrive on contentment."

"Tell me about your life in Mexico and Bolivia and Peru," he said, curious about her.

Grace talked quietly, then asked him about his life in California.

"You didn't answer me before—you don't approve of me, do you, Grace."

"I told you, I think you're a wonderful daddy for Megan."

"But you wouldn't eat with me tonight because you disapprove of my lifestyle, right?" he persisted, leaning forward and putting his elbows on his knees, narrowing the distance between them.

"We agreed to keep our distance since I'm your employee. I think I should stick with that," she replied coolly, but he noticed she licked her lips and sounded breathless when she spoke.

"You wouldn't stick with it if I asked you to do something with me and you wanted to be with me, now would you?"

"I suppose you're right."

"So it gets back to disapproval." He sighed and sat back in his chair. "That's okay. I've been surprised how friendly people in town are. Life changes, people change and money makes a difference. I think they like the Sawyer money enough to overlook my past. If you like money so much, I'm surprised that doesn't work for you."

"Money's important, but it's not that important to me."

He laughed softly. "So if I asked you out, you'd turn me down."

"Definitely, but I don't think you're really going to ask me out. I'd turn you down because I'm your nanny."

"Suppose you weren't my nanny. Would you go out with me then?"

"Tell me about all those businesses you inherited,"

she said. "What are you keeping and what are you disposing of?"

"I don't know yet," he answered, amused by her efforts to change the subject. She wouldn't go out with him under any circumstances. She was his nanny, and the heat must be getting to him because he shouldn't want to ask her out or ask her to join him for dinner or even spend the evening talking to her.

"Gabe's told me about the rumors in town," he said, knowing he shouldn't care, but wanting her approval. "Grace, I don't have any kids running around Stallion Pass."

She turned to look at him. "I didn't think you did. Those rumors sounded a little farfetched. If what I heard was true, you'd have a whole passel of kids."

"Nope. None. I've never fathered a child."

She looked at him sharply and he gazed back, guessing what was in her thoughts.

"I know all the stories, and you've heard why I left town."

"Yes, I have. They say that you left because you got someone pregnant."

"The girl who was involved died that summer in a swimming accident."

"I've heard that, too."

"Besides the girl involved," he said, "there were four others of us who knew the truth. Hank, Gabe, Josh and me. So now only two besides me. With Hank and Olivia gone, it no longer matters much. Hank was the father."

Startled, Grace stared at him, and he gazed back at her. "Your brother was the baby's father? Why would you tell everyone it was your baby?"

"Hank and Olivia were engaged. Olivia was a San Antonio socialite, and Hank was afraid if the truth came out, it would end their engagement. They had this big wedding planned, and Hank wanted to marry Olivia. He was afraid that if Olivia and her family learned about the pregnancy, there wouldn't be a wedding.''

''And you did that for your brother?''

''Yeah, I did,'' he said gruffly. ''It wasn't that big a deal. Everyone believed the worst about me, anyway, and most of the time I deserved it. I did a lot of wild things. I earned the reputation I had, but I never got anyone pregnant. My father was making my life miserable. I told Hank I'd take the heat because I was ready to get out of town, anyway.''

Grace still stared at him in amazement. ''That's really something—to bear people's anger for your brother. So you were close to your brother?''

''Yeah, as close as I've been to anyone in my family. Hank and I fought and we weren't alike, but we got along. I didn't want his engagement broken, so I didn't mind.''

''With the exception of your two close friends and your brother, you've never told anyone this, have you.''

''Nope, I haven't. I guess I care what you think about me. That doesn't happen often,'' he said, taking another long swallow of beer.

Grace felt a mixture of surprise and relief that he wasn't as terrible as she'd been told, and another feeling, a closeness, because he'd opened himself up to her and shared what must have been his deepest secret. She couldn't ignore the rush of pleasure when he'd said he cared what she thought about him.

''People in Stallion Pass will always think you were the father.''

''Doesn't matter. Like you said, you know yourself, your family—in my case, my brother—knows you, your friends know you and no one else matters. I've felt that way since I was a kid. My best friends, Gabe and Josh, knew the truth. They were the only ones who mattered to me. And as far as I know, she did die in a swimming accident. I know there were rumors of murder, but that was all they were, rumors. I was riding in a rodeo that night and Hank was with Olivia at a party. It was all a long time ago.''

''What did you do when you left here?''

''Odd jobs. The first summer I worked in an oil field because it paid well. I worked on ranches, gentled wild horses, rode in rodeos, hit a lot of bars and did a lot of partying and ended up in California.'' He took another swallow of beer.

''What did you do in California?''

''I began to make big money with my bull riding and met a man who talked me into going to work for him in commercial real estate. I knew a little about it because of my father's businesses here. I used the money from bull riding to get into the real-estate business. I took classes, took the tests, got my license and became a broker. That guy taught me all about the business, and when he retired, I bought his business. I got in when property was cheaper, and then prices shot up and I made a lot of money. I made good investments and made more money.''

''So commercial real estate is your first love.''

''Hell, no. It's just a good way to make money.''

''What's your first love?''

He grinned and set down his bottle and leaned toward her again, resting his elbows on his knees. ''Pretty women. We've talked enough about me. What's your first love, Grace?''

''I'm the nanny, remember. If I had a room that was

air-conditioned, I'd go to it now. Let's keep this impersonal.''

"Scared of me?''

"No, I'm scared of losing my job. And I made some
promises to you about that.''

"So you did and you've kept them, but let's just enjoy
the summer night and conversation. I promise, you won't
lose your job over us tonight. You're a very good
nanny.''

"Thanks.''

"So what's your first love?'' he asked again, leaning
closer and running a finger along her arm.

"Books, probably. Mr. Sawyer, you need to keep your
distance. I don't want to have to go inside.''

"Don't even think about going into that hot house.
And I would keep my distance if I thought I was repul-
sive to you, but I don't think that's the case.''

Grace's pulse was racing and she was thankful for the
darkness so he couldn't see what kind of reaction he was
getting from her. She leaned forward so that she was only
inches from his face, looking him straight in the eye. "I
think you're interested in me solely because I've said no
to you. If I had gone all starry-eyed and eaten dinner
with you and if I'd hung on every word you said and
flirted with you, I don't think you'd be sitting out here
talking to me now, nor would you give me five minutes
of your time. You're just interested because I haven't
been in a swoon over you, Wyatt Sawyer.''

"Maybe there's some truth in what you say, but that's
not why I asked you to join me for dinner tonight. When
I got home from work, I was enjoying your company,
and I'd had a lousy day that you were making me forget.
And nanny or not, sparks fly when we're together. You

have to be as aware of that as I am. Deny that one, Grace.''

''I will deny it. I don't think there are sparks every time we're together. There's nothing now. Bulletin for you: I'm not interested. I find it difficult to pretend, and even if I did pretend, I don't care to be another conquest, someone you get bored with after a while.''

''No sparks, huh?'' he asked, his deep voice like velvet. He slipped his hand behind her head and looked at her mouth. ''You don't feel anything?''

''Nothing,'' she said calmly, and started to pull away. His hand tightened and he leaned closer, his lips brushing hers.

''Scared of me?''

''Not at all,'' she replied calmly, but her pulse jumped and she could feel the sparks and the contest of wills. Her heart thudded, and she wondered if he could hear it. She didn't want to feel anything. She didn't want to be a summer conquest because he was stuck on the ranch with his new responsibility and bored with life, burdened with having to settle his brother's estate. But how impossible it was to sit quietly, to try to avoid responding to his light kisses, to try to keep her wits about her.

''Nothing yet, Grace?'' he whispered, pausing to look at her. His bedroom eyes would have sent her pulse skyrocketing without kisses. Add his to-die-for kisses, and fire raged in her veins.

He kissed her again, this time his mouth settling on hers, opening hers. As his tongue stroked hers, he lifted her easily onto his lap, his arm encircling her waist and pulling her close against him.

Her insides melted, and her resistance was gone, yet she fought to hang on to wisdom and to refrain from kissing him in return. But without thought she had wrapped her arm around his neck. She was pressed against his bare chest, and her body was having a different reaction from her brain.

She shifted away from him, looking at him. "See? Nothing. I'm not a sexy woman and I'm not exciting to men. Forget it." Guilt and desire besieged her. Had she ever told a whopper like that one? She could barely breathe, her heart still pounded, and she wanted to throw her arms around him and kiss him for the rest of the night.

She was trying to get off his lap. His chest expanded as he exhaled and his arm tightened around her waist. "You are sexy and you are exciting and there's no way I'm going to give up now." He kissed her again, throwing himself totally into it, his tongue taking possession.

Her pulse roared in her ears, and she felt devoured, on fire. How much resistance could she keep up? His kisses obliterated the world and ignited her deepest desires. She had never been kissed like this. His kisses stormed her barricades and demolished them. He possessed, demanded and won her response.

As she kissed him in return, she moaned softly, heard herself only dimly. Angry with herself, annoyed with him, she suddenly wanted to devour that impenetrable self-assurance of his.

She was on his lap and she felt his thick shaft press against her hip. Their kisses were escalating, and his breathing was as ragged as hers. Her fingers wound in his thick hair. Her breasts tingled and she felt a low throbbing ache deep inside her.

When his fingers trailed lightly along her bare thigh, she shook with pleasure. She knew she was committing folly, risking her job, her future, yet how could she stop kisses that turned her inside out and sent her pulse galloping?

Then he framed her face with his hands. She opened her eyes to look at him and met a solemn gaze.

"Now you feel something, don't you?" he asked.

# Six

"**H**ow can I keep from feeling something? You're the expert, and I've had very little experience. But I didn't invite your kisses and that was next to force—"

"Force!" he exclaimed, sounding appalled. "Grace, I have never used force in my life. Here—hands behind my back. Resist if you don't feel anything." He put his hands at his sides, releasing her, but he leaned forward to brush kisses on her throat up to her ear, his tongue tracing her ear and then trailing kisses to her mouth where he brushed his lips across hers again. Her insides were wound tight and she wanted to hold him and kiss him, and she wanted him to hold her tightly as he had been and kiss her as he had been kissing her. She knew the word *force* had been unfair, but to hang on to her self-control and not become mush in his arms, she had to use whatever tactics she could.

"Go on, Grace, stop me if you don't like this. I'm not

holding you. There's no force whatsoever,'' he whispered between kisses, trailing them around to the side of her neck, then back to her mouth.

She couldn't stop him. She wanted to resist, but she couldn't. "I know you didn't use force," she whispered, hopelessly lost. She kissed him, yielding, tightening her arm around his neck and leaning closer, kissing him with all her pent-up passion.

Then his arms wrapped around her and crushed her against him, and he kissed her long and deeply. His body was hot and hard and his kisses were fiery.

Finally she wriggled and slipped off his lap, moving swiftly back to her chair. Both of them were gulping for air as they stared at each other.

"We've got to stop, Mr. Sawyer. I'm your employee," she said, emphasizing the last word.

He hitched his chair close to hers, facing her, his index finger trailing circles on her knee. "Stop that 'Mr. Sawyer' stuff. It's Wyatt. You're a desirable woman."

She took a deep breath and stared at him. He trailed his fingers along her throat. "Your pulse is skyrocketing. Go out with me Saturday night."

She shook her head. "I can't keep from responding to your kisses, but you know we shouldn't take this further. Thank you about Saturday, but I'm sorry, no."

He stared at her and ran his fingers through his hair. "Why shouldn't we? There's no law that says a guy can't date his nanny."

"We shouldn't date because we're not the least compatible. We're as different as ice and fire. You don't like the things I enjoy, and I don't like the things you enjoy. I don't approve of the risks you take. I hear you at night, riding away on your motorcycle, and I've seen you—you go very fast. You like riding wild animals, you like a lot of daredevil things. Now you have a responsibility to Megan. You're her father now.''

He looked away and ran his fingers through his hair again. ''Hank didn't change his lifestyle, and he was her real daddy. I don't think I take giant risks. I can cut back on skydiving, but the other stuff isn't that dangerous. Anyway, that really doesn't have a whole lot to do with our going out Saturday night.''

''Do you not understand the word *no?*''

He grinned and ran his finger along her cheek and then leaned forward to kiss her briefly and lightly, yet setting her heart pounding again. He stopped abruptly and placed his hand against her throat. ''Your reaction is why I don't want to take no for an answer from you. If fireworks didn't go off when I kissed you, I wouldn't care or be interested.''

''Find someone else, and don't kiss me. Now, do I have to move into the hot house?''

He smiled at her. ''Nope. I know when I'm not wanted. I'll go join the guys for a while.'' He leaned close. ''But someday, Grace, you'll say yes to me,'' he said in that husky, velvety voice that was a caress in itself. ''Half of you already has.''

He stood and strode away toward the corral, and she watched his easy, long-legged stride. It had taken every bit of willpower she possessed to turn down a date with him Saturday night. She ached to go out with him, to kiss him more, to have him kiss her. Wyatt was exciting, sexy, appealing and nice. She had never dated a man like him. But she knew she was doing the right thing. If she wasn't careful, she was going to be in love with her handsome boss. Even if they both wanted a deep relationship, there was no future for them. She couldn't bear his wild hobbies, and he wouldn't be able to settle for her quiet life.

She stood and moved to the crib to look at the sleeping baby. Pulling her cot closer to the crib, Grace stretched out and lay looking at the stars and thinking about Wyatt. She knew sleep wasn't going to come, possibly for hours.

She had no idea how late it was when she heard Wyatt returning. She sat up to see if it was him.

"Grace?" he said softly.

"I'm awake."

"I'm going to shower and then I'll be back. Want a break from staying with Megan before I go inside?"

"No, I'm fine."

He passed her and she turned to watch him walk toward the house. Moonlight spilled over him and she saw a jagged, bleeding cut across his shoulder and back.

"Wyatt, are you hurt?"

"I was dodging a flying hoof and didn't quite get clear. I'm okay."

"I can't leave Megan, but bring something to put on that cut after you shower and I'll help you."

"It's okay," he said as he headed toward the house.

In half an hour he was back and she sat up, swinging her feet off the cot.

"Did you bring something to put on your cut?"

"No, I didn't. I don't need anything."

"Stay with Megan, and I'll go get it."

"Here," he said with resignation in his voice. He held out a small spray bottle and a dry washcloth. "I thought you might insist on getting something, but I don't need this."

"Turn around and sit," she said, looking at the long gash across his back. "This may hurt, but you need to put some antiseptic on that cut. It looks terrible."

She opened the bottle and sprayed it, dabbing at his back where the antiseptic ran. He had one deep cut and several smaller cuts across his muscular back. He sat without flinching, yet she knew it had to hurt.

"All done."

"Why can't you sleep?" he asked, turning to look at her. She sat in one of the lawn chairs again and faced him.

"I don't know."

"Liar," he said softly. "You can't sleep for the same reason I can't."

"Maybe, but we're not going to do anything about it."

"Okay, we'll sit and talk, but there are better ways to spend time. Tell me what you want out of life. You don't care about dating, so what do you want?"

"Eventually I want a family. For the past few years I've been concentrating on my education."

"Turn around and I'll give you a back rub. That'll help you relax and go to sleep," he said.

"I don't—"

"Turn around. It's just a back rub," he said. Grace turned her back to him and he scooted his lawn chair close behind her. She knew she should argue with him and avoid any physical contact, yet a back rub seemed ridiculous to argue about.

His hands began to gently massage her shoulders. She became aware of his knees on either side of her and realized he was sitting quite close behind her and she sat between his legs.

"You're taking accounting. What do you want out of that? If you have money, what will you do with it?"

"I want to own my own home. My parents have never owned a home."

"No kidding?" he asked, and she could hear the surprise in his voice.

"No. Dad was a minister and Mom was a choir director and a lay minister. They moved and lived in houses furnished by the church. Then when they started going on missions, they sure didn't need a house here. They still live in church housing wherever they are."

"I hadn't thought about that. Except for the years in California, I've been on this ranch all my life. My great-great-grandfather built this place. I own my home in California, and now I've inherited Hank's San Antonio home and this place."

"Wyatt, are you going to live here or in San Antonio or in California?"

"Probably here and sometimes in San Antonio. I'll spend time off and on in California, but I'm not moving back out there to stay. I like Texas too much."

"Where will Megan go to school? In San Antonio?"

"I hadn't thought about it yet. She'll probably start school in Stallion Pass like I did."

"If that's the case, you should socialize with young couples who have little children so Megan will have friends to play with." Grace turned to look at him. "If you had a wife, she would get to know other mothers around here. You already have some close friends. I think you ought to have a party, have people out here who have young children and make some friendships for Megan's sake. She's the one who is isolated."

"I hadn't thought about it, but I guess you're right."

"Do you go to church?"

"Church never has been much in my life. It sure wasn't growing up."

"Maybe you should attend one, so Megan will have that in her life, too. Then she'll know kids through church."

Grace had turned around again, and Wyatt kneaded her back, working lightly, too aware of her fine bones, her slender body, wanting to slide his hands a few more inches around her and cup her full, tempting breasts. He knew if he did, he'd probably lose a nanny. He was only half thinking about what she was discussing, yet he realized she was right.

"Maybe I should have a party, but what'll I do with Megan, and suppose no one comes?"

"People will come. You said yourself that people had been nice in Stallion Pass. You're sexy, appealing, established, wealthy—they won't turn you down. And your close friends will come for sure. As for Megan, I'll be there to take care of her, and you can show her off. No one can resist a sweet little baby. Let everyone bring their children. That's more fun, anyway, and this house looks able to take kids."

"I'm sexy and appealing?"

"Don't push it, Wyatt. You know you are."

He grinned. "So if you and I have a party, what about rumors starting about us?"

She glanced over her shoulder at him, giving him a smile. He knew she didn't mean to, but it was a provocative pose and he had to fight to keep from sliding his arms around her waist and pulling her close. Instead, he tried to pay attention to what she was telling him.

"Don't be ridiculous. No one will notice me. I promise, you won't have any problems about rumors."

"You'll help me plan this?"

"Sure," she said, turning around again.

He rubbed her shoulders, his thumbs gently massaging her nape, and then he worked his hands down her back, his imagination stripping her bare.

She scooted her chair away. "Thanks, Wyatt. I'd offer to give you a back rub in return, but you're too cut up."

"I'm not cut all over and it's been a tedious day. I'll

take you up on that rub." He turned his chair around. His interminable day had ended when he'd stepped into the nursery this afternoon with Megan and Grace, but he wanted Grace's hands on him.

In seconds her hands began to knead his left shoulder, carefully avoiding his injury. Her slightest touch caused a jump in his pulse, and the back rub was making his breath catch and his heart pound. He was amazed by the effect she had on him. Too easily, she could tie him in knots. He'd had experience with women since too far back to remember, so why was Grace with her light touches, her reluctant presence, her standoffishness, keeping him tied in knots? Why did he want her so badly?

Was it a perverse streak in him for conquest? He didn't think so. He thought it was a scalding mutual attraction that she felt far more than she would admit to him. She was right about making friends with locals for Megan's sake. He needed to have a network of friends because Megan could easily be isolated if he stayed on the ranch.

On the other hand, he could move to San Antonio and put Megan in private school, and a lot of the social problems would solve themselves.

"Wyatt, earlier you said the real-estate business isn't your first love, but you never answered me about what *is* your first love."

"This ranch. I missed it like hell when I left. I love it."

"Then why don't you sell the businesses you don't want and get someone competent to run the commercial real estate for you? Take over the ranch. It's yours now."

"Jett's totally capable of running this place."

"It isn't big enough for the two of you?"

He could hear the incredulity in her voice. "Well, a

lot of the time, yes, it is. But there are decisions that he makes that I would if I came back.''

"Have you talked to him? He might be ready for you to take charge. How old is Jett?''

"Early fifties, I think. He's the one person on this ranch my dad didn't mess with.''

"He might be ready to let up a little. Some of this looks like hard, physical work.''

"It is, and I think that's why I like it," Wyatt replied, wondering about Jett and if he might not mind stepping down a little. Wyatt thought about the ranch and knew he would love to have it as his full-time work.

Grace's hands were at the small of his back, rubbing and kneading, and the effect was far from relaxing. "Thanks, Grace," he said, and pulled his chair slightly farther from hers, knowing he had to put space between them or she would be in his arms again.

"Let's plan the party. What weekend would be good for you?''

They talked for two more hours, making plans for a barbecue with friends, talking about a variety of subjects, until Grace was exhausted. She moved to her cot, stretching out on the cool sheet. "Wyatt, I have to go to sleep now.''

"'Night, Grace," he said, his voice deep.

She lay down and in seconds was asleep. Wyatt sat in the dark, sipping his beer and studying her. She was stretched out on the cot, one arm flung overhead, her skirt hiked higher. Her long legs were smooth and shapely. His gaze ran over her curves and he inhaled deeply. Another sleepless night. He moved to his cot and stretched out, staring at the stars and glancing at the baby who had changed his life forever. He thought about running the ranch, getting someone for the real-estate business in town and in California. In half an hour his thoughts shifted to the party and he began to plan.

Ten o'clock the next morning Grace received a phone call from Wyatt, who was at his office in San Antonio.

"Are you melting?" he asked.

"Actually, we're doing fine. I gave Mrs. Perkins the day off. I hope you don't mind."

"I'm glad you did. It's too hot for her to cook. The earliest I can get someone out there to look at the air conditioner is eleven this morning."

"I'm amazed you've managed that," Grace replied.

"It took bribery, but the guy is a friend of Gabe's and he's coming. I think we'll need a new unit, so it probably means another hot night."

"We'll manage."

"I'm getting the house here aired out and then cooled down. I'll come get you two for dinner and we'll stay here in town tonight. I can't get to the ranch until around four."

"We're doing great. When she had her bath, I let Megan play in the water this morning for a long time and then we went outside where there's a breeze. The crib is still outside in the shade. I'll be careful and see that she doesn't get too hot."

"Sure. The house in town has a pool. Bring your swimsuit."

"Thanks, Mr. Sawyer," Grace replied dryly, trying to remind him of their employer-nanny relationship. "I believe I promised I wouldn't wear anything like a swimsuit around you."

"That was before the air-conditioning broke down. I won't pay any attention to you and even if I do, you won't let it do me any good. Bring your suit and enjoy yourself. Think you can take the heat until four?''

"Yes, Wyatt. Tonight you and Megan should go to your place and I can stay—''

"See you at four. I have to run. We can talk when I see you," he said, and broke the connection.

Glaring at the phone, she replaced the receiver. Her pulse skittered at the thought of eating dinner with him and spending the evening with him.

To her surprise, Wyatt was home by half-past three. From the moment he entered the house, she was acutely aware of him. After showering, he changed to a blue, short-sleeved shirt, jeans and his snakeskin boots. He looked incredibly handsome, and she again reminded herself to keep things impersonal and cool between them.

Grace had dressed in one of her plain jumpers and white, short-sleeved blouses, and she had Megan in a pink sundress.

As they drove to town, he talked about his day at work again, about the air conditioner and listened to her tell him every detail about Megan. They ate a long, leisurely dinner in a casual restaurant on the River Walk, and Megan seemed to enjoy the outing as much as the adults. Grace fed her bites from a jar of baby carrots, orange soon dotting the bib tied around Megan's neck.

"It's a small world, Grace," Wyatt said, standing and dropping his napkin in his chair.

A couple approached, and a smiling, slightly graying man shook Wyatt's hand. An attractive, older blond woman, dripping with jewelry, gave Wyatt a frosty smile and Grace a cold stare.

"Grace, I'd like you to meet Megan's grandparents, Alexandra and Peter Volmer. This is Grace Talmadge. And there's Megan."

"Would you like to hold her?" Grace offered, wiping puréed carrots off Megan's chin.

"No, thank you," Alexandra Volmer replied. "I don't believe I want carrots down my front. Another time. She has gotten much bigger. We'll leave you to your date, Mr. Sawyer."

"It's Wyatt, ma'am. I'm Megan's uncle and y'all are her grandparents, so there's no need to be formal."

"It was nice meeting you," Peter Volmer said to Grace, looking one more time at Megan and then nodding at Wyatt before he turned to follow his wife out of the noisy restaurant.

"You should have told them I'm just the nanny. She seemed incredibly cold. How could they not want to hold their granddaughter?"

"Hank said they weren't interested in Megan. I guess he knew what he was talking about," Wyatt said, sitting back down. "I called them the first week I had Megan and told them to come out whenever they wanted to see her."

He gazed after the Volmers and shook his head, then looked at Megan and touched the top of her head lightly. "At least, she doesn't have any idea that she was just rejected. I love you, Meggy," he said, leaning closer to her across the table.

Megan blew a mouthful of carrots at him and he and Grace laughed as she wiped up the carrots. "Good thing you kept your distance there."

"I don't care," Wyatt replied. "I'll wash."

After dinner at dusk, Wyatt drove to a residential area of palatial homes on well-tended lawns. He turned into a wide, circular drive to a sprawling two-story redbrick mansion.

"This is a beautiful home, Wyatt."

"Thanks. My grandfather had it built, and it's been in the Sawyer family ever since."

As soon as they had Megan down for the night, Wyatt gave Grace a tour of the beautifully furnished rooms, with their priceless antiques, gleaming silver and polished hardwood floors, far more elegant than the ranch house. The enormous family room, as well as the dining area and kitchen, all opened onto a long patio. Beyond it was a blue-tile pool with a nearby cabana, lawn chairs and tables and potted plants.

"We can sit in here where it's cool," he said.

"I did bring my swimsuit and since you will be with Megan, I think I'll take this chance to go swim. That pool looks gorgeous and too inviting."

"Sure," he said, nodding.

She smiled at him and hurried out of the room, going upstairs to the bedroom he said was hers for the night. The decor was shades of burgundy and beige with a four-poster bed. Swiftly she changed to a one-piece deep-blue swimsuit, slipped into a terry cover-up, grabbed a towel and left.

The pool was well lit and blue and inviting. She dropped her things on a chair and jumped into the cold water. Her hair was naturally curly, and she didn't worry about getting it wet. She swam laps and then circled leisurely, enjoying herself, when she looked up to see Wyatt seated on the edge of the pool, his bare legs dangling in the water.

Startled, she stared at him. Her mouth went dry and her pulse jumped. He was in a black swimsuit and she could see almost every inch of his sexy, muscled body. She became aware of herself and how little she was wearing, and she didn't want to get out of the water. Less than a foot away, slightly to his right and behind him,

Megan slept peacefully in the baby carrier. Grace had never considered Wyatt's bringing the baby down to the pool. She swam over to him and stood on the pool bottom, water slightly above her waist.

"Want me to take her back upstairs so you can swim?"

"Nope," he said, sliding into the water beside her. He was close, only inches away, his body almost totally bare, and Grace wondered if he could hear her heart pounding.

"We can't both swim and abandon her here by the side of the pool!"

"Wasn't going to," he answered calmly. "You go on with your swim. I'm just cooling off. When you're tired of swimming, if you don't mind, you watch her and I'll swim. There's an intercom on the patio, but I'm not sure we could hear her if we were both swimming and she was upstairs, so I brought her down."

"Good. You swim now. I've already had my turn," she said, and moved closer to the edge of the pool. He stepped in front of her, sliding his arm around her waist.

"Wyatt—"

"It's been a delightful evening, Grace," he said solemnly, and her heart thudded. He pulled her against him as he leaned down to kiss her. His mouth covered hers and his tongue played over hers.

The moment their mouths touched, her insides cartwheeled and an ache started and her breasts tingled. The water was cold, but his body was warm against hers, hard with flat planes and angles. One hand held her head while he kissed her passionately, hot, sweet kisses to create a lifetime of dreams. She knew she should stop him, stop herself, push, move, resist. Instead, she wound her arms around his neck and returned his kisses. She felt his arousal press against her. She wanted to keep kissing, wanted to be in his arms, wanted to toss aside all the resistance to him she'd tried to maintain.

His body felt marvelous. His kisses sent her into a dizzying spiral. There was no way to keep an impersonal relationship between them. Her fingers stroked the strong column of his neck. She shifted closer, pressing her hips against him. When he slipped his bare leg between hers, her heart thudded again. Every touch tore down barriers of resistance, every second of kissing took them headlong into a different relationship.

His hand moved to her breast and his caress shot through her like a lightning bolt. She gasped, too aware, even through the swimsuit, of his hand on her, too conscious of his seductive touch.

She twisted her head. "Wyatt," she whispered.

"Tell me you don't like it, Grace," he whispered in return, bending to kiss her throat while his hand slipped down over her hip and then along the curve of her bottom.

"Want my hand here?" he asked as he stroked her bottom. "Or here?" he whispered while his tongue played in her ear and he caressed her breast again.

She caught his hand. With all the effort she could summon, she opened her eyes to look at him. "Stop now, Wyatt. We had agreements about these things."

"I don't remember any agreement that I wouldn't kiss you," he said, nuzzling her throat.

She moaned softly, but she pushed against him and slipped out of his arms. "You have to stop."

He gazed at her and reached out to place his palm against her cheek. "I'll stop for now." He turned and swam away.

The moment he put distance between them, she

jumped up on the side of the pool to sit, her legs dangling in the water.

Wyatt turned to watch her and then swam over to her, catching her ankles in his hands, caressing her ankles and calves lightly. "I didn't want to ruin your swim. If you'll wait, I'll be just a few minutes and then I'll stay with Megan."

"Swim all you want. I don't mind," she said, too aware of his hands on her ankles and legs, of Wyatt so close, even though he was in the pool and she was out. Too aware of her wet swimsuit and all the exposed skin.

He smiled and swam away. Her heart was still pounding and her lips and her body still tingled. Desire was hot and intense. She should quit this job, but where would she find another job that would pay like this one? She looked at the sleeping baby and knew she was beginning to love Megan as if she were her own.

She touched Megan's soft curls. "You'll both break my heart, just like Virginia said." While Wyatt's powerful arms cut through the water, she remembered exactly how it had felt to be pressed against him, to have his bare leg between her legs. Handsome, sexy, charming, intelligent. It wasn't fair to have all that rolled up in one six-foot-four-inch package.

He climbed out at the deep end, walked away and then turned to run and dive into the pool. She shook her head, knowing even if it was his own pool, it wasn't safe to run on wet tiles. Did he always have to do something risky? And break rules? She suspected she was merely another challenge to him. Why else would he be interested in her?

Then he was splashing up out of the water in front of her. He jumped up to sit beside her on the edge of the pool. "I'm through. You can swim now."

"I'm going to bed," she said quietly, suspecting if she stayed, Wyatt would also stay.

"Okay, we'll all go in," he said cheerfully.

She stood, crossing to the chair to get her cover-up and slip it on. She turned to find Wyatt watching her. His dark gaze burned with blatant desire and she inhaled swiftly, her insides heating. She belted the cover-up and picked up her towel. "Good night, Wyatt."

He got to his feet, picked up the carrier and fell into step beside her. "I'm coming, too." As he held open the door, he said, "I've been thinking about this party we'll have—"

"Not we, Wyatt. You. Do I have to keep reminding you I'm only the nanny?"

"Right, Grace. Anyway, I think I'll ask Ashley Brant to help me with a guest list, because I don't know who lives here any longer and who doesn't, and who I should ask and who I shouldn't."

"I don't know who Ashley Brant is."

"She's Gabe's wife and her family lives on Cotton Creek. She went to school in Stallion Pass, so she has the same background Gabe and Josh and I do."

"Then she sounds like a good one to ask about a guest list."

As they walked down the hall, Grace asked, "Where did the name Stallion Pass come from?"

"It's an old legend. There was an Apache warrior who fell in love with a cavalryman's daughter. The cavalry killed the warrior, and according to legend, his ghost returned as a white stallion that roams this area. That's where the name originated. According to the story, whoever tames the stallion finds his true love."

"That's sad and romantic."

"What fuels the legend is that there have been wild, white stallions in these parts for years."

"Anyone try to catch and tame one?"

"Not that I know of. Guess no one wanted true love to come that badly," he said, and she laughed. "Want a glass of wine or cold lemonade before we turn in?" he asked.

"You're wearing me down, Wyatt. Yes, thanks. I'll take the lemonade."

He smiled. "Good." They entered the kitchen and Wyatt crossed the room. Wyatt had his towel around his neck; otherwise, the only clothing he wore was his swimsuit, and she was intensely conscious of him. Clothing was a slim barrier between them, but nonetheless, it was a barrier, and she hoped her long skirts and high-necked blouses cooled Wyatt's interest in her, but she knew her swimsuit wouldn't.

"Wyatt, I'll go change and put Megan into her crib. You know, I really shouldn't have accepted the glass of lemonade."

He crossed the room to her and touched her chin lightly. "Don't go all proper on me. I'll keep my distance. Just come back down and talk to me," he said, smiling at her.

"Wyatt, you're hopeless. I'm struggling to keep everything between us as impersonal as possible. This is a game to you."

"No, it's no game," he said solemnly. "And impersonal flew away back there in that first interview when you asked me about my experience as a daddy. Come on. Relax. I won't bite."

She felt ridiculous protesting when he was being easygoing and charming, yet she knew she was right. "All right, but I'm putting on my jeans and a T-shirt."

He grinned. "Scared I might peel you right out of that suit? Or does it disturb you to see me in a swimsuit?"

She knew he was teasing, and she laughed. "You like trouble, don't you, Wyatt."

"It's all I know."

"I don't believe that, and you'll have to be good for Megan's sake."

"You're right there, but I don't have to be good with you. You need a bad boy in your life, Grace."

"No, I don't."

"Someday I'll get Jett to come up to the house and stay with Megan and I'll get you to ride on my hog with me."

"I don't think so."

He stepped closer, his arm slipping inside Grace's cover-up and circling her waist to pull her close.

# Seven

"**W**hen you come back, you'll be covered up from chin to toe. Give me one more kiss while we're both half-naked, Grace," he whispered, pushing open the cover-up and pressing against her as he kissed her.

She didn't fight him this time, but wound her arms around his neck and kissed him in return, responding fully, feeling his arousal, too aware of their almost naked bodies pressed together.

He kissed her senseless. She lost awareness of their surroundings, of time, of everything except Wyatt and his hard body. When he released her, she opened her eyes to find him watching her.

His breathing was as ragged as hers and she stared at him, wanting to pull him back and kiss him more, but reason was swiftly returning and she knew she should be glad he stopped.

"We may be drawn to each other, Wyatt, but it doesn't

mean anything. *That* I'm sure you can understand. I'll see you shortly.'' She picked up the carrier with Megan and left without looking back. As soon as she had the baby in her crib and was in her own bedroom, Grace closed her eyes. One lie on top of another. Where had her impeccable honesty gone? His kisses didn't mean anything—to him. To her, they meant everything. His kisses changed their relationship, changed how she saw him, changed how she felt, changed her job and her life. Could she ever forget Wyatt?

Could she possibly be falling in love with him? She hadn't been with him a month yet and he was storming her senses, demolishing her defenses. She would call that Ashley Brant and ask her to make sure there were some beautiful single women on the party-invitation list so Wyatt could meet them or renew old friendships.

She walked to the mirror and stared at herself. Her lips were swollen from his kisses, her wet hair plastered to her head.

''Drink one glass of lemonade and go. Don't let him near you,'' she told her reflection. She hadn't worked for him very long and already their nanny-employer relationship was in shambles. At least she thought it was in shambles. Wyatt probably thought the situation was improving.

''Resist.''

She showered, dried her hair, dressed in jeans and a T-shirt. She went downstairs where she kept a distance between them and kept the conversation only on plans for a party. After one glass of lemonade, she went back to her room. He had looked amused at her abrupt departure, but had let her go without touching her again.

He, too, had changed into a T-shirt and jeans. He switched off lights and went out by the pool to sit on a chaise, putting his bare feet up. It was three in the morning now, and lights sparkled on the water, but all he saw was Grace and how she'd looked tonight at the pool. She was gorgeous, and he had wanted to take off her swimsuit that clung so revealingly to every curve.

Just remembering took his breath and made him hard with desire. He wanted her more than he could remember ever wanting a woman. And he liked being with her more than with any woman he had ever known. When he was at work, he was beginning to look forward to getting home and seeing her again.

This constant eagerness to see her and be with her, even just to talk, was proof that it wasn't just the challenge she presented that drew him. She was wonderful with Megan, managed everything about the house, and Mrs. Perkins liked her enormously.

He had been in love too many times to count in his life, and he knew he was drawn to Grace now. Love, excitement, touching, physical relationships, shared times—he liked them all, but he wanted his freedom to do as he pleased. Yet the thought of marrying Grace sent a ripple of excitement through him. Marriage to Grace. Was that so improbable? It would be good for Megan.

Marriage to Grace. He would have to think about that one.

Wyatt shifted, staring at the water and lost in thoughts about Grace. He wanted her in his arms, in his bed, in his life. The realization surprised him, and he knew he needed to know her better, to get to know his own feelings better.

He sighed. Between Megan and Grace he hadn't had a whole night's sleep in weeks. And he didn't see any improvement looming in the future.

\* \* \*

The next day a new air conditioner was installed, and Grace hoped their lives would get back on track and she would see little of Wyatt. That afternoon she was in the ranch yard swinging Megan in the baby swing when a pickup drove up. Wyatt emerged from the house and strode across the yard toward it.

Josh Kellogg climbed out of the truck and waved at her. Just as she waved back, Wyatt reached Josh and the two men faced each other. She was too far away to hear what they were saying, but she could see that Wyatt's friend was angry with him.

Wyatt could see the fire in Josh's eyes. Josh's fists were clenched, and Wyatt was ready to duck in case one of those fists came swinging.

"You go into town and talk to the bank," Josh was saying. "Dammit to hell, Wyatt, I know you meant well, but you can't pay off my loan for me. It's my problem, not yours."

"I didn't do it for you, so just calm down."

"The hell you didn't. You don't know Laurie, and if this is because we agreed to be Megan's guardians if something happened to you, you get Gabe and Ashley for guardians. You're not paying off my loan."

"I did it for your dad," Wyatt said quietly. He yanked off his shirt and turned around. "Remember this, Josh?"

He turned back to face his friend. "Your dad stopped those terrible beatings."

Josh gaze into the distance, a frustrated, angry scowl on his face. "Okay, I guess you're grateful for that, but that was my dad, not me. I didn't have anything to do with it. The damn bank won't redo the loan. As far as they're concerned, this is between you and me."

"I want to do this because of your dad. The money

means nothing. Do you want to see my bank books and savings and see how much I'm worth? I'll never miss the money, Josh. Never. And money by itself means nothing if you can't do what you want with it. And it wasn't just your dad. If it hadn't been for you having me over at your place so much, I wouldn't have known your dad. You two let me live on your ranch for months on end. Do you have any idea what that meant to me at that time in my life?''

''Wyatt, it just doesn't seem right.''

''Did it seem right for you two to give me a home when we were kids?''

''Of course it did. That's entirely different.''

''It was another mouth to feed. You did plenty for me back then. Now let me do this for you. I'm serious, Josh. I'll never miss the money. I had more money than my dad even before I came back here.''

Josh's brows arched. ''You made that much in California?''

''Yes, I did, and if it makes you feel better, you can look at my financial statements or you can talk to my California accountant. I think you can guess what the Texas inheritance is worth.''

Josh stared at him in silence.

''Come on, Josh, let me do this. I'm just sorry I didn't do something when your dad was alive.''

''Oh, hell. You always could talk your way into or out of anything. I'll feel like I owe you my life. But you're not getting my wife or my firstborn.''

Wyatt relaxed and grinned, reaching out to clasp his friend on the shoulder. ''That's fine.''

''You're something else, Wyatt.''

''Now do me a favor and keep this quiet. It's just between our two families. I don't want word out in town that I've turned rich and charitable.''

Josh laughed. ''All right. And you know my mare, Gladiola. Well, you can have her foal, her firstborn. That foal is going to be one great horse.''

''I might take you up on that.''

''Thanks,'' Josh said, offering his hand. His eyes sparkled. ''Now that we've got that out of the way, I can tell you my news. Laurie and I are expecting our first child.''

''Congratulations! That's great.'' Wyatt pumped his friend's hand.

''I'd like to see Megan now,'' Josh said. ''You know, I'm going to owe you my soul.''

Wyatt laughed as the two turned toward the yard. ''No, you're not. Consider it a gift to your dad, not to you. It's for days long gone, but they saved me from some hellish moments.''

''I'm glad. My dad wasn't very responsible when it came to running the ranch or making money, but he was a good man and a good dad.''

''He gave me hope.''

''Hey, Wyatt, I'll tell you what—I'll throw in another gift. Gabe caught a wild white stallion that has been running in these parts. He had gotten in with some of Quinn Ryder's good mares and bred them, and Quinn wanted him caught. Gabe couldn't tame him and gave him to me. I can't do anything with him. He's yours if you want him.''

''Sure. I'll take him.''

''You're not scared of the legend?'' Josh asked, grinning.

''Hardly.''

''Well, remember, Gabe had the stallion and now

Gabe's married. I have the stallion now and I'm married.''

"No danger. Give me that wild horse and I'll tame him and I *won't* end up married. It'll be interesting.''

"He's yours. You were warned.''

"I don't believe that legend and you don't, either.'' They reached the back gate and walked through it to join Grace and Megan who were on a blanket on the grass. A slight breeze cooled the air and the spreading branches of a tall oak shaded the area.

"Hi,'' Josh said to Grace as they approached. She smiled when he caught the swing and bent down to talk to Megan.

Then he straightened. "We'll have you over for supper soon, Wyatt. You bring Megan and you can look at my prize mare.'' He turned to Grace. "You come along, too, Grace. Laurie would love to talk to you about Megan, I'm sure.''

"Thanks, Josh. We'll do that,'' Wyatt answered easily.

"I better get home.''

He turned away and Wyatt walked with him back to his pickup. After he drove away, Wyatt returned to sit down beside Megan.

"I'm glad Josh seemed so happy when he left,'' Grace said. "He looked angry when he first arrived.''

"He had a bee in his bonnet over ranch stuff, but it's all smoothed out. They're going to have their first child.''

"Ah,'' Grace said. "I wondered why his wife would want to talk to me. We've never met.''

"You'll know her when you see her. She's a gorgeous woman, a model, and does a lot of commercials for this area. She probably wants to ask you questions about baby care.''

Grace laughed. "So now I'm an expert.''

"You're getting to be one. You'll meet her at our party."

"*Your* party, Wyatt. Not ours."

"It was your idea. You're helping me plan it. You'll be my hostess, so that makes it our party."

"Do you ever lose arguments?"

"Yep. About eighty percent of the time with you," Wyatt replied, touching the tip of her nose lightly. "Josh is giving me a wild, white stallion. Gabe caught the horse and couldn't tame him and gave him to Josh who doesn't want him."

"Is it tame now?"

"Not at all."

"And you want the challenge of taming him?" she asked.

"Yep. Josh wanted to know if I was scared of the old legend."

"That's ridiculous," she remarked, gazing into Wyatt's inscrutable dark eyes. "You won't fall in love because you own a horse."

"I don't think so, either," he said.

Megan began to fuss, and Grace picked her up. "Come here, sweetie."

"I better head to town. See you tonight." He leaned over to kiss Megan. "Bye, bye, darlin'."

"Say goodbye to Daddy," Grace said, waving the baby's hand.

Wyatt looked at her sharply. "Daddy?" he asked.

"I've been meaning to ask you—do you want her to call you Uncle Wyatt or Daddy? You'll be Daddy to her. You already are. Your brother Hank wouldn't object, would he?"

"No, he wouldn't. I'll tell her about her real mother

and daddy when she's old enough to understand, but, yes, I'd like it if she called me Daddy.''

"That makes sense to me. So Daddy it is. That's what I've been saying to her, anyway.''

"One more decision out of my hands,'' he said dryly. "Bye, sweet stuff,'' he said, brushing Megan's cheek with another kiss. Bye, Nanny,'' he added, and brushed Grace's cheek with a quick kiss, too.

"Wyatt, if Mrs. Perkins sees you, there'll be wild rumors all over this ranch.''

"I'm trying to reform, but there are moments when it isn't going to happen.'' He stood and was gone, striding toward the garage. He usually left in the sports car, but today he got on his motorcycle, waved at her and then with a roar and stirring up of dust, he sped out of sight.

For the next week he was gone during the day, but he spent every evening with Grace and Megan until Friday night after supper. Grace was in the family room with Megan when Wyatt appeared at the door. He had changed to a T-shirt and Jeans. "Josh is bringing the stallion over now,'' he announced. "Want to bring Megan and see the new horse?''

"Yes, I do,'' Grace said, picking up Megan.

It was a warm summer evening and while they waited for Josh to arrive, they sat on the porch. Wyatt held Megan, playing with her until Josh drove into view, pulling a horse trailer behind his pickup.

They all went to the corral where Wyatt opened the gate for Josh to drive inside. Standing outside the corral, Grace watched the muscles ripple in Wyatt's back and arms as he worked and her throat went dry. Sexy man. Just the sight of him could make her heart race.

Wyatt waited while Josh drove inside and then he entered the corral and closed the gate behind them.

A terrible racket shook the horse trailer, and Grace realized the stallion was kicking and fighting to get out. When he whinnied loudly, she drew a deep breath, watching both men who acted as if nothing unusual was happening.

"I'll let him out," Wyatt said. "You stay in the pickup."

Josh nodded and waited. Wyatt opened the trailer and the animal burst out, whirling to run.

Wyatt slammed shut the trailer and then ran to the gate. While Josh drove out, the horse reached the fence. He reared, whinnying loudly and then turned to run again. He bucked and reared and Grace thought he was a fearful sight, but she noticed Wyatt and Josh seemed to pay little attention to him.

"Thanks, Josh," Wyatt said.

"I don't think you're getting any prize. He's too wild for me."

Wyatt glanced at the stallion. "We'll see. It'll give me something to do in my spare moments. Come up to the house and have a cold drink with us."

"Sure, thanks."

They all went to the porch where Wyatt once again took Megan and Josh held her for a few minutes. Grace enjoyed sitting and listening to the two friends talk about old times and their ranches. Wyatt was charming, relaxed and constantly attentive to Megan until she began to fuss, and Grace knew Megan was growing sleepy.

"I'll take her to bed," Grace said, taking the baby from Wyatt, conscious of her hands brushing his.

When she returned, they sat on the darkened porch for another hour before Josh left for home.

Then, as they had done every night as soon as Megan was asleep, Wyatt discussed the upcoming party with Grace.

Later that night when she couldn't sleep and went to the window, she could see lights at the corral and Wyatt moving around inside with the wild stallion. One more wild thing that he was involved with.

Ashley Brant had helped with the guest list for the party, and the Saturday night of the barbecue, the last of June, finally arrived. It was a blessedly cool night, so they could enjoy the patio and yard, as well as the inside of the house.

Before the guests arrived, Grace dressed Megan in a frilly pink dress, a pink hair bow, lace-trimmed pink socks and tiny white sandals.

"Let's go show you to Daddy," Grace said. "C'mon, sweetie." She picked up Megan and went to the family room and then to the dining room to find Wyatt. He was having the dinner catered, and men and women in uniforms moved through the house, setting up the food and bar.

"Wyatt."

He turned and Grace's heart missed a beat. He was dressed casually, yet he looked incredibly handsome in jeans, a plaid, short-sleeved shirt and snakeskin boots.

"Hi, sweet baby," he said, crossing the room to take Megan. "She looks adorable."

"Yes, she does."

He stared at Grace's outfit, which was frumpy to the extreme—plain brown dress of the kind of fabric that looked better suited for flour sacking. It was loosely belted over a thick waist.

He poked her middle. "What the hell, Grace?"

"It's padding, but I think it'll prevent any rumors about us being an item."

"I'm not worried about rumors. You don't need to come to this party looking like someone's elderly aunt." He reached out to remove a pair of ugly black-framed glasses from her nose.

"No, this is better, Wyatt. Think about Megan. You told me a long time ago that because of Megan, you didn't want a whisper of scandal connected to you now."

He studied Grace's hair, which was slicked back in a bun behind her head. No tendrils escaped. With the padding, glasses, old-lady shoes and flour-sack dress, she wouldn't get a second glance.

"There'll be a few nice single guys here tonight. Sure you want to meet them looking like that?" he asked dryly, thinking it suited him fine if his single friends didn't give her a second glance.

"I think I remember you saying something about no boyfriends out here, so it's just as well I don't meet anyone I want to start dating. Right?"

He handed her the glasses and watched her put them back on. "I don't know—at a glance, you're right. No rumors, but if you get up close and talk to anyone, I think they'll be able to see past the glasses and dress and all."

"You didn't that first day."

He laughed. "All right. Wear your fake glasses and sit in the corner and be obscure. You'll be missing all the fun at the party. You'll see."

The doorbell rang and he left her, carrying Megan away with him, and from the arrival of the first guests, he was busy. Grace faded into a corner and watched, seeing Wyatt at his most charming. Once he entered the room with a beautiful woman beside him, and he shot

Grace an angry glance before he turned to introduce the woman to other guests.

Grace could guess the reason for the annoyed look, and in minutes, her guess was confirmed when Wyatt came over to her to hand Megan to her. "I think she needs changing. Grace, I thought I took all these single women off the guest list."

"I dug the list out of the trash and put them back on," she said sweetly as she took the baby from him. "You need to meet some women you can date. You won't be so lonesome and bored out here."

"Grace, I get about three calls a day from single women. They bring me casseroles to the office. They ask me out. That's one reason I don't want to live in town. Now, dammit, I don't want to encourage any—"

"Wyatt, just get to know them. You might have a lot of entertainment, and you need the diversion in your life. And then you wouldn't simply hit on the nearest available female." Grace smiled and left before he could reply.

As she walked away, Wyatt swore under his breath.

"Wyatt, your home is beautiful," a tall, slender blonde said, slipping her arm through his. He turned, trying to smile, yet wanting to follow his nanny and give her a lecture about interfering in his life and reminding her that he hadn't hit on her simply because she was the nearest available female.

Kids ran through the house, and it was filled with his neighbors, old friends, people who hadn't spoken to him that last summer he'd been at home, but who seemed to be enjoying his hospitality now.

Later in the evening he was standing with his best friends looking at Gabe and Ashley's two children as they moved about the room. Five-year-old Julian was carrying his eleven-month-old baby sister. "I can't believe how your kids have grown," Wyatt said.

"Ella makes Julian look all grown up. He's not such a little boy any longer," Gabe Brant said.

"Wyatt, does Grace Talmadge work all week for you?" Ashley asked. "Does she have any free days?"

"She's off on weekends."

"She's wonderful with children," Ashley said. "I was hoping she had some days when we could hire her for Julian and Ella. We lost our nanny when she graduated from college." They stood watching Grace, who was at one of the long tables in the dining room. Five small children were clustered around her, and she was assisting each of them to get second helpings of food.

"Sorry, but I've got her full-time."

"If she ever quits, please let us know," Ashley said. "And she's so considerate of you. She asked me to put some extra single women on the guest list."

Gabe grinned at his wife. "Why? Does she think Wyatt needs help meeting women? That'll be the day."

"I think she just thought he'd been away so long and was a little isolated out here on the ranch—"

Gabe and Josh both laughed. "Isolated—Wyatt?" Gabe said, and Ashley laughed.

"I didn't stop to think. I suppose you're right," Ashley admitted.

"Who are you dating, Wyatt?" Gabe asked. "Anyone here?"

"Nope. I've been dating a woman in California."

"You should have brought her out here for this party," Gabe said.

"I'm sorry, Wyatt," Ashley said. "Although I see you did invite the women I had on the list."

"Grace did that. I scratched their names off."

"You're lucky to have her," Ashley said.

"I am lucky," Wyatt answered, watching Grace. He shifted Megan in his arms, barely aware of his friends' conversation as he thought about Grace. In minutes everyone moved away except Josh, who studied Wyatt.

"I don't think you're about to let your nanny hire out to someone else even if she wasn't full-time here."

"Why do you think that?" Wyatt asked. He looked at Josh and saw the sparkle in his eyes.

"I saw her the last time I was here. I don't remember any glasses and I seemed to remember she had a more appealing shape."

"You're damned observant."

"And what the two of you do is your own business. I'm not prying, but I think there's one good-looking nanny under that disguise."

"I hope you're the only person here tonight who knows that. I'm trying to avoid the sort of scandal that's always followed me. I don't want more scandal in Megan's life."

"I'd guess I'm the only person who's noticed the disguise. Gabe hasn't. But then, he's never seen her before. No, tonight I don't think anyone would look twice. And Megan, too, lends you an air of respectability. Ah. Here comes Gretchen, one of those women your nanny thought you should invite. I'm getting out of the way now, because I know Gretchen wants to talk to you, not me."

"You stay right here."

"Nah. I've been away from my wife too long. She's over there talking to her dad, and I haven't gotten to say hello to him tonight."

"Did I run Josh away?" Gretchen said, gazing up at Wyatt. She was a brunette with big blue eyes and a lush figure, yet Wyatt just wanted to escape.

"No, of course not. Gretchen, would you excuse me? I need to change Megan."

"I think it's the sweetest thing the way you've become such a caring parent. Let me go with you and see the nursery. This house is just beautiful."

Wyatt barely heard her. He didn't know whether Megan needed changing or not, but as an escape ploy, it had failed. As he crossed the room, Gretchen at his side, Grace glanced at him. He gave her a meaningful look, wanting to shake her for inviting all these single females.

She smiled sweetly at him and then bent over a child's plate. He sighed and tried to listen to Gretchen.

Three hours later he stood on the front drive and waved goodbye to the last of the departing guests. He walked back inside to find Megan tidying up the few things the caterers had left undone.

"Don't clean," he said, catching her hand. "Let's sit on the back porch and have a drink and relax. We can hear Megan over the intercom if she cries."

In minutes they were on the porch and he had pulled off his boots and unbuttoned his shirt. Grace had been to her room to change to cutoffs and a T-shirt, and she sat beside him.

"It was a very nice party, Wyatt."

"It was a good idea, so thanks. You're right. I need to do things so Megan will have friends."

"She'll have friends when she goes to school and gets into activities, but it's good for you to get to know people now."

"I'm not even going to think about those women you invited—you did me no favors there. Don't you know I can find someone to date on my own?" he said, setting down his bottle of beer and turning his chair to face hers.

He reached for her and pulled her onto his lap. "I've wanted to do this all evening."

"Wyatt!"

"I want you, Grace. And having all those women around here tonight just made me more aware of how much I want you and you alone."

"Wyatt, stop. I'm not your kind of woman. We have nothing in common. You've never dated anyone like me, have you? Someone quiet and bookish. You don't even like to read. You drive too fast, you fly your own plane—"

"You talk too much," he said, and kissed her.

Grace wanted to resist, but it was impossible. Wyatt could melt her resistance with the stroke of his tongue. He leaned away. "I'm going to Houston Tuesday," he said. "I'm flying down. Come with me for the day."

"No. Surely you don't want to take Megan on a plane!"

"Megan will be fine. If there's any bad weather, we won't go. It'll be interesting. C'mon, Grace, live a little. I promise I'll get you both there in one piece."

She put her fingers on his mouth. "Don't make promises like that. You can't control life."

"I sure as hell can't control you. Come with me, please," he whispered, showering kisses on her throat and ear. "Go with me, Grace. Stop living in a bubble."

"Some bubble," she whispered. "All right, Wyatt. You win. I'll go. I'll be terrified of flying in a little plane, but I'll go."

Tuesday morning Wyatt fastened Megan into her carrier in the back seat of his pickup. As soon as he and Grace were buckled in, they drove away. It was a gorgeous day, deep-blue skies, a slight breeze and bright sunshine, and Grace bubbled with anticipation at spending part of the day with Wyatt.

She glanced at him swiftly, taking in his jeans, white shirt and black boots. He had a sports coat with him, which he would probably wear to his appointment. She smoothed her navy skirt, thinking most people would still give her little notice.

"I reserved a hotel room so you'll have a place to relax while I take care of business. It's in a good shopping area, too."

"Thank you," she said. "Megan loves to go out—she must get that from her uncle—so she'll be happy."

As they left the ranch, Grace turned to him. "I thought you said you have your own runway and hangar on the ranch."

"I do, but I need to see Ashley Brant this morning."

"Your friends are wonderful. And Ashley seems to adore Megan."

At Gabe's they slowed at the back gate. Ashley and Julian came out of the house and approached the truck. Then Quinn Ryder, Ashley's father, stepped out of the house with Ella in his arms. "Here comes the family to greet us," Wyatt said. He got out and reached back in to unbuckle Megan and pick her up.

"Are we going in?" Grace asked, and he grinned.

"I have a surprise. Ashley's keeping Megan for me so you and I can have a day in the city on our own."

# Eight

"**W**yatt Sawyer, you didn't tell me that!"

He grabbed Megan's bag and shut the pickup door, leaving Grace sputtering. She climbed out just as Ashley and Julian arrived, both of them smiling at her.

"Hi, Grace," Ashley said. "I'm looking forward to watching Megan today. Laurie is coming over to learn a few things about babies. Although Megan and Ella aren't tiny babies any longer."

"Ashley," Grace said, "I only just found out that Megan would be staying with you. I'm—"

"It's a surprise," Wyatt interjected easily. "I thought my nanny needed a day of relaxation, and Grace hasn't been to Houston in a long time, have you?"

She gave him a stormy look and stood with her hands on her hips.

"Well, enjoy yourself while Wyatt works," Ashley

said. "And don't worry about Megan. I'll take good care of her."

"We'll all take good care of her," Quinn Ryder said, smiling at Grace, and she had to smile in return.

In minutes she was back in the pickup with Wyatt, waving at everyone as they turned and drove away.

She faced Wyatt. "Of all the deceitful, low-down tricks—"

"No worse than you asking all those single females to our party without telling me," he said, reaching for her hand. "Stop getting your feathers in a fluff over a day in town. Relax and enjoy it. I'll be working and you can do as you please."

"Wyatt, men don't take their nannies off on plane trips without the baby just to be nice."

"This man does."

"Well, that will not be how the Brants and Mr. Ryder will see it."

"So how will they see it?" Wyatt asked.

"You know darn good and well they'll think we're going off to spend the day in bed."

"Now there's a thought!"

"Wyatt!"

He laughed. "Don't be ridiculous. We can spend the day in bed at my house, if that's what's going on. No, they'll think we're going to do just what I told them. I said you'd do some shopping."

She threw up her hands. "I still think it was sneaky to not tell me."

"Was it sneaky for you to avoid telling me about fishing that guest list out of the trash and inviting all the women I had scratched off the list?"

"All right. We're even."

"So smile."

She looked at him and laughed. "Wyatt, you're something else."

"Nope. I'm just a guy wanting to have a good day."

And soon she was buckled into the private jet beside Wyatt and on the way to Houston. Once there, they drove first to the hotel and he went up to the room with her. She gave him a look as he unlocked the door and motioned her inside ahead of him.

"You're coming in?" she asked. "I thought you had business."

"I do. I have an appointment in thirty minutes and I'll be on time. I'm just coming in for a few minutes so we can make plans."

She walked into a large suite that overlooked the patio and pool area. She crossed the room to look below and then turned to face Wyatt, who was poking through the briefcase he carried. He set it down and faced her.

"Here's where I'll be if you need me," he said. "Here's my cell phone."

"I won't need you and I'm not calling you while you're engaged in business."

"Suits me if you do. I'll be through about three today. We can go out for an early dinner tonight and then head home."

She planted her hands on her hips. "What other surprises have you got, Wyatt? Do you have this hotel room for the night?"

"No, I don't. You heard me tell Ashley that we'd see her tonight."

"So when do we check out of here?"

"I asked if we could keep the room until four. We'll go to dinner—no one knows us here so no rumors will start—then we'll fly home. Now, does that meet with your approval?"

"Yes. I don't know why you bother asking. If it didn't, you'd talk me into it."

"I do have something I want to talk you into."

"Oh, brother, here it comes," she said, narrowing her eyes.

He smiled and took her purse to open it and slide a card inside. "Here's a credit card of mine. This isn't a bribe. There are no strings attached." He put her purse in the chair. "Go shopping today. I don't see any reason for you to work in those awful dresses you wear. I'm going to notice you whether you do or you don't, so why don't you come into this century and get some other clothes? Buy something to wear to dinner tonight."

"Wyatt, I'm not going to become your sleep-in nanny. You're irresistible to women and you know it, but I will not move into your bed. We've kissed and I knew we shouldn't have, because look what it's led to—this."

"You sound like I'm asking you to jump out of the hotel window this afternoon. Just buy some cute clothes, something besides that schoolmarm stuff to go out in tonight."

"Thanks, Wyatt. You're very generous, but you've been running around with women who've warped your view of life. They are entirely different from me. He stepped closer and she glanced at her watch. "Don't you have to be somewhere now?"

"I'm not late, but I need to go." He reached into his pocket. "Here's a list of nice shops where I have accounts—they know you might be in today. Get whatever you want. I'm going to make some money this afternoon and you can spend some."

"How long have you been planning this?"

"For about a week. Didn't you enjoy the flight this morning?"

"Yes, I did. You were right about that, but you're still not getting me into your bed with all this, even if your kisses *are* irresistible."

"I didn't know for sure they were irresistible," he said quietly, dropping his briefcase and closing the distance between them. "If that's the case, kiss me goodbye." He wrapped his arms around her and leaned down to kiss her, smothering her protest and kissing her until she clung to him and kissed him back.

When he stopped, she opened her eyes and stared at him.

"And you *will* be in my bed," he said in a husky voice. "I want you." He picked up his briefcase and strode to the door. He glanced over his shoulder at her. "See you at four. Go buy a pretty dress and some pretty dresses to work in. Something that doesn't cover you from chin to ankles."

Annoyed beyond measure with both herself and him, she snatched up a small vase on a nearby table and threw it at the closing door. The door shut and the vase struck it, shattering into pieces.

Appalled at her loss of temper, Grace stared at the bits of glass, unable to believe what she'd done. She couldn't recall losing control like that ever before. Not with her sisters or anyone. Suddenly the door opened and he thrust his head inside, looked down at the smashed vase and then at her.

"Wow! I didn't know you'd do something like that. They'll just put it on the bill. Let them clean it up, too. So it seems you can let go when you want to, darlin'," he said, chuckling as he closed the door.

"Tarnation, Wyatt Sawyer," she said, glaring at the closed door. Contrary to his suggestion, she crossed to it to kneel and pick up the broken pieces of china. Then she moved restlessly around the hotel room, looking outside at the beautiful day. At last she picked up her purse. He wanted her to go shopping. Okay, that was what she would do. But she wasn't going to climb into bed with him. She wasn't going to be a live-in nanny, as well as a live-in lover. She just hoped she had sense enough to stop letting him kiss her and to stop kissing him back.

She thought about Megan. She missed her. She'd never told Wyatt, but when she left on weekends, she missed Megan. She'd given up her apartment in San Antonio to save money, so on weekends she stayed in a cheap hotel or with friends. Weekends were usually long, sometimes lonely, and she missed Megan dreadfully. She hated to admit it, but she missed Wyatt, too.

Grace pulled out the list of shops, squared her shoulders and left the hotel.

She spent most of the day buying clothes, but she also went to a bookstore to get herself three new books and one for Wyatt. She spent her own money for the books. He might pitch his book into the trash, but there was a chance he'd read it. She returned to the hotel by two and showered, getting ready for her early dinner date with Wyatt.

"All right, Wyatt Sawyer, you want me to wear something that isn't schoolmarmish," she told her reflection in the full-length mirror.

She had bought black lace underwear, which she stepped into. Then she pulled on a black dinner dress. It was clinging, short enough to stop inches above her knees and had a soft drape around the neckline to plunge to her waist in back. She piled her hair on her head loosely, letting curls fall around her face. Finally she stepped into high-heeled black sandals. She studied herself as she put on makeup.

She twisted and turned and didn't see how he could call this dress schoolmarmish. She bought a small black envelope purse. Glancing at her watch, she saw he was ten minutes late and she wondered what he was doing.

She'd had his book gift-wrapped, and now as she stared at it, she suspected he would be disappointed. She had bought him a box of chocolates, too, and those she knew he would like.

Wyatt knocked before he unlocked the door and stepped inside. He was late, tired of dealing with business and eager to see Grace. "Hi, darlin', I'm home," he called, remembering how Grace had tossed a vase at the door.

All evidence of it was gone now, the carpet swept clean.

Grace strolled through the door from the bedroom, and he sucked in his breath at the sight of her. He'd known from that first night that she was gorgeous, but most of the time, she kept that beauty hidden. Not tonight. He stared and his temperature spiked up twenty degrees. He wanted to stay right here in the hotel room and take her out of the fantastic black dress.

She had done what he wanted beyond his wildest dreams. The dress molded her full curves, revealed long, luscious legs and her slender arms and throat.

"You look beautiful," he said, moving toward her. "You take my breath away."

"You approve of the dress?" she asked, turning for him. When he saw the plunging back, he wondered if she wore anything beneath the slip of a dress. The dark hose and pumps showed off her legs.

"I more than approve."

"Thank you. I bought you a present—with my own

money," she said, smiling at him and picking up a small sack.

It was an effort to stop staring at her. He knew she had tried to get something to please him, but all he wanted to do was look at her and touch her. He took the sack, sat in the nearest chair and caught her wrist to pull her down on his lap. "Come here while I open my present."

She sat perched on his knees while he opened the sack and ripped wrapping paper off a box of chocolates. "Yum," he said, looking at her mouth. "Thank you." He opened his other present and pulled out a book entitled *History of the Lone Star State*.

"I know you don't read much, but I thought you might enjoy parts of this about the time when your great-great-grandfather settled in Texas. I've read it before, and it's a particularly interesting book."

"If you gave it to me, I will love it." His arm tightened around her waist, but she slipped off his lap quickly and stood.

"Now are you taking me to dinner?"

Amused, he gazed up at her. He wanted to pull her back into his arms and kiss away all her protests and seduce her. But he would stick to his plans for the evening and take her to dinner and dancing. He wondered if she even danced. He'd find out soon enough.

"Yes, we'll go to dinner. Let's get your things. I've already checked out of the hotel."

"I'll pay for the vase, Wyatt."

He grinned. "No. I wouldn't have missed that for the world. I didn't know you ever let go like that."

"I don't. You drove me to losing my temper, but it's not going to happen again."

He grinned and touched her cheek. "Want to make a little wager?"

"No! I don't bet. And never with you. Now, let's not get into another hassle because I've had a wonderful day and I'm looking forward to dinner. I skipped lunch."

"Why did you do that?"

"I was busy shopping. I spent two hours in the bookstore."

"Two hours with books?"

"You should try reading. Books are wonderful."

"Grace, I didn't finish high school."

"That doesn't have a thing to do with reading. One of my grandfathers didn't finish high school, yet he read constantly, and he read to me and my sisters when we were little. I think he's why I like to read."

"Well, I'll read the book you gave me."

"Don't read it to be polite. Only read it if you like it. The world is filled with good books."

"The world is filled with exciting things to do, too. Let's go."

He drove the car he'd rented to a restaurant a few streets away. The place had soft lights, dark paneling, a piano player and linen-covered tablecloths with pink rosebuds in vases on each table.

Wyatt ordered steaks for them and was charming through dinner. At one point she asked him, "How was your business deal today?"

"Not what I'd hoped in some ways, but I did make the sale and I'm rid of an albatross."

"Why did you tell me to go out and spend money when you didn't know whether you would get the money you wanted from this deal?"

He smiled at her and reached across the table to take her hand. "Because the money I made today doesn't matter. Grace, I had more money than my dad from my businesses in California. Then I inherited all the Sawyer properties and businesses.''

She stared at him wide-eyed. ''That's wonderful, Wyatt. Megan will be well provided for, then.''

''There are a lot of women I would never tell one word about my finances, but you I can tell. First of all you have a healthy appreciation for money. At the same time, that doesn't make me have one iota more appeal to you, does it.''

''No. Your money really doesn't have anything to do with how much you appeal to me.'' She smiled. ''But you probably don't believe that, in spite of what you just said.''

''I do believe it. Your values aren't the same as those of a lot of people.''

''Might not be. But I do appreciate money. Except I hope you don't spoil Megan when she's older.''

''I hope by then I'll have a wife who'll keep me from it.''

''I thought you didn't ever want to marry.''

''Life changes. I'm changing. You and Megan are changing me.''

The piano player had been joined by three more musicians, and several couples began to dance. Wyatt stood and took her hand. ''Dance with me.''

Grace walked to the dance floor and into his arms. Wyatt held her lightly, his hand holding hers and his other hand in the small of her bare back. As they danced together, she gazed up with her wide, green eyes, and his pulse thrummed. He wanted to pull down her hair, kiss her, peel her out of that bit of a dress.

He knew she didn't want to be a live-in lover. He suspected that in spite of yielding to his kisses, she might stick with what she said. But he also thought he could seduce her. He wanted her as he had never wanted any other woman. But he wanted more than just a lover. He wanted her friendship. He wanted her with him at the end of the day. Today he'd liked having her with him on this jaunt.

Marriage. Something he'd always said he didn't want, but now he did. He always thought marriage would take away his freedom, but he didn't want to be free from Grace.

He promised himself that he wouldn't rush into proposing to her until he was sure of his feelings, but he grew more certain by the hour. He hadn't known her a long time, yet each day added to his desire to have her in his life. She constantly surprised him. She was a great companion. She was gorgeous, sexy, intelligent. And she was wonderful with Megan.

He circled the small dance floor with Grace, still gazing into her eyes, forgetting his surroundings and everything else except her. She was light in his arms, following his lead perfectly. He was too aware of the warm skin on the small of her back. He was on fire with wanting her.

He suspected if he did something she really didn't like, she would quit working for him. "You know how to dance, Grace. Who've you dated?"

"No one important. Who've you dated?" she shot back.

"No one important," he answered, and she smiled.

The music changed to a fast number and she was equally adept at that. She must have dated someone sometime, gone dancing with him a lot, a thought he didn't care to dwell on. The next slow number, he couldn't resist. "You're a great dancer. You've dated enough to get that mastered."

She smiled at him. "Jealous, Wyatt?"

Surprised, he stared at her and then laughed. "I guess so."

"Well, you don't need to be. I'm from a strong church family, remember? I've spent a thousand hours at Sunday-school dances and church-sponsored events that included dancing."

"Now that's good news. I don't remember feeling any kind of jealousy before."

"Phooey. I find that difficult to believe."

"It's true," he said, pulling her closer.

They danced until dusk, and he knew they should start home. Reluctantly he led her from the dance floor, and in minutes they were speeding to the airport and boarding his jet.

She was fascinated by their takeoff, looking at the twinkling lights of Houston below and exclaiming in delight.

"Could it be that you like flying?" he asked.

She turned to smile at him. "The weather is perfect. I figured you would know what you're doing, so it's okay. It's still risky, but not high risk. And you told me you have a will and a guardian appointed for Megan, so she's covered if something happens. This seems safer than your motorcycle. That I'll never like."

"Bet you ride on it with me."

"Bet I don't."

"I withdrew from the bull-riding competition in California."

She turned to stare at him. "Why?"

"Why do you think?"

"Because of me? Because I don't approve of it? I don't think so, Wyatt. Why did you?"

"I can give up some of my activities. I canceled the skydiving I had scheduled. That one I can give up easily. In the future, I thought I'd switch from bull riding to bronc riding. Broncs aren't as dangerous as bulls. I have one more—I can't get out of bull riding in the rodeo in San Antonio."

She stared at him, and he had to smile. "Speechless?"

"Yes, I am. You don't mind giving up those things?"

"Nope, or I wouldn't have done it. I care what you think."

"Oh, my!" she exclaimed.

"Don't look so totally undone. Isn't that what you wanted?"

"It's what I think is best for Megan because you're her daddy now, but I'm amazed you'd do it just like that."

"Megan doesn't give a rip if I ride bulls or jump out of airplanes. That wasn't why I did it," he said quietly.

"Wyatt, I'm stunned. You can't have done that for me. We're not that important to each other."

"Well, I did do it for you, and you're getting to be important in my life. I should have told you all this when I wasn't having to keep my attention on piloting this plane."

"You keep flying. Thank you, I guess."

They lapsed into silence, and then he changed the subject, asking her about her shopping.

It was eleven before they picked up a sleeping Megan and drove home, then put her to bed.

Wyatt tiptoed out of the nursery and switched off lights. He caught Grace's hand. "Come downstairs and have a drink with me."

"It's been a wonderful day and night, Wyatt. I had a marvelous time and thank you for the dress, but I should say good-night now."

He swung her up in his arms and carried her into her bedroom, setting her on her feet and wrapping his arms around her waist. "I get a good-night kiss," he said in a husky voice. He leaned down to kiss her and she wrapped her arms around his neck.

"You're so beautiful," he whispered. "Grace, I want you. You're going to be mine."

"This is all wrong," she whispered. "You should go right now."

"You don't like to kiss?" he asked, kissing her and tightening his arms around her. He wanted to devour her. He wanted to love her the whole night long and felt there was nothing wrong about anything involving her.

Grace trembled, knowing she should be strong and send him on his way, but she couldn't. She'd never known a man like Wyatt, and she knew she never would again. She wanted his loving, wanted him. She couldn't resist his kisses. She stopped arguing with herself, flinging aside worries momentarily and tightening her arms around his neck to kiss him back.

He was trembling, too, and she was startled by the knowledge, just as she had been surprised earlier to learn he was giving up some of his dangerous activities. *For her.* That was what was so stunning, though she hadn't fully accepted that he'd changed his life for her alone. Was it something temporary? Something he would regret later? Or go back to later? If he had quit permanently, she was awed, amazed and frightened that she had become that important to him.

In spite of great times together or compatibility or wild, passionate kisses that set them both on fire, he was not the man for her and she wasn't the woman for him. He wasn't the marrying kind, and even if he was, she didn't want to tie her life to a daredevil. He had changed some, but he wasn't ever going to change completely. He'd never stop riding his motorcycle or flying or riding wild animals or myriad other things that involved risk. And he would become bored with her quiet ways.

But right now, however fleeting, was so incredible! She stopped thinking, just lost herself in a dizzying spiral of sensation. She felt his hand on her back and before she knew it, her dress was puddled on the floor at her feet. She wore only panties and panty hose now, and Wyatt inhaled sharply, leaning back to cup and caress her breasts in his warm hands and gaze at her. "You're so lovely," he whispered.

As his thumbs circled her nipples, she trembled with desire. She fumbled with the buttons of his shirt, pushing it away and running her hands over his marvelous chest.

Then he was embracing her again, kissing her wildly. She wound her fingers into his hair, aware of his hands in her hair, pulling down her curls.

She struggled for reason, for sanity. She had to stop and he had to stop. She pushed against his chest. "Wyatt, wait."

He straightened. His breathing was raspy, and the desire in his eyes made her heart thud.

"Wyatt, we have to stop. I'm not ready to go further. I can't."

He leaned down to take a breast in his mouth, stroking her nipple with his tongue.

She gasped, moaning softly with pleasure, holding his strong shoulders. "Wyatt—"

He straightened again. "You're the most beautiful

woman I've ever known, Grace," he said solemnly. "I want you more than I've ever wanted anyone."

"Oh, Wyatt, don't. We don't belong together."

"I don't know why you think that. But if you want me to go, I will."

"I do want you to leave. I'm not ready for this."

He clamped his lips together, turned and was gone.

Grace moved to the door, leaning her forehead against it and hurting. Tears stung her eyes. She wanted Wyatt. Every inch of her body ached for him. She would never again know a man like him. He had brought excitement, joy, exuberance into her life. He was the sexiest man she would ever know. Yet she couldn't be his lover, couldn't involve herself with him.

She knew she'd done the right thing. If she had good sense, she would quit this job, yet the thought of leaving Megan and Wyatt tore at her.

She heard the roar of the motorcycle and knew he was leaving on one of his midnight rides. She picked up her dress and moved stiffly around the room. Her body ached for him, for his hands and mouth and lovemaking.

She pulled on her nightie and sat in a chair by the window. An hour later she saw him return. He was bare-chested, speeding up the drive and whipping in a circle to stop and climb off.

"I love you, Wyatt Sawyer," she whispered, knowing she had indeed fallen in love with him. Hopelessly in love. They didn't have a future, but she couldn't change her heart.

Take him as a lover, an inner voice urged. Just once. She would never know lovemaking the way she would with Wyatt. She shook her head in the darkened room. If she gave herself to him, how would she ever get over him? She wasn't certain she was going to, anyway. If they made love, how could she work with him daily, knowing such intimacy?

"Wyatt, you've complicated my life," she whispered.

Outside, Wyatt strode across a field heading for the horses, then swung onto the bare back of his bay to ride to the gate. He slipped off and opened the gate, whistled the horse through and closed the gate, then jumped on again. He locked his hands in the mane and urged the horse forward, riding without seeing, his thoughts lost on Grace while he waited for his body to cool down.

He wanted her.

He thought about her full breasts, touching them tonight. His body burned with desire for her. But it went deeper than desire—was this really love?

What could he do Saturday night? Where could he take her that would be special? Could he get someone to keep Megan again? He needed to find a nanny so he could go out with his nanny.

He wouldn't sleep tonight. Images of Grace taunted him. Memories plagued him. Imagination set him on fire.

He rode for an hour, then went to the barn to feed, water and brush his horse, finally turning him out to pasture again.

Later, Wyatt sprawled in bed and opened his new book to read, munching some of the chocolates Grace had given him. It was almost dawn before he fell into a fitful sleep filled with dreams of Grace.

The next morning he picked up the mail from the day before and carried it to the kitchen to join Megan and Grace. It was Mrs. Perkins's day off and Grace had cooked a breakfast of eggs and toast. She sat feeding Megan. Wyatt's gaze slipped over both of them, and his brows arched. "Grace, I thought I told you to get some other clothes yesterday."

"I did. That black dress was new. As far as what I wear when I'm working, my clothes are just fine. I'm not spending your money to buy shorter skirts and tighter blouses."

He grinned at her and sat at the kitchen table, plopping the mail down in front of him. "Scared you'll get me all hot and bothered if you do?"

"No. It just seems a ridiculous waste of money when I have a closet of nice clothes."

Wyatt opened an envelope, staring at the contents before he started swearing.

Grace glanced at him. "I'm glad Megan can't understand you." One look at Wyatt's face, and she knew she shouldn't joke with him. "What's wrong, Wyatt?"

"Olivia's parents want my lawyer and me to meet with them. They want custody of Megan."

# Nine

―――――

"I can't believe it! You told me that you called them and said they could come see her."

"I did and they said fine and that's the last I've heard until this." He waved the letter. "They've shown no interest in her. Hank told me that they seldom saw Megan."

"They can't get custody, can they?"

"I don't know. I'll have to talk to Prentice. I'll fight them as long and as hard as I can."

"What about Olivia, their daughter? Did she have a will?"

"Yes. She and Hank had identical wills and she named me as Megan's guardian, too. Olivia didn't want them as guardians."

"It would be a crime for them to take Megan from you."

He smiled at Grace. "I don't think they can. I'll go call my lawyer now."

"Do you have a good lawyer? You haven't lived here long."

"I think so. Prentice Bolton was Hank's attorney, and his firm is highly recommended by a lot of people I deal with. He's Gabe Brant's lawyer, too."

"Good."

As Wyatt left the room, she gazed after him and then hugged Megan, saying a swift prayer for Megan and Wyatt.

Wyatt made an appointment to see his lawyer that afternoon. He left for his office, and Grace and Megan were alone.

Grace waited that night to eat with Wyatt. She heard his car arrive and in minutes he came striding into the house, crossing the room to pick up Megan and hug her. She squealed with delight.

It wasn't until they were seated over baked chicken that Grace brought up the custody question. "What did your lawyer say today?"

"He said not to worry. Olivia and Hank had solid wills."

"Good! Do you still have to meet with the Volmers?"

"Sure. We have to go through the motions. If we can't work things out, they can take me to court, but hopefully, it'll be dropped before then. Now, what happened here today?"

"I took Megan to Stallion Pass with me and I got our pictures." She reached behind her to retrieve the envelope and then handed it to him.

Wyatt pulled out the pictures taken the day he'd come home from work and found Grace playing with Megan, making her laugh. As he ran through the stack of pictures,

Grace watched him. He was still in a white shirt and jeans. His hair was a tangle above his forehead and with summer, his skin was getting deeply tanned.

"Nice pictures," he said, smiling and handing them back to her. "Grace, will you go to dinner with me Saturday night? I have a sitter lined up for Megan."

Torn between wanting to accept and knowing she should refuse, Grace stared at him. "Wyatt—"

"Come on. Just dinner and dancing. Wear your pretty black dress, or go buy another one."

She laughed. "I don't need another dress! All right, Wyatt, but you know as well as I do that we shouldn't date. It'll only lead to trouble."

"If it's trouble, then it's the best kind of trouble," he said softly. "Seven o'clock, Saturday night. Okay?"

"Okay. Who's watching Megan?"

"Jorene Ryder. She's one of Ashley's cousins, and Gabe and Ashley have used her before. She said just to bring Megan to her house, because she has sisters who will help. Then we'll pick Megan up on the way home."

"Wyatt, it's crazy for us to date."

"It would be crazier for us not to. You'll see. You'll have a good time Saturday night."

"That's what's worrying me."

He grinned. "Try life on the wild side and see what my world is like." He strode out of the room whistling a cheerful tune, and she stared at his back in consternation. He could get her tied in knots while he was enjoying himself on a trail to seduction.

*"Try life on the wild side and see what my world is like."* His words rang in her ears. Maybe she should. At least a degree more than she usually did.

That afternoon she buckled Megan into the carrier in the back seat of the car and drove to San Antonio. Laurie

Kellogg had told her about dress shops there. Grace shopped for about an hour and then returned home, this time buying a red dress with her own money.

That night she awoke to Megan's cries. They had agreed she would get up weeknights with Megan and Wyatt would take the weekends, so she rolled out of bed. Since that first night, she had never again seen Wyatt in the nursery and so had long ago stopped throwing on a robe. Besides, her cotton nightgown covered her from chin to toes.

She picked up Megan and switched on a small light. She changed her diaper and then went to the kitchen to get a bottle, returning to Megan's room to sit and rock her.

Megan finished the bottle and Grace quietly rocked until the baby was asleep. She carried her to bed. "Good night, sweet baby. You're my little love. I love you, Megan," she said softly, and leaned over the crib to kiss the baby.

"Need help?"

Startled, she looked up. Wyatt stood in the doorway. He was bare-chested, dressed only in jeans that had the top button unfastened. As he came into the room, her pulse jumped and she clutched the neck of her nightgown.

"No, she's asleep now. I thought I was the one getting up on weeknights."

"I couldn't sleep." He stopped beside Grace and looked at the sleeping baby. "I never knew I could love someone the way I love her."

"You're a good daddy, Wyatt."

He raised his head and her heart thudded as his dark eyes met hers. Desire was obvious in the dark depths.

"She's asleep now. Come here," he said, taking

Grace's hand and walking backward toward his bedroom door.

"Wyatt—"

"Shh, Grace, just for a minute."

She slipped her wrist out of his grasp. "I'm going to bed, Wyatt," she said.

He caught her around the waist and pulled her to him. "Don't be in such a rush," he whispered. He leaned down to kiss her.

What good did it do to protest? Every time, she not only yielded to his kisses, she returned them.

"Ah, Grace," he said, holding her head with one hand while his other arm banded her waist and he kissed her deeply. He walked backward, a silent, slow dance to passion, and then they were in his bedroom. He closed the door behind them.

His hand went to her breast, stroking the taut peak through her nightgown. She felt his fingers at the buttons and then he slipped his hand beneath her gown to cup her breast and stroke her nipple with his thumb.

She moaned softly, pleasure rippling through her. Tonight, she thought, love him tonight. Take his loving and let it be a memory forever. Yet if she did, could she live under the same roof with him and ever again say no to him?

Questions were dim, like annoying bees buzzing nearby, and growing dimmer with each caress and kiss.

He framed her face with his hands and looked at her intently. "I love you, Grace."

Her heart thudded violently and she stared at him. Then she remembered it was Wyatt, the man with a past filled with women. Words of love probably rolled off his tongue as easily as breathing.

Words that even if they'd been true, would never

change one iota of the circumstances between them. An impossible situation. Yet tonight, just tonight, she wanted to know him fully.

"You can't love me," she whispered.

"Yes, I can and I do," he said. "I love you," he repeated, and pulled her close and kissed away any reply. His kisses escalated. Hot, demanding, never-to-be-forgotten kisses that burned away every thought in her head. She clung to him, kissing him in return while her body ached for his loving.

"I want to take all night to pleasure you, Grace." He caught her gown and with a twist, it was over her head and tossed aside.

His broad chest expanded as he inhaled. His gaze was a caress, trailing over her scalding body. His hands rested on her waist as he leaned down to take her nipple in his mouth, to stroke the bud with his tongue.

She clung to him, running her hands through his hair and across his strong shoulders. His body was a wonder to her, something to discover and relish. He peeled away his jeans and stepped out of them, then pushed away his briefs.

Wyatt picked her up to carry her to his bed, coming down over her to trail kisses across her flat stomach to her breasts.

He moved between her legs and his hands drifted lightly over her, feathery touches that left trails of fire. And then he kissed her leg, behind her knee, letting his tongue slide up her inner thigh, his hot breath on her while he watched her.

She was far beyond the point of going back. Tonight he would make love to her as much and as long as he wanted to. And then his hand caressed her intimately, rubbing and stroking, taking her to a peak as she clung to him and cried out, wanting him beyond her wildest dreams.

She pushed him down and moved over him, showering kisses over his muscled chest, his throat, his ear and then down across his flat belly, down, stroking his thighs, breathing so lightly over his thick shaft, touching him with slow caresses that made him shake and gasp.

He came off the bed to turn them so he was above her, kissing her again, his hands everywhere, giving her pleasure every way he could.

He ran his hands through her hair. ''You're beautiful, Grace. I can't ever look at you enough. Sexy, gorgeous.''

He turned her onto her stomach and began to caress and kiss her back, moving down, his hands stroking her bottom, moving over her thighs and the backs of her knees.

With a cry she twisted and turned over to sit up, taking his shaft in her hand. She kissed him, stroked him, tried to pleasure him until he groaned and pulled her into his embrace. He cradled her in his arms, leaning over her and kissing her with unbridled passion, kisses to make her faint, kisses to make her want him more than anything else in life.

He pushed her down, moving between her legs again. As Grace looked at him, her breath caught. He was aroused, ready, a male in his prime filled with sexual energy. Her heart thudded in anticipation.

Wyatt took a deep breath, looking at Grace. She was ready, eager for him. He felt he would burst with his love and need for her. He wanted her to be his woman, wanted to love her senseless, wanted to share everything with her. Never had he felt like this.

''Wyatt, I want you!'' she exclaimed, and sat up to pull him to her and kiss him.

Wyatt shifted, and moved away to retrieve a packet and when he returned, his gaze held hers steadily. His mouth covering hers as he kissed her hard, shoving her back down on the bed and lowering himself over her.

She watched him, running her hands along his strong thighs. Then she wrapped her arms around him when he lowered himself between her legs. His shaft touched her, teasing, touching.

"Wyatt!" she cried. "Please!"

"I want you to want me like you've never wanted anything or anyone before."

"I do! Come here."

He kissed her, stopping her words. He entered her slowly and she gasped, but her cry was muffled, taken with his kisses.

Grace thought she would faint with need, wanting all of him, needing to move, to satisfy this urgency he had built inside her.

Hot and hard, he filled her slowly. She locked her legs around him, rocking with him, wanting him, needing release. Tension built as he moved in.

"Wyatt!" she cried before his mouth again muffled her cries.

Wyatt felt the tightness, knew she was a virgin. He tore his mouth from hers. "I don't want to hurt you."

"Wyatt, love me," she whispered, her hands on his firm buttocks, her legs pulling him closer.

Sweat rolled off him as he tried to go slowly, to build her up to a frenzy, but then his control slipped away and he thrust inside her, going deep, covering her mouth with his to take her cry.

They moved together and she was abandoned in his arms, thrashing and twisting, driving him beyond conscious thought. All control had vanished, hers and his.

And she was in as big a frenzy as he was. When release burst in him, Wyatt shuddered, pumping and relishing her passionate responses.

He never knew how long before they slowed. Both of them quieted, gasping for breath, their hearts pounding together. He showered kisses on her, knowing that for the first time in his life, he was truly in love.

Grace clung to Wyatt, feeling his hard length stretched against her. They were one, united, and for this moment, he loved her with all his body. And maybe, for now, with all his heart.

He was the first man in her life and, she suspected, the only one forever. She was as certain of her love for him as she was of its hopelessness.

Running her hands over his strong back, she pushed away her thoughts. Time for reality tomorrow. Tonight she was in Wyatt's arms and she wanted his loving, his kisses. She wanted to touch and feel his body, to revel in his lovemaking.

Wyatt kissed her throat, her temple. Then he rolled over, holding her close and keeping her in his arms, his legs wrapped around her. He smiled at her. "You're perfect."

"Oh, Wyatt, I didn't know it could be like this!" she exclaimed, tightening her arms around him.

He kissed her again and then raised his head. "It will get a lot better than this. You'll see. What we have, Grace, is special. So incredibly special."

She placed her fingers on his lips. "Stop talking, Wyatt. Take the moment and keep tomorrow shut away for now."

"Suits me fine," he whispered, still showering her with light kisses, his hands trailing over her. "I want to memorize every inch of you, kiss every inch of you, love every inch of you. You're gorgeous, Grace.''

"You're crazy or blind. That wasn't your first impression of me.''

"I guess not, since you did everything you could to hide your beauty." He leaned away to smile at her, stroking damp tendrils of hair from her face. "This is paradise.''

"Yes, it is.''

"You're my woman now, Grace. Mine.''

She stroked his face, feeling the rough stubble on his jaw. His hair fell in a tangle over his forehead, black locks curling damply. There was a fine sheen of sweat on his shoulders and chest and she ran her hands lightly over him. "It goes both ways, Wyatt. I can't get enough of touching you. This magic night is a special treasure.''

"You're the special treasure," he whispered. "It's never, ever been like this. Not once, not ever.''

While her heart skipped beats, she tightened her arms around him, placing her head against his chest and listening to the steady rhythm of his heart.

He stroked her back, running his hands from her shoulder to her bottom and then up again, while his other arm banded her waist. "I don't want you out of my arms tonight," he whispered. "I want to know that you're here, letting me love you. I've dreamed of this, Grace, since that first night.''

"You can't have!''

"Oh, yes, I did.''

"Well, that was nothing but lust.''

"Might have been, but it's more than lust now. Did you know that I haven't had a peaceful night's sleep since I inherited Megan—first because of her and then because of you.''

"I don't believe you," Grace said, raising her head.

He held up his hand, palm toward her. "I swear it's the truth."

"I don't know why. I did everything I could to keep you from noticing me. At least now you can sleep peacefully."

"Why do I doubt that?" He shifted slightly. "I'm re-energized. Let's get in the tub."

"You're crazy, Wyatt."

"You'll see. We'll have a great time." He stood and scooped her up in his arms and carried her into the bathroom. In minutes he was in the tub seated behind her with his arms and legs wrapped around her while he soaped her all over. "How's this? Pretty good, huh?"

"Mmm, better than books," she murmured, closing her eyes while he rubbed her back lightly with a warm, wet cloth.

"Better than chocolate, too," he said huskily. "I love your hair," he added. He played with her curls while he soaped her back with his free hand.

As he rinsed her off, she closed her eyes, relishing the relaxing rub, the warm water, and Wyatt wrapped around her. When he reached around with his hand to stroke a nipple, she inhaled swiftly. "Wyatt!"

"You feel so good," he whispered, cupping her breasts in his wet hands and caressing them. Gasping, she closed her eyes, leaning back and twisting around to kiss him.

In minutes she turned, and he moved her over him, settling her on his manhood, holding her tightly while they moved together.

Her eyes closed, Grace returned his kisses and clung to him until she cried out her release. Then she felt his shuddering release. She sprawled against him and he held her tightly, stroking her hair and murmuring soft endearments.

Thirty minutes later they were back in bed, wrapped in each other's arms. Through the night Wyatt loved her, and she was amazed at his energy and stamina.

Near dawn she lay in his arms. The night had been bliss and she didn't want it to end, but she knew it must.

She turned to look at him. He lay on his side with one arm beneath her and the other arm wrapped around her waist. His dark lashes were feathery shadows above his prominent cheekbones. She smoothed locks of his black hair away from his forehead. She loved him and she would love him the rest of her life. The knowledge hurt because their lifestyles and their futures were poles apart.

He had told her he loved her, but she didn't take him seriously. He had been in the throes of passion, and she suspected he had told a fair number of women the same thing. She didn't want to think about that. Right now she just wanted to cherish Wyatt and the night and moments that had already become memories.

She kissed his head lightly, trying to keep from waking him, yet unable to stop touching him. She shifted and found herself looking into his dark-brown eyes.

"I didn't mean to wake you," she whispered.

"I'm glad you did. I have something I bought for you when I was in town this week. Don't go away. Promise."

"I promise," she replied with amusement, wondering if he thought she might get up and run to her room the moment he let go of her.

She watched him walk across the room casually as if unaware of his nudity. His body was male perfection. Tanned, rippling muscles, lean and hard. Her mouth went dry and her pulse began to race as she looked at him, and she wanted him again, wanted to hold him, wanted to feel his body against hers, wanted his loving.

He fished something from a drawer and returned. She saw that he was aroused again, a perpetual state through the night. She held out her arms, wanting him, his gift forgotten.

He lowered himself to the bed and pulled her close. "I love you."

"I love you," she replied solemnly in return, stroking his cheek.

"Grace, will you marry me?" he asked, and held out a ring.

# Ten

Stunned, she stared at the ring that sparkled in the glow of the one small lamp. She sat up, staring at Wyatt in amazement.

"Wyatt, this is so sudden."

"It might be sudden to you, but I've been thinking about it for some time. It never takes me long to make up my mind about what I want. Especially something I want badly."

Everything in her cried out to throw her arms around him and say yes. But wisdom said no. A lump formed in her throat, and tears stung her eyes.

"What happened to all that freedom you said you cherished?" she asked.

"I wanted freedom from people I didn't love. It's different when you love someone. My freedom is with you in my life. I don't want to be away from you. I want you part of my life always."

"Oh, Wyatt! We're so incredibly different! I love you and you're wonderful and maybe I'll always love you."

He frowned. "I'm not getting the reaction I'd hoped for here. What's wrong? You told me you loved me. I love you. It's pretty simple to me."

She shook her head. "I can't accept."

"Why not, Grace?" he asked, his heart plunging. An ache started and he wondered if it would ever end.

"I've told you before—our lifestyles. You can't change completely for me and I can't change completely for you."

"Can't we go on like we are now? We've been doing just fine together."

"Wyatt, the more I love you, the more I worry about you. When you go out the door, I worry about you. I don't want to go through life like that. And I don't want you to change for me. You wouldn't be happy."

"Ah, hell, Grace. I've given up skydiving and bull riding. I don't take chances like I used to. And when you've flown with me, you liked it. Tell me you didn't."

"It was fine, Wyatt, but the weather was good. We didn't take Megan with us. If I marry you, I'll be a mother to her and I won't be able to stand watching you teach her to fly and ride and do all those things."

"It's life. It's just living."

"What you do is more than just living. It's life on the wild side. You drive too fast. You ride that motorcycle without a helmet. I just know that there'd be endless arguments and worry and neither of us would be happy."

"I think I could be very happy," he said solemnly. Her words hurt him, and he thought she was being foolish and ridiculous. She had already changed a lot since she'd moved to the ranch. And he had changed.

"I can't say yes. I just can't."

"We're both changing," he argued. Her tumble of curls framed her face and cascaded over her silky shoulders. She had the sheet tucked beneath her arms, and it clung to her curves. One long leg was out from under the sheet. She looked lovely to him and he ached with wanting her.

"But we're not changing enough," she answered sadly.

He wiped away her tears. "I've never really been in love before. Not like this. This is going to hurt, Grace. It's going to hurt badly."

"It does hurt."

"Well, it's needless. I'll try to keep from worrying you. Maybe after you've lived out here awhile, you'll get used to some of the things I do. But I can't sit in the house on summer evenings with my nose in a book."

They stared at each other and then he pulled her into his arms to kiss her as if he'd been deprived of kisses for a year, instead of only minutes. He bent over her, his demanding kiss silencing their argument, making her heart pound as she wrapped her arms around him and responded.

Wyatt wanted to devour her. To drive all the doubts away and make her see that they belonged together. He needed Grace with every fiber of his being. He was incomplete without her. And yet he couldn't alter his entire life. And he couldn't expect her to alter hers. He wondered now if he was really kissing her goodbye.

In spite of the tears that streamed down her cheeks, Grace clung to him until finally she pushed against him and he released her. "I can't, Wyatt. I just know I can't. But I do love you."

She slipped out of bed, grabbing her nightgown and rushing back through the nursery door. She crossed the room to the crib, looking at Megan and knowing she was saying no to Megan, as well as to Wyatt. She would lose them both.

Fresh tears streamed down her cheeks. "Marry him. Take a chance on Wyatt and life. You'll have Megan," she whispered to herself, but she thought about the future and knew she would be in knots every time Wyatt went on his bike or flew or rode a bronc. And she couldn't bear to think of him teaching Megan that lifestyle.

She went to her room and sat in the dark, wanting to hold Wyatt and be in his arms, wanting to hold Megan. She loved them both, but how could she let go of feelings and worries she'd had for a lifetime?

If she married Wyatt, she was afraid that in time, they would be unhappy with each other. He didn't like books or the things she did. He wouldn't want to do the things she liked. She would hate some of the things he liked to do. She wouldn't want him taking Megan with him.

Grace rubbed her temples. Her head had started to throb. She loved Wyatt with all her heart, but that didn't change daily living and what they each liked to do.

Could she adapt to his ways? Could she let go of worries and fears and her conservative lifestyle? Could she give up some of the things she loved so deeply? She didn't think she could change enough.

And she was certain Wyatt couldn't.

So how could she stay here if she didn't?

She looked at the closed door to Megan's room. She adored that child.

The thought of Wyatt wanting to take Megan on his bike with him sent chills through her. She would never adjust to that. She knew she had to find another job and move away from Wyatt, Megan and the ranch.

The realization hurt. Her head throbbed more than ever

and she couldn't stop crying. She wanted Wyatt and Megan and the glittering, wonderful life he offered, but it would never work.

She would have to leave. Unless she accepted his proposal, there was no way she could stay. And the sooner she left, the easier it would be on all of them.

Grace hurt so much she could barely breathe. How could love hurt like this? Wyatt was wonderful and marvelous and terrifying all at the same time. He seemed to have no fear of anything.

She stared into the gray early dawn, still crying and hurting and wanting to run back into his arms. She moved to the bed and cried herself to sleep.

A couple of hours later she heard Megan. She climbed out of bed and went to get her. Holding her close, she murmured, "I love you, Megan. You'll never know how much. I want to marry your daddy and live with both of you. But I don't think we could last, and when I marry, I want it to be forever."

She put Megan on a blanket on the floor while she swiftly dressed, and then she took her downstairs. Grace's pulse jumped at the prospect of seeing Wyatt, but it seemed he was already gone. A note was propped on the table.

"See you at dinner," was written in his bold scrawl.

She picked up the note and put it in her pocket, wanting him, wanting to kiss him, wanting him to hold her. Was she making the most foolish mistake of her life?

Yet every time she thought about Megan growing up and Wyatt teaching her to do the daredevil things he did, Grace knew she could never learn to tolerate it or avoid continually worrying and constantly arguing with Wyatt.

She would help Wyatt hire another nanny, so he wouldn't have to go through all those interviews again.

It hurt to think about getting another nanny, but Grace knew that was the only thing to do. She would tell him when he got home tonight.

"I love you, Megan," she said through her tears, picking up the baby to hug her.

The day seemed a thousand hours long to Grace, but she began to make plans to move.

Wyatt called once while she was in the yard with Megan. He left a terse message that he would be late, and she wondered if he was staying away on purpose. She knew she had hurt him and she was sorry. She suspected he would rebound far better than she would.

That night he wasn't home until late, and Megan had already gone to bed. When he came in, Grace was reading in the family room. Watching her solemnly, he dropped his jacket on a chair and crossed to her.

Her pulse jumped as he approached. He leaned down, taking her hands and pulling her to her feet. As she stood, he put his arms around her. "I missed you and I hope you've thought about my proposal and our future."

She wound her arms around his neck and kissed him hungrily. He tightened his arms around her, kissing her hard, taking her breath and setting her aflame. She stopped thinking. For this moment she was back in Wyatt's arms, kissing him, holding him, and he was kissing her. A scalding urgency made her fingers shake as she peeled away his shirt.

Reason, fears, doubts, vanished. Desire and love were everything. Driven with need, she kissed him.

He pulled her T-shirt over her head and tossed it aside, unclasping her lacy bra to drop it, then cup her breasts. He bent to take a nipple into his mouth.

She shook with need, unbuckling his belt and then unfastening his slacks. They fell in a heap around his ankles. Releasing her, he sat on the sofa and peeled off his boots and then the rest of his clothes. He caught her wrist to pull her to him.

She sat on his lap, feeling his thick shaft pressing against her bare hip. Retrieving a packet for protection, he shifted her to the sofa and moved between her legs.

He was virile, so incredibly sexy, ready for her. As he entered her slowly, she arched to meet him.

"Wyatt, love me!" she gasped, wanting this moment because she didn't think there would be many more times like this. And she wanted to give herself to Wyatt, give him memories to last a lifetime. She tightened her legs around him, clinging to his strong back, moving with him.

If only…

She knew she couldn't follow the reasoning of other possibilities. They couldn't marry. It was that simple. She tasted salty tears, certain that this time she was telling him goodbye.

He lowered himself, entering her, and desire scalded her as she held him. He kissed her passionately, and then they were caught in an urgency that built until she thought she would explode with her need for him.

"I love you, Grace!" he cried out.

"Wyatt, oh, my love," she said, clinging to him and moving wildly with him.

Release came in a burst of ecstasy, then she felt his shuddering release.

As they slowed, their breathing gradually became natural. He crushed her to him, showering kisses on her, murmuring endearments. "Marry me, darlin'. It'll be so good between us, Grace. I love you."

"I love you, too, Wyatt," she whispered, kissing him.

In minutes he shifted and moved. "When I get the

strength, I'll carry you upstairs and we can take a long, leisurely bath together.''

"I can walk upstairs by myself," she said, smiling at him, too aware that for the moment, they were skirting the subject of their future.

"Go run the water. I'll get a cold beer for myself and a glass of wine for you and be right there."

She didn't want to argue now, so she watched him grab his clothes and leave the room. She picked up her things and hurried upstairs, checking on Megan and then going to Wyatt's bathroom and running water.

They bathed, ate a late dinner, made love again and then long into the night as she lay in his arms, she asked him about his day.

"You don't want to know. What happened here?"

Grace sat up and pulled the sheet beneath her arms. "I've thought about the future. Wyatt, I always come back to the same thing."

He looked as if she'd struck him a hard blow. He grimaced and reached out to stroke her arm. "Dammit, Grace, I love you. Really love you. But I can't give up my flying and rodeos and my bike. I can't change, especially when, to me, it seems ridiculous. Live a little, Grace. Are you going to tell Megan and me goodbye because you're scared of life?"

His question hurt, but she nodded. "I'm scared of it the way you live it. I can't bear to go through life watching you do risky things."

While they stared at each other, a muscle worked in his jaw. "So where do we go from here? Live like this?"

"No, of course not. All day I've thought about it." She took a deep breath, knowing that with her next words, she would be telling him goodbye. "I'll help you hire a new nanny and then I'll leave."

She saw the pain in his expression. "Just like that, you're gone?"

"I don't see anything else we can do," she replied.

"Whatever happens, we need a new nanny, but if you move out, Grace, it's over."

"It was over before it started, Wyatt. I'm sorry. And we can't go out Saturday night." She slipped out of bed and reached for her robe, wrapping it around her and leaving without looking back. Tears streamed down her cheeks and she knew that this time they had truly said goodbye. Now they would just go through the motions and do the things necessary for her to move away.

She didn't know she could possibly hurt so badly. Half an hour later she heard the roar of the motorcycle.

Wyatt raced away into the night, tearing down the county road, letting the wind whip against him. After an hour he returned to the ranch. He needed to move, do something physical. He drove to the pasture where he kept the white stallion that he had named Legend. Taking out a bridle and saddle, he stood quietly, talking to the horse, which was a hundred yards away. Wyatt had worked with the stallion enough now that the horse was becoming accustomed to him.

Moonlight bathed the powerful animal as the two stared at each other. Wyatt turned and walked away, standing quietly, waiting, finally hearing the horse moving behind him. It was another half hour before he reached out to touch the horse.

He had ridden the stallion three times now without getting bucked off and knew he better focus on the horse because he was still dealing with a dangerous animal.

Two hours later, he drove back to the house and the moment he left the stallion, his thoughts jumped to Grace. In his life he had left some broken hearts behind, but they mended, and he suspected no one had ever been deeply in love with him.

He kept telling himself he would get over Grace, but he didn't believe it. It was the same as telling himself that in the future, he wouldn't need air to breathe. He loved her desperately. At the same time, he knew if he promised her he would change completely and do what she wanted, he would never be able to keep the promise.

Tears stung his eyes and he wiped at them angrily. How could it hurt this much to love someone? The day had been pure hell. His lawyer was trying to avoid having to go to court over custody of Megan, but Olivia's parents were being hateful. They wanted Megan, and in his lawyer's opinion, they wanted her trust fund and inheritance. Since Hank had always said they never had any interest in Megan, Wyatt wondered if Prentice was right.

Wyatt realized he was losing Grace and he was going to have to fight to keep from losing Megan.

As he sat on the porch, he tried to think what he needed to do next. Monday morning he had another appointment with Prentice Bolton. Tomorrow was the Fourth of July. He had intended to take Grace and Megan to a picnic at the country club in San Antonio and then watch fireworks afterward, but that was out of the question now. There was a little rodeo in Stallion Pass. He would go to that, get away from the ranch and Grace. He would run an ad for a nanny. Grace had said she would help him hire someone. The sooner he did, the better it would be, because it was going to tear them both up to live under the same roof.

He swore steadily, wondering if the hurt would ever end. He knew Grace well enough now to know that she would stick to what she said.

He knew he'd better put the hurt behind him, because

he had another big battle looming that might be the fight of his life. He couldn't change Grace, but he could fight for Megan.

In the next few days Grace saw little of Wyatt. She knew he was busy selling some of the businesses Hank had owned. He flew to California and was gone a week. During the time he was away, the ad for a nanny ran and Grace did the early interviews.

By the time Wyatt returned, she had five likely candidates for him to interview. And then the second day he was back, she interviewed a woman she thought was exactly what Wyatt wanted.

Sonya Madison was an older woman whose grandchildren were all in college, and she loved little children. She'd been a nanny for the past ten years and had excellent references. She had kindly blue eyes, wore bifocals and had white hair.

After an interview with Wyatt, Sonya was hired and agreed to begin work the following Monday. July was more than half over.

As soon as Sonya moved into the house, Grace could devote herself full-time to finding an apartment and a job in San Antonio. Grace rarely saw Wyatt these days. He kept late hours and left early. When they were together, the air was filled with tension. She loved him and wanted to be in his arms. All of this was dreadful, yet she continued with her plans.

Grace found an apartment in San Antonio and then a job in an accounting office. She packed and got ready for her move.

On Thursday she worked all day, cleaning and getting her apartment ready. When she returned to the ranch, she climbed the stairs. She wore cutoffs and sneakers and had her hair in a thick braid. Tendrils escaped and curled around her face.

She went to see Megan, tiptoeing into the room in case the baby was asleep.

Dressed in a white shirt and a navy suit, his tie loosened, Wyatt stood beside the crib holding Megan in his arms. When Grace entered, he looked up. She was startled to see that his eyes were filled with tears.

His lips thinned and a muscle worked in his jaw as he turned away. "I just came in to see her," he said gruffly.

"Wyatt, what's wrong?" Grace asked.

When he turned to face her, he had control of his emotions.

"Things just aren't going well. You want to see Megan?"

"Yes, but I can come back later."

"You can see her now." Crossing the room, he handed the baby to Grace. "Sonya has gone early for the weekend. I told her I could watch Megan."

"I can watch her for a while if you have something you want to do."

He nodded and left the room. Grace stared after him, thinking about his answer. What was bothering him?

She set Megan down with her toys, then sat on the floor to play with her. In another half hour she heard Wyatt leave in his pickup. Later Grace fed Megan and put her to bed. Too aware of the empty house, Grace showered and changed into fresh cutoffs, T-shirt and sneakers. She went downstairs to find Wyatt on the porch in the dark. He had a bottle of beer and sat with his feet propped on the porch rail.

"Can I join you?" she asked.

He stood and waved his hand. "Sure. Come out. Want something to drink?"

"I have iced tea." She sat in a chair near his and he sat back down, propping his booted feet on the rail again.

"Wyatt, what's wrong?"

"Doesn't concern you now, Grace," he said, and she realized he was beginning to shut her out of his life.

"I didn't mean to pry," she said, suddenly feeling he didn't want her sitting with him. She stood and started inside. "'Night, Wyatt."

"Sit down. I have to go to court next month. The custody battle is going full force. The Volmers want Megan, and they have the money and the law firm to pursue this. They say I'm an unfit father, and they're dredging up a lot of old stuff."

Appalled, Grace stared at him. "That's terrible! How can they say you're an unfit father? You're a wonderful father."

"You might have a biased view," he said dryly.

"Can't I testify about your fitness as a father?"

He turned his head to look at her. "I don't think so, but thanks."

"Why not?" she asked, hurting for him. "You don't want me to try to help you? Wyatt, don't let your anger at me get in the way of letting me help you."

"Grace, you're part of the problem. They've accused us of living together out here, parties—remember my party? I don't think you can say one thing that will help. Remember, they saw us together at the restaurant in San Antonio. But thanks. I'll tell Prentice you offered to testify."

"That's terrible! And so wrong. Surely they don't stand a chance."

"They're blood relatives, too. They've been married a long time. I'm single, considered wild and unpredictable, not daddy material. I'll fight it legally as long as I can, but Prentice said we may not be able to stop them. A lot depends on the judge we get. They have a big legal outfit from Austin. Prentice knows their lawyers.''

''I'm sorry,'' Grace said, still aghast.

Megan began to cry, her wails coming clearly over the intercom. ''I'll get her,'' Wyatt said, rising to his feet. '''Night, Grace.''

When he left, Grace thought she'd never felt so alone. She hurt for Wyatt and for herself. His losing Megan was too terrible to contemplate. He was an adoring, wonderful father.

She sat staring into the dark for hours, but Wyatt never returned, and finally she went to her room. She lay in bed in the dark, mulling over his situation, mulling over the possibility he might lose Megan.

All her life family had been the most important thing. Nothing else mattered. Now Wyatt and Megan had become her family—Wyatt had asked her to become family forever.

She couldn't walk out on them. Could she accept Wyatt as he was? If she stayed, she would have to. With some deep soul-searching, she knew she was willing to try. She understood fully that if she married Wyatt, she was going to have to accept him as he was, with all his wild ways. Deciding that she would, she wondered if she was too late. And after making her decision, her heart leaped with eagerness. She wanted to run to Wyatt right then.

Instead, she forced herself to think it over more, wanting to be certain. Eventually she fell asleep.

The next morning, after she'd showered and dressed, she went downstairs to search for Wyatt, but he had already left and she learned he had taken Megan to Ashley

Ryder's for the day. Mrs. Perkins was there to cook and clean, so Grace was free to go.

She hurried to her room to change, dressing in a short navy skirt and sleeveless navy blouse and high-heeled pumps. She looped and pinned her hair on her head, told Megan goodbye and left word with Sonya and Mrs. Perkins where they could find her.

She drove to Wyatt's San Antonio office, stopping in the lobby to call him. It took a few minutes until he answered because his secretary had long ago been told to put Grace straight through to him.

"Can I come see you now?"

"I have an appointment in fifteen minutes. If you're at the ranch, we'll have to make it this afternoon."

"I'm in the lobby of your building."

There was a momentary pause. "Come on up."

She rode to the top floor where Sawyer Enterprises, Incorporated, was located. She entered a spacious reception room with lush potted plants, thick rugs on polished hardwood floors and leather furniture. In seconds, she was told to go ahead into his office.

She opened the door to a corner office with floor-to-ceiling windows that looked out over the city. Wyatt stood behind a polished wood desk, and his gaze swept over her swiftly as she entered and closed the door behind her.

"What brings you here, Grace?"

She walked across the room. Every nerve she had was raw. She wanted to run and throw herself into his arms, but he had thrown up a wall between them.

His brows arched as she kept walking around his desk to him. She stopped only inches away, and her heart was thudding.

"Wyatt, you may have lost interest now, but if you haven't…I want to marry you."

Stunned, Wyatt stared at her. His heart pounded and he wasn't sure he'd heard her correctly. He had been trying to shut her out of his life, out of his mind and heart, yet he hadn't been able to even slightly. Now she stood gazing at him, her green eyes pulling at him, telling him she would marry him. But she was too solemn, her voice too full of regrets.

"What brings this on, Grace?" he asked, trying to stop thinking about the possibilities, feeling there was a catch somewhere. "Yesterday you wouldn't even consider marrying me."

# Eleven

**"I**'m sorry. I know I hurt you," she said quietly. Her eyes filled with tears, which she wiped away swiftly before they fell. "I don't blame you and I know you've been trying to forget me."

"I believe you're the one trying to distance yourself from Megan and me as fast as you can."

"Wyatt, I thought about it all last night. Near morning I fell asleep, but I meant to catch you before you left for work today. Family has always been the most important thing in my life. We've never owned a home, never lived one place long, so I never had long friendships. Family was it. Now you and Megan are my family."

"I may lose her soon, Grace." His eyes narrowed. "You're doing this to help me keep from losing Megan, aren't you?"

"That was why I stopped to think about us and the future and the possibilities, but that isn't why I'm here.

If you could tell me right now that the custody suit was dropped, I'd still be here.''

"Why do I find that hard to believe?" he said sharply, certain she was doing this to help him keep Megan. He was angry and hurt. He could fight his own battles, and he didn't want sympathy. "All my life I've had to fight for what I wanted," he snapped. "This isn't any different now, but I don't want your sympathy. Thank you, but no thanks. I've got an appointment."

He turned away, putting papers in his briefcase, hurting and angry and aware she hadn't moved. Dammit. Why did she have to look so beautiful? He struggled, fighting every urge inside him to throw aside hurt feelings and worries and accept her offer.

When he turned around, she was gone. He felt as if his insides were crumbling into a million pieces. He thought he'd hurt as much as it was possible to hurt, but he'd been wrong.

That night when he got home, Grace had moved out. She had left a phone number and address, which Wyatt tossed into the trash.

With steely determination Grace drove to the Sawyer ranch on Saturday. She knew where to go and knew Wyatt was away for the afternoon because she had talked to his foreman, Jett Colby.

She reached the pasture that adjoined the road to the ranch house. This was where Legend was kept, and Grace stopped her car at the gate. At the sound of the engine, the stallion came trotting into view, his ears cocked forward.

"Watching for Wyatt, aren't you? We've both fallen under his spell," she said quietly as she opened the gate, drove inside and then got out to close the gate.

Wyatt had let her watch once when he had been working with the horse at the corral and she remembered every moment of that evening. She parked and got out, going around to open the trunk of her car and get out the saddle she had borrowed.

She looked at the horse. He stood watching her, his ears still cocked forward. She talked softly, getting out treats she had ready for him. She had spent the past two days at a San Antonio stable, learning about horses, how to saddle one, how to ride. She had decided to live life a little more fully and to stop being afraid of so many things. This seemed as good a place to start as any.

She waited patiently, knowing the horse was moving closer until he was finally only yards away. While she talked quietly to the horse, she turned to hold out her hand with apple slices. He moved closer and in minutes took the treat. She fished more out of a bag, held them out and then patted the horse.

Taking lots of time, she finally got a saddle on Legend and after a few more minutes, placed her foot in a stirrup and mounted him.

He shook his head and she realized she was trembling. "You can do this," she said to herself, patting his neck. She flicked the reins slightly and he began a sedate walk. She inhaled, wanting to get down, thrilled to be riding him, realizing maybe she should let go of so many worries and fears. If she could ride this horse, how much more likely for Wyatt to ride him without qualms. Of course, she knew Wyatt didn't care whether the horse was wild and hostile or docile.

She inhaled another deep breath, aware of the blue sky, the sun beating down on her above her floppy straw hat. She had worn a T-shirt, jeans and new boots. And she had plans to wear those boots again in a few more hours.

She ached with a terrible longing for Wyatt and then pulled her mind sharply back to the horse, knowing she needed to stay alert.

A pickup came along the road and too late, she realized she should have ridden away from the road and not toward it, but she knew from Wyatt's secretary that he had an afternoon appointment with his lawyer.

The pickup passed her, then turned and whipped off the road, bouncing over the ground toward the pasture gate.

She turned the horse to ride toward the gate, knowing that whoever it was, the driver was coming to see her.

The pickup stopped and Jett Colby climbed out, coming into the pasture. He stopped and stood at the gate.

"Grace, can you get down off that horse, please?"

She reined in and dismounted, leading the stallion with her until she was closer to Jett. "I just wanted to see if I could ride him."

"Grace, just drop the reins and get in your car and let me take it from here. I'll open the gate for you."

She smiled at Wyatt's foreman. "I can unsaddle him and I have some treats for him."

"You let me unsaddle him and forget the treats. Just get in your car. That horse is dangerous."

"You mean dangerous for an amateur. I've been out here a long time now," she said, glancing at her watch.

"Well, cut it short, please."

She heard the worry in his voice. With a glance at the horse, she turned and went to her car. She drove out and Jett opened the gate, closing it behind her. She cut the engine, stepped out and waited, watching Jett unsaddle Legend.

He carried the saddle and she opened the gate. He came through and put the saddle in the trunk of her car.

Suddenly the horse reared, pawing the air, whinnying loudly. He came down, pawing the earth, then turned and galloped across the pasture.

Jett turned to face her. "Grace, please don't ever ride him again—especially out here alone. He threw Wyatt last night and he's as unpredictable as spring weather. That's not a horse for you to be around at all. He may never be completely gentled."

"I just wanted to see if I could," she said. "I won't be out here again. Thanks for helping me."

"Sure," the older man said, his blue eyes studying her. "Wyatt is mighty unhappy. And he worries about losing Megan."

"That shouldn't ever happen."

"Nope, it shouldn't. Wyatt's a good daddy."

"Well, again, thanks. It was good to see you." She climbed into her car and started the engine, driving away and glancing in the rearview mirror to see Jett watching her.

Hot tears ran down her cheeks and she wiped them away angrily. "Wyatt, I love you," she whispered.

That night Wyatt slid onto the back of a bull at the rodeo in San Antonio. He wrapped the rope around his hand, but he didn't tie himself on. He had done that once and suffered a broken arm because of it.

The buzzer sounded and the gate opened and all thought stopped as the big animal lunged into the arena. The world was a blur, the roar of the crowd dim, as jolt after jolt shot through Wyatt. Yet he relished it and clung to the animal and let his anger and frustrations release in the battle between man and beast.

An eternity later the buzzer sounded. He heard the roar

of the crowd as cowboys tried to help him off the back of the bull.

He slid onto a horse and then dropped to the ground, running for the fence when the bull charged. He climbed the fence, perching on top to see the bull trot out through an open gate. His gaze swept the crowd and then returned to a box right on the front row.

Grace sat there watching him, and even across the big arena, he felt as if he was looking straight into her green eyes.

He dropped off the gate and crossed the empty space while they announced his time and everyone cheered. He was in the lead for the evening, but he barely heard anything. He didn't stop to think; he just kept walking, and when he reached her box, he jumped up, caught his hands on the wall and vaulted over to land on his feet. He sat down beside her. "What are you doing here?"

"I'm trying to change."

"It's a little late," he said.

She flinched as if he'd hit her. "It might be, but I decided you're right. I need to let go of some of my fears, and I thought the best way might be to come watch you ride. I love you, Wyatt."

He stared at her. "I've never been hurt like you hurt me."

"I'm sorry," she whispered, and closed her eyes.

"And I don't want to marry someone who wants me to change completely. I don't want to marry someone who feels sorry for me and is doing this out of charity."

"Charity!" Suddenly fire blazed in the depths of green. "Wyatt Sawyer, I would never marry a man out of charity. You're the last man on earth who needs a woman's charity. I love you! Just the way you are. Can't you understand that?" She threw her arms around his neck and kissed him, her soft lips on his, her tongue darting into his mouth as she pressed herself against him.

Wyatt was stunned momentarily, but then his arms wrapped around her and he kissed her back. He pulled her onto his lap, taking kisses that were salty with her tears. "Will you marry me?" he asked.

"Yes! Oh, yes. I love you!"

"Grace, you're going to drive me crazy." He kissed her again, and then he wanted to be alone with her. He wanted to make love to her, to peel away her clothes to make sure he wasn't dreaming. But there wasn't anything dreamlike about her kisses.

"I may lose Megan. You still want to marry me even if I don't have her?"

"Yes! And we're not going to lose her."

Some knot inside him loosened and fell away, and his world righted. "Let's get out of here." He stood and took her hand. People around them applauded and whistled, and he realized he'd forgotten where they were. He grinned, draped his arm across her shoulders and pulled her closer.

At his pickup, he hauled Grace into his arms to kiss her long and hard again. "Let's go home, darlin'. We have some making up and some celebrating to do."

# Epilogue

**W**yatt stood at the front of the sanctuary with Josh beside him as best man, Gabe next to Josh and Jett Colby as yet another groomsman. Grace's white-haired grandfather, Jeremy Talmadge, was officiating, and he smiled broadly, waiting for his granddaughter to appear.

Wyatt waited, watching Grace's sisters come down the aisle, followed by her good friend Virginia. Wyatt was barely aware of them or the crowded church. He glanced once at his soon-to-be mother-in-law, who held Megan in her arms. It was September now, only weeks since Grace had accepted his proposal, yet he felt as if he'd waited forever for this moment.

And then Grace appeared on the arm of her father, and Wyatt couldn't look anywhere else but at her. His heart thudded with joy.

Dressed in white, her thick, red hair pinned on top of her head, she looked lovelier than he'd ever seen her. He met her gaze, a gaze as direct as the day he'd first opened his door to meet her. Only now, her eyes were shining with love, and he felt a lump form in his throat. He loved her beyond measure, beyond anything he had ever dreamed. She had laid to rest so many skeletons of his past, helped him over hurts, solidified a place in the community for him. And won him Megan. Then Grace was beside him, her father placing her soft hand in his.

Wyatt drew a deep breath and squeezed her hand. He solemnly repeated vows with her, knowing he would love her forever.

Grace looked up at him as they were pronounced husband and wife, and then they hurried back down the long aisle. The day became a blur. First they had pictures taken at the church. Then they were driven to the country club for the reception, where more pictures were taken.

Wyatt had one taken with his groomsmen and then another with just Gabe and Josh, the three men looking happy, handsome, and still the closest of friends. Grace looked at Wyatt in his tux and white shirt. He was the handsomest man present, actually the best-looking Texan in the state, she thought, and she was still amazed how in love with her he was. Why had she thought she couldn't live with his wildness? That was part of what made him so exciting to her. Maybe she was indeed letting go of some of her conservative ways.

And he'd read the book she'd given him.

Next, Wyatt had another picture taken with his friends and their wives and children. Wyatt held Megan and Gabe held Ella, while Julian stood in front of them. The instant he was told he could go play again, Julian was off, rushing outside onto the large terrace where the other children were.

Later, the newlyweds were talking to their friends. "As

soon as you get back from your honeymoon," Gabe said, "we'll have a barbecue and we'll all get together."

"Sounds good to me," Wyatt replied.

"Then we'll have something at our place," Josh said, smiling at his wife as he hugged her thickening waist.

"When Megan gets a little bigger, she'll be able to play with Ella," Ashley said. "I'm glad your custody battle is over, Wyatt."

"Grace rescued me. I wondered at first if that's why she agreed to marry me," he said with a smile at his bride. He had his arm around her waist, and Grace was aware that any time he was near her, he held her hand or arm or put his arm around her—which suited her fine.

"But you knew better," she said, looking up into his dark eyes.

"As soon as I got engaged—especially to an upstanding, model citizen like Grace—the battle was over. They dropped the case. Their strongest point had been that I was a swinging bachelor. Grace ended that."

While everyone laughed, Wyatt gave her a squeeze. "I invited them to the wedding," he continued, "because as I told them, I didn't want to cut them off from their granddaughter, but they declined to come."

"Megan has other grandparents that love her," Josh remarked. "I don't think your mother has put her down all day, except when she's been wanted for a photograph."

"Mother's happy to have a granddaughter," Grace said, looking across the room at her mother and Megan.

"Our baby won't have grandparents," Laurie said, "but I think our baby's aunts will be good substitutes."

"I'm lucky to have my dad," Ashley remarked. "He has Ella right now."

"Well, Wyatt, that white stallion proves the old legend was true," Gabe said.

"Maybe so. Look at the three of us. His name is Legend now—really, Legend," Wyatt said grinning, and the others laughed. "It ought to be Maverick because he's a maverick," he said, looking down at Grace, and she remembered when Wyatt discovered she had ridden Legend. Wyatt had been angry and stunned, yet she thought maybe he had realized then that she had really begun to let go of her conservative ways.

In minutes other guests joined the group, and then Wyatt and Grace were separated. Once Wyatt was standing alone when his new father-in-law walked up.

Tom Talmadge smiled at Wyatt. "I want to thank you again for your more than generous donation to our mission work in Bolivia. It'll build a school and get us a small bus, among other things."

"My dad was tight and mean and never tried to help others," Wyatt said. "I like to think it's his money I'm giving. I guess I can't outgrow that feeling of wanting to get back at him. Something you'd never understand."

"I like to think it's your money, Wyatt. You're kind and generous beyond measure. You're a good person and you'll help children more than you can ever imagine."

"I was glad to do it. Would you two ever consider coming back here? There are kids in San Antonio who need help, too. I'd be happy to put up money, but I don't know anything about what to do."

Tom Talmadge glanced across the room. "I'll talk it over with Rose. We'll need to oversee your gift for the coming months, but once things get up and rolling, we might come back here. Megan is our first grandchild, and both of us want to get to know her."

"That would be great," Wyatt said, feeling a bond with Grace's father.

"Thanks for the offer. And don't worry about Megan while you're on your honeymoon."

"I'm not going to worry for a minute. She's in good hands. Thanks for keeping her and watching the ranch house while we're gone."

"It's been wonderful to get all the family together again. You've got a big family now, Wyatt."

"I'm glad. When I can find Grace, we'll be getting out of here, so I'll tell you goodbye now. You have all the phone numbers and hotels, and we'll call you tonight and every day."

The two men shook hands and Wyatt left. It was half an hour before he got Grace away from the party. They rushed out a back door to his waiting car, and he drove to his home in the city, where Grace changed into a green sheath dress and pumps and rushed back to the car.

In another half hour they were airborne, Wyatt piloting his jet as they headed to Houston. They would spend the night there and leave in the morning for ten days in Paris.

When they were finally alone in the bridal suite in Houston, Wyatt handed her a glass of champagne and raised his. "Here's to a lifetime of happiness, Mrs. Sawyer."

"I'll drink to that," Grace answered.

Both sipped their champagne, and then Wyatt took her glass from her and set it on the table beside his. He shed his coat and tie.

His dark eyes ablaze with love and desire, he slipped his arm around her waist and pulled her close. "Mrs. Sawyer. My wife. My love. Grace, I love you beyond words," he whispered.

She looped her arms around his neck and held him, standing on tiptoe and pulling his head down to kiss him.

Wyatt tightened his arms around her, his fingers caressing her nape and then pulling the back zipper of her dress slowly down. The material fell with a soft whisper around her ankles, but Grace was barely aware of it as she tried to unfasten the studs on Wyatt's shirt and unbuckle his belt. "Wyatt, I love you," she whispered.

He bent over her, and she clung to him while he kissed her deeply. Grace's heart thudded with excitement and joy as she held her reckless, handsome cowboy, the man she would cherish the rest of her life.

She leaned away to look up at him. "Now, wild man, let's see you really let go. I'm ready for a little excitement."

He grinned and his dark eyes glittered. "Always a challenge, Grace!" His arm tightened around her. "I'll see what I can do."

*　*　*　*　*

# SILHOUETTE®
# DESIRE™ 2-IN-1

## AVAILABLE FROM 21ST NOVEMBER 2003

### AMBER BY NIGHT  Sharon Sala

Sexy playboy Tyler Savage knew that prim Amelia Beauchamp and flirtatious Amber were one and the same. As for their romantic dinners and long, moonlit nights together, they were things he wanted to turn into reality...

### PRINCESS IN HIS BED  Leanne Banks

The minute he saw beautiful Mimi Deerman crash into his property Jared McNeil knew he was in trouble. For Jared sensed she had secrets, but Mimi drove him crazy. Before long she was in his bed and tearing down his defences.

### EXPECTING...AND IN DANGER  Eileen Wilks

One passionate night with Rafe Connelly, and Charlotte Masters was pregnant. But she couldn't accept Rafe's proposal, for to a woman with secrets, Rafe was as dangerous as the killers at her heels...

### CHEROKEE MARRIAGE DARE  Sheri WhiteFeather

Luke didn't believe in love, but he knew desire—and Maggie dared him to feel, to want, to hope—to *marry* her! But Luke had to resist her, for if he took Maggie in his arms, he knew he'd never let her go.

### SKY FULL OF PROMISE  Teresa Southwick

When Sky Colton agreed to be Dominic's pretend bride, she'd never expected his passionate 'fake' kisses would set her on fire. But when danger threatened could Sky trust Dominic to make her the one *real* promise that would save them both?

### THE WOLF'S SURRENDER  Sandra Steffen

Stranded and in labour in hardened bachelor Grey Colton's office, Kelly Madison was surprised by her desire for the man who was helping deliver her baby. But could Kelly risk a future with Grey when he was unaware of her past?

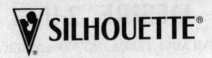

He is every inch a Desperado.
But this time the job is personal.

*Diana*
*Palmer*

DESPERADO

**On sale 21st November 2003**

*Available at most branches of WHSmith,*
*Tesco, Martins, Borders, Eason, Sainsbury's*
*and all good paperback bookshops.*

1203/047/SH60

**SILHOUETTE®**
**SPECIAL EDITION™**

*proudly presents*

a brand-new five-book series from
bestselling author

# SHERRYL WOODS

# The Devaneys

*Five brothers torn apart in childhood,*
*reunited by love.*

### RYAN'S PLACE
*December 2003*

### SEAN'S RECKONING
*January 2004*

### MICHAEL'S DISCOVERY
*February 2004*

### PATRICK'S DESTINY
*March 2004*

### DANIEL'S DESIRE
*April 2004*

1203/SH/LC75

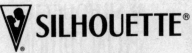 **SILHOUETTE**®

*is proud to present*

a brand-new series

# The

# *Country Club*

**Dangerous, intense and seductive.
These stories are ready to introduce the
unsuspecting into a world where wealth
is power and deception is rife.**

*December 2003*
**Once a Father by Marie Ferrarella**
Silhouette Sensation

*January 2004*
**In the Line of Fire by Beverly Bird**
Silhouette Sensation

*February 2004*
**Moment of Truth by Maggie Price**
Silhouette Sensation

*March 2004*
**The Country Club: The Debutantes
by Ann Major, Christine Rimmer & Beverly Barton**
Silhouette Books

**Now prepare for more action with the twelve-book series...
Coming in March 2004.**

# FREE!
## 2 Book
### and a surprise gift!

We would like to take this opportunity to thank you for reading this Silhouette® book by offering you the chance to take TWO specially selected titles from the Desire™ series absolutely FREE! We're also making this offer to introduce you to the benefits of the Reader Service™—

- ★ FREE home delivery
- ★ FREE gifts and competitions
- ★ FREE monthly Newsletter
- ★ Books available before they're in the shops
- ★ Exclusive Reader Service discount offer

Accepting this FREE book and gift places you under no obligation to buy; you may cancel at any time, even after receiving your free shipment. Simply complete your details below and return the entire page to the address below. *You don't even need a stamp!*

**YES!** Please send me 2 free Desire books and a surprise gift. I understand that unless you hear from me, I will receive 3 superb new titles every month for just £4.99 each, postage and packing free. I am under no obligation to purchase any books and may cancel my subscription at any time. The free books and gift will be mine to keep in any case.

D3ZEF

Ms/Mrs/Miss/Mr ......................................................Initials ...................................
BLOCK CAPITALS PLEASE

Surname ................................................................................................................

Address ................................................................................................................

................................................................................................................

................................................................Postcode ......................................

**Send this whole page to:**
**UK: The Reader Service, FREEPOST CN81, Croydon, CR9 3WZ**
**EIRE: The Reader Service, PO Box 4546, Kilcock, County Kildare (stamp required)**